Breaking THE ICE

BETH BOLDEN

AUTHOR NOTE

Breaking the Ice AND the Portland Evergreens series take place in the wider Beth Bolden universe: a universe that is more inclusive and welcoming than our own.

In Beth-world, the first professional athlete to come out of the closet was Colin O'Connor (*The Rainbow Clause*), and after this happened, approximately ten years ago, there have been numerous players, coaches, and even owners who are living their best queer lives freely.

1. The Quad
2. Lewis Dorm
3. Clark Dorm
4. Hazel Hall
5. Beard Dining Hall
6. Bachelor
7. Jefferson
8. Hood
9. Hoover House
10. Knight Athletic Complex
11. Harrington Field
12. Gym
13. Lovejoy Apartments
14. Jimmy's Joint
15. Darcelle's Bar
16. Star Signs Arcade
17. Sammy's Subs & Smoothies
18. Koffee Klatch

CHAPTER 1

June

Zach was sweating. A lot.

He wiped a damp palm on his thigh, but the material of his shorts was slippery and it didn't feel any drier after. Nothing felt drier. Sweat beaded at his hairline, under the brim of his hat, at the back of his neck, and under his arms.

It was the high eighties in Michigan, and humid as fuck, but that wasn't why he was currently a soupy mess. He considered cranking up the air conditioning again, but he already knew that wouldn't help.

"You can do this," he said out loud to his reflection in the rearview mirror. But the pep talk didn't do much to help. He still wanted to turn around and go back to Traverse City and, also, hit the accelerator and arrive at his destination in the next oh-point-five seconds.

Get it over with.

Zach turned down another road, this sign even more faded than the last. The gravel under his tires gave way to dirt ruts, and the rental car jolted over the dried lumps of mud.

He imagined in the winter this road was basically impassable.

In the fall or the spring, this road was *probably* impassable.

Zach tried to be grateful that it was June and he wasn't going to get stuck all the way out here, but it was hard to be relieved when he was this fucking nervous.

Finally, his rental car jolted down the lane, passing one mile marker and then another until he made it to the one he was looking for.

Without it, he'd never have seen the turnoff. It was half-buried in the surrounding foliage, and Zach wasn't stupid enough to think that wasn't one-hundred-percent on purpose.

The person who lived down it didn't want to be found.

But Zach had found him, anyway.

Hayes, his best friend, had told him that this was a fool's errand. But because he was ride-or-die, loyal to the absolute core, he'd been the one to call in half a dozen favors to help Zach figure out exactly where he was going.

Zach tried to feel gratitude, but all he felt was a sick, nauseating lurch in the base of his stomach as the cabin came into view.

Despite the foliage surrounding it, the building was clearly well cared for. Windows glistened in the sunlight, and the screened porch running along the entrance side was neat, only a table and a single chair. There was one pair of boots with muddy soles by the front door.

Zach stopped the car and tried to unclench his white-knuckled fingers from the steering wheel.

"You can do this," he repeated to himself, and it worked a little better the second time, because he actually got his seat belt undone and the door open.

He was halfway out the car when the front screen door swung open.

Zach stared down the barrel of a shotgun and sweat slipped down his spine, dampening his T-shirt even further. Holding up his hands, he said in a shaky voice he barely recognized as his own, "Hey, it's just me. Uh . . .Zach. Zach Wheeler."

The shotgun barrel wavered and then lowered, giving Zach his first glimpse of Gavin Blackburn in four years.

Dark scruff covered his jaw, the same mahogany as the too-long wavy hair on his head, sprinkled at the temples with gray that hadn't been there the last time they'd met. His dark stare was flat, equally dark circles under his eyes, and he shaded them with a hand. He wore a ratty T-shirt clinging to his broad shoulders and even rattier basketball shorts, exposing still-muscled legs.

Zach couldn't say he looked *bad* exactly, but then Gavin Blackburn would have to be halfway into a grave for him to ever think that.

"Zach?" His voice sounded rough with disuse, and more than a little shocked. "Is that you?"

Zach risked another step closer. "Yeah, it's me. Zach." His hand twitched at his side, tempted to wave hello like a complete fucking idiot.

You're not handling this, the Hayes-voice inside him said bluntly.

Zach told the Hayes in his head to fuck off and cleared his throat. "Can we talk?"

Four years ago Coach would've smiled and gestured Zach inside.

Now, he just shot him a hard look. "What are you doing here?"

"I just want to talk."

"I've got nothing to say." Gavin didn't need to add *to you* but Zach heard it anyway.

It shouldn't have hurt. Dozens of people hadn't even made it this far. Hayes had told him that the last scout who'd come out here, the one he'd gotten the directions from, hadn't even gotten ten words out of Blackburn. He'd only gotten the shotgun barrel and a hissed warning to get the fuck off his property.

"Well, *I've* got something to say," Zach said, shifting his weight uncomfortably. Half-expecting the shotgun to rise again. "You gonna let me say it?"

He—and the athletic director at Portland University—were both counting on his ex-coach having a tender spot for one of his ex-players.

Coach—*Gavin*, Zach told himself, he was Gavin now, because they weren't anything, and Coach hadn't been his Coach in a long fucking time—shot him an unimpressed look.

"You wanna say it out here?" Gavin asked.

He didn't. Not really. But Hayes had told him that *nobody* had ever made it onto the porch, even.

Zach's competitive streak, the one he'd thought was long-dead, killed by the grind of the NHL, flared to life.

"No," Zach said.

Gavin's dark eyes flashed a warning, and it occurred to Zach that he looked more alive now than he'd looked in the last five minutes. Pissed off, sure, but pissed off was better than that dead-eyed look he'd been wearing before.

"You should get back in your car and turn around. Get out of here." Gavin's voice was gruff.

"No," Zach repeated.

Gavin tilted his head, appraising him. He was quiet for so long that Zach was afraid he *might* get shot, and no matter what he'd discussed with Sidney Swift, the Portland U athletic director, this was *not* worth a hole in his chest. He had the assistant coaching job, no matter what. Swift had promised him that.

"You grew up," Gavin said flatly.

How long had he waited for Gavin to say that to him? A whole fucking long time. But then Zach had always imagined that it would occur under a lot different circumstances—if it ever happened at all.

For one, he'd hoped Gavin would utter it in a dreamy, mesmerized voice, rough around the edges with awe, not rough with disuse and annoyance.

Nevermind that he'd imagined it would be offered as invitation, not a way to slam the door shut between them.

"It's been years," Zach said, shrugging, burying his disappointment deep down, in the same place he'd always shoved his inconvenient and never-to-be-returned feelings.

It was true. The last time he'd seen Gavin had been four years ago, when his NHL team, the Los Angeles Mavericks, had played Gavin's team, the Seattle Sea Monsters.

They'd greeted each other with a warm hug and a few words pre-game and a few more after the game. It had felt like every other chance meeting between an ex-coach and his old player.

Six weeks later, Gavin's wife was dead and he'd disappeared. Zach had kept waiting for Gavin to rejoin the land of the living, but he never had.

"Has it really?" Gavin scrubbed a hand across his jaw. "I guess so."

Zach had known this was a fool's errand. If he hadn't known it himself, Hayes' frank assessment of his chances would've convinced him. But he was here, anyway, wasn't he? He'd come regardless, and he wasn't going to let his offer stay unsaid.

"I just want to talk."

"You know I'm going to say no," Gavin said bluntly.

"Probably, yeah, but I told Swift I'd say it anyway." But he wasn't going to make the offer because Sidney Swift wanted him to. He was going to make it because *he* wanted to. Because Gavin deserved more than to bury himself in the middle of nowhere, where he probably couldn't even *leave* October through April.

And that, more than anything, was fucked up.

"Swift?"

Shit. He hadn't meant to give that away. Not yet. Not until he made it onto the actual porch. More sweat slipped down Zach's spine. The cotton of his T-shirt was probably glued to his back by now.

He was sure Gavin would really tell him to fuck off now. Lift the shotgun again, maybe. Threaten him the way he'd threatened so many representatives who'd actually made it all the way out here.

But Gavin only sighed, like it was inevitable, and gestured towards the door. "Come on," he said.

Zach could barely believe his luck. He wondered if he could take a picture of the porch. Prove to Hayes—and everyone who'd doubted him—that he was *here*.

But he dismissed the tempting possibility. This wasn't about *winning*, though that was great too. It was about having the opportunity to make his pitch.

Nobody else had ever done that either.

Gavin had never let them.

He didn't move towards the door to the cabin, only leaned against one of the columns on the screen porch and waved at the single chair. "Sit," he said.

Zach didn't want to sit. He felt shaky with adrenaline and success—and well, something else he didn't want to look at too closely.

He'd told Hayes he was over his crush, had been over it for a long, *long* time, but that wasn't quite true, was it? He'd just not had anything to feed it for so long it had atrophied, and now there was blood pumping, hard and strong, into it, and it was roaring back to life like it had never been dead at all.

"So?" Gavin said after Zach had reluctantly taken the chair. He crossed his arms over his chest, that threadbare T-shirt barely hanging on for dear life, and even though he was buried out here, in the middle of fucking nowhere, his body was impossibly hotter than it had been seven years ago, when it had starred pretty exclusively in all of Zach's late-night jerkoff sessions.

"So?" Zach swallowed hard. He needed to fucking focus.

"So why are you fucking here?" Gavin asked.

Suddenly, Zach was reminded of why he'd initially been so nervous. The *pitch*.

"I'm the assistant coach at Portland now—"

"What?" Gavin interrupted, looking shocked. "You're not playing?"

Oh. That would make sense. Gavin wouldn't know that he'd quit the NHL after six years. Wouldn't know he'd given up. Gone back to school. Tried to make something out of the mess his life had become.

Zach swallowed hard. "No," he said.

Gavin actually had the nerve to look pissed now. *More* pissed. "Why the fuck did you stop playing?"

"You're assuming I *chose* to stop playing," Zach said, even though that *was* true. He could've kept going, for another contract and maybe even another. At least his agent had thought so.

"Don't be stupid, you were too good for nobody to pick you up," Gavin said.

Had he been good? Zach tried to think back to a time when he'd believed that was true, before the machinery of pro hockey had worn him and his confidence down.

"I went back to school. Got my degree. Working on my masters, now," Zach said, looking anywhere but at Gavin's face. He didn't want to see the disappointment in his eyes. The resignation. *You gave up,* he could imagine his old coach saying. *You couldn't hack it.* Somehow those words would hurt even more coming from him than they did coming from his own fucking brain.

"What about *hockey*?" Gavin demanded.

That was fucking rich, considering that Gavin had buried himself out here without hockey.

"Yeah, *what about hockey*?" Zach retorted, his temper shredding under the pressure. He wasn't proud, but he was kind of a mess here.

Gavin's mouth compressed together. "Fair," he said flatly. "So you're here to recruit me?"

Zach shrugged. Suddenly he wanted to leave very badly. It had been a mistake to come here. To see the ruins of his life reflected back at him in the eyes of the one person he'd admired more than anyone else. The one person whose approval he'd always craved.

"I thought you were going to give me some big speech?" Gavin continued. He started to pace back and forth on the screen porch.

Zach absolutely did not check out his ass in those shorts. He was a grownup, and grownups didn't do that shit.

"Would it matter if I did?"

Gavin made a face. "Nobody's ever gotten this far before, and I feel . . ."

"I wasn't going to go away and you weren't going to shoot me," Zach said, suddenly *very* sure about that. "Though, if they knew you at all, you weren't ever going to shoot anybody."

Gavin choked out a laugh. "How do you know that?"

"Come the fuck on," Zach said. "I bet there aren't even shells in that."

Gavin's hip collapsed against the pole again and he was *almost* smiling.

Much later tonight, Zach imagined he'd get himself off to that half-smile and in the morning he'd have to text Hayes and tell him, **I fucked up.**

"I'm not interested in coming back," Gavin said primly, his tone at odds with the sly curl of his lips.

Yeah, Zach wasn't imagining that mouth doing anything at all.

Fuck.

It had been bad enough when Gavin was married to Noelle, his high school sweetheart, who Zach had genuinely *liked*, and now it was worse, because Noelle was dead and Gavin's grief had transformed him into this man that Zach both knew as well as the back of his hand and not at all, anymore.

"What, you're gonna stay out here in the middle of nowhere and *rot*?" Zach demanded. Because it was such a fucking waste, and suddenly the destruction of it actually really pissed him off.

Nobody would ever see that half-smile again. He'd be the last. He'd be the last one to wonder, *what if.*

Gavin would never organize another power play, never make anyone bag skate until they were throwing up all over the ice. Never stand implacably behind the bench, or lean in and cajole his players to get their shit together. Never once inspire one of his players to make goals—even if they were goals bigger than they could bite off and chew.

That was such a fucking crime Zach could barely take it.

Gavin didn't say anything for a very long time. Zach almost worried that he'd not heard him but then he'd practically bellowed it so how was that even possible?

"Sure," Gavin finally said quietly. With resignation.

The joke was on Zach though, because despite the dark circles under his eyes and the scruff and the too-long hair that looked like he was chopping it off with a hunting knife or something equally ridiculous, Gavin looked so fucking alive.

He wasn't rotting.

Not dead. Not by a long shot.

"Why?"

Gavin shot him a hard look and fell silent.

And okay, yeah, he didn't want to talk about it. Well, *Zach* didn't want to talk about it either.

The day he'd found out, he'd crawled under the covers and cried until he'd felt like a dried husk of a human being. For Noelle, of course, who'd been so kind and sweet to him, practically a second mother when he'd been on the team, and for Gavin, who'd lost his touchstone, his soulmate.

Hayes had held him for hours, until he'd been all cried out.

Maybe that had been the beginning of the end for Zach.

He'd gotten over it—how could he do anything else?—but that driving hunger inside him had never felt the same. Noelle's death had been a rude reminder that hockey wasn't everything, that once it was over, once Zach was done, he'd have a whole life stretched out in front of him, empty and blank. Waiting for him to fill it with *something*.

But even if he didn't want to talk about it, Zach was *here* to talk about it.

"So, that's it?" Gavin finally spoke up. "You come all the way out here, and that's all you're gonna say? That I'm 'rotting' out here? Come on, Wheeler, you can do better than that."

Gavin didn't remind him again that he'd actually let him onto the porch, and nobody else had ever gotten that far, but then he didn't have to. Zach could feel the pressure of it. Wanted to rise up and meet it.

Where should he even start?

At the beginning, of course. But not Gavin's beginning. At *Zach's* beginning.

"I didn't know I wanted to coach, at first," Zach said. "But I went back to school, and some guy in my econ class figured out I'd played in the NHL. It didn't take long for him to start trying to persuade me to join their beer league."

Gavin chuckled. "You didn't."

Zach shrugged. "One or two of them had played in juniors, it wasn't *that* ridiculous." But okay, it had been. He'd skated circles around everyone. Had multi-point nights basically every time he took the ice.

"I'm sure your ego was very stroked." Gavin said it with a straight face, but everything inside Zach went hot and tight.

He pushed the feeling away. He'd never *wanted* to want Gavin Blackburn. He only had, helplessly. But back then he'd been eighteen. Now he was twenty-seven. He could control himself.

"But if I wanted to play the way I knew we could, with me on the roster, we couldn't just go out there and push the puck around. We needed—" Zach made a frustrated noise, remembering how after the first dozen or so games the casual attitude had begun to make him a little crazy. "We needed plays. Practices."

"You started coaching 'cause you wanted to dominate your beer league?" Gavin was laughing again, and it sounded rough, like he hadn't done it in awhile. Zach wondered, before he could stop himself, just how long it had been since he'd had anything to laugh about. Since he'd had anything he *wanted* to laugh about.

"It sounds really stupid when you put it that way, but yeah."

"So you started coaching your beer league, and then what?" Gavin might pretend disinterest in hockey, but Zach could see the light in his eyes. Whether it was because of hockey or Zach, he *wanted* to hear this story.

"A season. Then two. We won the city championship. But then I moved back to Portland for grad school, and I discovered I actually missed it—"

"Of course you did," Gavin muttered.

Zach wasn't going to touch that with a ten foot fucking pole.

"The scoring and the bullshit way everyone loved and hated and admired me, yeah, a little, but mostly just the coaching, actually. Coaxing the best out of those guys. Watching them bring that to the ice, every game we played? That I missed. More than scoring over fifty goals in twenty-five games."

"Jesus," Gavin said, scrubbing a hand over his face. "How many penalties did you draw?"

Zach laughed. "Enough. Never stopped me."

"I bet."

"But that's the thing, right? I liked playing. I *love* coaching." Zach forced himself to meet Gavin's dark eyes. The way he almost never had, the way he almost never could, starting when he'd been eighteen and then nineteen and in thrall to the most persistent crush in the history of the world. "Then I thought about what coach I'd want to learn from. The coach I'd like to be most like, and . . ." Zach shrugged, because he knew he didn't need to say it.

Gavin didn't say anything. Not for a long time.

Zach let him have his moment. He'd told the truth, yes, but he'd laid it on a little thick, once it had really sunk in that the reason Gavin was really interested was that this pitch wasn't about *him*. It was about Zach.

That was probably the other thing nobody who'd come out here had ever realized.

"I thought I'd like that story more," Gavin said flatly, finally.

But he had liked it. He hadn't liked the ending.

"Lie to yourself if you want," Zach said, standing up. Suddenly very tired of all this bullshit. The front that Gavin was so committed to. The front he didn't quite believe. "But don't lie to me."

He didn't look at Gavin as he walked by him.

Hayes had been right; this was a fool's errand.

Gavin wasn't rotting out here in the middle of fucking nowhere because he wanted to. He was rotting out here for something else, and until he figured out how to be honest? Well, he was just going to continue rotting and there was nothing Zach could do about it.

He was nearly to the screen door when Gavin's voice stopped him. "Wait."

Zach turned.

Gavin's face was full of anger. Regret. Frustration. Resignation.

"Come inside. Let's . . .we'll talk."

Some of Zach's disbelief must have leaked out because Gavin just rolled his eyes. "I can dismiss everyone else easy, without breaking a sweat. I don't give a shit about them. But you . . ." Gavin just shook his head and pushed off, heading towards the other door. The door into the house.

There'd been a time when hearing those words would've made Zach giddy for hours. For *days*. Even if he knew that Gavin only saw him as a player. One of *his* maybe, but still a player. Maybe, in some ways, a pseudo son.

Gavin held the door open and Zach took it, taking care, like he always did, not to touch him.

It took his eyes a second to adjust to the darkness once they were inside.

It was simple, but not as simple as he'd been initially expecting. After all, Gavin had been living here for *years*.

It was mostly one room, though Zach could see a doorway to another room, the corner of a bed with a dark green plaid coverlet visible. He looked away immediately, taking in the rest of the place.

There was a small kitchen on one side, with a big white ceramic sink sunk into the plain butcher block countertops. A living room on the other. A big comfortable-looking couch, opposite a surprisingly large TV setup.

Maybe it was neat, but it was clearly lived in. This was Gavin's *home*. There was a half-drunk bottle of red wine on the counter, the cork shoved into the bottle crookedly. A worn book on the table next to the couch. A sweatshirt draped unceremoniously over a barstool.

"You want a beer?" Gavin asked, heading towards the refrigerator.

"I . . .uh . . .sure," Zach said. He'd never been of-age when Gavin had been his coach and he was having to remind himself he was twenty-seven—not eighteen—the longer he spent in his presence.

Maybe because he suddenly felt just like he had back then, overwhelmed and shaky and very sure that none of it mattered at all.

Gavin pulled two bottles out of the fridge and popped the tops off easily. Slid one across the kitchen counter.

"So, uh, what did you want to talk about?" Zach asked stupidly. He picked up the beer and drank because he needed to do something with his hands.

Gavin shot him a look. "Did you really come all the way out here just to *kind of* make me an offer?"

"I'd make it official and everything. Contracts. Salary. About a dozen persuasive sub-points." Zach shrugged. "You said you didn't want to hear it."

"I don't." Gavin drummed his fingers on the countertop. "Tell me anyway."

CHAPTER 2

Zach had grown up.

When he'd first pulled himself out of the car, Gavin had barely recognized him.

Still the same height, but his build had changed, almost completely. He'd filled out, bulked up. His face had done the opposite—morphing and thinning out, leaving him chiseled and handsome.

Gavin felt a jolt go through him at the realization that he *was*. Big and tall and handsome, with his kind blue eyes and wheat-colored hair, long but not as long as Gavin's, clearly cut by someone who knew how to frame his face.

And that *face*. Jesus.

Gavin had always known he was into both men and women but he'd fallen in love with Noelle so young he'd never had a chance to do more than look. And he'd certainly never, *never* looked at Zach that way, but the jolt of *something,* deep in his belly, at how good Zach had grown up, was fucking him up.

In so many ways, Zach was that shy, scared nineteen-year-old he'd last coached. He was that kid Gavin had sent to the NHL.

He was the pro player with so much talent and potential that he'd prepped his own team to play against.

And he was someone else, entirely.

Someone else Gavin wasn't sure he knew anymore.

Right now, he was carefully outlining the selling points that Swift had probably sent him, referring to his phone that he'd set out on the counter.

Gavin stayed standing, on the other side of the long counter that stretched most of the length of the house. Zach had slipped onto one of the barstool seats, like sitting down made this whole conversation more official, like he was *really* offering Gavin this contract and Gavin actually wanted to hear about it. Like he might be truly tempted into considering it.

They both knew the truth, but Zach was committed to the charade anyway.

Not once had he considered that Zach, of all the guys he'd coached, might be better at leading than playing.

You could've been there for it, for all of it, but you made sure you weren't.

He had. For a lot of reasons. Reasons that still felt solid, if not *good.* He had a decent life out here. It wasn't terrible, but then it wasn't the life he'd had, either, and that was the most important thing.

Gavin interrupted Zach when he was between points six and seven. Something about performance-based bonuses. Extra money if he led the Evergreens to the playoffs, and won there, too.

"What happens to you if I say no?" Gavin asked.

Zach looked startled. "Uh . . .what do you mean?"

And Gavin realized the interruption hadn't been the surprising thing, but instead the concept that Gavin might actually be considering the job offer.

Suddenly he felt shitty that he was making Zach do this, and he didn't even want it. He didn't even *mean* it.

At least that had always been true, but then he'd never let anyone get this far before. He'd dismissed them in the clearing outside his house, the weight of his unloaded rifle always on his shoulder.

He had another gun he carried on long hikes, a lightweight pistol, because there was still wildlife out here, deep in the forests. But the rifle was showy and impressive and made all the slick NHL suits panic in a way that amused him at first and now only felt simpler. Easier.

"I mean, did they hire you thinking you could get to me, and if you can't—"

A frown creased Zach's face. "They didn't hire me to get to you."

"No?" Maybe it wasn't fair, but Gavin didn't really believe that.

The NHL didn't like loose ends, and he was the ultimate loose end. No longer easily folded into their systems, into their development programs, into their coaching hierarchies.

"This was all my idea," Zach said stubbornly. "Sidney wanted to approach—" He cut himself off. "It doesn't matter who he wanted originally."

It kind of mattered, in a way that Gavin hadn't considered in a long, long time.

Before, *before*, he'd been competitive. He'd wanted to be the best. The most sought after. The idea of the Evergreens going after anyone else to be their new head coach would've kept him up nights.

But then he'd discovered there were a lot worse things.

"I was the one who suggested it." Zach shot him a look. "Swift thought I was crazy to even come here, but I told him, I told him I *had* to try, to see you, to make sure . . ."

Zach didn't have to finish the sentence for Gavin to know what he meant. That he was alive. That he was well. That he hadn't drowned himself in booze or silence.

He couldn't say that either of those things hadn't seemed appealing at the beginning. But he'd grown out of self-destruction. Now numbness came naturally, without any assistance whatsoever.

"Well, you're here. I'm here." Gavin spread his arms wide. Ignored the guilt pulsing in his gut. It was easier than it should've been. "I'm fine. Even if I'm apparently rotting away here."

"Why did you let me—" Zach stopped abruptly, expression suddenly angry. "I get it."

If Zach got it, then that was one of them, because Gavin still wasn't sure why he'd invited Zach in or why he'd been stupid enough to let him make an actual job pitch.

Maybe he'd been tempted by life, by *real fucking life*, for the first time in four years. Now *that* he should feel guilty about but like a cosmic joke played on Gavin, of course he didn't. Not even a little bit.

"They won't fire you, then?" Gavin changed the subject, back to his initial question. It was easier to stay focused on Zach and his future, maybe not the future he'd imagined for him, back when he'd known that nineteen-year-old, so fucking full of promise, but still undeniably bright.

Zach looked incredulous. "No," he said bluntly.

"Okay. Good."

"Do you want to hear the rest?" Zach asked cautiously.

He didn't. He hadn't wanted to hear the beginning or the middle either, but like an idiot, he waved his hand for Zach to continue.

It was really stupid but he couldn't seem to stop himself.

Zach finished and then for a long moment, there was silence.

Zach still looked a little angry, like he couldn't quite believe Gavin had made him go through the whole thing. Gavin couldn't really believe he'd done it either.

"Well," Zach finally said. "That's it."

"I listened to it," Gavin said as diplomatically as he could. It should be very easy to get the next word out. The *no*. The *no* had come very easily to him for the last four years, but now the word was stuck in his throat. Instead, he cleared it and said, "So, since I listened, I think you should tell me why you quit playing hockey."

Gavin leaned over, pulled the fridge open, and grabbed two more beers. He shouldn't care about this, shouldn't feel like something he'd wanted, that he'd believed in, had turned out to be false. This was *Zach's* life, not his.

But it still stung.

"And," Gavin added, "don't tell me the beer league where you demolished everyone was *really* playing hockey. Why did you quit the NHL?"

"I didn't *quit*," Zach said mulishly. "I fucking retired."

"If you're not even thirty, you didn't retire."

"I didn't expect that you'd be an asshole about this." He didn't tell Gavin what he'd expected he would be an asshole about, but then it was obvious, wasn't it?

He'd actually been pretty nice about the job offer. He'd let Zach get through the whole spiel. Hadn't actually said the word *no*, even.

Gavin pushed that thought away. "I'm not being an asshole."

"Kind of looks like it from here."

"I just wanna know why it didn't work out. When . . ." Gavin swallowed hard. He'd meant it, earlier. He didn't want to talk about it. He *could,* but he never *wanted* to. "You were playing. Playing well. Second line, if I remember. The Mavs had high hopes for you. Maybe not the foundation of the franchise, but the future looked promising. *Your* future looked promising."

Zach huffed. "Am I allowed to say *I* don't want to talk about it?" He took a long drink of beer.

It was inexcusable, and he *should* feel guilty about it, but he pinned on his best "fuck around and find out" Coach look and shook his head.

"You've got a funny way of not being an asshole," Zach muttered.

"Just tell me. Not everything just . . .*why.*"

Because if he didn't, Gavin was going to dig out his tablet when Zach left and Google it, and he really, really didn't want to go down that rabbit hole.

He couldn't say he'd *never* gone down it, but he'd gotten better about resisting. About realizing that the hole inside him and its accompanying agony was always worse when he let himself do it.

"I didn't . . .I didn't *like* it," Zach said.

Gavin's jaw dropped. That was not what he'd expected Zach to say.

"You *love* playing hockey, though."

"Yeah, I love playing hockey. I didn't love playing it as a job. All that corporate bullshit. The trades. The pressure to win. Never sure what's going to happen the next day." Gavin watched as Zach's throat, strong and tanned, worked. He wanted to press his fingertips to his skin and *feel* it.

He looked away, shaky and suddenly unsure.

"And," Zach added, like he didn't want to even say it, but he couldn't *not*, "the gay thing really fucking sucked."

Fury coalesced inside Gavin. He knew what Zach had been saying about the corporate bullshit. The intense highs of winning. The catastrophic lows of losing. But he'd never imagined Zach's sexuality was going to be a problem. He'd listened intently when Zach had come out, stammering and blushing, and reassured him that he wouldn't be alone. That there were others. That nobody would give him shit. He'd shown him articles about the out players in professional football. About the Riptide and the Piranhas. How the new owner of the Charleston Condors was gay and in a relationship with one of his ex-players. Zach had nodded intently, and later Noelle had teased Gavin, gently suggesting that Zach had probably been more aware of all of this than Gavin himself.

Had he been wrong? Had Gavin *lied* just because he hadn't known any better? Because he was stupid and clueless and ridiculously hopeful?

"Did—" Gavin swallowed hard. "Did people give you shit?"

"Nothing obvious, and well . . .there was another guy on the Mavs, too. He wasn't out either, so we had each other. It could've been worse, I know that. But it was that, on top of everything else. It was like I could never relax and just remember why I liked, why I *loved*, playing hockey."

Gavin didn't know what to say. "Shit."

Zach chuckled under his breath. "Yeah, basically. It was shit. I was miserable. Course then I quit and I was miserable not playing, at first."

He didn't want to know what that felt like, but he did. When he'd first come out here, it had been so quiet and he'd been so alone, and the pain, already intense, had grown and grown until it was excruciating, like hundreds of nails shoved under his skin.

Eventually, Gavin had found ways to blunt it, to dull it. Until he could bear it.

"But you figured it out." Zach was standing there, whole and hearty, looking so fucking alive, with none of the sourness of depression or sadness around him. He didn't need to tell Gavin he was okay, but Gavin discovered he wanted the words anyway.

"Yeah," Zach said. "Took time. But things fell into place. I finished my degree. Decided to go to grad school. And the coaching thing? That was unexpected but good."

Unexpected, but good.

Kind of like how it had felt to Gavin when he'd woken up this morning and hadn't known that hours later, he was going to be sharing a beer with Zach.

"Good," Gavin said. Not sure what else he should say. Not sure what he *could* say. He didn't want to take the job; he *couldn't* take the job.

But the temptation tugged at him, anyway.

He drank more of his beer. Tried to think of something else to say, and just when he thought he couldn't, his brain snagged on something Zach had said.

"So, this other guy, on the Mavs, who was out? You guys stuck together?"

Zach nodded, picking at the label on his bottle.

"You get together with him?"

Zach's eyes shot to his, looking shocked. "No, *no*. God, no. Hayes is just . . .he's my best friend. It was never like that between us."

Hayes. *Hayes.*

The only Hayes Gavin could remember was Hayes Montgomery. His brain was still stuck on the fact that Hayes Montgomery was gay, but then Zach kept talking.

"Few years ago, he was traded from the Mavs to the Sentinels, so even if I'd stayed, signed the next contract, and the *next* contract, he wouldn't have been there, anyway, and I'm so glad . . ." Zach trailed off. "It was just better this way."

He didn't sound like he quite believed it, but Gavin let that go. He understood. Sometimes things that were better—like him moving here, letting the world fall away around him—didn't always feel awesome.

But that didn't mean they were *wrong*.

"You're still friends, though?" Gavin wanted to skirt the counter sitting between them and put a reassuring hand on Zach's shoulder or, *fuck*, something. But it had been years since they'd casually touched like that, and before, when they had, everything had been totally different.

He didn't know how to touch Zach now.

Zach smiled. "Yeah. He's actually the one who figured out where you were."

It was almost automatic instinct to say, *well fuck him then*, but then Gavin realized he wasn't angry Zach had shown up today.

"Yeah? Well, I'm glad he knew," Gavin said.

"You actually mean that." Zach sounded shocked.

"I didn't shoot you, did I?" *I asked you to the porch. I invited you inside. I listened to the whole job offer.*

Zach rolled his eyes. "We established already that you weren't gonna shoot anybody. Definitely not me."

"Fair." Gavin cleared his throat. He still hadn't said the words out loud. *Thanks but no thanks.* He knew once he did, Zach would have no reason to stay. He'd made the offer. He'd told Gavin why he'd left the NHL. There was nothing else to do, nothing else to *say*.

But Gavin realized that he didn't want him to leave. Not yet.

He would eventually, of course. His life was in Portland. Zach would fly back to the west coast and he and Sidney Swift would go to that other coach, the one Swift had wanted in the first place, and hire him instead.

It shouldn't have stung. It did.

Maybe it was that realization or maybe it was the fact that he'd be leaving anyway, regardless, so there was no harm in it.

"Hey," Gavin said, "you should stick around. Have dinner with me."

Zach's eyes widened. "You eat dinner? With *people*?"

Gavin wanted to tell him he wasn't people; he wasn't even close to *people*. But it was too weird, even for him, because the last time they'd even been in a room together had been four years ago.

And that hadn't even been a room; it had been a rink.

"Not with people, no, not usually." Though occasionally, now, he did go into the little town closest to his cabin and eat at the diner. But that wasn't really eating *with* people. There were people around. Sometimes they said hi and smiled at him, familiar now with his presence, but it wasn't a social event. It was just food. Fuel.

"But you want me to stay." Zach sounded uneasy now.

"Yes," Gavin said. Maybe *he* should be the uneasy one, but it felt like the most natural thing to offer. A glance at his watch told him it was past four.

"I'm sorry, but *why*?" Zach burst out. "You don't want to take the job—"

"I didn't say that," Gavin said, but obviously he didn't. He *didn't*.

If he went back to coaching, it would be the same, all over again. And if he went back to Portland, when everything in his life was fundamentally different now, he'd never be able to be numb again.

And the only thing that kept him alive, kept him moving, was that blessed numbness.

Zach shot him a sharp look. "You didn't have to say no. I know you don't want it, I knew it before I even got out of the car, but I came here anyway, and I realize now, I . . .I shouldn't have."

"No," Gavin said and discovered he was rounding the island before he realized he was doing it. Tugging Zach into a quick hug. And it *was* different. Totally different than how it had been seven years ago and then four years ago. Maybe because they'd become two different people than they'd been before. "No, you should've come. I'm glad you came."

Zach still looked at him incredulously when he pulled back. "What the fuck," he said.

Gavin smacked him lightly on the arm. "Language," he teased. "You were better behaved at nineteen."

"I was scared as fuck of you at nineteen," Zach muttered.

"Really?" Gavin chuckled.

"*Really*. You were fucking terrifying."

"Not me, maybe. Everything was probably terrible." Gavin sighed. "I mean it. I'm glad you came. I'm glad I got to see you."

"It didn't have to be me promising at least a dozen or so open-ended favors to Hayes to find out where the hell you were and then driving all the way out here for it to actually happen." The moment the words were out of his mouth Zach looked like he regretted them.

But no. This was good. This was honesty.

Gavin had forgotten how bad—and good—the truth could feel. Like sharp blades cutting through a flawless stretch of ice.

Lancing all the aching pain inside and letting it bleed out, finally.

"I know. . .I'm sorry."

"You're not sorry," Zach said. "You're really not. Don't say it if you're not. I'm not . . .I'm not mad. I get it. You had to do what you had to do."

"I did," Gavin said softly. "I *am* sorry that it hurt you. Me doing what I needed to do."

"It didn't . . ." Zach cleared his throat.

"It *did*, and I'd probably be mad, somewhere inside, if you didn't give a shit," Gavin said, trying to laugh, because it was easier than the alternative.

And this is why he didn't do this. Because that comfortable numbness was impossible to find right now, but he figured Jon, his therapist, whom he hadn't seen in at least six months now, would probably tell him that was a good thing, the *best* thing. That was why he'd stopped seeing him. He kept pushing Gavin and Gavin didn't *want* to be pushed.

"Well, I give a shit," Zach said, laughing too, now.

"Then stay for dinner. We can watch . . ." God, suddenly Gavin didn't know what they *could* watch. Definitely not hockey. Except hockey had been the one thing connecting them, all those years ago, and now hockey was . . .well, hockey was difficult for Gavin.

He craved it, still.

Couldn't let himself have it.

But for one night, you could.

Zach gestured towards the TV. "What *do* you watch?" he asked, because he was clearly assuming it wasn't hockey. It *wasn't*.

"Uh, stupid reality TV. Brainless movies. Lots of explosions." Gavin made a *boom* noise under his breath and Zach laughed again, and it was easy. Well, *easier*.

"I can get behind that," Zach said.

It felt natural then, to head to the fridge, find the chicken he'd defrosted. There was plenty for both of them, because Gavin hated cooking for just himself and often made enough leftovers he could skate by for a couple of days.

He pulled out two more beers, and he told himself that it was easier that way, to deal with Zach, with this new grownup, this *handsome* Zach, when there was a layer of booze sanding down all their newly sharp edges.

Zach agreed to chop veggies for a salad, and it felt way too normal, marinating the chicken and then taking it out onto the back patio to grill.

They ate at the counter, Zach's leg brushing against Gavin's once, then twice. Not on purpose, he didn't think, but accidentally. Like he was just loose now, from the beer and the food and the company.

After, with more beer, they retreated to the couch.

Zach had hesitated when Gavin had handed him a new bottle. "I shouldn't," he said apologetically. "I'm driving and—"

"Stay. Couch is comfortable," Gavin said, before he could think better of it. For a split second, he almost considered saying, *so is my bed*. But that was *insane*. And Gavin had been working very diligently for the last four years to *not* be insane.

Zach *would* be leaving in the morning. He wasn't going to maroon himself out here, not like Gavin. He had no reason to do it. But it was already too soon, and the morning felt safer, like he'd have adjusted to this new reality by then.

"Sure," Zach said, like it was easy. Like it was nothing to stay on Gavin's couch.

Like that wasn't its own kind of insanity.

Maybe Jon would tell him he was losing it, finally. Or maybe Jon would tell him this was the sanest he'd been in awhile.

In four fucking years.

They watched one of Gavin's stupid explosion movies. Then another. Gavin's shoulder brushing up against Zach's big one.

God, he *had* gotten big. And tall. Taller even than Gavin.

Maybe it was the beer. Maybe it was the darkness falling around them.

But it felt right to press his thigh against Zach's and keep it there. To absorb all that warmth that he'd been living without forever.

When the credits of the movie rolled, Zach didn't move and Gavin sure as fuck didn't move. He was comfortable, lulled into a sense of total complacency by the beer and the food and the actual physical touch.

"Hey," Zach said and turned his head. God, was he really *that* close to Gavin? He should *really* move back. Put another few inches between them.

But it was like the last four years hadn't happened. None of the pain. None of the distance and the special agony *that* had brought Gavin, and he didn't have the motivation to do it.

"Hmmm?"

"I want you to see something," Zach said.

"What is it?" Gavin felt so comfortable, so relaxed, he might just float away on a cloud of serotonin.

For the first time in what felt like hours, Zach tensed, and then it was like he forced himself to relax. "You haven't been following hockey at all, have you?"

"No," Gavin said. "I mean . . .I'll occasionally, like . . .I don't know. Fall down a rabbit hole. I know better, but it happens. And then after I . . ."

"What if I was here after?" Zach asked quietly. Somehow his hand—and God, his hands had gotten big, too, as big as the rest of him—was on Gavin's knee, squeezing lightly.

It would not suck as much, that was for sure.

He'd have someone to pull him back out. And *God*, Gavin wanted it.

"I just want to show you something," Zach said. Then suddenly he was gone, his warmth missing, and Gavin nearly complained about it.

But that would be weird. Even weirder than this was, anyway.

Thirty seconds later, Zach was back, and he was carrying a backpack. He pulled a laptop out of the bag and set it on the coffee table. "I'm not trying to convince you, I just . . .I just want you to see. Why I came here."

"You came here to see if I actually put shells in my rifle," Gavin said drowsily.

Zach chuckled, but when Gavin focused on the screen he could see that Zach was queuing up some game film.

Gavin would have to have buried himself out here for a lot longer than four years to not recognize the Evergreens' green and white uniforms.

"This is from last year," Zach said, gesturing at the screen. "Second to the last game of the year."

There was a part of Gavin that really wanted to look away. That wanted to shut the laptop and tell Zach he didn't want to see. He didn't *want* to be convinced. But he couldn't, because Zach cared enough about this to come out here.

There was a line change on the screen, and Gavin straightened, because the energy on the ice suddenly shifted. The team, while not sluggish before, began driving harder, faster towards the net, finding a new gear.

Pushing them was a smaller guy, the right winger, but the center and the left winger were right there with him. Gavin remembered, abruptly, why he didn't let himself do this, because he was leaning forward, eyes glued to the screen, watching the play unfold.

Watching the three of them pass the puck like they were born to do it, and the right wing take a brilliant fucking shot, top shelf, the goalie not having a chance in hell of stopping it.

Gavin didn't say anything, because he knew Zach was going to tell him what he wanted to know.

"That's Elliott Jones," Zach said. "He was eighteen there. Nineteen now. He spent the whole season on the second line, but the Evergreens were on a five-game losing streak, getting outscored and outplayed, so the coach changed the lines up."

"He's . . ." Well, Gavin didn't even need to say it. Zach could see it. You could probably see it from the freaking moon. The kid was probably going to be a big star. Drafted-in-the-first-round big star.

"Here's the thing," Zach said. "He wasn't that good on the second line."

"What?"

"I mean, he wasn't *bad*. He couldn't ever be bad, probably. But he went from decent to extraordinary with those two."

Gavin didn't want to ask. He asked anyway. "Why?"

"See the left wing?"

Gavin nodded.

"That's Malcolm McCoy. He'll be a senior. Drafted by the Leafs, but wanted to stay in school. He's solid, reliable, but when Jones gets out there? He's better, too. He turns from a guy barely hanging onto being drafted into Jack freaking Hughes. Jones and McCoy only played on the same line for the last two games. But in those two games? They had five goals and six assists."

"So you have two guys who make each other better. A *lot* better." Gavin was turning this over in his head, even though he didn't want to. He wanted this to be someone else's problem.

"Funny though, when I met Mal for coffee a month ago, after they'd hired me, you know what the first thing he said was?" Zach chuckled dryly. "*Don't you dare put me on the same fucking line as Jones.*"

"Huh. They don't like each other?"

Zach sighed. "That's the theory. I don't know how to deal with this. And we get any kind of coach in there who doesn't get it, they're gonna fuck this up. And the two of them—the *three* of them out there, really, 'cause Ivan's a big part of it, too, keeps them focused and centered, honestly—could be something special out there."

Gavin knew it. He'd seen it, too, immediately.

"I saw it," Zach continued, "and I knew *you* could handle it."

Gavin swallowed hard. He didn't want to be Zach's savior. But there was no question this was an intriguing problem.

"What about the rest of the team?"

"Solid defense. Two guys who will definitely end up in the pros. Brody's really a pure defenseman, one of the best I've seen. Give him five years, and he's Jaccob Slavin."

"And the other guy?"

"Ramsey Andresen. He's like a freaking chess master out there. When the five of them are on the ice, it's pure fucking magic."

"Goalie?" Gavin told himself to stop asking. He didn't want to know how good this team could be. How good they could be if they had a coach who understood, who knew how to bring disparate parts together into one well-oiled machine.

"And that's where things get really interesting."

Gavin's jaw dropped. "They weren't interesting before?"

"I know," Zach said, laughing. "We just got a new transfer. Finn Reynolds."

Even buried in the wilds of Michigan for four years, Gavin knew that name. "He's not. *No.*"

"Yeah, Finn's Morgan Reynolds' son."

"Shit."

"What I'm trying to tell you is that we *need* a coach who's gonna be willing to be . . .well, unorthodox? Who's willing to work with these kids and make them better. Help them live up to their potential." Zach didn't need to add, *like you helped me live up to my potential,* but Gavin knew they were both thinking it.

Gavin had never wanted to be a different person, with different baggage, more than he did in this moment.

He could see it now. Putting that logo back on his chest. Coaching these guys to the one thing he'd never won before—a national championship.

Taking one deep breath and another, Gavin scrubbed a hand across his face. "Why didn't you lead with this?"

Zach shut the laptop and turned to him, and suddenly he was just as close as he'd been before. Maybe even closer. His thigh pressed hot and inevitable against Gavin's.

Gavin could pick out the individual cerulean and green flecks in his blue eyes. He seemed flushed too, skin warm and golden, lighting him up inside.

It was that he was so familiar and so strange, too—creating a weird mix churning inside him. Making him unsettled. Making him temporarily lose his mind.

"I . . .I didn't think I'd even make it to the porch," Zach confessed softly. "And then I did and you . . .and I . . ."

Gavin thought he understood. This whole evening had taken him by surprise. Maybe Zach had known some of it, because he'd been the one to come here, but clearly he hadn't expected to end up here.

"Yeah," Gavin said, barely getting the word out, his throat suddenly thick.

The air was sluggish, hot even, and hotter between them. Zach leaned in another half an inch and if he did it again, well . . .Gavin wasn't going to think about that.

He *couldn't*.

No matter how good it felt, to be this close to someone else again, to someone he knew and *liked*—though Gavin could at least acknowledge the affection hadn't felt like this before, tinged with heat—he should move away. He should move away, *because* it felt so goddamn good.

Because it *hadn't* ever felt like this before. Zach had been a player of his, and he'd loved him in that way, exclusively. Gangly, self-effacing, well-meaning Zach, who looked out for everyone and just wanted someone to do the same for him.

Back then, he'd even considered himself a pseudo-father figure.

Well, the fucking joke was on him now, because four years later, the rumblings in the base of his stomach felt anything but fatherly.

Shit.

That was the thought that propelled him backward. Away from temptation.

Did Gavin see disappointment flash across Zach's face? If he did, he pretended he didn't.

Pretended his heart wasn't beating double-time.

"Well, uh, it's late," Gavin said awkwardly.

Zach nodded. Like he didn't trust his voice.

Well, Gavin didn't trust his whole fucking body now, because it hadn't been Zach leaning in, gobbling up the space between them. Gavin had been right there, not even caring that it was insane to be doing this.

That it wasn't a betrayal of everything he . . .that he . . . Gavin shut that thought off with a relentless thud.

Never to be examined again.

"Let me get you some blankets," Gavin said, lifting himself off the couch.

"Not sure I'm gonna need them. It's . . .uh . . .a warm night."

Gavin flushed, glad he'd already turned away so Zach wouldn't see. He was hot too, sweaty palms, moisture trickling down his back, just from sitting too close on a couch.

"It can get cold at night." He crossed over to the chest, pulled out two blankets that he often used deep in the winter when he cuddled up alone on the couch and didn't feel like dragging himself all the way to the bedroom. He set them on the far end of the couch—as far away from Zach as he could manage.

"There's a bathroom, through. Spare toothbrush, in the drawer," Gavin said, gesturing towards the bathroom door. He could hear the fear, the panic in his voice. "If you need anything . . ." *Don't need anything. Don't come to my bed. Please God, no.*

But Zach only nodded slowly. "I'm sure I'll be fine," he said.

There was no other word for it. He couldn't even pretend it wasn't something it absolutely fucking was. Gavin *escaped*, closing the bedroom door behind him. Leaning against it, breathing heavily.

What the fuck had just happened? What had he nearly done?

And now Zach would be there in the morning, sleepy and warm, on Gavin's couch.

Gavin nearly groaned.

It *had* to be better in the morning. With the bright sunlight exposing everything, making it impossible for him to feel that way again.

He'd get up early. Set an alarm. Make breakfast. Keep the counter between them. Feed Zach and then send him on his merry way with a firm no.

CHAPTER 3

"You ever going to tell me how it went?" Hayes asked lazily, shoving a hand through his damp hair, leaving it sticking straight up in little wet spikes.

They were in Hayes' outside pool, soaking up the sun.

Zach had been here in Florida nearly six hours, and he was impressed that Hayes had waited that long to ask.

"I . . .there's nothing to say," Zach said, even though that was the biggest lie he'd ever told his best friend.

There was a whole fucking lot to say.

Gavin invited me into his house. Made me dinner. Practically cuddled with me on the couch. We almost—oh my God—kissed. And then he panicked, and the next morning it was like nothing had happened. He made me breakfast and then sent me on my way.

And in the last moment, when I was getting in the car, he compressed his lips together, shoved his hands into his pockets, and wouldn't look me in the eye when he said that he wasn't going to take the job.

It was a whole lot.

So much that Zach's hands had been shaking on the wheel as he'd driven out of the woods. So much that when he'd gotten to the airport, he'd convinced the nice lady in Traverse City to rebook his ticket from Portland to Tampa.

He'd come straight to Hayes. To tell him everything? To tell him *something*, certainly. Zach had never hidden anything from Hayes.

But it turned out he didn't know how to even begin telling this story.

"What the fuck, man, you come out here all of a sudden, and now you won't even tell me why?" Hayes didn't sound mad though. He sounded worried.

Maybe he should be.

Zach's hands had stopped shaking, but his insides hadn't.

Every time he thought about that five minutes on the couch, after he'd showed Gavin the game film, he quivered like a tree in a storm.

It shouldn't have been like that. It had never been like that before.

Sure, Zach had hero-worshipped Gavin. He'd had the unfortunate crush. But it had never felt like it could ever go anywhere. Even after Gavin's wife had died, he'd never once thought, *oh, now he's free, something might happen.* First, because Gavin had clearly been too devastated. Second, he'd never appeared to see Zach as anything but his player. And then there was the minor fact that Gavin had never said he was interested in guys like that.

He'd definitely never appeared to be interested in Zach like that.

"It didn't go how I expected it would go," Zach finally said.

Hayes made a face. "Well, no shit. So you made it onto the porch, huh?"

"I made it into the house. I . . .I spent the night."

Hayes' jaw dropped. "You didn't freaking sleep with Gavin Blackburn. Tell me you didn't."

"No, *no.*" Zach laughed self-consciously. "No, of course not. I was on the couch. It wasn't . . .it wasn't like that."

Hayes punched him in the arm lightly. "I was about to give you about a hundred high fives and then lecture you about what a terrible fucking idea that would be."

"Awful," Zach agreed.

It was one thing to say it out loud. It was another to believe it, deep down, though.

"You always had a ridiculous hockey crush on the guy."

"Kind of like the one you had on Morgan Reynolds?"

Hayes punched him again, harder this time.

"And that's why I'd be giving you the lecture," Hayes said. He didn't sound as bitter as he usually did. More resigned.

Zach shouldn't have brought up Morgan. He was a sore spot, always, with Hayes. Zach couldn't even blame him, considering what he knew about what had happened between them.

"And don't think I missed that you're trying to distract me," Hayes continued. "You stayed the night on his couch? I can't fucking believe it. Nobody's ever made it to the porch before."

"He was never going to shoot me." *Wasn't ever going to shoot anyone. If they actually thought that, they were stupid enough they didn't deserve Gavin, anyway.*

"Not you," Hayes agreed. He was quiet for a long moment, floating in the water. His eyes were covered by sunglasses, and his expression was thoughtful, but opaque. "I'm guessing despite you two becoming reacquainted, he's not taking the job."

"No," Zach said quietly. He hadn't texted Sidney Swift yet, but it was only a matter of time. He should've already done it. It wasn't like Gavin was going to change his mind.

He'd gotten everything he was ever going to get from Gavin Blackburn, and frankly, Zach knew he should be happy about it. It was more than he could've possibly expected.

But it still sucked.

"Not surprised," Hayes said. "But you gave it a solid effort. B+, I'd say."

"Do I wanna know what I'd have had to do to get an A?"

Hayes turned, fingers latching onto the edge of the pool. "Seduced him, maybe? Though that wouldn't have convinced him to take the job. Probably would've freaked him out. Big gay freakout, for sure. And then probably the big widower freakout—"

"That's not a thing," Zach interrupted.

"Oh, it's totally a thing. And then even after all those freakouts, he definitely wouldn't have taken the job."

"Thanks, Monty. That's super helpful," Zach said dryly. "I can see why the Sentinels send you on so many recruiting trips."

Hayes shrugged. "You show him Jones and McCoy?"

"Yeah."

"Okay, well, A- then. But that's as good as you're getting."

Zach smacked him on the shoulder. "You're such an overperforming, overachieving asshole. Do you ever turn it off?"

"Baby, you know I don't," Hayes said, batting his eyelashes in Zach's direction.

"You're the worst."

"Which is why you came to *me*," Hayes said knowingly.

"Maybe I missed you."

"Bullshit," Hayes retorted. "So did the most brilliant genius coach in the universe have any super special insights on Jones and McCoy?"

"No," Zach said. And okay, sue him. He did think Gavin was the most brilliant genius coach in the universe with all the super special insights. It wasn't really fair of Hayes to bring that up, but then *he'd* brought up Hayes' ex-fling, so possibly they were even now.

"No? Not even one? Well, that's disappointing. I thought maybe he might agree with me," Hayes said.

"They're not fucking," Zach said.

"But they *want* to be," Hayes said knowingly.

"That's your theory."

"You have to admit it's a good theory. You showed me the game. The one where they started on the same line for the first time? It was like Jones finally thought he could make McCoy pay attention to him." Hayes shot him a look. "Don't tell me you've never felt that way before."

He had. *He had.* Too many times when he'd been in college, for those two years, when Gavin had been his coach. He'd wanted his eyes on him more than he'd wanted to breathe sometimes.

But was that Elliott?

If it was, it could backfire so spectacularly. Zach had figured out how to find that edge without Gavin coaching him, but everyone couldn't do that. You had to do more to make it than play good hockey to impress a cute boy.

"You know I have." Zach told himself not to say it, but he said it anyway. "And so have you."

"Yeah, which is why I said it," Hayes said calmly.

"It could be catastrophic," Zach said. It wasn't the first time Hayes had suggested this theory, but Zach had been more willing to dismiss it outright. But it was harder today, because he'd just been forcibly reminded of how strong that pull could be. Despite knowing better, despite knowing everything he did about Gavin and his situation, when they'd been on the couch together last night, he'd have gone along with anything Gavin wanted.

And it had been *years*.

"Isn't that your job? To figure that shit out?" Hayes wondered.

Zach made a face. "Yeah."

Hayes fell quiet after that, and Zach drifted in the pool, enjoying the sun and the water and the quiet companionship he always had with Hayes. But he still found it hard to force his mind to dismiss last night from his memory.

He wanted to hang onto it, to build a castle around it, to assign it a meaning it didn't deserve.

Maybe he *should* tell Hayes. Hayes would set him straight. Tell him flatly that there was no future and he needed to get over it.

But before he could, Hayes turned to him. "Did you think I couldn't handle talking about it?" he asked.

"I don't know what you mean," Zach said, but it was mostly a lie.

"I saw the transfer," Hayes said bluntly.

"Please tell me you don't still have him on Google alert," Zach said. "If you do, I'll have to stage an intervention—*another* intervention—and we know how well that went last time."

"It wasn't that bad," Hayes grumbled.

"You ended up with some guy you didn't even really like, who made you come out of the closet to prove some bullshit about how committed you were. And then he dumped you."

"Thanks for that reminder," Hayes said dryly. "And the answer is *no*, I do not have Morgan on Google alert. Or Finn, for that matter. A teammate told me."

"A teammate who doesn't know?"

"You forget, *nobody* knows," Hayes reminded him. "Just you."

"And him," Zach said, even though that was not exactly helpful.

"I don't know, it was a long time ago," Hayes said, a trace of bitterness in his voice. "Maybe he's forgotten about it."

Zach smacked him in the arm. "Don't get all moody and melancholy, okay? This is why I didn't bring it up—"

"So you *weren't* telling me," Hayes said triumphantly.

"I can't believe you," Zach said. "Of course I didn't tell you. You get all weird every time Reynolds comes up."

"This is his son, and he's transferring to the college you're coaching at. We *should* talk about it." Hayes glanced over at him.

"How is this any different than the Sentinels drafting him? You're gonna have to face him someday."

"*Someday*," Hayes said knowingly. He didn't need to add that so many things could happen to players in development. Finn might never make it to the NHL. Never make it to the

Sentinels. Hayes might never have to face the son of the man he'd fallen wildly in love with.

Zach shrugged. "Just like I said on draft night, what is there to talk about? I know you're like—"

"Don't say it," Hayes interrupted him, his voice hard.

"I *know* you're fucked up about him. You always have been, even before, well . . .even *before*. If you want me to talk about it, all there really is to say is that I have a feeling Finn's just as fucked up about his dad."

"In a different way," Hayes said.

Zach rolled his eyes. "Obviously."

"So what are you gonna do about it?"

What *were* they going to do about it? Zach didn't know yet. He knew how it felt to have expectations riding on you. He'd learned to balance that pressure, though not as well as others he knew. If he had, maybe he would've enjoyed playing professional hockey more.

"It's still new. I haven't even talked to the kid, yet."

Hayes didn't say anything. He seemed annoyed, but then he'd been the one who brought it up in the first place.

It was definitely time to change the subject. It had been time to change the subject before it ever came up in the first place.

"I almost kissed Gavin—or he almost kissed me."

Hayes froze, halfway to reaching for his can of beer on the side of the pool. "Seriously? *Seriously?*"

"I mean, yeah. Pretty sure. It didn't happen, but it might've, if I'd grown a pair and actually gone for it before he panicked."

Hayes took a long drink of his beer and shot Zach a look. "Okay. Rewind. Tell me the whole fucking story, okay?" He shook his head. "I can't fucking believe you didn't *lead* with that."

Zach did. From the moment he'd gotten out of the car, to the invite to the porch, to the house, to dinner and the beers they'd drunk.

"And in the morning," Zach finished, finally, "he was really weird. Could barely look me in the eye. Practically shoved me out of the house and into my car. On my way out told me he didn't want the job."

"Ouch," Hayes said.

Zach had been telling himself since it happened that it hadn't sucked. But it kind of had, actually.

He'd gotten used to nice Gavin until cold shoulder Gavin had unexpectedly shown up.

"Yeah," Zach said morosely. "It was probably the first and the last and the *only* chance I'd ever get. I should've just gone for it."

Hayes floated closer. Slung an arm around Zach's shoulders. Hayes was an inch shorter than him and built a little smaller, but it felt good to have his best friend pull him in and comfort him. "Listen, no. You shouldn't have."

"Really?"

Hayes nodded. "Really. Imagine if you'd actually kissed him and he'd kissed you back? How insane would his freakout have been?"

"But I would've *known* then. What it felt like." Zach knew he was whining.

"And what, you think you'd have been better off? No. No, you wouldn't have been. Take it from someone who thought, once, that something was better than nothing. It's not. It's . .

." Zach could hear the pain in Hayes' voice. But he kept going anyway. "It's not better. It's worse. 'Cause you know what it's like, and you can't forget it, even if you never get it again."

Zach didn't know what to say to that. He just hung onto Hayes harder. Hugged him tighter. "God, man, I'm sorry."

"Don't be sorry." Hayes' voice had gotten lighter, but it sounded so forced. "I'm glad I learned for both of us. Maybe after this you'll be able to move on."

For half a second, he nearly considered asking Hayes if that had ever helped him, but he didn't. Because the answer was obvious.

"Well, I don't have much of a choice. Why would I see him again? He's not taking the job."

"Imagine if he did though?" Hayes was smiling now, like he was contemplating what an utter clusterfuck that would make of Zach's life.

"Let's not," Zach muttered.

"I'm just saying—the guy probably thought he was straight. How old is he again? Fifty?"

Zach made a scoffing noise. "He's almost forty. Unlike—"

Hayes interrupted him before he could say it. "So he went his first *almost* forty years thinking he was straight, and then he lost his wife, and the grief fucked him up so bad, he moved into the middle of fucking nowhere and quit the job he loved. Then his ex-player shows up, all grown up, and reminds him he's not dead, yet."

"It wasn't like that," Zach argued, even though he could see it.

"I think it was *exactly* like that," Hayes retorted. "It's kind of amazing he didn't have a meltdown in front of you."

And suddenly, Zach was worried.

Maybe he shouldn't have been, but Zach was wishing he'd gotten his new phone number or something, because now he couldn't even check in to make sure he was okay.

Of course, checking in to make sure he was okay would also mean acknowledging what had *almost* happened, and now that Zach was thinking about it, he wasn't sure he could've.

"Now you're freaking out," Hayes said bluntly.

"Well, what if he *isn't* okay with it? What if he doesn't have anyone to talk to?" And okay, Hayes was at least partly right; he was panicking about this, now.

"He's a grown ass man. He got through his wife dying. I think he can get through a little sexuality crisis."

"Is it little though?"

Hayes laughed and made a big deal out of trailing his gaze up and down Zach's body. "Maybe not so little."

Zach elbowed him in the side. "Don't be an ass."

"It's my turn," Hayes said calmly.

"I did leave my card there." When he'd pulled it out of his pocket, he'd thought it was a mistake to do it. But Gavin had barely been able to look at him and if Zach was being very honest, he'd barely been able to look back. The crush he'd believed long-dead had come roaring back with such ferocity it made him a bumbling nineteen-year-old again.

But he'd tucked it half under his breakfast plate.

Maybe when Gavin found it, he'd throw it away.

Or maybe he'd keep it.

"Oh yeah?" Hayes waggled his eyebrows.

"It was stupid—really, really stupid. But I thought . . .well, anyway, if he wants to talk to me about it, he'd be able to."

"You think he's gonna text you—sorry, *call you*, 'cause he's old—and be like, *please Zach, pretty please talk me through my sexuality crisis?*"

"Now that you say it, it sounds very stupid," Zach grumbled.

"You're worried. It's cute."

"No, it's stupid," Zach argued. "I'm . . .well . . .you know."

"Yeah, if anyone knows what *that's* like, it's me," Hayes said.

"I just hope he has someone to talk to," Zach said.

"Man, you are *gone*."

Ugh, he wanted to tell Hayes he was wrong, that it was just the remnants of an old childish crush, that he'd be over it so fast—that there wasn't even anything to get over—but Zach wasn't sure.

Because it had lingered for the last four years, in the back of his mind, and that was before he'd ever believed, even for a second, that Gavin might be attracted to him.

And now? As much as Zach might try to deny it, something *had* happened last night.

He just needed to remind himself that nothing else was ever going to happen again. That was the first and last time.

"Come on," Hayes said, patting him on the arm. "Let's get out. Shower. Grab some food."

Zach knew what Hayes was trying to do—this was why he'd come here, anyway. He'd known Hayes would be honest and then do a good job of distracting him.

He just needed to let himself be distracted.

CHAPTER 4

GAVIN FOUND THE CARD a few minutes after Zach drove away.

He stared at it, sitting so innocently on his kitchen counter, and mentally debated about what to do with it for way longer than he should've.

"Just throw it out," he said to himself.

He knew why Zach had left it. He'd hoped, no matter what Gavin said, that he'd consider—or reconsider—taking the job.

Or maybe, that deep down uncooperative voice said, *he's thinking about you offering something else.*

But that was crazy. He wasn't interested. He *wasn't.*

That had just been the beer he'd drunk, plus him being alone for a long time, *plus* the shock of realizing that Zach had grown up.

But he didn't crumple up the card, even though he thought probably he should. He didn't even slide it over to the far end of the counter. He left it where it sat, right there in the middle of the goddamn space, no way to distract from it or ignore it entirely.

It was stupid. But apparently Gavin was being very stupid these days.

After he cleaned up from breakfast—taking extra care to scrub the pans and set them on the drying rack and wipe every single crumb from the almost-empty counter—Gavin only hesitated briefly before grabbing his hiking boots and shoving his feet into them. He gave himself a quick once over with sunscreen and bug spray, filled up his water bottle, shoved on his hat, and was out the door in under five minutes.

He took one of his favorite trails, winding his way through the forest, enjoying the silence.

Or *trying* to enjoy the silence.

When Gavin got to the lake, he was surprised to find it fairly empty, only a few people to be seen on the far shore and a handful of canoes dotting the placid water.

Normally, he'd make it all the way out here, sweat slicking his skin from the humidity and the exertion, and be glad there wasn't anyone out here to ruin the perfect silence.

But today, he wanted more than the chirping of the birds and the slow swish of the water against the shore.

He wanted something to distract him. That would make him stop running Zach's visit over and over and goddamn *over* in his mind. The way he'd grown into his body and his height. The confidence in his stance. His earnestness as he'd relayed the job offer. How his eyes had lit with excitement as he'd talked about Jones and McCoy.

Then there was the warmth of his big thigh pressed to Gavin's. The heat that had streaked through him. The wonder and awe in Zach's face as they'd leaned in closer . . .

"Shit," Gavin said out loud, annoyed with himself. A little annoyed with Zach, too.

He hadn't needed to look so eager. Or so disappointed when Gavin had pulled away.

Nineteen-year-old Zach hadn't possessed any kind of poker face. Twenty-seven-year-old Zach was better. Years of NHL media training would do that.

Of course, all the media training in the world wasn't going to be enough to hide that Zach *had* been on board with whatever was happening between them on Gavin's couch.

Maybe a switch had been flipped, and not just for Gavin.

"This is not helping," Gavin announced, and somehow, shockingly, that did not help either.

He stayed out for another hour, hiking partway around the lake.

By the time he got back to the cabin, his head felt marginally clearer.

At least until he let himself back inside and there, staring at him from the counter accusatorially, was Zach's card.

Goddamn it, why had he *kept* it?

He should throw it away.

But his fingers still hesitated over it.

Finally, he fisted them and left it.

Took a really long shower. Ate a plate of leftovers without tasting anything, and then switched on the TV, picking another big, stupid movie full of explosions. But by the time the credits rolled, Gavin felt like he hadn't really seen any of it.

Went to bed and even though he was tired after last night's restless night, couldn't find a comfortable position.

The next day, rinse and repeat.

Again and again and again.

He had things to do. Wood to chop for the winter. A handful of emails he should answer. Supplies and groceries to buy.

But even when he took care of everything on his list, including going into town and sitting at the diner, he felt restless. Itchy. Weird.

On the fifth day, he caught sight of himself in the bathroom mirror. His eyes were sunken, dark circles underneath them. Nothing had felt right since Zach had left.

It wasn't Zach necessarily—though he couldn't argue that it *wasn't* Zach, either—but it was like he'd exposed the complete uselessness of the life he'd built here.

What was he even *doing*?

On the sixth day, he sent an email to Jon, and twenty minutes later, Gavin answered a call on his tablet.

"Hey," his therapist said. "Long time no talk."

It had been six months. At first, Gavin had felt guilty about not answering his emails about scheduling new appointments. But then he'd considered the alternative and even ghosting felt better than pushing himself into places he had no intention to go.

"Yeah, about that," Gavin said, rubbing his neck and feeling shame wash over him.

"I get it. I pushed you. You got pissed. You hide when you don't know how to deal with emotion."

Gavin rolled his eyes, even though it was a well-documented fact by now.

He'd come all the way out here after Noelle had died, hadn't he?

He'd called it re-prioritizing, but he could look back now and see it for what it was: *hiding*.

From people he hadn't known how to talk to anymore and a world he hadn't wanted to rejoin.

"Right," Gavin said.

"So, what's up? You said you were having trouble sleeping?"

That was the bare minimum. The least of the problems that he could confess to Jon to get him on a call.

"Yeah. About the last week."

Jon looked non-accusatory. He *never* looked angry or hurt or upset. Sometimes a flash of judgment crossed over his face, but it was always when Gavin deserved it.

He'd have deserved it now, but it was missing in action.

"Anything new?"

Gavin took a deep breath. He was going to talk about this. "Someone came to see me."

"That happens, still?"

"Not like this," Gavin confessed. "It was one of my old play-ers, that I coached when I was at Portland U. One of my . . . well, we weren't supposed to have favorites, but it happens, and he was one of mine. He's working for the university now, as an assistant coach, and he wanted to offer me the head coaching job."

Jon raised an eyebrow. "And you didn't pretend to shoot him?"

"No." Gavin grimaced. He knew Jon had thought the way he'd built up his walls hadn't been healthy. *You can say no, and create firm boundaries without being so freaking dramatic, Gavin.*

And he *knew* that, obviously. But the dramatics ensured that people didn't come back. That the stories and the legends grew. That he became like the hockey boogeyman, and eventually people would just stop bothering him.

That had happened.

Until Zach.

"I let him in the house," Gavin continued. "I invited him for dinner. We watched a movie. Drank some beers. I . . ." He didn't know how to say this so he just fucking said it. "He grew up."

Both Jon's eyebrows raised now.

"How old is he now?" he asked neutrally.

And yeah, that was a hell of a lot easier question than the one he knew Jon *wanted* to ask.

"Twenty-seven." Gavin tapped his fingers on the counter in a relentless rhythm. "He's quit playing hockey, professionally, and that really bothered me, at first. His explanation makes sense, and he seems happy, but it . . .it was like a jolt to the system. Realizing that he's grown up. Making his own grown-up decisions."

"So he showed up, offered you a job, and you two caught up. And now you're not sleeping."

Maybe there wasn't any judgment in Jon's tone, but Gavin felt like he deserved a whole truckload of it.

"Yeah, that's the long and short of it," Gavin said.

"Any thoughts as to why?"

"I just . . ." Gavin squirmed, even though he didn't want to. He knew what was true. What he *should* say. But the words stuck in his throat. They were too similar to what Jon had pushed him to do, why he'd stopped seeing him six months ago. "After he left, I can't seem to settle back into my old life."

"But you never left it. You invited Zach into your life," Jon said.

"I did," Gavin said. And despite all this bullshit, he couldn't say he regretted it, even now.

"Is it possible," Jon asked, so carefully neutral, "that Zach exposed how this life you've chosen doesn't fit you anymore?"

Gavin didn't want to answer that. So he didn't.

"He showed me some hockey tape. Guys on the team. They're exciting. A lot of upside. So much potential." And as much as Gavin had been thinking about Zach and that moment on the couch, he'd been turning over the Jones and McCoy problem in the back of his head. Considering how a coach might approach Finn Reynolds and convince him to divorce himself from all the expectations inherent with his last name. How *he* might approach Finn Reynolds.

And that was the root of the problem, wasn't it?

Zach hadn't been wrong; this team would be a challenge, but an exhilarating one.

"You didn't tell him that you didn't watch hockey anymore?" Jon asked.

"I did . . .I . . .I could've said no." But he hadn't. He'd leaned in, just as interested and fascinated by the game as he'd ever been.

"But you didn't."

Gavin huffed in frustration. "You want me to say it? Okay, I miss it. I miss having a purpose. I miss . . ." *God, so many things.*

Numbness was a comfortable state of being now, but he missed being alive.

Missed *feeling* alive.

"It doesn't make *me* feel better to hear you say it," Jon said gently.

He could be an ass about this; he'd been right, after all. It had taken Gavin six months to see it, to *feel* it, but he couldn't deny it any longer.

"Well, that's something."

Jon was quiet for a long moment. So long, Gavin actually felt himself tense up, wondering what Jon was gearing up for.

"So what do you want to do about it?"

And yep, there it was. The million dollar question.

It wasn't that hard, actually, to answer it for himself. Harder to say it out loud.

Harder to know if he *should* do it.

Gavin took a deep breath. "I don't want to live here anymore. I don't want to do nothing anymore."

"There you go," Jon said, and now he *did* sound pleased. "What else?"

"I want . . .I want to take the job. I shouldn't want to. I *shouldn't—*"

"What do we say about *shouldn't*?" Jon interrupted.

"That this space is a place where we're honest, regardless of anyone else or what they'd think," Gavin repeated dutifully. He'd probably said it hundreds of times during over four years of therapy.

"The job, huh? Talk about diving right into the deep end." Jon didn't sound angry about that, though, or worried even, just contemplative.

"It's what I want. You asked me what I want." But there were caveats, too. Not just the worry about what he *should* do, but the whole thing with Zach.

If he took the job, how many more moments would they experience, just like the couch? He could be careful. Keep Zach scrupulously at arm's length.

But how long would that work?

How many times would he be tempted to cross the line that he'd sworn he'd never cross again? Nevermind with a guy. A *guy* who'd been one of his players.

"If you want it, that's important, Gavin," Jon said. He didn't need to add that Gavin hadn't *wanted* anything in a long time. But then he didn't know about the couch, either.

He wet his lips. "There's one other . . .complication."

They'd only talked about this once, about a year ago, when Jon had started making noise about Gavin getting out of the comfort zone he'd constructed here.

When he'd brought up dating again.

Jon had defaulted to women as an option, and Gavin shouldn't have bothered to correct him. After all, it didn't matter if Jon believed he was straight, because he wasn't going to ever date again. Anything in him that might be good for someone else had died with his wife.

But he had because it suddenly had felt very important that he *wasn't* straight.

"Hmmm?"

"Zach, who's going to be the assistant coach . . .I think there was . . .I don't know what to call it . . .but there was a . . .moment,

I guess, for lack of a better word. When we were sitting on the couch together."

It was galling how unsurprised Jon looked. "You said he grew up."

Of course, he'd remembered what Gavin had said about Zach to begin with. One of the best—and worst—things about Jon was that his mind was a steel trap and he never forgot a goddamn thing.

"He did. He's . . .well, it's four years since I've seen him."

"And he's attractive." Jon paused. "Attractive to *you*?"

God, Gavin wished he'd asked an easier question. "Yes. No. It's . . .it's complicated. I think it was just that I hadn't hung out with anyone in a long time, and we'd had a few beers and it was hot and late, and well . . ." He was only fucking human, okay?

He'd been convinced his libido had died with Noelle, but that wasn't how it worked, was it? He'd been regularly jerking off again, for the last eighteen months.

That was one of the reasons Jon had brought up dating again, because they'd worked through the guilt Gavin felt imagining someone else in his head when he touched himself. He couldn't think about Noelle—it always made him sad. Too sad to do anything about his bodily urges.

"Well?" Jon looked at him expectantly. "What are you looking for here, Gavin?"

"A reality check."

"You mean, a reminder that he's off-limits? Or a plausible explanation for why you had a 'moment' on the couch even though you're not attracted to him?"

"You suck," Gavin ground out.

"I think you want both."

"If I take this job, I'm not going to touch him," Gavin said.

"And you want me to agree with that assessment?"

Gavin nodded. He respected Jon's opinion—after all, he'd gotten him through the worst of the grief. Helped him build his numbness and then rightly pushed him when he'd gotten too used to it. He hadn't necessarily *liked* the process, but he couldn't deny how good at this Jon was.

If Jon told him he shouldn't—that he *couldn't*—do anything with Zach, then he'd believe it.

"I don't know him, so it's impossible to say what the right course of action is," Jon said.

Gavin ground his teeth together. "You don't have to know him. You know *me*. You know I can't."

"Why? Because you wanted to believe you were dead too? You're not. You're coming back to life—leaning into it. Why not this too?"

"Because it's . . .because it would be wrong. So fucking wrong."

Jon tilted his head. "Because he's younger than you? He's twenty-seven and seems to have a decent head on his shoulders. Is he your direct report?"

Gavin shook his head. "But that doesn't matter. I can't date again. I can't . . .I just can't." Gavin's throat closed over, panic streaking through him at even the idea of it.

"You did say that. Many times," Jon said. "Maybe it's not that you can't, it's not that you *shouldn't*, it's that you're not ready to take that step."

"Right, right. No." He wouldn't ever be ready, but maybe that was enough to keep himself in check. A necessary and vital reminder that nothing could ever happen, if he was tempted.

Jon shot him a look, and Gavin forced himself not to squirm on the stool. "Why do I sense that you're not really agreeing with me?"

"I don't know why you'd say that," Gavin protested.

"Right." Jon leaned a fraction closer to the screen. "I think this is going to be good for you. But it's going to be a shock to your system."

"Are you talking about Zach or the job?"

Jon looked unimpressed, like he'd figured out that Gavin had just been looking for another excuse to say *Zach*.

"I'm talking about rejoining the land of the living," Jon said.

"Yeah. Right. Well . . .how about I promise not to be a stranger this time?" If he went back and took the job, well, he'd *need* support. Maybe that was why he'd really emailed Jon. He'd already known he wanted to take it. Why else hadn't he been able to throw out that card Zach had left?

He'd even gotten jealous over whatever other coach they'd offer the job to next.

He should've realized all of these things. So much for all the work he and Jon had done on knowing himself.

He hadn't even realized what he wanted.

"That sounds good," Jon said.

That was the moment it hit him.

Other coaches.

Zach and Sidney Swift could've already offered the job to someone else. Six days later the deal could already be done.

Oh, God.

If Gavin had been looking for more proof he actually wanted this, that he wanted it *badly*, how terrible the realization was that he might've missed the chance was enough.

"Hey, I have to go," Gavin said hurriedly. Five minutes wouldn't change anything, but maybe if he knew, one way or the other, that feeling of being squeezed until there wasn't any breath left in his lungs, might ease.

"Sure," Jon said. "And email me your new schedule when you know it." He paused. "Good luck. I think this is a great move for you, Gavin."

"Me too. Thanks." He signed off and the next moment he was grabbing for his phone and for the business card. Pristine, uncreased, still, because he hadn't even had the courage to touch it.

His fingers were shaking when he dialed the number.

Zach picked up on the fifth ring. "Hey?" he asked.

"Zach, *Zach*," he said breathlessly. He sounded like a heroine in a romance novel. Gavin cleared his throat. "It's Gavin. Gavin Blackburn."

Zach chuckled, and frankly it was hilarious. Of course he knew who Gavin was. He'd come and tracked him down, hadn't he?

"I admit I'm surprised to hear from you," Zach said.

Don't say it. Don't say you hired someone else.

"I . . .uh . . ." Gavin cleared his throat again. "I wanted to ask if the job offer was still open."

There was a long interminable silence.

Surely Zach could hear his heartbeat rabbiting from wherever he was.

"You . . .you want the job?" Zach sounded shocked, and frankly, that made two of them.

"Yes," Gavin said, trying to sound as certain as he felt, deep down.

"Wow," Zach said.

"Is it . . .is it still available?"

Zach laughed. "Swift told me I was crazy."

"*Zach*," Gavin pressed.

"I've been putting him off. For six days. I . . .I just left Florida. Put it off forever. Hayes finally kicked me out, told me I had to face reality. Face whoever the coach was gonna be if it wasn't gonna be you, and I'd just accepted that. Landed in Portland this afternoon. Was going to go see Swift tomorrow morning. And here you call me."

"Sounds like it worked out." Gavin took a breath and then another. The bands over his lungs seemed to be loosening.

"Yeah, I think so," Zach said. He sounded delighted. Surprised, maybe, but delighted.

"You left your card for a reason. You knew I'd . . ." Gavin swallowed. "You were right."

"I think I should record you saying that," Zach teased gently.

"Probably," Gavin admitted. He didn't admit he was wrong very often. "Guess uh . . .I'm going to be flying to Portland now, too."

"Guess so."

Gavin told himself that Zach's smug tone was not attractive. Because he wasn't doing this. *They* weren't doing this.

"Good, uh . . .tell Swift to send me the contract. I want my lawyer to look over it."

"Will do," Zach said. Then the smug amusement bled into something sweeter. "I'm really glad you changed your mind."

"Honestly, I don't think I had even made it up, not til today," Gavin said.

"I'm gonna remind you of that, every chance I get."

That was fair. Gavin had almost fucked this up. But he wasn't going to come close to making any of those same mistakes again.

"And while you're at it, send me all the game tape you can get your hands on," Gavin said. "Especially everything with McCoy and Jones."

"Sure." He could hear the smile in Zach's voice. "Glad you're back on board, Coach."

"Me too," Gavin said and knew it was true.

CHAPTER 5

July

It was one of the wildest, most exhilarating days of Zach's life, and it still wasn't over yet.

The team had held a press conference this morning, introducing Gavin to the public, and like everyone had expected, it'd been absolute chaos.

Ever since the Evergreens had released an announcement that Gavin had signed the contract, the media had gone berserk.

It *was* a good story. Zach knew just how good of a story it was. Coach returns to the scene of his early success, after being off the grid and out of hockey for years due to the traumatic death of his wife?

Everyone was eating it up, even more than Zach—and he thought Gavin, too—had expected, and he couldn't help but worry that the fever-pitch excitement was actually going to scare Gavin off.

He was just rejoining the land of the living after all, and Zach imagined just being around people must be overwhelming. Nevermind the wild packs of press pushing him for his opinions on everything from the pedicabs dotting the Portland streets to the Evergreens' upside to if he was going to start Jones and McCoy on the same line.

Then there were all the questions about Finn. His dad had naturally opened his mouth and made a few comments during a podcast, because Morgan Reynolds was notoriously incapable of leaving anything alone.

"That guy," Gavin had muttered, after they'd finished the press conference and he'd gotten a second to catch his breath, Zach ushering him to a quiet room.

Zach couldn't say how he *really* felt about Morgan, because that was too tangled up in what he knew about what had gone down between him and Hayes. But he could still say, with one-hundred-percent honesty, "We need to do what we can to insulate Finn from all that."

Gavin nodded. He twisted the water bottle in his hands. "We'll see what we can do."

It suddenly occurred to Zach as he leaned against the wall that this was the first time they'd been alone together since Gavin had come to Portland.

It had been a whirlwind, no question. After a few weeks of negotiations, Gavin had come to town to sign the contract, but of course Swift had been there, along with about half a dozen PR representatives, making sure every second of it was documented.

They'd gone to dinner, after, and sure enough Sidney Swift had been there, along with several other members of the athletic director's staff.

There'd been no opportunity to get Gavin alone, to talk about what they were doing. To ask—if he managed to actually get up the nerve—if one of the reasons Gavin had come back to Portland had been for *him*.

Just the question was breaking Zach's mind apart. He'd never have even considered it, but that moment on the couch had happened. Zach might've dismissed it, but then unlike what he'd expected—unlike what Gavin had insisted, over and over again—Gavin had actually fucking taken the job.

Hayes had been the one to say it. Texting him when they'd gotten past the initial contract negotiation and Zach had felt like he could tell him what was going on: **I can't fucking believe I was right. Are you freaking out?**

Maybe Hayes was his best friend, and he'd *normally* tell him everything, but even typing it out felt too real.

Too much an *actual* possibility.

So he just sent Hayes a thumbs-up. He'd replied that he didn't know Zach was chickenshit now.

Honestly, that was fair.

But he was trying to *not* be chickenshit now.

It still wasn't the right time, but they *were* alone together.

"If I didn't say it," Zach said quietly, gaze glued to Gavin, like he could have ever looked away, "I'm really happy you took the job."

The corner of Gavin's mouth quirked up. "Me too, actually. Despite all that." He waved towards the door and the no-doubt ravenously hungry media that were still salivating on the other side.

"Yeah," Zach said. "I'm sorry—I knew it would be crazy, but I had no idea it would be *that* crazy."

"Me either." Gavin tipped his head back and let out an unsteady sigh.

"It'll calm down," Zach said. "This is the worst it'll be."

"Hope so." He sounded tired. Exhausted, really.

This must really be a shock to his system. For the last four years, by his own admission, he'd barely even shared a meal with anyone. And now he was dealing with dozens and dozens of people.

Zach wet his lips, feeling suddenly, horribly nervous. More nervous than he'd been even before he'd pulled up to Gavin's cabin in Michigan.

Hayes would tell him to stop being such a chickenshit. *He* was telling himself to stop being such a chickenshit.

"Why did you . . .uh . . .take the job?" Zach asked.

He certainly never expected that Gavin might just bluntly, blatantly, look at him and say, *because you asked. Because you're here.*

So he couldn't even be disappointed when Gavin said, "Because it was time to do something again."

"I get that," Zach said, nodding earnestly. Understanding that. When he'd first quit the NHL, he'd spent two aimless months living off his not-insignificant savings and wondering, without much urgency, what the fuck he was going to do with the rest of his life.

He couldn't imagine doing that for *four years*.

It was probably a fucking miracle Gavin hadn't lost his mind.

"I didn't even realize it, until you blew into my life," Gavin said wryly. "My therapist told me six months before that I needed to change things up, but I thought he was full of shit. Until it turned out that he wasn't."

"Uh, well, glad it was me," Zach said. He wasn't handling this. He wasn't even really *doing* this. At least not in a non-chickenshit way.

"Maybe it could only have been you," Gavin said with a quiet earnestness and a solemnity in his expression that made Zach's heart beat a little faster.

"I . . ." Zach didn't know what to say. He hadn't known they would do this, or do this so soon. He'd imagined he'd need to work a hell of a lot harder to navigate the conversation to what had nearly happened between them in Michigan.

But then Gavin kept talking, gesturing with the water bottle. "I wouldn't have let anyone else get close, but you were my player. I *knew* you. And I had so many good memories of coaching you. It was easy to let you in, even a little. Once I did, I realized just how fucked up I'd gotten."

This was not the way he'd hoped the conversation would go.

Not, *You grew up and I saw you differently than before,* but *you were my player.* And, *I had so many good memories of coaching you.*

For those handful of moments on the couch, Zach had been convinced Gavin no longer saw him as the kid he'd coached. But now, Gavin had gone out of his way to emphasize that to him, Zach still was.

It was frustrating and Zach didn't like it.

"Oh," Zach said. Not sure what else he could say that wouldn't make his disappointment obvious.

Because he couldn't deny that ever since Gavin had called him and told him he'd changed his mind about the job, he'd expected that *someday* they'd be back in that place. That the distance between them would shrink to nothing, and one day, Gavin would tilt his head up, that look would be back on his face, and Zach would close the distance between them. It might take time, but eventually they'd fit together like two puzzle pieces that had finally gotten out of their own way.

"Yeah, I'm glad you came to Michigan," Gavin said, chuckling easily, like the only possible reason Zach ever would've come to Michigan was to offer him the job.

It could still happen, Zach argued with himself. Yes, it could. But the more Gavin insisted that Zach was still a kid, still his player, the harder it would be to ever bridge that gap.

"Me too," Zach said, swallowing hard.

Hayes would tell him he was fucked, then probably add that he was better off.

But Zach didn't know if he agreed. Wasn't sure if he'd *ever* agreed, but now that he and Gavin were going to be working together for the foreseeable future, he already knew his crush wasn't going to go away.

Considering the way his heart had stuttered when Gavin had walked into the room this morning, hair cut, still curling just around the tips of his ears, freshly shaved, pressed slacks hugging his perfect thighs and a tight polo emphasizing just how wide his shoulders were, there was probably no hope for Zach.

He was *in* this, whether he wanted to be or not.

Whether Gavin was in it or not.

"Besides," Gavin said, smiling, "you left your card for a reason. You knew I'd reconsider."

Part of Zach wanted to tell the *real* truth. Why he'd actually left the card. Sure, yes, the job had entered into it. Had there been some faraway, nearly impossible fantasy of Gavin calling him for a hookup? He wanted to deny it, even to himself, but he knew the truth.

But he wasn't going to share that. It was embarrassing enough that Gavin was still mentally thinking of him as that nineteen-year-old kid. Awkward and gangly, without an ounce of game.

He'd been good on the ice, and that was it.

Twenty-seven-year-old Zach was different.

"Right, yeah. That's why I left it. The job," Zach said. His voice didn't even sound convincing to his own ears.

But if Gavin wasn't convinced, his poker face was too good to give it away.

He wanted to say something else, to make it clear that he'd certainly had other thoughts, other *non-coaching* thoughts, but between the way Gavin had shoved him back into the ex-player box to all his utterly platonic assumptions, Zach didn't even know where to begin.

Gavin hadn't left him any room.

The door opened, and Sidney Swift walked in. "Oh, good, you're getting some quiet," he said to Gavin, who nodded.

"I . . .uh . . .I need a moment," Zach said.

It was stupid, he was already *having* a moment.

But he couldn't confess to Hayes how wildly disappointing this was in front of Gavin.

Besides, Sidney was already going over the rest of the day's schedule and Gavin was nodding, clearly absorbed in what he was saying.

Nobody was going to miss Zach. Not for five minutes anyway.

He ducked out the door and went down the hallway, in the opposite direction of the media room, and to a bathroom in a section of the building that would be empty if the team wasn't playing yet.

Zach's memory was right; it was a single stall, with a locking door.

He pulled the door closed and dialed Hayes.

"Hey," Hayes said, sounding distracted. Like maybe he was in the car. "Everything okay?"

"No. Everything's not okay," Zach said in a rush.

"He just got there. How bad could it be going already?"

"Bad," Zach said darkly. "I finally got him alone, after the press circus, and I started saying how I was so glad he'd taken the job and gave him an opening to tell me . . .I don't know, *something*. But instead he fucking talked about how I was his player. How he'd coached me."

"Ouch," Hayes said. But he didn't sound particularly surprised.

"Yeah, it fucking sucked." Zach hated how despondent he sounded. "I didn't expect him to . . .I don't know, fall to his knees or something, but I thought he wouldn't deny the whole thing."

"Seriously? You thought he was just going to tell you, I know I spent the last four years alone because my wife died, and everyone thinks I'm straight, including probably me, but hey you wanna hook up sometime?" Hayes' tone was kind, but blunt.

And maybe that blunt honesty was what Zach needed to get his head screwed on right.

"Right," Zach said. "It was stupid. I was so stupid—"

"Not stupid," Hayes interrupted. "*Hopeful*. That's different."

"Doesn't feel very different right now."

"No, it wouldn't." Hayes paused. "I told you he was probably going to have two freakouts. The gay freakout of course. And then the widower freakout. And you know, you don't *have* to deal with either of those? It's not *your* baggage, Zachy."

"But, *ugh*," Zach said. "What if I want it to be?"

Hayes chuckled darkly. "You're kind of gone for him, aren't you?"

"Always have been." He could tell Hayes this, because Hayes understood better than anyone else.

"But it's worse now," Hayes said, not asking but stating. And yeah, it *was* worse. Because of those heart-stopping moments when they'd nearly kissed, and more, too.

Because this thing between them, if Gavin could move past his baggage, and if Zach was patient enough to let him, could be *real*.

Not just a late night fantasy or a childish crush.

"Well, yeah. It's an actual fucking possibility now. It never was before. It was just me being . . .well, stupid then, too." Zach made a face.

"Doesn't seem you've really moved past that," Hayes teased.

"Thanks," Zach retorted. "Pot, meet kettle."

"I never denied it," Hayes said lightly. And no, he hadn't.

"At least we're stupid together," Zach said. What Hayes said made sense. A lot more sense than Gavin showing up in Portland, ready and willing to hook up with Zach.

Hayes hummed his agreement. "You're gonna have to be patient. Really patient, probably. And you know what else? You don't have to do this, Zach. You can just . . .decide to be friends. Co-workers. You don't have to hold back, and wait for someone who might never be ready to acknowledge that you're more than just his old player. Or that you've grown up, and he's interested in you as more than just a professional acquaintance."

Zach knew he was right. But then Hayes had never taken his own advice. "How'd that work out for you?" he asked. Maybe that was unfair, but it was also true.

"It never did," Hayes admitted with a sigh. "You know that. But you're not in *that* deep, yet."

No, he wasn't in love with Gavin. Yet.

"I'm just saying. You could hold yourself back, if you wanted to."

Zach knew that Hayes probably believed that was true.

But he hadn't felt the way Zach had when Gavin had called him three weeks ago. Or the way his pulse had skittered when Gavin had walked in this morning. Or the way his gaze was always drawn to him, even when he wasn't talking.

Like they were both magnets. Zach didn't know if he wanted to avoid the pull, or lean into it.

No, that wasn't right. He *knew* what he wanted to do.

"I don't know if that's true," Zach said bluntly.

Hayes sighed. "Oh, Zachy."

"I know," Zach said morosely. "This is gonna be awesome and also is gonna suck hard, isn't it?"

The long pause before Hayes answered told him the truth.

"Yeah, probably," Hayes said. "But maybe, for you, it'll turn out differently."

Gavin should be exhausted.

Even though he'd spent the last three weeks during the contract negotiation trying to mentally prepare himself for how his life was going to be changing, it turned out that no amount of shopping malls and busy restaurants could've prepared him for having dozens of members of the press asking him questions.

The press conference had been organized chaos.

Then he'd had lunch with the university president and then dinner with Sidney Swift. Zach had been there, too, of course, but he'd been quiet.

Or maybe it was just that everyone else felt so freaking loud.

Gavin scrubbed a hand over his face and tried to close his eyes again and fall asleep.

But he couldn't.

Maybe it was the sound of a city still buzzing around him even though it was nearly midnight. Or maybe it was the sliver of streetlight peeking through the curtains.

If she was here, Noelle would've told him he was being very stupid and lying to himself.

Of course, if she was here, *he* wouldn't be here, in Portland. He'd still be in Seattle, probably, coaching the Sea Monsters.

Would he be happy? Gavin thought so. He'd been happy before. Distracted, though, and taking everything that was actually important in his life for granted. But they'd had a good life together, until it had been cut way too short. An infection, raging out of control. And then a week later, she'd been gone. No time to prepare. Barely even time to say goodbye.

Gavin opened his eyes again. Stared at the wedge of light. He'd need to get better blackout curtains, for sure.

He rolled over, grabbing his phone from its charger on the nightstand.

To look for new blackout curtains, he told himself, but that wasn't the app he switched to.

Gavin's fingers hesitated over the screen for a long moment. He'd never actually texted Zach before.

During the three weeks of contract negotiations it had been inappropriate, and Gavin hadn't wanted to put him in a difficult position. And after, Gavin had flown into Portland, and there'd never been a need because if he needed to talk to Zach, he was right there.

His new assistant coach.

God, he was coaching again, and he was coaching again with *Zach.*

More than once, he'd thought, *What the fuck are you thinking?* Followed immediately by, *You're thinking straight for the first goddamn time in years.*

Followed by, *Maybe you're not thinking 'straight' at all.*

And wasn't that the problem?

Zach was so big and quiet and *there*.

Gavin had been much more sure he could dismiss that moment on the couch. It was just a moment. Less than five minutes. Nothing had happened. It should be easy to re-align his thinking back to Zach as being under his protection.

But Zach didn't need his protection.

He'd grown up and Gavin was struggling more than he expected when it came to stuffing him back into that box.

Maybe if you say it enough times.

But he'd said it today, repeated it *twice*, straight to Zach's face, who'd barely batted an eye, and that hadn't changed anything.

If anything, it had gotten tougher. He'd gotten caught up at dinner, when he was supposed to be listening to Sidney blow hard about the upcoming season, watching Zach in the dim light of the restaurant.

The nick underneath his chin, from shaving. The thick strength of his neck and the vulnerable skin at the hollow of his throat, once he'd lost the tie he'd been wearing all day. The deepening shadows under his blue eyes.

The way Zach looked at him. The way Zach lingered at the entrance of the restaurant with him, like he hadn't wanted to say goodbye either.

Gavin had forced himself to walk away, to take the car Sidney had called for him.

He didn't know if he had it in him again.

He sent, **You up still?** before he could change his mind.

A second later, to Gavin's surprise, Zach called.

"Yeah?" he answered. He'd thought Zach would be down with the texting, so the phone call was unexpected.

"Hey, sorry." Zach's voice was quiet. Intimate. And this was why Gavin had texted, not called. Because it was impossible to forget who he was talking to, when he could hear his voice.

"It's alright," Gavin said. He probably sounded just as hushed.

Maybe even exactly as he'd sounded *that* night.

"I realized I didn't grab my glasses from the bathroom when I took my contacts out," Zach said apologetically. "It's hard for me to see my phone to text without them."

"Oh, I'm sorry—"

"Don't apologize," Zach interrupted gently. "It's alright. I just wanted to make sure you were okay. It was . . .it was a long day."

"Then why can't I sleep?" Gavin questioned.

It wasn't Zach's job to lull him into complacency, into sleep. But suddenly, inexplicably, he wished it was.

"Ah, that's it, then?"

"The noises, and the lights, and just . . .*ugh*," Gavin said, aware of just how whiny he sounded.

"You could've stayed out of town, a bit."

Yeah, he could've. But he hadn't been sure, even though he'd signed the contract for three years, if this would work out, and he hadn't wanted to buy again. The small bungalow rental right down the street from the rink had seemed a better choice, at least in the short term.

"Didn't seem like the right choice, when I'm trying . . ." Gavin swallowed the rest of the sentence. *When I'm trying to rejoin the land of the living.*

Because in some ways Zach had been right; he *had* been rotting out there.

He knew that was true, but part of him shrank back from admitting it out loud. From admitting to *Zach*.

"To actually exist in civilization?" Zach's tone had morphed from concerned to quietly teasing.

"Right." Gavin told himself he'd started this conversation, he could actually say what was really on his mind. Well, most of it, anyway. "I just want this whole circus to stop so we can actually start working on the team."

"I want that too," Zach said earnestly.

"Sidney's just…enthusiastic." Gavin said it as diplomatically as he could.

Would he have changed his mind if he'd known how much insanity he was inviting into his life? No, probably not. But he might've put his foot down more, and much, much earlier.

At dinner, Sidney had pointed out that his office had scheduled several more podcasts for Gavin to go onto, and he'd finally had to say *no*, that was not going to be happening.

"I'm here to coach your hockey team, not to single-handedly publicize it," Gavin had said.

"It's just such a great story," Sidney had wheedled.

And it was. Right now anyway. How good of a story would it be six months from now, when the Evergreens couldn't win any games because he was too busy recording podcasts and circle-jerking the hockey community?

"That isn't how I'd put it," Zach said bluntly.

"Hopefully what I said at dinner will solve that problem," Gavin said. He wished he was more confident that was true.

"Might've been easier for you to go coach someplace else," Zach said, even though he didn't exactly sound that enthusiastic about the idea. "Less history, someplace else."

"No, it wouldn't have been," Gavin said. "I would've been . . .well, it wouldn't have worked, anyway."

Zach was quiet. Gavin almost wanted him to ask if it was because *he* was here, but surely he'd made that clear enough this morning.

"Well," Zach finally said, "the morning's clear tomorrow. You wanna go to the rink?"

"Just the two of us?"

"Bet you haven't had skates on in forever," Zach said.

And no, he hadn't. He'd barely even worn them when he'd coached in Seattle.

"You don't need to," Zach added hurriedly. "I know coaches don't typically—"

"And when have I *ever* been a traditionalist?" Gavin asked archly. "You came to me because I'm not. Because I might see a way forward that nobody else does. We can get on the ice. Then watch some tape."

"You already watched everything I sent you?"

Gavin chuckled. "Yeah, you know I did. It wasn't that many games. Why did Nichols take so long to put Jones and McCoy on the same line?"

"I wasn't coaching here then," Zach said, by way of explanation.

"Oh, come on, you have a theory," Gavin said.

"Do I?" Zach sounded downright amused now. "You must know me really well."

Gavin's grip on the phone tightened. Was Zach *flirting* with him?

Oh God.

His heartbeat shouldn't be accelerating just at the thought of it.

"I do know you," Gavin said earnestly. He was shitty at flirting anyway.

"Uh, I think . . .I think he listened too much to Mal arguing. And then he bought into how Elliott was playing on the second line. He couldn't see the path forward, the *right* path forward." Zach sounded adorably awkward now. Enough for Gavin to believe that *yes*, he had been flirting. And even though Gavin should hate it. Should shut this down. It was late and he was tired and maybe for ten minutes, he didn't have to fight this.

After all, this whole conversation was harmless. It wasn't like they were even in the same room.

"He should've at least *tried* it," Gavin complained.

"He should've," Zach agreed. "So you're definitely going to put them on the same line, then?"

"Well, *yeah*," Gavin said. "And Ivanov, too, as the center. He grounds them."

"Not McCoy?"

"Are you kidding me? When Jones pushes him, it's like he finally forgets about all the shit he's not supposed to worry about."

"What about Finn?"

Gavin sighed. "Did Morgan *have* to fucking open his mouth?"

"I think you already know the answer to that."

"Jesus fucking Christ. Save me from hockey dads."

"I'd save you from anything," Zach said earnestly.

He probably meant it too. He'd go on all those podcasts Sidney had signed him up for, and he'd do it without arguing. He'd take one for the team. For *Gavin*.

"He's got real upside. I like the way he tracks the puck. But the moment the other team scores, it's like he gets too deep in his own head."

"Yeah," Zach agreed. "That was my assessment too. I talked to one of the assistants over at Syracuse, where Finn was before he transferred to Portland, and if you think Morgan opening his mouth to ESPN now is bad, prepare yourself."

"What do you mean?"

"He's going to be *here*."

"No, he's not. He's going to push his son right out of hockey."

"Then you're going to have to talk to him."

"For fuck's sake," Gavin complained.

"Do you know him?"

Gavin sighed. "He's Morgan Reynolds. Of course I know him."

"I mean, did you ever play with him?"

"I coached him once. I was an assistant during the Four Nations Tournament five years ago." Gavin hesitated. "And before you even ask, *no*, he was not particularly coachable."

Zach laughed.

"He was the captain, and—"

"Oh yeah. I remember that one now. Hayes was on that team."

"Yes, he was. They won the whole thing, a beauty of a goal from Morgan to your friend Hayes." Gavin pursed his lips. "I'll reach out to him. I'm sure he'll take my call, if only because he's going to want to convince me to play Finn as the starter."

"Wouldn't you play him as the starter anyway?"

"Yeah," Gavin said. "No question. The other kid's too young. Too inexperienced. Finn's our guy. But if Morgan interferes, we're going to have issues."

"Good luck with that."

Gavin groaned and for a second, everything went very quiet on Zach's end, except for his breath, a little quicker than normal.

After replaying the sound in his head again, Gavin wanted to smack himself. Why had he sounded like that? When it was *Zach* on the other end of the line?

He'd gotten carried away. He knew he'd gotten carried away.

It didn't matter that they weren't in the same room now. Because he was *thinking* about it.

"I . . .uh . . .should go," Gavin said, painfully aware of how awkward he sounded.

At least, positively, it would be basically impossible for Zach to find *that* attractive.

"Yeah. Gonna get you back on the ice in the morning. You need your sleep."

"I don't have skates—"

"I'll take care of it," Zach said.

"Oh. Thanks."

"I've got the equipment guys in my back pocket. One of them is a major Sentinels fan and Hayes sent me a signed jersey."

"Oh. Um. Good."

Zach had told him that he and Hayes were only friends, and even if they were more than friends, it wouldn't matter, because it wasn't like Gavin was going to cross the line.

But he didn't *like* it.

He wasn't stupid; that was an even bigger problem than Morgan Reynolds interfering with his hockey team.

"Yep," Zach said, clearly unaware of how Gavin felt about this, which was *good*. A relief, honestly. "I'll see you at . . .what, let's say nine?"

"Yeah," Gavin agreed.

"Night," Zach said softly.

And even after he hung up, Gavin couldn't fall asleep. It was worse, even. Because now he knew what Zach sounded like, when he said *goodnight*. Would it sound the same if Zach was tucked up next to him in this bed?

Gavin had shied away from even the *thought* of it with anybody else. He'd essentially ghosted his fucking therapist for only suggesting he go on a few dates. Nevermind sleeping next to someone again.

But he was thinking about it, anyway.

Zach was so big and broad. He'd dominate this queen bed, sleep way too close to Gavin, their sides pressed together, warm and inescapable.

"Fuck." Gavin deposited the phone back on the charger and rolled over.

Talking to Zach shouldn't feel that good. Maybe it was just that his mind was coming back to life, turning the hockey problems on his new team over and over in his head.

Or maybe it was just Zach.

"You're not going to do anything," Gavin said out loud. Then repeated it again, with more confidence. "Even if you want to. It's not going to happen. Doesn't mean you can't be his friend. Doesn't mean you can't enjoy him."

That was allowed.

But the line he was drawing—nothing physical, nothing that could even remotely be construed as dating or hooking up—felt solid in his mind.

He could keep it intact. He'd done a lot harder things in his life, after all.

CHAPTER 6

Zach woke up at six with the alarm, feeling refreshed even though he'd barely gotten five hours of sleep.

By the time he was out of the shower, he had a text back from Marcus, the equipment guy. **All set, I'll take care of it. Be ready by eight.**

Zach sent Marcus a thumbs-up and then texted Hayes. **Your bribery is coming in really handy.**

Hayes replied: **Do I wanna know?**

I'm just saying if this guy pinged my queer radar at all, I'd say he has a massive boner for you.

So just a hockey boner, then. Disappointing.

Even if it was the regular kind of boner, you'd still be disappointed.

Dating just sucks :(

No, dating just sucks when you're hung up on someone else. Ever think about getting over it?

Oh, why didn't I think of that? I'll get on it right away.

Fuck you.

In your dreams, asshole.

Zach grinned. It was going to be a great fucking day. He was going to get back on the ice. He was going to get *Gavin* back on the ice.

By eight, he was at the rink, heading towards Marcus' office. After Zach rapped on the doorframe, Marcus looked up, grinning.

"Hey, Zach," Marcus said. "I've got everything you wanted together, in the coaches' room. That good?"

"Yeah, yeah, I just wanted to thank you again."

"Well, of course. Anything for you, and you know, for a friend of Hayes." Marcus' eyes glazed over.

Maybe the guy did have a boner for Hayes. Zach should tell him it was impossible, because Hayes only had a boner for one person.

"Too bad he got traded to the Sentinels," Zach said. If he hadn't been, they could've done better than a signed jersey. The Evergreens traveled down to LA several times a year, and even if the timing hadn't worked out, for a front row seat to Hayes Montgomery, he had a feeling Marcus would have bought a plane ticket.

"Worst day of my life," Marcus said.

"Yeah, I miss him too," Zach admitted.

On his way to the locker room, he pulled his phone out and sent Hayes another message. **Might be a regular boner. You want his number?**

A second later, Zach saw he'd read the text and then the little typing bubbles popped up and then disappeared three times.

He shouldn't have asked. He was about to say, *nevermind, it's kind of a terrible idea, I don't know why I thought it was,* when Hayes finally replied.

Is he cute?

Would I have suggested it otherwise?

Marcus wasn't *Gavin* levels of hotness, sure, but Marcus wasn't doing too badly for himself. And he was nice. Nicer than some other ex-NHL player Zach could mention.

No. Being with a fan would be weird.

But that wasn't all that Hayes wanted to say apparently, because three more texts appeared in rapid succession.

That's what I was to him, wasn't I?

Some pathetic fan?

God, I'm sorry. Ignore me.

Zach wished he hadn't said anything, but he could tell it wouldn't have mattered. Hayes was in a mood. A Morgan-induced mood.

You didn't tell me everything, but from what I heard, no. It wasn't like that. Maybe he's Morgan Reynolds, but you're Hayes Montgomery. Even now, Hayes was close-lipped with the details, but sometimes it was more about what he *didn't* say, so he hadn't even had to confess it all for Zach to know the truth.

Sure, there'd been a light dusting of hero worship, but Hayes was a superstar in his own right.

Every time Hayes forgot that—and it happened regularly—it was impossible not to be annoyed about it.

Sorry.

You're not the one who should be sorry.

For being way too fucking dramatic? Yeah, I should. Good luck today! Kick ass! Take some names! Don't kiss Gavin Blackburn!!!!!

Zach was still laughing as he pulled open the door to the coaches' locker room.

And then he stopped abruptly, nearly swallowing his tongue.

Gavin was already here. Shirtless. Back turned to Zach. And *God*, what a back it was. Firm with muscle, wide shoulders sloping down towards his trim waist.

He turned, and Zach hoped he'd managed to rearrange his expression into something that wasn't him panting like a dog in heat.

Hayes had reminded him—and he'd reminded himself—that he was going to need to be patient, but right now the last thing he felt was patience.

"Hey," Gavin said. "I grabbed an early workout and I know we said nine, but I'm here, and you're here . . ."

"I wanted to get started too." It was good that Gavin felt the same way he did. They were going to lead this team, and Zach thought he'd never wanted anything more.

Okay. Well, *almost* anything more.

"You took care of all the equipment," Gavin said warmly. "Thanks."

"Hayes comes in handy."

Gavin still hadn't pulled on a shirt, and the front view was even worse than the back. Zach felt his tongue must be hanging out; his crush—and his *boner*—showing.

How did someone who'd spent the last four years in the middle of fucking nowhere have honest-to-God *abs* like that? Zach wanted to lick them up and down. Jerk off on them.

Finally, *finally*, Gavin pulled on a shirt, though it didn't help much because it was a clingy underlayer, so tight Zach could still see every ridge of muscle.

"Bet he does," Gavin shot him a weird look. "Are you going to get ready?"

Oh Jesus, he'd just been standing here, completely fucking useless and *staring*, hadn't he?

Fantasizing about jerking off all over Gavin. Even doing that, without Gavin touching him, might be the best sex he'd had in years.

Zach flushed. "Uh, yeah. Of course." Getting naked in a locker room was something he'd done for so many years, it shouldn't mean anything. But that had been then, and this was now, and it didn't matter how many times he'd stripped down in front of his then-coach, it was entirely different to do it now, at twenty-seven.

He shucked his clothes quickly and efficiently, trying not to think about it. Trying not to look up even once, to see if Gavin was looking.

He *wouldn't,* of course. Even if Zach wanted him to. Even if Zach knew he had nothing to be ashamed of.

"Ready to go?" Gavin asked when he was dressed.

Zach glanced up, and Gavin's gaze was warm and his face a little flushed. *Had* he looked? Well. Now Zach almost wished he'd caught him doing it.

"Yeah, let's get out there," Zach said.

Zach wasn't going to make a big deal out of it, only glancing out of the corner of his eye as he led Gavin out onto the rink. They looped around the ice in slow, careful swaths at first, just warming up.

Hayes always told him it was like riding a bike and that had been true for Zach, and it seemed now it was true for Gavin.

"Feeling good?" Zach said as they came to a stop by the goal.

"Yeah, actually. Feels great." Gavin was smiling now, wide. "I didn't think . . .I didn't think I'd ever have this again. Didn't know if I . . .well, you know."

Zach wasn't sure he *did* know, and actually he wanted Gavin to tell him. But maybe the most important thing was that Gavin himself knew.

"Yeah," Zach said. Patted him on the back in the most bro-y, *hey I'm your ex-player and now your assistant coach* way he could. "Good to have you back."

"Can't be as good as it feels to *be* back." Gavin sighed happily. "You wanna shoot some pucks?"

Zach wasn't ever going to say no to that.

He grabbed his stick and a bucket of pucks and headed out, doing a more involved warmup, the way he used to before games.

Gavin continued making slow-ish laps around the ice, staying out of his way, but clearly keeping an eye on what Zach was doing.

"I can only imagine the circles you ran around those guys in the beer league," Gavin said after he'd shot his first batch of pucks.

"Sort of," Zach said.

"Come on," Gavin scoffed. "You look great out here. Like you never left."

Zach felt himself flush. "Well, it's one thing to shoot a puck into a net when there's no defense and no goalie."

"Can't do much about the goalie," Gavin said, reaching behind the boards and grabbing the second stick Zach had stashed there, "but I might be able to do something about the rest."

Zach told himself not to look—or sound—shocked. "You wanna go?"

Gavin's shrug was self-deprecating but his eyes were gleaming bold silver under the fluorescent lights. "Why not?"

"Why not?" Zach muttered under his breath and took off, not as fast as he possibly could, but fast enough. He half-expected to lose Gavin after the first dozen or so feet, but to his surprise, there he was, right with him, after he caught up. Zach pushed harder, breath coming out in short pants as they whipped around the net. Gavin shoved his stick in, attempting to steal his puck.

Zach muttered a quiet *fuck* under his breath and pushed him away with an elbow. But Gavin kept coming, right until Zach finally pushed the puck into the net.

"Shit," Gavin exhaled sharply, but his smile was even wider now. "Forgot how good you are." He paused and slid a knowing look towards Zach. "Guess you forgot how good *I* was, too."

It wasn't hot. It shouldn't be hot. But Gavin still being good at hockey after all this time still lit him up inside.

"Guess I did," Zach admitted. "Again?"

Gavin smirking at him shouldn't have been hot either, but it was. "Sure."

Twenty minutes later, they were both sweating. Zach had discarded his sweatshirt, wiping his face with it, and yeah, they were both a little rusty, maybe, but the skill was there—and the love.

"I missed this," Gavin admitted, as he leaned against the boards, trying to catch his breath. "Didn't know I did—no, that's not true, either. I *did* know, but I thought . . .I thought I couldn't have it. Not again."

Zach wasn't going to ask why he'd believed that. Obviously it had something to do with his wife's death, and with Gavin smiling like that, he wasn't stupid enough to bring it up.

"Well, I'm glad you could find it again," Zach said.

"You wanna go over some plays I've been drawing out?" Gavin asked.

"Sure," Zach said.

It wasn't easy with only two of them, but it was enough to get a good idea of the offense they could implement with their new top line.

"I'm meeting with McCoy next week," Gavin said, when they were heading into the locker room to shower and change.

"You gonna tell him then?"

Gavin shrugged. "I don't think I'm gonna need to, necessarily. He knows, he *has* to know, he's better and the team's better with Jones on his line. I've seen his grades. Watched his tape. He's smart *and* he's got a great hockey IQ. I don't think he'll do either of us the disservice of pretending he doesn't know it's coming. There's a reason that was the first thing out of his mouth when you met with him."

"Fair," Zach said. He could see it. Mal was tough and set in his ways and he didn't like Elliott, but he *did* put the team first, always.

"He's going to bitch about it, though."

Zach laughed. "No question about that."

"He can bitch all he wants to. He's still gonna do it." Gavin sounded very sure about this, and Zach was reminded of the two years Gavin had coached him.

Gavin had always been a tough coach. He'd had a reputation for being hard but fair. But, *always*, despite that steel backbone, he'd put his players first. Team was the most important thing, and he'd always, no question at the back of anyone's mind, been able to get the locker room to buy in to what he was selling.

That was why Zach believed Gavin would be the best possible coach for this team.

This year the Evergreens had a lot of disparate, difficult pieces. Not just Elliott and Jones, but besides Ramsey and Brody, a fairly young defensive group, and a goalie who felt like he was only a few bad games away from quitting entirely.

"Yeah, he is," Zach agreed.

They showered and changed, this time Zach being smart enough to avert his eyes.

He didn't need to fuel his fantasies with any more front row views of how absolutely rocking Gavin's body still was.

He'd thought it, the moment he'd seen him at the cabin, and today had only confirmed that hypothesis.

"Do you want to be there?" Gavin asked later, when they were in his office, Zach trying to pull the game tape up on the big TV there.

"For?"

"When I talk to McCoy," Gavin said, tapping his fingers on the desk. "It occurs to me that I've got a unique advantage. You're more these guys' age than I am. You could be like a transitional buffer."

"You want me to be their friend?"

"Not in a behind their back kinda way," Gavin clarified. "More like I think they could trust you a fraction more than they might ever trust me."

Zach wanted to tell him that he was crazy—that part of Gavin's coaching magic was gaining that trust in a seemingly effortless way. But he had a point.

"Um, yeah, I could do that. It wouldn't be hard. But for McCoy . . .that's the kind of thing a coach would tell him—not a friend."

Gavin's eyes lit. "Ah, I get it. You want me to be the coach, lay down the law, and then he can go bitch to you."

Zach nodded.

"Okay, we can play it that way. How's Jones gonna take it?"

"Like you just handed him the keys to everything he's ever wanted. He's not gonna be an issue."

"I can see that."

Zach didn't want to bring up Hayes' theory, but he *should* say something. Maybe it wasn't true, but Gavin should still know.

"Now, about Finn . . ." Zach trailed off.

"I'm gonna have to talk to Morgan."

"Yeah."

Gavin made a face. "I've been putting it off."

Zach just didn't want to be the one to do it—he couldn't say that Morgan Reynolds had ever been his favorite player, even considering how good he'd been in his heyday, but the way he'd fucked up Hayes had permanently cemented his opinion that Morgan was an asshole.

They needed someone who'd be nice and flatter Morgan's not-insignificant ego. That was *not* going to be Zach.

"Well, I don't want to do it," Zach said bluntly.

Gavin raised an eyebrow. "No?"

"He's not my favorite person," Zach said. He hoped that Gavin didn't ask why.

"Not mine either," Gavin admitted. "But I know why *I* don't like the guy. What's your deal with him?"

"He . . .uh . . ." Zach paused. How could he say this and not be just as much of an asshole as Morgan? No matter what the guy had done to Hayes, he didn't deserve to be outed. "He dated a friend of mine and it ended badly."

"So not just 'cause he's an egotistical jerk then?" Gavin chuckled.

"Well, that too."

Gavin sighed. "We gotta get Finn some space. He's got real instincts. A knack for the net. I've been watching a lot of tape of him. Let's get him up there." He gestured towards the TV.

"Done," Zach said. He didn't mind starting with defense.

They were almost through the third game when there was a knock on the door.

Zach looked up and Ramsey Andresen was standing there, grinning and leaning against the doorjamb like he belonged there.

Which, from everything he'd heard about Ramsey, that was probably true.

"Hey, you must be Coach," Ramsey said, extending a hand, and Gavin stood, shaking it. "I'm Ramsey."

They'd only briefly talked about Ramsey—long enough to talk about his defensive skills and then to agree that he should at least be on the short list for captain.

Mal was the other choice, but Zach was pretty sure he'd be a bad choice—well, not a *bad* choice, exactly, because he was definitely leadership material—but the wrong choice. He'd be too inflexible, and the thing this team needed more than anything was flexibility and understanding. What was the point of working so hard to get Gavin to coach the team if they just let a hardcore guy take the C?

"Good to meet you," Gavin said. He glanced over at Zach. "You know Zach?"

Ramsey nodded, but shook his hand too. Maybe he had a reputation for being a loose cannon, but he seemed fairly respectful right now.

Then he opened his mouth again.

"Marcus texted me you guys were here," Ramsey said, "and I thought I'd stop by. Say hey."

A crease appeared between Gavin's dark brows. "Marcus?"

"Marcus is the equipment manager. The guy who helped us out today?" Zach couldn't explain why he felt the need to intercede and explain instead of Ramsey, but he did, anyway.

"Yep," Ramsey agreed. "He's great."

"You bribe him too with a signed Hayes Montgomery jersey?" Gavin asked, chuckling.

"Nope. With a blowjob," Ramsey said without a trace of shame on his face.

Gavin's jaw dropped. Zach had a feeling he looked similarly shocked.

"A damn good one, too," Ramsey added, smiling. He nudged Zach, who was still shocked into silence. "Not all of us have famous NHL player friends, so we gotta make do."

"I . . .uh . . .well, you gotta do what you gotta do," Zach said weakly.

"Damn straight. You get it," Ramsey said.

Gavin still looked like he had no idea what to say. Zach hoped he managed to get *something* out of his mouth soon, or else Ramsey was going to think his problem was with the gay part of the "gave their equipment manager a blowjob as a bribe" and not the "gave their equipment manager a blowjob as a bribe" part of it.

"So I should expect anything I ask him to do, he's gonna text you first?" Gavin raised an eyebrow.

Ramsey, still without a trace of embarrassment, just nodded and looked smug. "Yep."

"That's strategic," Gavin said.

Ramsey's smile grew. "Yeah, it was, wasn't it?" Like he was just discovering that, but the truth was, Zach had a feeling he'd known that before he'd ever gone to his knees, and he'd known what he was doing too, when he offhandedly brought it up less than five minutes after meeting his brand-new coach.

Ramsey was definitely living up to the reputation Zach had heard about him.

"I'm glad you stopped by, though," Gavin said, digging in now. "Zach and I wanted to talk to you about this year's team leadership."

"Yeah?" Ramsey asked casually, leaning against the corner of Gavin's desk like it was nothing.

"You're not the only senior on this team, but I think you might be exactly the kind of leadership we need," Gavin said. They had only talked about it briefly, but clearly whatever had just happened in *that* exchange had convinced Gavin that Ramsey would be better than Malcolm.

"Well, I'm flattered," Ramsey said modestly.

Zach was impressed he'd dredged up that tone and made it seem real. Because honestly, Ramsey didn't seem to have a self-deprecating bone in his body.

"Would you be interested in taking the C?" Gavin asked.

Zach almost laughed, but he held it back at the last moment. Because he was beginning to realize that not only would Ramsey be interested, he'd designed this entire encounter to make sure he got it.

"I'd be honored," Ramsey said.

"Well, think about it," Gavin said.

"You're not interested in giving it to McCoy? He's a real boy scout."

"A little boy-scouty for this team, maybe," Gavin acknowledged.

Ramsey nodded, like he understood. Honestly, he probably did, better than the two of them.

"Besides," Ramsey said, "Mal's gonna have his hands too full with Elliott, anyway."

"Probably," Zach agreed.

"You're putting them both on the same line, right? Don't fuck it up the way that Nichols did, last year. They were born to play together."

"It didn't take us very long to figure that one out," Gavin said dryly.

"Good," Ramsey said with a sharp nod. "Well, I can't say I hadn't already thought about captaining this team so you might as well put me down as a yes."

"Excellent." Gavin held his hand out and they shook again. "We'll be in touch."

"Good." Ramsey shot Zach a look. "Next time, if you're here, I don't wanna find out from Marcus."

"No, no, there'll be a whole schedule and we'll make sure you're aware of it," Gavin agreed, still faintly flushed along his cheekbones, like he wanted to point out that bribing the equipment manager with a blowjob wasn't the best way to stay informed, but then he'd have to say it *out loud*, and he didn't think he could.

Zach hoped he wouldn't. He didn't think he'd survive Gavin saying the word, *blowjob*, even if it was to Ramsey.

"Awesome," Ramsey said. "I'm off to the gym, then."

When he was gone, Gavin waited five seconds, then ten. He turned to Zach. "Did I just hallucinate that conversation?"

"No," Zach said, barely able to get the word out, because he was suddenly laughing so hard and he wasn't sure he could stop.

God, Gavin's *face*.

"Did you know, uh . . ." Gavin flushed again, brighter red this time, like he'd been willing it back while Ramsey had been here.

"Hell no," Zach said. "Though I had heard some stories about Ramsey. You know the regular loose cannon stories. But no, I didn't know about Marcus. Though that does make sense, in some ways."

"It does?" Gavin still looked flabbergasted.

"Well, I told Hayes his boner was for more than just hockey, and it turns out I was right." A second too late, Zach realized he'd just said *boner* to Gavin, and then *he* went bright red.

"Guess so." Gavin cleared his throat. "I was not expecting that, I'll say that."

"But you couldn't have hated it. You offered the guy the C right after he told you." Zach knew Gavin was open-minded—he'd certainly been supportive when Zach had come out to him—but he hadn't expected him to be *that* open-minded. But clearly Ramsey had, because the more Zach thought about it, the clearer his machinations looked now.

It was a good trait in a captain, and maybe that was what Gavin had seen too.

"I was surprised, sure. But . . .I admired his brazenness too. He's not going to hide. He's going to be honest. The guy in the room who speaks up, even when it's not something anyone wants to hear. That's valuable."

"And you figured out that's why he did it," Zach finished.

"Yep. I agree. That kid could probably run a small country. Why not have him run the team?"

"Exactly," Zach said. He stretched out, back cracking as he pushed his arms as far above his head as they could go.

When he was done, Gavin was still flushed. From remembered embarrassment? Or the flash of skin Zach had given him when his shirt had ridden up?

Patience, Hayes had told him, but he didn't feel patient at all. He already felt like he was splitting apart at the seams.

You're just going to have to get used to it, that Hayes-voice in the back of his head reminded him.

"You're okay with it, then?" Gavin paused. "I didn't mean to just do it without talking to you first—"

"We talked about it, and this is *your* team, Gavin," Zach reminded him. But it made him all warm and tingly and fucking *seen* that Gavin had made sure he was on board.

"Only 'cause you gave it to me," Gavin said quietly, meeting Zach's eyes and the warmth inside tripled then quadrupled, turning from a sweet heat to a whole fucking conflagration.

He wanted to confess, and to yell, and to hug and to kiss.

But he didn't do any of those things. Hayes would be proud of how he just shot Gavin a smile and said, "Of course I did. Nobody else I'd trust with it."

CHAPTER 7

GAVIN HAD BEEN PUTTING this off, but he knew he couldn't anymore. He'd met with Finn two days ago, and he liked the kid already—but the dad was going to be a problem, and there was nothing to do about it but to deal with Morgan.

He dialed the number he'd gotten from his agent and waited as it connected, ringing over and over again.

Considering Morgan's stature, he wasn't surprised when he never answered and the call went to voicemail. He kept it short and sweet as he left a message, explaining that he was the new coach of the Evergreens and he hoped to chat with him soon.

Maybe someone else wouldn't have called him back right away, but Gavin wasn't particularly surprised when less than ten minutes later his phone rang.

He'd known that was probable if not guaranteed, so he'd deliberately not started any projects in his office that he wasn't going to finish.

In fact, he'd been sitting there, in his chair, staring at the window, thinking of how attached it would make him look if he texted Zach.

They'd started texting—or to both of their surprise—calling each other at the end of every day.

Even on days they spent the whole day together, it didn't
feel like it had been a good day if he didn't get to talk to Zach
while they both lay in bed.

They dissected the day. Talked about future plans—both
long-term and what tomorrow would bring—and about
other things, too. What stupid movies Gavin was watching.
The classes Zach was thinking of taking during the next
semester. How Gavin had burned his toast this morning
because he'd been too busy watching (again) the video of
Elliott and Mal playing together.

It was everything and it was nothing, and Gavin liked it so
much he was worried he should stop—but it was harmless,
wasn't it? They were just making friendly conversation. It
was totally okay that Zach was becoming his favorite person.
Your assistant coach *should* be someone you liked. The job
was hard enough on its own, without Gavin having to deal
with someone he didn't give a shit about.

"Hey," Gavin said, picking up the call.

"You called me," Morgan said.

Typical Morgan response. They didn't have a *lot* of experience together, other than the national tournament he'd
coached five years ago, when he'd been an assistant and Morgan had captained the USA team. He'd fed Hayes Montgomery that gorgeous pass so he could score the winning
goal in the championship game.

"I did," Gavin said. "You got a minute?"

"Wouldn't have called you back, otherwise," Morgan grumbled. "Before you say anything, I want to make a case for Finn starting this year."

Gavin wanted to say he was surprised, but was he?

No. Not really. This was why he'd called Morgan in the first place. This was the whole fucking problem.

"Don't you think Finn's made a good case on his own for starting?"

"Well, obviously," Morgan said, like Gavin's question was top ten in the dumbest questions he'd ever been asked.

At least, Gavin figured, there was that. He didn't have to convince Morgan that Finn was good. He just had to convince Morgan to leave Finn alone, hoping that without all that constant fatherly pressure, he might be not just good, but *great*.

"That helps," Gavin said bluntly.

"Helps what?"

"Helps what I'm about to say to you," Gavin said. "You gotta leave him alone."

There was nothing but silence on the other end for a long, interminable moment. Gavin actually thought he might've hung up on him. That wouldn't be that out of character.

"You trying to tell me how to father my own goddamn son?" Morgan finally asked, bordering on belligerent.

Gavin sighed. "No, I'm not telling you how to father him. I'm telling you to stop coaching him. Let me do that."

More silence.

"You actually gonna do it?"

Gavin considered telling Morgan that now *he'd* asked the stupid question, but that would only piss him off, and he was on thin ice anyway.

"That's the plan," Gavin said, keeping his tone as neutral as possible.

"Well, if you do it better than that fucking idiot at Syracuse, then, sure, I'll be happy to leave it to you."

"What did he do?"

Morgan sighed, long-suffering. "All the wrong shit, okay? It was like he didn't know how to deal with Finn at all. Kept pushing him. When he doesn't get that we push *ourselves*."

Gavin wondered if Morgan even knew he'd said *we*, like Morgan and Finn were a matched set, or if it just came naturally.

"What did Finn think about that?" Gavin could guess. He could also guess that when it came down to it, if asked, Finn would claim he'd transferred to get farther away from his father. Not that he hadn't liked his coach.

"Oh, you know. He didn't get it." For the first time conversation, Morgan sounded human. Like a real fucking dad, who'd gotten blamed in full for something that he was undoubtedly partially—but not entirely—responsible for.

"He's young," Gavin said.

"Yeah. *Yeah*." Morgan exhaled sharply. "So you're gonna coach him?"

"Yes. The way he should be coached," Gavin said. He was sure the Syracuse coach had promised similar things, and there was no way he could guarantee to Morgan he would be better. There was only his word.

Hopefully, that would be enough.

"You were a decent enough coach, back at Four Nations," Morgan admitted. He didn't sound entirely convinced, but he didn't sound doubtful either.

"That was a ten day tournament, five years ago," Gavin reminded him, though now that he was thinking about it, why *had* he brought that up?

"Believe me, I know," Morgan said dryly. "But still. You were good. I . . .I'm not gonna leave him alone entirely, though."

"You shouldn't. You're his dad."

"If I overstep and you find out, let me know, okay?" There was suddenly a vulnerable note in Morgan's voice. "He's got a mom, right? But she's busy. Remarried, had more kids. I want to be there for Finn, but sometimes . . .it's like the only thing we have that connects us is hockey."

Gavin sighed.

"I know, right?" Morgan sounded almost amused now. "It was easier when you thought I was just a total asshole."

"I'm sure at some point you're going to remind me of that fact again," Gavin retorted dryly.

Morgan barked out a laugh. "Oh, probably. I won't be a stranger, so yeah. I expect it'll happen."

"I hope you'll come to town and give our guys something to aspire to," Gavin said.

"Definitely." That smug tone of Morgan's was back. The one that he'd always had, that screamed, *yeah, I know just how fucking good I am.*

The worst of it was he *had* been. Probably still was, even though he'd been retired for a few years now.

"Good," Gavin said. He stood and made approximately thirty more seconds of small talk—but they both knew why Gavin had called and he'd dealt with it so there was no point in prolonging the conversation.

By the time he'd hung up with Morgan, he was already packed up and walking out of the rink, heading home.

He could wait until he got home, ate dinner, and pretended to watch a movie before he called Zach. Or he could just call *now*.

It wasn't hard to know what he wanted to do—besides, wouldn't it be *less* bad if he did it now, when he was upright and walking, and not when he was lying in bed?

That was all the justification Gavin needed.

Dialing Zach's number, he realized as his heart beat just a little bit faster, that the fact that he was needing excuses to call his assistant coach was probably not good.

But then Zach answered, with an out of breath, "Hey."

Gavin pushed all those uncomfortable thoughts away and focused on Zach.

"Hey," Gavin said, suddenly and inexplicably happy in a way he couldn't remember being in so long. "Did I catch you at a bad moment?"

"No, no, I'm just—" He cut off, breathing even harder all of a sudden. "Just finishing up a workout."

Gavin's skin prickled with heat.

"I can call back—"

"No, no, it's all good," Zach said, and Gavin didn't want to tell him, *the way you're panting is making me crazy. Is making me think of things I don't want to think about. That I shouldn't be thinking about.* "What's up?"

"I just got off the phone with Morgan."

"Oh yeah?" Zach's breath was finally evening out, but Gavin still felt infused with heat. Or maybe that was just the air outside. It was hot for Portland, nearly eighty still, even though the sun was going down.

It was a decent enough justification that Gavin's mind snapped it up, accepting it as fact.

"It wasn't terrible. He's not terrible. Wasn't even unreasonable about it."

"And here you were dreading it so bad," Zach joked lightly, even though Gavin had barely mentioned how much he wasn't looking forward to making the call.

Like he'd just *known*, because he knew Gavin.

"Yeah," Gavin agreed, squeezing his eyes shut.

It had been a very long four years since he'd felt *seen* the same way he felt seen right now. It would be so easy to just lose himself in this feeling. But it wasn't fair to Zach to do that. Not when he didn't know if he could give it right back.

And he didn't know—was still partially convinced, in fact—if his ability to do that was completely and utterly destroyed. After all, part of the reason he'd removed himself from people was that he wasn't sure he had anything left in himself to give to anyone.

"So he's gonna give Finn some space?"

"So he says," Gavin said. "Apparently the coach at Syracuse was partially to blame for this whole situation."

"Yeah?" Zach sounded surprised. About as surprised as Gavin had been. "Finn didn't mention the coach when I talked to him. I mean, he didn't mention his *dad* either, but that was sort of a given. He just said he needed to get away. Have a change of scenery."

"I think maybe Reynolds interfered because he thought the coach was fucking Finn up."

"And he fucked Finn up more as a result?"

Gavin winced. This poor damn kid. He needed to catch a break. "Yeah. Basically."

"Well, we're gonna have to fix that. We should tell Ramsey to reach out to him."

It was a good idea, and Gavin was about to say so when he remembered the other thing he knew about Finn Reynolds. "Isn't he gay though?"

"Yes," Zach said cautiously. "As far as I know. No official statements, but I don't think he's really been hiding it, either."

"I'm not worried about that, I'm worried about Ramsey deciding to seduce the kid," Gavin snapped. Maybe a little harder than he should've. Because yeah, it annoyed Gavin that every time it came up, Zach acted like *now*, this was the time Gavin was going to reveal himself to be a homophobic asshole.

"You really think he would?"

"Well I just called him a kid, but he's not, right? He's twenty, nearly twenty-one. And Ramsey is . . ." Gavin trailed off. Had he sort of admired the balls of Ramsey's stunt with Marcus? Yes. But he also didn't want the guy fucking up the chemistry on the team because he couldn't keep his dick in his pants.

"Ramsey's not an idiot," Zach soothed. "I shouldn't need to tell you this."

"No, no, you don't need to." He didn't. Normally, he'd have looked up a full bio of whoever he'd asked to be captain, ahead of time, but this time he hadn't done it until he'd already offered it to Ramsey. But everything he read about him afterwards had only solidified his decision.

"Good," Zach said approvingly.

"We talked about this," Gavin said. "I . . .I just know interpersonal relationships can fuck up a team. And ours could be *so* good."

"Yeah, but if anyone fucks it up, it's not gonna be Ramsey." Zach didn't need to say who was more likely to fuck everything up—Elliott and Malcolm.

Ramsey on the other hand? Gavin thought about what he knew about him.

A lifelong foster kid, who'd ended up at nine years old, in a semi-permanent situation with a guy who coached hockey. He'd taken to it immediately, and by sixteen, he'd been off in the OHL, living with a billet family and playing for the London Knights.

Then at eighteen, he'd decided to go to college and been recruited by every powerhouse hockey college in the country. He'd been drafted at twenty by the Sabres and from what Gavin could figure out, had been invited to prospect camp before every year, but seemed satisfied to stay in school, for now, and to graduate, then join the team.

This was a guy who was searching for something, always, and Gavin wasn't sure he'd found it yet.

"No way. Not Ramsey. He loves this team. Like it's his family."

That was what kept convincing Gavin that even if Ramsey could be restless, he was also committed to the Evergreens, and that was the most important thing.

Zach had also mentioned that his best friend, Brody, always played with him, and that from what he could see, Ramsey had semi-adopted Brody as his family.

"I'll reach out to Ramsey, see if he wants to connect with Finn. I know he's getting into town soon," Gavin said.

"He will," Zach said confidently. "I'm gonna talk to Ramsey, too."

"About?"

"Oh come on, Coach," Zach teased, "don't you trust me to handle this? I thought I was the good cop. The *friend*."

It should have done the opposite but Zach calling him *Coach* sent a thrill up his spine. And as much as he tried to pretend otherwise, it was not a platonic kind of thrill.

Gavin couldn't remember the last time he'd felt this weak-kneed, stomach-clenching delight with someone else, but it was probably back in high school. When he'd realized the girl in orchestra who could play the flute like an angel kept smiling at him.

"I do," Gavin said, wavering. Feeling weak all over. Not just his knees.

This was so much the same and yet so different, because he knew what those feelings turned into, and he didn't want that. Not with Zach. Not with *anybody*.

"Good," Zach said, a little smugly, like he knew just how much Gavin trusted him. How much he *liked* him.

Fuck, that shouldn't have been hot, either, but it was. Gavin's fingers were trembling as he gripped his phone. This was supposed to be *safer*. More public. More upright. Less intimate.

But maybe it didn't matter how or why he talked to Zach. Maybe it was always going to feel like this.

"I just was . . .curious. I . . .uh . . .wanted to know how you'd approach it." He hadn't wanted to say goodbye. Walk inside his empty bungalow and eat dinner by himself, with only silence for company.

He craved Zach's voice in his ear. Deep and rumbling and *sure*.

"Well, first thing I planned to do was appeal to Ramsey's need to be right. Let him figure how to help Finn. He likes a challenge; a problem to solve. I'm going to give him one."

"That's smart," Gavin said, wetting his lips as he let himself into the house with his key. His mouth must be so goddamn dry because it was hot out today. "I like that."

"Yeah? Thought you might." That teasing edge was back in Zach's voice, and Gavin wanted to eat it up.

"You're good at this," Gavin said.

"Learned from the best."

Gavin caught sight of his reflection as he walked into his house, on the mirror hanging in the little hallway off the front door and ignored how flushed he looked.

"I'm not the best," Gavin blustered, even though he *loved* hearing Zach saying it. Especially like that. "I'm . . .I'm out of practice. Just feeling my way around here."

"Doing a damn good job of it," Zach said.

"Doing a better job 'cause you're here," Gavin admitted. He didn't think he needed to say there was no way he could've done this job alone, not after all his time in Michigan. He wasn't even sure he could've done it without Zach even if he hadn't taken so many years off.

They made a fantastic team, working together like they'd never done anything else. Like it hadn't only been six weeks since Gavin had come to Portland.

Gavin squeezed his eyes shut. Willed his crush to stay contained.

He didn't want to be the one to fuck this up.

"You wanna get breakfast tomorrow morning?" Zach changed the subject, and Gavin nearly took a heady breath of relief. But he knew it was only a temporary reprieve.

"Yeah, I'd like that," Gavin said. "Meet at Jimmy's at eight?"

"Sure," Zach said. "I gotta go. Need to take a shower and change. Meeting a friend for dinner."

"Sure. Yeah. See you tomorrow," Gavin said and hung up almost immediately after Zach had said goodbye. Hating how jealousy curdled hard and tight in his stomach. A friend? Or a date?

Zach was allowed to date. Zach *should* date.

Why then did it feel like glass being ground in his stomach as he puttered around the tiny kitchen, putting together his own pathetic meal?

He tried to distract himself with a new Jason Stratham movie. It didn't work.

Gavin went to bed and lay awake, staring at the ceiling.

It was obvious Zach had told him about his dinner not only because he did need to go get ready but also to let him know, gently, there wouldn't be a late night phone call tonight.

He shouldn't be so used to them that he couldn't live without them, but damn it, he *liked* them. The phone calls helped Gavin relax. Helped him to empty his mind out of all the stupid minutiae of his day, properly categorize it and then put it away so he could sleep.

When he'd mentioned it to Jon, Jon had only said, "Well, isn't that what you always did with Noelle?"

He had. Goddamn it, he *had.*

It was so fucking unfair to cast Zach into that position. Unfair to Zach. Unfair to Noelle's memory. Unfair to Gavin, too, if he was really going there.

Because he wasn't ever going to be able to do it in person. Wouldn't ever be able to roll over and see Zach's sleepy face and ask him whatever burning question was eating up his brain late at night.

That was a line he couldn't cross, no matter how much his body craved it.

"This is good," Gavin told himself out loud, feeling undeniably pathetic. "This is better than good. You're gonna get used to this new reality."

But the new reality had *Zach* in it. Zach in his ear. Zach laughing under his breath as he teased Gavin. Zach being his friend. Zach being his favorite person.

Gavin squeezed his eyes shut.

He could fall asleep without that. He *could.* There weren't any options. He just had to do it.

But just when he was getting to the point where he wasn't actually sure he could, his phone vibrated with a text.

He snatched it from the bedside table so fast, it was a miracle he didn't get a cramp.

It was from Zach.

Is it weird that I miss talking to you at night?'

Goddamn it.

It was easier to deal with this if Gavin kept telling himself it was just him. Maybe he'd even be able to let it go if he could paint it as his own selfish desires.

But here Zach was, smashing that assumption to fucking dust.

No, it's not weird.

It should be weird; Gavin *knew* it should be weird.

He texted again, refusing to think about why he couldn't stop his fingers from moving. **I missed it too.**

Missed you, too.

Okay. Not just me then.

Ugh, this would be easier if Zach seemed less into it.

No.

A second later, his phone rang.

"I . . .uh . . ." Zach stammered. "I thought it would be easier to talk than text."

Gavin smiled, unable to help himself. "It's alright. I like this too."

"Good. Good." Zach was smiling, too. Gavin could hear it in his voice, and that did something to his insides. Made him feel like he was glowing from the inside out.

And that was fine, it was *fine*, as long as the line between them didn't get crossed. Besides, how could it, like this? They were just talking. It was just talk.

"How was your dinner?" Gavin hesitated briefly over the last word. Wondering if he should've called it a date instead. Hating the flare of envy that someone else had gotten to take Zach out. Not that it could ever be him; he knew it couldn't be. But that didn't change the electric pulse of *want* that he always pretended he didn't feel.

"Fine. It was just a friend. My friend Jill. We hang out sometimes. She's in a lot of my classes."

"Oh." He felt stupid now. It was Jill, not *Jack*.

"You didn't think I had a date, did you?" Zach's voice was teasing now. Cute. Intimate. But this was still only words.

"No, of course not. Of course not." Gavin heard how stupid he sounded.

"You totally did." Zach sounded delighted. "And you thought I was dating Hayes. *Hayes*."

"Well, in my defense, he's gay and you're gay, and he's not like *unattractive*." Certainly not as attractive as Zach, but Gavin wasn't going to say that, out loud.

"Yeah? Hayes is your type? Yours and Marcus', apparently."

"In Marcus' defense, he's apparently got more than one type," Gavin joked weakly.

"True. Good thing Hayes isn't the kind of guy to get jealous." Zach paused for a long moment. "I don't think I've ever heard you say you found a guy attractive, before."

One minute everything was fine, no worries whatsoever about crossing the line, and the next, they were edging right up to it, and Gavin was floundering trying to ease back from it.

It wasn't that he didn't want to be honest about his bisexuality—especially when Zach had come out to him even though he'd clearly been semi-terrified about it—but how could he separate the truth from his attraction to Zach?

"I . . .uh . . ." Gavin hesitated.

"It's okay," Zach said, like it was. Like Gavin wasn't a total chickenshit.

They'd almost goddamn kissed on his couch in Michigan. Zach *had* to know he had some form of attraction to men.

"It's . . .it's not, actually."

There was a long, terrible silence.

"Not that I don't think it's okay," Gavin said quickly, when he realized how fucking awful that sounded. God, he needed to do better. He could just tell the truth. He *should* tell the truth. Zach deserved that much.

"Really—it's okay," Zach said.

"No. That's what I meant. It's not okay for me to not be honest. I don't think it's a big deal. I just . . .always knew I liked both? But I met Noelle so young that it wasn't ever a thing that I could explore. It was just . . .it just *was*."

"Okay," Zach said.

Gavin huffed out a frustrated breath. "Is that all you're gonna say?"

"Congratulations?"

"You're not the first person I came out to," Gavin said, but he could still hear how hopelessly fond he was.

"Good," Zach said.

Gavin squeezed his eyes shut, wishing he could've done a way fucking better job at that. Even half out of his mind, Zach had done a better job coming out to him.

But then, Zach hadn't been coming out to someone he was attracted to.

That had made it awkward. Or at least, that was what Gavin wanted to tell himself.

"That really sucked, actually," Gavin admitted.

Zach laughed. "Did it?"

"It really did. Not me telling you, obviously. But how . . .God, tell me it gets less awkward."

"Sort of," Zach said. "I know everyone says, *it gets better*, but sometimes I think that's something we tell ourselves so that we don't approach each and every time like it's gonna really fucking suck."

"Fair," Gavin said.

"But I'm glad you told me."

"I should've told you before, but it felt . . ." Gavin took a deep breath. "Felt unnecessary."

He didn't have to say why. Zach got it.

"How old were you when you and Noelle met?" Zach asked quietly.

Gavin swallowed hard as pain flared deep inside. It was less agonizing than it had been, but it still hurt. "Fifteen."

"God, I'm . . .I'm sorry. I'm so sorry, Gavin."

"Yeah. I know. I . . ." Gavin trailed off. Four years after losing her, he still didn't know how to accept people's sympathy.

"It must be hard, to know what to say to people," Zach said, like he could read Gavin's thoughts.

"Yeah, it really was. *Is*, I guess," Gavin confessed.

"Was for me too," Zach said. "And she wasn't my wife."

"I didn't know you felt anything when . . .when it happened."

"Are you fucking kidding me? She was so great, Gavin. So great. Nice to me when she didn't have to be—"

"Yeah, she did," Gavin interrupted. And yes, it hurt. It always hurt. But now that the pain was breaking through the numbness it wasn't as horrific as it had been, at one point.

It was a pain he could, well, Gavin couldn't say he could *live* with it, but he was, wasn't he?

He was living with it right now, and he didn't want to even admit it to himself but Zach was helping, too, every single day.

"Well, she was nice. And when I found out . . ." Zach swallowed hard, audible clicks over the line. "And when I found out, I hurt for you, G."

It was Gavin's turn to swallow that lump in his throat, forcing it down. "Thanks."

"I wanted to tell you but I didn't know how and maybe it was better that I didn't."

"It was better," Gavin insisted. "I didn't . . .obviously I'm total shit at accepting sympathy."

"It's okay," Zach said. "I like you anyway."

And Gavin really believed that might be true.

Not like *that*, maybe—or else Gavin hoped it wasn't like that, because it wouldn't matter if Zach had those feelings or not, because nothing was ever going to happen.

"You know, I like it when we talk about nothing, but this was nice too," Gavin said.

"Yeah, it was," Zach said. "I'm sorry if I didn't say any-thing before."

"Don't be," Gavin insisted. Back then, he hadn't needed Zach to tell him. He'd only needed everyone to leave him the hell alone. And now that Zach was? Well, he wasn't sure he'd ever be *ready* to hear these things, but it wasn't as awful as it might've been, once.

He could live with it.

"Okay," Zach said. He sounded relieved, like *not* saying anything had been bothering him. "I'm glad you came out to me." His tone went softer then, almost intimate, and Gavin felt them edging towards that line again.

The line he didn't want to even acknowledge to himself, while also depending on it entirely.

"Guess there were a few things we needed to say to each other," Zach mused.

"Guess so."

"You wanna skate again tomorrow morning after break-fast?"

"Sure. And then I have a lunch with Sidney."

"Again?"

Gavin made a frustrated noise. "He's not unhappy or anything. Just . . .nosy."

"Great," Zach said sarcastically.

"I know. When I was here before, he was only the assistant AD and he wasn't so . . .well, you know."

"Pushy? Gossipy? Interfering?"

Gavin laughed. "Yeah. But I wouldn't call him interfering, not exactly, anyway. He's letting us do what we want."

"He'd better," Zach said.

Gavin couldn't help it; he laughed *again*.

This was why he hadn't been able to deal without this. He *liked* feeling this way. He wanted to feel this way all the time.

Content and happy and *seen*.

Something he should probably talk to Jon about. But surely, there was no harm in it. Because Zach was getting something from it too, clearly. They were friends. Gavin was his coaching mentor. It was him and Zach, against the whole world.

And nothing had felt more right than that.

"See you tomorrow. Breakfast at Jimmy's," Gavin said like Zach might've forgotten.

"Right, yeah. See you tomorrow."

After he hung up, setting his phone back on the charger, Gavin realized that he was sleepy now. Settled.

A second later he fell asleep, a smile still on his face.

CHAPTER 8

September

Zach didn't think he'd been so happy in his whole goddamn life.

Not when he'd been drafted. Not when he'd taken his rookie lap. Not when he'd scored his first NHL goal.

Not even when his beer league team had won the city championship or when he'd graduated with his bachelor's degree.

Nothing felt as good as this—Gavin pressed to his side on the bench, the last thirty seconds of their first game ticking down.

The Evergreens were up five to zero, and the Cougars hadn't even pulled their goalie, because one—even *two*—goals wasn't going to make a bit of fucking difference.

Not tonight.

Gavin was practically vibrating next to him, and he knew that if he turned and looked, he'd see pure joy on his face.

He almost did it, but then Elliott leaned back and caught his eye, and he leaned in to check in with him instead.

"You good?" Zach asked.

Elliott nodded. He was beaming, too. And why shouldn't he be? He'd had two goals and an assist on Ivan's goal. The hopes for the first line, with Elliott and Ivan and Mal, had been high, maybe even too high. Last night, he'd mentioned to Gavin that maybe they'd put too much pressure on them. Maybe they wouldn't be able to deliver at the rate everyone was expecting them to.

But he shouldn't have worried.

Elliott was glowing, and even Malcolm didn't look nearly as disgruntled as he normally did.

"Hey," Elliott said, "how 'bout that power play goal?"

Zach grinned. "You know it was sick."

It had been. The way Mal had tipped him the puck, barely even glancing in Elliott's direction before it had connected to his tape, Elliott sniping it right into the upper right of the net.

That was going to end up on some highlight reels, for sure.

The horn sounded, the game ending officially.

Elliott gave him one more delighted look, before shooting off the bench with the rest of the team for the handshake line.

"Well, that was delightful," Gavin said as Zach followed him down the tunnel towards the locker room.

"I'm trying to think of how it could've gone better," Zach agreed.

"Ivan could be snappier on his faceoffs," Gavin said, scratching his chin. "Work with him on those this week?"

"Yeah, we'll do that."

"And the penalty kill—"

"Yeah." They could tighten that up a bit. The Cougars hadn't scored, but there had been a handful of dicey moments. If Ramsey hadn't deflected a shot off his skate at the last moment, they definitely would've gotten that one in.

"But Finn was solid. He recovered from that and got the shutout," Gavin said under his breath as they walked into the locker room.

Zach nodded. "Hey . . ." He shouldn't even suggest it. But how many breakfasts and lunches had they shared over the last six weeks? So many. Zach was learning patience, in a way he'd never have imagined he might when Gavin had first come to Portland. The late night phone calls were now a staple—but they almost never did it in person. Occasionally, there were later nights at the office, but that was the office.

Zach told himself he was being smart. Giving Gavin the time he needed to adjust to the idea of Zach being more than just his assistant coach.

But in the last week or so, he couldn't pretend he wasn't frustrated at how slow it felt. How little progress it felt like they'd made.

Maybe Gavin would be perfectly happy to keep things exactly as they were, but Zach knew *he* wouldn't be.

He wanted more. And Zach believed that if he could shift them out of this rut even a little, Gavin would want more, too.

"Yeah?" Gavin was distracted and didn't look at him, bumping fists as the guys trailed into the locker room.

"We should grab a drink after this. To celebrate." Zach couldn't quite form the words to add, *at my place, where we'd be all alone.*

But he was thinking it.

He was *wanting* it.

Gavin actually looked disappointed. "Ugh, Sidney cornered me this afternoon and said there's some booster get-together tonight, after the game. At Sullivan's?" He named one of the upper end restaurants right on the edge of campus. "You should come with me."

Zach didn't want to spend his evening glad-handing with boosters and watching as Sidney dragged Gavin around, showing him off to every single person who'd ever given money to the university. But it was also better than sitting in his empty apartment, waiting for Gavin to call him so he could lie in bed, make meaningless small talk and wish that they were there together.

That he could roll over and Gavin would be right there, easy to touch. Easy to kiss.

"Sure," Zach said.

"I'm sure it'll be—good job, Finn," Gavin said, abruptly interrupting himself to greet their goalie. Finn's helmet was pushed back, his hair sweaty and looping in dark curls over his ears and forehead, but he was smiling.

"Thanks, Coach," Finn said.

He looked just about as light as Zach could remember seeing him, and he thought, *maybe this'll all be okay.*

It was too early to know that for sure, of course, but it was a nice thought.

Nicer than spending his evening with Sidney Swift anyway.

Music started playing, guys shedding pads and equipment and heading towards the showers.

A damp patch was forming on his lower back, making his shirt stick to his skin so he headed in that direction too. He was just out of the separate coaches' showers, changing into a pair of jeans and pulling an Evergreens polo over his head when Gavin walked into the room after dealing with the media.

He still looked happy, but he looked tired, too.

"You good?" Zach asked as he ran a hand through his damp hair.

Gavin shrugged. He'd already lost his jacket and loosened his tie. Now he pulled it the rest of the way off and began to unbutton his shirt.

Zach looked away. It was only polite. But also he didn't know how to look and not want to touch all that naked skin so badly his hands shook with it.

If he'd thought his crush was bad, back when Gavin had been his coach, it was nothing compared to how it felt now, taking up so much inside him Zach thought he might choke on it.

Hayes had stopped suggesting he get over it.

Now he was just a stoic presence on the other end of the phone line and in his inbox. Reassuring Zach that he could be patient. That he could do the right thing and wait until Gavin was ready.

If he would ever be ready.

"I'll be in my office, alright? Just come grab me when you're ready to go." Zach was still looking in the vicinity of his shoelaces, no matter how much he wanted to just fucking *stare*.

"Sure," Gavin said.

Zach retreated to his office. Just as he was leaving, out of the corner of his eye he thought he saw a flash of pale skin, and he swallowed hard as he collapsed onto his chair.

There were texts on his phone. Mostly of the congratulatory variety. His mom had texted for both herself and his dad. Several guys—still friends—he'd played with in the NHL and in his beer league.

Hayes, of course.

He thumbed over to their convo.

I'm going out of my mind.

Hayes had stopped telling him it was going to get easier a few weeks back, which strangely felt better than the alternative.

It wasn't going to get better. He didn't want useless platitudes.

He was in so deep he didn't want to crawl out again. Even if someone showed him the path, he wouldn't take it.

Maybe, at some point, he might've, but that was before Gavin had come out to him, and he'd known then, no question about it, that this was actually a solid, real possibility.

Winning is still better than losing, Hayes texted back. Zach knew it was late in Tampa, so he was surprised. But then, maybe he shouldn't be. Hayes wasn't exactly sleeping well either, these days.

And Jesus, Hayes had been doing this for *years*.

Zach didn't know how he'd survived.

Of course, Hayes didn't have Morgan around all the time—or at all, actually. Maybe that made it easier. For a stupid split second, Zach considered asking him that, but at least he realized before he sent the text that it was shitty.

Hayes probably *wanted* Morgan around all the time.

If Morgan had been around all the time, their fling probably wouldn't have been so short-lived.

Yeah, except when you have to look in his face and see how goddamn happy he is.

Zach took a deep breath and added: **I'm still being patient, tho.**

Of course, what else are you gonna be?

I tried asking him to come over to my place for a drink, but somehow instead, we're going to some booster event where Sidney fucking Swift is going to monopolize him all night long.

Hey, at least you have your phone calls.

The phone calls were great. Infuriating, yes, but also great. When he did finally fall asleep each and every night, Gavin's voice was echoing in his ear.

Of course, that usually meant he woke up from hot and unsatisfying dreams, hard as a rock and leaking in his boxer briefs, wishing that the other side of the bed wasn't empty.

Cold fucking comfort.

Remember when I said in July you were in deep? I didn't mean it. You're in deep now.

You'd know.

Don't worry, I'm not staging any interventions.

Yeah, well, it wasn't my fault your ex is an asshole. Not yours either.

Hayes didn't answer right away. Zach groaned under his breath. He hadn't meant to piss Hayes off, and now he was going to be worrying all night that he'd inadvertently made his best friend feel even worse about his personal life when he'd only been trying to help Zach with *his*.

There was a noise in the doorway. Zach glanced up and Gavin was standing there.

"Everything okay?"

Zach realized he'd been sitting here in the dark, staring at his also-dark phone.

Well, that wasn't weird or anything.

"Oh yeah, I'm good," Zach said, plastering on a smile. It wasn't even that hard, really. He *wanted* to smile whenever he saw Gavin. Wanted to do a whole lot of other things, too. The frustration only came because he *couldn't*.

"Good," Gavin said.

It wasn't a very long walk to Sullivan's. They were probably close to halfway there, when Gavin said, "I'd rather be grabbing a drink with just you, you know. I . . ."

"Yeah," Zach said uselessly, when Gavin didn't quite finish that sentence. Not that he'd probably have finished it the way he wanted him to, but the thought was nice.

"Sidney is annoying," Gavin said, chuckling under his breath. "And if this team keeps playing the way they did tonight?"

"He's gonna be on your ass constantly."

Gavin sighed. "Constantly."

"Winning's better than losing?" Zach offered, repeating what Hayes had just said.

"Always," Gavin said, the corner of his mouth tilting into a smirk. "But if that's true, you have to tell me what you were doing in your office, frowning at your phone."

"I . . . uh . . . it's Hayes."

"He's okay?"

"Oh yeah. He's good. Probably gonna have another fifty goal season, frankly. But . . .well, I think he's lonely."

"No boyfriend?"

Zach barked out a laugh. "No. *No.* He's sorta hung up on someone, someone he can't have, and it's fucked him up, forever."

Gavin shot him a knowing look, intense and a little hot around the edges. "It's not you, is it?"

"For the hundredth time, Monty and I are just friends."

"Well, it would be okay if you weren't."

Zach wanted to stop right in the middle of this sidewalk and shake Gavin until he got it. Or *kiss* him until he got it.

"We're just friends," Zach said dryly. "He just . . .he had a fling with a guy, a *player,* awhile back. Pretty much the stupidest thing he could've done. I told him it was a mistake, but he didn't listen, and now he's fucked up and in love forever."

Funny how history repeats itself.

"That really sucks."

"Yeah," Zach agreed.

"Maybe you *should* give him Marcus' number," Gavin teased. "He could get anyone out of a slump."

"Maybe Ramsey," Zach joked and Gavin choked out a laugh.

"God, don't," Gavin said. "Can you imagine—"

"Yes, and I wouldn't ever, because what a clusterfuck," Zach finished for him.

"He's such a beast on the ice," Gavin mused, and by the time Zach pulled open the door to Sullivan's, they were chatting easily about the game.

Not surprisingly, the moment they entered the lounge area, crowded with people in Evergreens gear, Sidney swooped in.

"Gavin, there you are. And you brought Zach."

"He's a very important component of what we're doing here," Gavin said stoutly.

"Well, of course, he's the one who got you here," Sidney said. "Now I've got a number of people who're just dying to meet you."

Gavin shot Zach a look that spoke volumes.

"I'll just grab us some drinks," Zach said, touching Gavin briefly on the arm. He tried to avoid touching him most of the time—or at least being the *first* one to touch—but he swore Gavin leaned into it and that pinched anxious look in his eyes faded.

"Great. Whatever beer you think I'd like," Gavin said. "Thanks, Zach."

There was a line a few patrons deep at the bar, but Zach didn't mind waiting. No doubt if more people recognized him, or if he'd been Gavin, the line would've melted away like it had never existed in the first place, but he decided it was better this way.

Let Sidney get his claws into Gavin for a bit, usher him around, and then by the time Zach had their beers, he could steal him away.

Sure enough, by the time Zach had two bottles in his hands, Sidney had Gavin at the third group he'd ushered him towards and that pinched look was back in Gavin's eyes.

"Hey, I've got to steal Gavin away for a second," Zach said, as he walked up to the group.

There was a blond woman there, eyeing Gavin with the kind of hunger Zach felt but never let show. "Oh, that's too bad," she cooed. "But who are *you*?"

"My assistant coach, Zach Wheeler. You were talking about how good the power play was tonight," Gavin directed towards the other side of the group, tilting his body away from the woman. "That was all him. He got McCoy and Jones there."

"I think it's going to be the best power play in the conference, if what we saw tonight is any indication," one of the men said.

Gavin tilted his head. "We'll see," he said. "It's early still."

He turned away, towards Zach, and Zach pressed the bottle into his hand.

"Here," Zach said. "Let's go find a quiet corner."

"God, I forgot how proprietary these people can be," Gavin said under his breath, shaking his head as Zach led him away to an empty high top table. They might not have a lot of privacy here, but it was a start, at least.

"It was a really good power play," Gavin said after he took a long sip of beer.

"It wasn't *all* me," Zach argued, though he *had* done a lot of work with Elliott and Mal and the rest of the group.

"It was enough you. Power play can be tough. Too many people who don't play together, too many players who run their own lines, not wanting to work together. But you made it work." Gavin paused, one of those smiles that he didn't seem to give anyone else but Zach blossoming across his face. "More than made it work, honestly. It was absolutely fucking amazing."

"Thanks," Zach murmured, ducking his head, hoping that Gavin wouldn't see how flushed he suddenly was at the praise.

"You're great at this," Gavin said. "Gonna eclipse me, at some point."

That seemed both improbable and impossible.

"No way," Zach said. "I don't wanna be anywhere else—"

"Someday. Not anytime soon," Gavin soothed, putting a hand on Zach's shoulder this time and to Zach's delight, his touch lingered. Like he didn't want to let go.

"Good, 'cause I don't want to go anywhere." He didn't. And if he *was* going somewhere, it was closer to Gavin.

He wanted to get closer *now*, and normally Zach might have fought against that compulsion, but he didn't want to any longer. Not tonight, anyway. He slid a few inches closer. Felt the heat of Gavin's arm pressing against his.

Gavin didn't move away, just smiled at Zach. Like he understood.

Like he wanted it too.

And every single goddamn time Zach thought this was too hard, that he didn't know if he had any more patience to give, this was why he kept going. Putting one foot in front of the other.

Because nothing else felt this good.

Someday, it might be even better. But until that day . . .Zach was going to wring every ounce of enjoyment out of every moment.

There was a sudden commotion in the front, near the door, and only Gavin looking away from him forced Zach to do the same.

"Well, this isn't that surprising," Gavin murmured when Sidney exclaimed loudly.

Zach realized that the man he was staring at, that *everyone* was staring at, was Morgan Reynolds.

"Well positively, you're no longer the most important person at this party," Zach said. *Might make it easier to sneak out with me.*

"Yeah, except it's Reynolds. Did you know he was coming into town?"

Zach shook his head. If Finn had known, he hadn't mentioned it.

"He didn't tell me either." Gavin sounded exasperated.

"At least he didn't tell Finn ahead of time, so he couldn't angst about it," Zach pointed out.

"Or Finn didn't tell us," Gavin said heavily.

"I don't think he would've been able to keep that under wraps," Zach said. "But let me check in with Ramsey. Maybe he told him instead." He pulled out his phone and sent Ramsey a quick text. **Hey did Finn say anything about his dad being here for the game?**

Ramsey's reply was nearly instantaneous. **No. He surprised him after the game. Asshole. It's okay. He's with me, now.**

Zach tried not to smile. Ramsey was as good of a protector as he and Gavin had hoped he would be.

"He didn't know," Zach confirmed. "And Ramsey's with him. He's got this."

"Good, good." Gavin was still looking over at where Sidney had an arm around Morgan. Sidney looked like he'd just won the lottery, and Morgan was laughing, amused by something.

Maybe how half the party was practically genuflecting at his appearance.

It was so weird, being in the same room as him—this man Hayes loved even though he didn't want to.

"I guess I should go over there. Say something to him." Gavin didn't seem like he actually wanted to do it.

"Or we could just leave." Zach didn't want to talk to him. What would he even say? *Hey, by the way, Monty is my best friend. Do you even know how much you fucked him over? How much you fucked him up?*

Hayes would kill him.

Gavin looked shocked. "Just . . .leave?"

"Why not? You did your rounds. You made nice with Sidney. Even dissected the power play."

"But Reynolds—"

"He's distracting everyone."

Gavin's mouth quirked up in a smile. "Yeah, he really is." He paused for a long second. Then immediately poured the rest of his beer down his throat. "Come on. There's a back door here, somewhere, if I remember right."

Less than thirty seconds later, they were pushing the door open, falling into the courtyard behind the restaurant, empty now, except for a small knot of smokers at the corner.

Next to him, Gavin tensed, like he was worried they'd recognize him too, but they didn't even glance over as they passed by them, and then they were free.

"I can't believe I just did that," Gavin murmured as they passed by the front of the restaurant. If Zach squinted, he thought he might see Morgan in there, signing everything any-one shoved in front of him.

No, it was so much better this way.

Not just because it was just the two of them.

"Oh, you weren't going to stay that long, anyway," Zach teased, nudging him.

"This is what you hated about the NHL," Gavin said, chang-ing the subject which said it all.

"Didn't you?"

Gavin shrugged. "I didn't love it. But I was used to it, I guess."

"I just wanted to play hockey. Now I just want to coach hockey." Zach didn't need Gavin to tell him that there was no way to do that. That once you were good enough—at playing or coaching; didn't matter which—the noise came with the territory. You couldn't turn it off.

"Missed a lot of things about this. Didn't miss any of that," Gavin agreed.

Zach didn't know where they were going. They were just wandering, aimlessly. It was like their late night phone calls, except they weren't in two separate houses. Gavin was right here, with him. Close enough to touch, if he found the courage.

"Anytime you wanna sneak out, I'm happy to be your ex-cuse," Zach said, meaning it.

"Yeah, I might take you up on that," Gavin said.

"Anytime." Zach nudged him with his shoulder, but didn't move away after. Enjoyed the way their arms brushed once, then twice.

They weren't touching *that* much, but it still felt like explo-sions detonating just under his skin. Zach craved more, but he didn't know if he should take it. If he even *wanted* to just take it.

They turned down another street and then another and another. Walked through the campus.

It was a nice night out, warm but breezy, and they found themselves on the quad, lingering near one of the picnic tables by Hazel Hall. When Zach had been a student here, he'd spent hours in this exact spot, eating lunch and studying and goofing around in the long, endless afternoons.

But nothing could match this. The starlight picking out the handful of gray hairs at Gavin's temples, the shadows turning his handsome face into Greek statuary.

Zach wanted so badly he burned with it, even as he told himself to be patient.

To let Gavin make the move if he wanted it, too.

But he didn't. Not really. But he did sit down on the table, feet on the bench, elbows resting on his knees.

Zach joined him, deciding that it was okay to let his thigh brush Gavin's.

He hadn't pulled away from his touch. Not once.

"It's funny how the season feels endless right now. Perfect, all stretched out in front of us," Gavin mused quietly.

"But by the time we hit January, it'll only feel like an endless grind?" Zach smiled. "Yeah."

He loved both feelings, actually. The excited anticipation when anything felt possible and even the point where it felt like almost too much, like if he had to go to another game, he was going to scream. Terrible, almost, but in the best possible way. Like someone touching him after he'd just come.

"Like you said, winning feels better than losing," Gavin said.

"The start of a season's never felt like this before, though." Zach knew why. It was his crush, too many feelings crammed into too small of a space, and how they overflowed everywhere.

"For me either." Gavin glanced over at him now. "Probably because I haven't done it in so long."

Zach wanted to argue, to tell him that wasn't why at all. That it was *him*. That it was him and Zach together, that was making every moment feel so precious, like that breathless split second before they swan dived right off the cliff into the unknown.

It was supposed to be scary—terrifying, even—but it didn't feel that way with Gavin. It just felt inevitable, and not like everything closing or anything ending, but instead like the world was opening up. A thousand different possibilities, with one single golden thread of commonality holding them together.

Him and Gavin, *together*.

But Zach wasn't stupid; he couldn't say any of that shit.

"Yeah," he agreed.

Gavin tipped his head back and looked up at the sky. "Maybe it's how good I think this team could be."

With Gavin not looking at him, Zach could look his fill without any embarrassment. Without any guilt. And he did, eyes glued to Gavin's face. To his lips.

God, he wanted to kiss him so bad.

He'd always wanted to. Even back in college, when he'd been eighteen and enjoying that first heady freedom, getting to make out with guys at frat parties and hook up after, he'd thought about Gavin way too much.

More than he probably should've.

And now? It was so much worse, a clamor in his blood, making his hands tremble.

"We're going to do great things," Gavin kept talking. Like Zach wasn't a hair trigger away from saying fuck it, grabbing Gavin's face between his hands, and not letting him get away from him this time.

But then Zach remembered Hayes saying *his big widower freakout*, and Zach couldn't do it.

He should move away. Put some space between them, so he was no longer tempted.

Before he could, Gavin's head tipped back down and then his face was right there, catching Zach right in the act.

And suddenly, *God*, they were right back in that same moment, when they'd been on the couch in Gavin's cabin.

Gavin was staring at Zach's mouth, his own dropped open a little. It was dark but Zach swore he could see the pink of his tongue just resting there, and he felt lightheaded. With desire. With the force it took to hold himself back.

"Zach," Gavin murmured, and then his hand was curling around Zach's shoulder, and he was hyperventilating, because Gavin was leaning in and this was everything he'd ever fucking wanted, condensed into a single endless moment, flawless like a diamond.

Gavin's fingers dug into his shoulder, and he tugged him another inch closer until they were pressed together.

He wanted to do a cheer and yell, *it's finally happening, it's finally happening*, but if he did that, he'd have to move, and there was no way he could do that. He was transfixed, frozen right in place.

Waiting.

Nervously, he licked his lips, wondering how long Gavin would make him wait.

Too long apparently.

Because suddenly, Gavin let go and that open, needy look on his face shuttered closed.

He leaned away.

Zach felt lost. What had just happened? Had he done something wrong?

No, Hayes told him, *you just have to keep being patient.*

If that had been hard before, it felt fucking impossible now. Weeks, maybe even months. *Years,* possibly, of this impossibility stretching out in front of him.

And maybe at the end of it, whenever it ended, it wouldn't even be the way Zach wanted.

"Sorry," Gavin murmured, looking away. "I . . .sorry."

It was like hitting rock bottom at the base of the cliff.

Zach shook his head, trying to clear it from the panic shooting through him, but he couldn't.

He could end up just like Hayes.

Stuck in shadows. Loving someone he couldn't ever have.

You don't know that. But the pep talk didn't work as well as it might've once.

"What are you sorry for?" Zach hadn't intended to ask the question, but he felt stripped bare of artifice.

Gavin slid off the table. Shoved his hands into the pockets of his jeans. Still didn't meet his eyes. "I don't mean . . .I didn't mean . . ."

Part of Zach wanted to retort that he sure fucking did mean it. That he'd meant it less than five minutes ago. That they'd been a breath away from meaning all kinds of things.

But then he remembered how Gavin had just emerged from four years in the middle of fucking nowhere, mourning his wife. How he'd sounded when he'd told Zach how old they'd been when he'd met her.

It was unfair for Zach to expect him to just *stop* mourning her.

No matter how he felt about it.

"It's okay," Zach said, even though he wasn't sure he one-hundred-percent meant it.

"We should—*I* should, uh, get back home. It's late."

It wasn't that late. It wasn't even midnight yet, and they'd talked on the phone that late plenty of times.

But maybe . . .well, *maybe* it would be a good idea to go their separate ways. Zach wasn't sure his heart—or his dick—could take any more close calls tonight.

"Alright," Zach said, trying to sound casual. Like he wasn't still half-living in that moment five minutes ago.

"Well, I'll see you tomorrow, yeah?" Gavin waved awkwardly in the general direction of his rental house. Zach's wasn't really in the opposite direction, and part of him wanted to argue they could walk at least some of the way there together. But forcing himself on Gavin wasn't going to do him any favors.

"Yeah," Zach agreed. They didn't have an official practice on the books—just the game on Sunday. But he knew he'd be in the gym, and at the rink, and in his office, going over the tape from tonight's game.

"Okay." Gavin gave him one single nod, and then Zach was just about to turn away when he heard a whispered obscenity under Gavin's breath and suddenly Gavin was pulling him into a tight hug.

It was quick—almost before Zach realized what was happening, it was over.

"Great win tonight," Gavin said and then he was striding off, like if he stayed then he might do it again. And longer, this time. And *more*.

Zach waited until he was nearly out of sight and definitely out of hearing range before he pulled his phone out.

"I don't want to talk about it," Hayes answered on the first ring.

"Talk about what?" Zach was confused. Hayes couldn't possibly know what had happened tonight—that was why he was freaking calling. To tell him that he and Gavin had nearly kissed *again*.

"Ugh." Hayes made a horrible disgruntled noise. Like a wet cat.

It suddenly occurred to Zach what Hayes was whining about.

"You didn't delete the Google alert, did you?"

Hayes made the noise again.

"You deleted it but then you *added* it *back*?"

"I'm doing it to be informed about Finn," Hayes said, clearly attempting to find some dignity. Zach didn't want to tell him he'd left that behind *ages* ago.

"Right," Zach said. Now he didn't know whether he should share *his* drama, not when Hayes was angsting so hard over Morgan.

"He was drafted by the Sentinels and I'm going to be his captain, eventually," Hayes said, like he needed to explain himself.

"Yeah, probably," Zach said. And that was going to be a fucking trip.

He could only imagine the meltdown phone calls he was going to get from Hayes once *that* happened.

"Ugh, *why*?" Hayes asked, even though there wasn't really a question there.

"Because fate and the NHL hate you?"

Hayes made the dying wet cat noise again.

"Hey, at least I didn't tell him to his face that he was a friend-destroying asshole," Zach said.

Only when Hayes went totally silent did Zach realize he'd just made a huge mistake.

"You wouldn't," Hayes finally said, quietly.

"No, of fucking course not. I didn't even talk to him. I didn't think I could, without punching him in the face."

"It wasn't—*isn't*—his fault, Zachy."

"No, of course not," Zach retorted sarcastically.

"I mean, how else was it supposed to work? We'd have been in the same zip code like what...twice a fucking year?"

"And the offseason?"

"Okay, so twice a year and three months out of twelve. Sounds like a good basis for a relationship." Hayes sounded like someone was stabbing him slowly in the gut and he just kept fucking *bleeding*.

Before, Zach would've mentioned that three years ago, Morgan had retired and there'd been nothing stopping him from moving to Tampa and showing up at Hayes' house and telling him he loved him and wanted to be with him. But he hadn't.

And that, more than anything else, Zach knew, was why Hayes sounded like he was bleeding out.

Zach would've done just about anything to staunch Hayes' hemorrhage. So it wasn't too much of a stretch for him to say, "Gavin almost kissed me again tonight."

"Oh yeah?" And he already sounded better, so Zach kept going.

"He didn't, of course. *Of course*. But *almost*? And that's something, right?"

"Right," Hayes agreed easily.

"I only had a minor freakout afterwards, when he *apologized*."

"He apologized? Ouch."

"I mean, he didn't say what for. Maybe he was apologizing for *not* doing it?" Zach wanted to believe that was true, but he didn't quite buy it. Still, it was easier to say that than to say the alternative, which was that Gavin was apologizing for *almost* kissing him.

"Sure," Hayes said but it was obvious he wasn't buying it either.

"What if we end up like this, together?"

"You mean happy and shit? I don't know. Enjoy it," Hayes said moodily.

"I mean *you and me*. What the fuck are we going to do?"

"Grow old and grumpy together. Marry platonically," Hayes said so quickly that it was obvious he'd thought about it, too. "Maybe adopt a dog."

"I like cats," Zach said, more to annoy Hayes than because it was true.

"Okay, we'll adopt a dog and a cat and be one big happy gay family."

"No offense but that sounds kind of awful," Zach said. "I love you and that still sounds awful."

"I know," Hayes agreed despondently.

They were both quiet for a long moment. "Tell me we're going to be okay," Hayes said finally.

"You're gonna be just fine. I'm going to give you Marcus' number. You're going to fall madly in love and have the best sticks in the league," Zach said, even though he knew none of that was going to happen.

As for himself, he didn't even want to spin any insane fantasies. If he ended up like Hayes? He'd lose his fucking mind.

He'd never be able to stay here, and he'd never want to leave, either.

It was so fucked. *He* was so fucked.

"I don't think so," Hayes said, but Zach could hear the smile in his voice and took that as a win.

"Sounds good, though," Zach said.

"You're gonna be okay too." Hayes sounded like he meant it, and Zach really wanted to believe he was right.

So he did.

CHAPTER 9

October

Gavin kept telling himself this would get easier.

That one morning he'd wake up and see Zach—at the diner or in his office, at the rink, or at the gym, and his heart wouldn't race. That his stomach wouldn't flutter.

But it kept happening.

And after he lost his mind two weeks ago and nearly kissed him *again,* after their first game, Gavin began to think that maybe it *wouldn't* go away.

That was terrifying, because what the fuck was he going to do about it?

He didn't know.

It was obvious he should talk to Jon about it—he *knew* he should—but he hadn't yet. He hadn't even known how to bring it up, and whenever Jon did, he was as bland as possible and then changed the subject.

Gavin didn't think he'd really fooled him, but at least he hadn't forced him to talk about it yet.

"Hey," Zach said, catching his attention as he flopped down onto the weight bench.

It had also been a whole lot fucking easier before Zach's classes had started up and his gym schedule had changed. Somehow he always ended up in the staff gym at the exact same fucking time as Gavin.

And well . . .Gavin wasn't blind.

Zach was very attractive. And when he was sweaty and hot, worked up from physical activity? It was like staring into the sun.

"Hey," Gavin said, nodding at him. He turned back to the leg press he was using, hoping that Zach would get the memo that he was ready to focus now.

Usually Zach was equally focused in the gym—and Gavin didn't want to appreciate the results of that, but it was hard not to, these days—but to his surprise, he sauntered over, appearing in the corner of his vision as he began another set.

"You talked to Brody recently?" Zach asked.

"All the time," Gavin said, grunting, definitely feeling the extra ten pounds he'd slid onto the rack.

He didn't want to use the phrase *sexual frustration,* even in his own head, but it was definitely something that sent him to the gym this often and saw him working this hard.

"I mean, about more than just regular hockey shit," Zach said. He was leaning against the machine now, hip cocked. He was wearing thin basketball shorts, riding high on his thighs, and an old T-shirt he'd cut the sleeves out of.

Gavin could see a lot of skin. Skin he was trying really fucking hard not to look at.

"No, not really, I guess. Is there a problem? Is he okay?" Gavin hadn't been worried about Brody. They were winning. The top line was producing at a ridiculous rate, even as Elliott and Mal continued bickering. The defense was tight. Finn seemed stressed and anxious at points, but overall, seemed to be handling it.

Zach hesitated. "I think so? I don't know. He seems . . .off to me. Quiet."

"He's always pretty quiet," Gavin offered. At least that was the impression he'd gotten over the last two months.

"Yeah, he is. But I think even quieter the last week."

Gavin finally finished his set and let out a gust of breath. His quads were burning, in a really good way that *almost* distracted him from the little flashes of biceps-pecs-abs that he kept trying to ignore.

"You want me to talk to him?" He finally couldn't put it off anymore and looked up at Zach.

He looked a little worried—that crease between his eyebrows that Gavin wanted to reach up and smooth away—but also really, really good.

Too good.

It was so much easier to compartmentalize these feelings when they were working or Zach was completely clothed or when they were in their respective houses, on the phone at night.

"No, I'll do it. I think it'll be better coming from me," Zach said. "Or maybe I should ask Ramsey."

"Ask Ramsey. That's probably the best place to start."

Zach nodded. "It's not his hockey. That's solid."

"Agreed," Gavin said. "I know he's taking a pretty serious load of classes."

"He is—you know he's a bio major, right?"

"Yeah."

Zach's expression was a little wistful. "Sometimes I wonder if I didn't make a mistake, not taking school more seriously when I was here the first time around."

"You knew what you wanted," Gavin said. Zach *had*. He'd been incredibly focused, only seeing college as a necessary steppingstone to the NHL. They'd both worked hard to make his dream a reality.

Was it any wonder how shocked he'd been when Zach had come to him this summer and admitted he wasn't playing professionally anymore?

"Funny how that changes," Zach said wryly. "How what we think we want isn't what we want at all." His gaze slid over Gavin, the look in his eyes knowing, and Gavin flushed.

After the second aborted kiss, he really should've said something to Zach. Something other than *I'm sorry* anyway. Because that implied . . .well, that he wanted to, but that he couldn't.

And that's true. You want to. But you can't.

It would be better for both of them if he verbalized this line between them and emphasized that he wasn't ever going to cross it, but Gavin didn't know how even to start that conversation.

So he just kept . . .not.

"Yeah, I uh . . .thought I wanted to stay in Michigan forever," Gavin said.

Zach grinned. "No, you didn't."

It was impossible not to join him in smiling, not when he looked like that. "Well, I *did*, until you showed up."

Until you offered me a job I couldn't say no to.

Until we almost kissed and it turned me inside out.

"You're welcome." Zach was still smiling smugly. Maybe it shouldn't be so attractive, but Gavin was having trouble convincing himself of that fact.

Gavin rolled his eyes, even as he was charmed.

"I'm gonna . . ." Zach gestured at the mat behind them.

"Alright," Gavin said.

He wiped his face and then the machine, taking his time making his way over to the treadmill.

He always did his weights and then cardio, but today, he really regretted this well-established schedule because that meant he was facing the workout mat now and had a front row seat to Zach doing his ab work.

He'd pulled his shirt off, and his chest and his stomach were both rippling with muscle—muscle he'd put on the hard way. Muscle he was working on the hard way, now, sweat dotting his brow and making his skin shine, a siren's song that Gavin didn't know how to look away from.

Zach's abs flexed as he lifted the medicine ball over and over again, and Gavin felt like his tongue must be hanging out. Imagining how they'd feel under his hands. How soft but firm his skin would be, that trail of hair bisecting his abs and arrowing lower, leading towards . . .

Gavin huffed out a frustrated breath.

It was hard to even put one foot in front of the other, nevermind to do it jogging on a treadmill, without killing himself accidentally.

"You good over there?" Zach called over. "You taking it easy today?"

Had he noticed that Gavin had been staring? God, he hoped not. But maybe it would be good, because then Zach might make a move, an *obvious* move, and that would give Gavin an opportunity to shut this down once and for all.

"Oh yeah. I'm good." Gavin pushed the speed up, praying he wouldn't trip over his own goddamn feet.

He couldn't keep going this way. *They* couldn't keep going this way.

Zach chuckled, a little out of breath, and that sent a spike of sexual heat through Gavin again. It wasn't fair. He *liked* Zach. He was so easy to hang out with—low-key and funny and smart. Great at hockey. Even better at coaching hockey. He'd not let Gavin down once since he'd started this job.

But he also had to be fucking hotter than the sun.

He wanted to just enjoy Zach without all this other *noise*.

Maybe no matter how much he didn't want to, or how awkward it was probably going to be, he should talk to Jon about this. Because the feelings he didn't want to have kept intruding, kept bleeding into every single everyday interaction.

Someday Gavin was afraid that he wouldn't be able to contain them. Wouldn't even be interested in denying them any longer. And that was impossible. He couldn't do anything about this. He didn't even *want* to feel this way.

Had never wanted to feel this way again.

Gavin finished his run and forced himself to look away as Zach worked on his lats, the muscles on his back gleaming as he pulled the bar down.

Grabbed his phone and sent Jon a text. He could duck home between his lunch meeting and practice this afternoon. Normally he might take a therapy call in his office, but there was no way he could talk about this at the rink. Even with his door closed, he couldn't take the risk.

"See you at practice this afternoon?" Gavin called out.

Zach nodded, not even glancing behind him, and Gavin told himself firmly he wasn't running away.

But he kind of was.

"So what's going on?" Jon asked, leaning back in his office chair.

Maybe with other clients Jon was more formal, but for awhile now, Gavin's sessions with Jon had felt more like chats with a friend than therapy sessions.

"Um, well not much. We're winning. Things are going good." Gavin knew he was fucking prevaricating. He'd asked Jon for this session. He needed to just open his mouth and spit it out.

Jon raised an eyebrow and looked unimpressed. "And you ask for a session *today*, just to tell me everything's fine?"

Gavin sighed. "It's Zach," he admitted.

"You guys having issues?"

"Uh, no. No. The fucking opposite." Gavin barked out a laugh. "I . . .I like him more than I should."

Jon didn't look surprised at all. And okay, probably he'd known this whole fucking time, and he'd just been waiting for Gavin to break and actually *talk* about it.

"What's wrong with that? Assuming it's not going to cause a problem with the team—"

"It wouldn't, ever. Swift is more his boss than I am. In fact, I think Swift even set it up that way," Gavin said. He knew he was still delaying the inevitable.

"Okay, so it wouldn't be necessarily inappropriate," Jon said. "What's the issue?"

Gavin's jaw dropped. "*What's the issue*? Are you joking?"

"Gavin," Jon soothed. "You're not even forty years old. It's not a requirement of grief to spend the rest of your life alone."

"I know that." Gavin bristled. "But that's not for me."

"Why not?"

Gavin made a face. "Because it just isn't for me. I don't want to date again. I *can't* date again."

"Sounds like you want to, though," Jon said kindly. Probably kinder than Gavin deserved.

"I don't, I *don't*," Gavin argued. Dating. Love. A relationship. That was the thing he'd had with Noelle. It couldn't be duplicated. He didn't even want to try. This thing with Zach was just . . .chemical.

"You just said you liked him more than you should. You like him. I think based on the few things you've mentioned, it might be likely that he likes you, too. Why shouldn't you date him?"

This was why Gavin hadn't wanted to talk to Jon about this. Because he would act like it wasn't a big deal; like this wasn't fucking monumental.

"I just can't," Gavin said stubbornly.

"If you can't tell me why, can you at least tell *yourself* why that is?"

Yes and no.

Gavin didn't say it though. The words felt stuck in his throat.

Jon sighed. "Alright, how about this? Could you spend some time together outside of work? Maybe not a date, but more than just co-workers?"

It was annoying how Gavin's heart leapt at that possibility. They'd done that two weeks ago, after that first game. Shared a drink, even if it was at a work function, and then they'd walked together through the dark, quiet campus.

It had been so good, until Gavin had lost his mind and nearly kissed Zach again.

"I don't know if that's a good idea," Gavin said.

"Why not?"

God, this was so embarrassing. "I'm not that good at uh . . .controlling myself," Gavin said. "There's a line and I've told myself there's no crossing it, that I don't even want to cross it, but . . ."

"But you want to," Jon finished for him.

He wanted more than anything to say *no,* he never wanted to cross it, but that would be a lie, because he wanted to cross it all the fucking time.

It was unfair to him. Even more unfair to Zach.

"I almost kissed him again," Gavin confessed.

"Yesterday? Today?"

"Two weeks ago."

Jon's eyebrows went up. "So you've been agonizing about this for two weeks."

I've been agonizing about this since June. Since it happened the first time.

"I thought I would . . .get used to it. Or I would get over it. Or I would—" Gavin broke off with a muttered curse.

"You spend a lot of time together."

"At *work*. We're working," Gavin emphasized.

"Right. And you enjoy that?"

"Yeah, I do. He sees me. And I think . . .I see him?"

"Okay. That's good. That's really good, Gavin." Jon was nearly smiling now and Gavin wished that he'd not done this at all. But if he didn't, what was he going to do about it? He'd run out of ways he could avoid it on his own.

"Why does it feel so shitty then?" Gavin wanted to know.

"Because you're not giving yourself what you really want. You're holding back." Jon paused. "Are you attracted to him?"

Gavin groaned. "I don't want to talk about that."

"That's a yes, then."

"It's a . . .it's a yes," Gavin admitted, flushing bright red. He couldn't deny it. Especially not after they'd shared the gym today.

"Okay, are you masturbating? Giving yourself the release you need? I know you were, but what about recently?" Jon asked so matter-of-factly that Gavin wanted to die.

Gavin stared at the laptop screen, *very* glad that he'd proactively decided to take this call at home and not in his office at the rink.

It was terrible no matter where they were discussing it, but *God*, imagine if Zach—or anyone else—overheard?

"We've talked about this," Jon chided gently as Gavin tried to avoid looking at his brick red face on the laptop screen.

"Yeah, and funny, it doesn't seem to get easier," Gavin croaked. It had been, at least before Zach had arrived on the scene.

"You going to answer the question?"

"No, I thought I could just die of embarrassment instead."

"It's a normal human body function, Gavin."

Gavin took a deep breath. "No," he said.

"No, it's not a normal human body function or *no*, you haven't been."

"The latter," Gavin ground out.

Jon raised an eyebrow. "Is it the same problem or a different problem?"

He was going to have to say it. Out loud.

"I don't want to, because I'm afraid," Gavin said in a rush.

"Not that you're going to think about Noelle. That you're going to think about Zach?"

God, it felt so wrong to nod his agreement, but that was the case, wasn't it?

Four weeks ago, after a particularly late night at the office, he'd been so keyed up, he'd lain in bed and thought, *I should*. Hoping that maybe it would help calm him down enough to sleep.

But the moment his hand had drifted down to touch himself, Zach had appeared in his mind, as he had earlier that night, stretching his arms over his head, a sliver of golden stomach and abs peeping out from under his T-shirt.

Gavin had yanked his hand back like he'd been shocked.

He was *not* going to jerk off thinking about Zach. That wasn't just nudging up to the line—that was skating right across it.

And he hadn't tried since, because he already knew what was going to happen if he did.

"You're allowed to think about him, Gavin," Jon said quietly.

"No, I'm really not," Gavin said.

"You know the difference between what's happening in your mind and what's happening for real."

"Of course I do." But if he kept *thinking* about it, if he let himself *really* go there, all of this would just get way fucking harder.

"It's not a betrayal," Jon said, like he hadn't even spoken. "You know my opinion on this. She wouldn't want you to be unhappy and alone forever."

"And she doesn't get to have an opinion, because she isn't here," Gavin snapped.

Jon sighed.

"What about finding someone else? Someone else with less history? A stranger?"

"That sounds awful," Gavin said. He didn't want just anyone. If he let himself, what he wanted was Zach.

It might be terrible and wrong, but that didn't change the fundamental way he felt.

"Then I want you to try it."

"Dating—" Gavin started to argue.

But Jon interrupted him before he could. "No, not dating. Simpler than that. Just . . .when you go to touch yourself, let yourself think about whatever you want. Even if it's Zach."

"I don't know," Gavin said doubtfully.

"I think it would be good for you."

Gavin didn't agree with that at all, but Jon was the expert here, and he'd been right about everything so far. Even about him supposedly never working in hockey again.

"Fine, I'll try it," Gavin said grumpily.

"Good. Let's set up another appointment, and we'll discuss how it went."

Gavin flushed again. "Do we have to?"

"You think you can manage single words?"

"Yeah. Yes. I can do that."

"Alright." On the screen, Jon pulled out his tablet, where he kept his calendar, and Gavin pulled out his phone, doing the same.

After they made the appointment for a week from now, Gavin hung up and grabbed his keys, heading towards the rink for practice.

Okay, in the next week, he was going to have to make time to get himself off. And he was going to have to do it without putting any restrictions on himself.

No big deal.

But it seemed like the moment he'd given himself permission, that was *all* he could think about.

How soon after practice could he get home and get naked and get his hands on himself and finally, *finally* let all those mental restrictions go?

"You look distracted, Coach," Ramsey said as they leaned against the boards, watching as the team and Finn took penalty shot practice.

"I'm fine," Gavin said.

"Yeah? So it's just me, then?" Ramsey asked, a knowing glint in his eyes.

Ramsey was a great captain. Sharp and observant, never letting things go, but also never harping on them when the players weren't ready to deal with whatever the issue was yet.

Across the ice, Mal yelled at Elliott, and Elliott snarked right back, the heat between them at its usual low-level simmer.

"Just you," Gavin said steadily. "So Morgan didn't tell Finn he was going to be at the game?"

"I believe he thought he was being low-key," Ramsey said. He made a face, which told Gavin they both agreed on how stupid that was.

He was *Morgan Reynolds.*

"I'll talk to him," Gavin said. "And I appreciate you taking point with Finn when he shows up."

"He's a good kid. A great goalie. I don't mind, really. He's becoming a friend," Ramsey said.

Gavin cut him a look.

"Just a friend, I swear," Ramsey said, laughing. "I'm not the one you should be worrying about."

"Oh, who should I be worrying about?" Gavin asked, hoping he wasn't going to hate the answer.

Gavin followed Ramsey's gaze to where Brody was laughing with Ivan.

"Ivan? Really?" Ivan was the steadiest player Gavin had ever coached. He did everything he needed to anchor that first line, barely letting Mal and Elliott's shenanigans faze him.

"Nope. Brody."

Just this morning, Zach had expressed concern over Brody. He'd said he'd talk to Ramsey, but here Ramsey was, before he could have.

"Did you talk to Zach?"

"No. But I'm not surprised he noticed too."

"What's going on?"

"He's playing as well as he ever has, but . . .well, you can see it too?" Ramsey sounded half-heartbroken about this. God, Gavin hoped that Ramsey wasn't actually in love with Brody. He had his hands full enough with the rest of the team.

"Not as well as you, probably. I wasn't here last year."

"Before he hurt his knee, he was . . ." Ramsey let out a hard breath. "He flew across the ice like he didn't ever want to be anywhere else, but it's changed. *He's* changed."

"Do you think his knee's still bothering him?" The reports Gavin got from the medical staff said the knee was fully repaired and functional, but this wouldn't be the first time a player lied to a trainer.

"No," Ramsey said. "I think he wants something else, now, and . . ." Ramsey didn't usually sound bothered by any of the team's issues. He faced them all matter-of-factly, like he was above them. But this seemed to genuinely worry him.

"And?"

Ramsey sighed. "Brody's brilliant. He could do whatever he wanted. I just thought . . .I just thought he wanted *hockey*."

"More to life than hockey."

"Coach!" Ramsey made a faux-shocked gasp.

He just shrugged. "We just gotta be here for him."

"I also think . . ." Ramsey sighed again. "I did something I thought would help him and it *would,* if he'd get out of his own way."

"What did you do?" Gavin asked suspiciously.

"Gave him a new roommate. You know Dean Scott? He plays football, is like the star on their defense?"

Gavin nodded. He'd heard of the kid, because Sidney couldn't spend all of their lunches talking about the hockey team, though he sure tried.

"Well, I thought they'd get along, you know?" Ramsey made a face. "I thought he might loosen Brody up some—they might loosen each other up, if I'm being honest—but all it's done is make him tense and irritable."

"For the love of God, Ramsey, stop trying to matchmake everyone," Gavin said, but he was chuckling.

Ramsey laughed then, too. "I can't really help it. I just like . . .fixing things. If only they'd get out of their own way."

"Maybe they still will." Gavin paused. "Please don't interfere with Mal and Elliott."

"But—"

"I mean it, Andresen. They're . . .it's a delicate balance."

"You mean, between wanting to kill each other and fuck each other?" Ramsey asked.

Gavin told himself very firmly not to blush. "That's not . . .*no.* I'm just saying, leave them to me."

Ramsey had the nerve to actually look disappointed. "But Coach—"

"You wanna keep them scoring on the ice?"

"Well, yeah, we all do. They're a machine out there."

"Then let me handle it. But you try to talk to Brody, okay?"

Ramsey nodded. "I can do that. Honestly, I just thought they'd fuck and it would loosen him up and that would be it, I didn't know he'd get all angsty and *pine* about it. I mean, Dean's just some big dumb football player."

"Just like all our big dumb hockey players?"

Ramsey laughed. "Fair."

Gavin gave him a friendly pat on the back. "Come on, go give Finn some work."

He watched the rest of practice, trying to keep his mind on what his players were doing.

His conversation with Ramsey had been a good distraction, if not a little terrifying. That kid was going to chess-master their team right out of playoff contention if he wasn't careful.

But then practice was over. He went to his office because if he let himself go home immediately, he was terrified of what that would mean about him. Dealt with some emails. Watched some film on their upcoming opponent. And none of that was nearly distracting *enough*.

Picked up a sub sandwich on his way home and picked at it as he watched a movie on the couch. Jon had set the appointment for a week from now, after Gavin had claimed that he was busy and that he might also need time to work up to what he'd promised. But well . . . there was no way Gavin was going to need a week. He was already half-hard in his jeans.

He wanted to go to bed. But he also *didn't* want to go to bed.

Gavin was in the middle of his mental debate about whether he should talk to Zach before or after when his phone dinged. Zach had texted him.

Talked to Ramsey. He said you already talked to him about Brody.

Gavin fumbled with his phone and dialed.

"Hey," Zach said. "You already talked to him?"

"It just came up at practice," Gavin said. "I knew we'd be talking later so I didn't mention it."

"You seemed distracted today."

"You and Ramsey are both worrying too much about me." Gavin really didn't want to talk about what was distracting him.

Zach chuckled. "But I *like* worrying too much about you."

Zach had never explicitly crossed the line either. They'd never discussed the two aborted kisses—and whether or not he'd have returned them.

But Zach also was making it clear enough, in a hundred little ways, that he'd definitely be into it.

Gavin's hand trembled around the phone.

"I'm fine," Gavin said. "Did Ramsey tell you the bullshit he tried?"

"With Brody and his roommate? Yeah, I yelled at him a bit. I don't care if he thought Brody needed shaking up or some kind of sexual revolution or whatever. He's messing with shit he shouldn't be messing with."

"Agreed," Gavin said.

"Brody'll be fine. And as for him not loving hockey the way he did before the injury? It'll either come back or it won't. Or he'll end up like . . ." Zach didn't finish the sentence, but he didn't need to.

"Like you?"

"Yeah," Zach said. "And that's okay, too. I'm happy. I told Ramsey that. Brody needs to do what makes him happy."

"Imagine if the NHL could hear you now. They'd have a heart attack."

"Probably. Only one way to do hockey, right?" Zach sighed. "It's such bullshit."

"He's got time. I'm definitely not kicking him off the team if he doesn't want to go pro. He's too good of a player."

"Never thought you would." Zach's voice was low, intimate.

It already felt like Zach was slumped next to him on the couch—or even worse. Like they were already in bed together. Stripped naked, or close enough that they would be soon. Anticipation and apprehension warred inside Gavin.

Jon hadn't told him to do this a bunch of times, but he knew once he let the dam break, he wasn't going to be able to hold back.

He was going to want it all the time; he was going to *do* it all the time.

"It's only right," Gavin protested weakly.

"And somehow you're one of the few who actually believe it. And follow through," Zach said.

"I'm not some kind of hero," Gavin argued.

"The fact that you don't see it means you kinda are." Zach hesitated. "I was so lucky before, when you were my coach. And I'm even luckier now."

Gavin didn't want Zach's hero worship. He wanted Zach to understand he was just a man, trying to do his best in an uncertain and unfair world.

"Me too, you know?" Gavin had said it before, and he didn't think he needed to say it again. *I wouldn't want to do this without you.*

There was a long quiet moment. Gavin could hear Zach breathing. Imagined he could hear the same. Not an awkward silence, but a comfortable one.

"I have to go work on a paper," Zach finally said reluctantly.

And I have to go jerk off, thinking about you.

"Hope it goes well. See you tomorrow?" He might've suggested breakfast at the diner, but he didn't know how he'd feel about seeing Zach first thing in the morning after . . .well, *after*.

He didn't think he'd want to throw Zach down onto a table-top at Jimmy's and kiss him until it seemed like the most natural thing in the world, but you never knew.

Gavin was in uncharted waters these days.

"We should get breakfast," Zach said.

Gavin should say no. He'd already decided it was a bad idea. But somehow he found himself saying, "Eight? I'll see you then."

Zach agreed and then said quietly, intensely, "Good night."

The moment he tossed the phone down, Gavin knew he wasn't going to make it to the bed.

He reached down and pressed at his cock, erect and aching.

It was easier than he'd thought it would be to unbutton and unzip and push his jeans down. He palmed himself in his boxers and gasped out loud. It was annoying how right Jon was, because he was desperate and gagging for it, twitching in his palm as he pushed his boxers down next.

It was even easier to turn his head and imagine that Zach was here. Comfort and heat in those soft blue eyes as they stared at him. Acceptance and desire, too.

It's okay, he could hear Zach say. *Do it. Let go. I want you to.*

His cock was so wet at the tip he didn't even need the lube in his drawer. He just slicked it down and let his mind keep wandering.

Zach there, still, eyes intent on him, on his body, on what his hand was doing. Then he reached over and didn't even touch his dick, just put his palm, hot and steady, on his belly, right above where Gavin was stroking himself, and then slid lower, down to Gavin's bare thigh. Squeezed.

God, you're hot, Zach might say. *I want you so much. I've been waiting for you to want me.*

And Gavin wouldn't hold back. He'd say, *I've been wanting you too.* He imagined leaning over and just letting his lips brush easily across Zach's. No pressure. No angst. Just pleasure—the two of them floating through it so easy as the kiss deepened, Zach's tongue brushing against his.

Zach murmuring against his mouth, *let me. I want to.*

Pleasure was burning in his stomach, mounting in his balls, and it would only take a little bit more to tip him over the edge. Zach's fingers, tangling with his own, stroking him together, and Gavin shuddered, coming so hard it was a miracle he didn't fucking pass out.

For a long moment, Gavin didn't think, he just *felt*.

How good it had been. How right.

The most natural thing in the world to want to cross that line, and then to just *do* it.

It would seem almost innocent, except for the cooling stripes of come on his stomach.

Or how much he wanted it still, despite just coming his brains out.

CHAPTER 10

It was so frustrating.

Zach thought he'd get used to pretending that everything was fine and normal. He'd been doing it for weeks, for fucking *months* at this point, but sitting across from Gavin, both of them acting like they hadn't talked to each other last night like *that*. Ignoring the way the air crackled between them. Evading even the slightest mention of the two times—the *two* times—they'd almost kissed.

But he wasn't used to it.

He leaned back in their booth in Jimmy's—they had a fucking booth now, one they sat in multiple times a week, sharing breakfasts and lunches and dinners and even occasionally a late night snack—and stared at Gavin opposite him.

Gavin didn't look at him, just kept his eyes pinned to his egg white omelet, and Zach wanted to deny it, even to himself, but he fucking *craved* Gavin's gaze.

Wanted to know, without a single doubt, that he was as affected by this crackling tension as Zach was.

"Good eggs?" It was a stupid question. Gavin always got the same breakfast order and ate it like it was going out of style. Today wasn't an exception.

Gavin glanced up, and Zach felt a thrill when their eyes met, *finally*.

He must've felt it too, because Gavin flushed a little, high on his cheekbones.

"Yeah," Gavin said. "Yours good?" He gestured towards Zach's plate. He'd been pushing his corned beef hash around not because it wasn't good, but because he was getting really fucking tired of not talking about this.

Zach nodded.

Hayes would tell him to keep being patient, and he *could* be patient, but he also needed something.

A tiny sliver of hope, to make the waiting easier.

"So . . .uh . . .about what we talked about last night . . ." Zach trailed off. Their phone call last night hadn't been *that* different than a dozen or so other phone calls, which really, that said it all, didn't it?

"Hmm?"

Zach swore that Gavin's flush was deepening. And okay, he'd been kind of obsessed with how soft and earnest and serious Gavin had sounded, how *into* it Gavin had been, even during a throwaway convo that wasn't all that much different than so many of their others. But to know Gavin was equally into it?

Was it any wonder Zach was losing his fucking mind?

"I mean, it was nice, you know?" Zach didn't know how to say, *it was better than nice; it was everything.*

And it hadn't been anything special. That was why he was so fucking stuck on this.

"Yeah," Gavin agreed. But then his eyes dropped back down to his stupid egg whites.

Zach wanted to scream.

Hayes would still tell him to be patient, but it was way too easy to just push that voice aside.

"It was more than nice," Zach said. Hating how silly he sounded. *You can do this. Break through the polite fucking platitudes.* "Every time we talk, like that, I think, it can't feel any better, but it does." He dropped his voice lower. Trying to find that intimacy they effortlessly built every night. "Every time we talk, I don't want to hang up."

That got his attention—in a major way. Gavin glanced up, looking shocked and astonished, like he actually thought he and Zach could keep going like this forever, edging around it, but never fucking talking about it.

Well, Zach was done with that. He was cutting through the bullshit.

"I don't know—"

"Don't say you don't know what I'm talking about," Zach said in a low voice. "You know. It's okay. I feel it too. I felt it in Michigan, and two weeks ago, when we walked through the quad, and every fucking night, on the phone."

Gavin's mouth opened and then he snapped it shut again.

Zach knew he was begging with his eyes for Gavin to say something. But he didn't, so Zach kept talking—like once the self-imposed dam was gone, he couldn't stop himself.

"I didn't think you might feel the same. Like it was really fucking crazy to even imagine it, but then you told me you liked guys, and I could just *feel* it when you looked at me. And then the other night, in the quad—"

Gavin interrupted him. "Me being bisexual doesn't mean I like you, Zach. Like that, anyway."

Zach couldn't believe it. Well, he *could*, that was the whole fucking problem. This was the same idiot who'd leaned into him once and then twice and pulled away both times.

Well, Zach wasn't going to let him be idiotic. "So you wanting to kiss me *twice*, was just . . .what exactly?"

Gavin's fork clattered to his plate. "Not what you think," he muttered.

"Bullshit," Zach said. "I saw the way you looked at me yesterday. You couldn't tear your eyes away from me when we were at the gym. I'm not stupid. I know when a guy is attracted to me."

"It's . . ." Gavin sighed, deeply. "Maybe it's a little bit like that, Zach, but that doesn't matter."

Zach wanted to do a fist pump of joy. But he didn't, because it wasn't like Gavin seemed to *want* this. Instead he seemed to still really be fighting against it. It was the worst time to remember Hayes saying, *his big widower freakout*, but maybe this was what this was, still.

"Seems like it matters from where I'm sitting," Zach insisted.

"Zach." Gavin said it so gently, but the letdown was coming. Suddenly, Zach could feel it and he wanted to run away before Gavin could actually do it. "We can't do this. We can be co-workers. You can be my assistant coach. I can be your mentor. We can be friends, even, but we can't be more."

Zach swallowed hard. "Because I'm your assistant coach?" He'd go quit tomorrow if that was the case, but he had a feeling that wasn't it, at all.

"There's so many reasons why but sure, let's start with that. Then add in you're too young for me—you were my *player*, for God's sake. Then I just . . .I can't do that again. I won't ever date again." Gavin cleared his throat and picked up his fork. "I hope you understand that."

He did. And he didn't.

"I . . ." Zach swallowed hard. "Okay."

"It's not you, it's me?"

Zach rolled his eyes. "Is that supposed to make me feel better?"

"Maybe it's supposed to make *me* feel better," Gavin said so gently, like he thought Zach might actually break. And the worst thing was he *might*.

Hayes had told him not to push. And he'd pushed and look what had fucking happened.

"But, what about in the future . . ." Zach trailed off.

It wasn't hard to see the finality in Gavin's expression, and after he'd witnessed it, it was nearly impossible to keep going.

"No," Gavin said.

"But you said you didn't want to coach again and look what happened there." Zach knew he was pushing too hard, but then he'd done that too, with the job, and that had turned out. Gavin had actually been *happy* he'd pushed right into his space, not letting him rot away in the wilds of Michigan.

Maybe this would turn out the same way.

But Gavin just shook his head, his expression tentative, like he was incredibly worried how Zach might react.

For a second, Zach wanted to tell him he was right. That he was going to stomp out of Jimmy's and throw a hissy fit and quit in a fit of disgruntled rage.

It sucked. It *hurt*. But at the same time, Zach got it. He'd seen Gavin and Noelle together. He knew how deeply Gavin had loved her.

He didn't want to remember that or understand why Gavin might convince himself he could never date again. But he couldn't help himself.

"I'm sorry, Zach," Gavin said. "I wish—sometimes I wish it could be different. But it can't."

Zach swallowed down a whole bunch of bitter disappointment. Maybe having Gavin as a friend and a mentor would be enough. Especially if he knew there was no chance. If he truly believed there wasn't any hope.

Hayes would probably tell him it would majorly suck. But then not having Gavin in his life would definitely suck worse.

"It's okay." Zach took a deep breath. "It's . . .I'm glad we talked about it."

Gavin didn't look like he necessarily agreed, but this had to be better than going around, torn between wild hope and heart-racing anticipation.

"Me too," Gavin said, and Zach was pretty sure that was the only lie Gavin had told him during the whole conversation.

"You've been avoiding me," Hayes said, the next time Zach picked up his call.

It wasn't the first time Hayes had called in the last two weeks—not by a long shot—but it *was* the first time Zach felt like he could relay the bare minimum of the conversation without breaking down and crying or throwing something or letting anger and frustration overwhelm him.

It was so much easier not to talk about it. So much easier not to think about it.

To just exist day-to-day—classes and practices and games. Taking one day at a time, putting one foot in front of the other.

It didn't feel good but Zach also didn't want to give Gavin the satisfaction of seeing how much his rejection had fucking sucked, so he tried to pretend to the world—and to himself—that everything was fine.

But he couldn't pretend to Hayes.

"Yeah, I have," Zach admitted. He stretched out, back stiff after sitting at his desk for hours, working on a paper for his advanced psychology class.

"You gonna tell me why?"

"I told you last week, when you texted me if you'd done something to piss me off, the answer was no. It wasn't about you. Not everything is about you. God, Monty." He could hear how grumpy he sounded.

"You fucking idiot," Hayes said, "I'm not worried about *that*. I'm worried about you. You're not usually this quiet. For a second I thought you might have fallen into bed with Gavin and just hadn't come up for air."

Zach choked a little. Tried very hard not to imagine what that might've been like—if his conversation with Gavin in the diner had gone in the opposite direction.

He wanted to say no, but he couldn't quite force the word out of his suddenly uncooperative throat.

"Oh shit. Shit."

He didn't even have to say it. Hayes got it anyway.

"Yeah," Zach breathed out unsteadily. "I was really fucking stupid. The way you told me not to be."

"Zachy, I'm so fucking sorry," Hayes said.

"It's . . .it's fine," Zach said. He was *fine*.

"It's okay if it's not. If *you're* not," Hayes pointed out.

"He said—it wasn't *me*. That he . . .well, that he *would*. But that he's never dating again."

Hayes was quiet for a long moment. "Is that better, or worse?"

Zach made a frustrated noise. "I don't know. I don't fucking know, okay?"

"Well, he *could* change his mind—"

"Don't do that," Zach interrupted him, frustration leaking into his voice and making it harsher than he'd intended.

"Don't do what?"

"Give me fucking hope. You said it, back at the beginning of this whole thing. He was going to have his big widower freakout." Zach took a deep breath. "But you were wrong, it's not a freakout. Freakout implies that it's got a beginning, a middle, and an end. And I don't think it will."

"Shit. I didn't want to be right," Hayes said earnestly.

"God, I know that. I *know* that. I shouldn't have said any-thing." He'd only been agonizing over this for weeks now. Had it been better that he'd spoken up? Or would it have been better to keep the hope buoying him as long as possible? Maybe if he hadn't forced Gavin to make a choice, he'd have eventually changed his mind.

But who was he fucking kidding? He'd heard the closed door in Gavin's voice. Saw it in his eyes. When he said he wasn't ever dating again, he meant it.

"Yeah, you should have," Hayes said, voice soft. "If you hadn't, imagine what would've happened? You'd have hoped forever and fallen in even deeper, and I think that would've sucked even harder."

"Yeah," Zach said. But he wasn't quite sure he believed it. That was the whole problem.

"You didn't quit, did you?"

"No. No way. I . . .it's not *his* fault, you know? I'm not even mad at him. Not really. He's as much a victim of this as I am," Zach said.

Hayes' silence was telling.

"So yeah, no, I'm still here. We're still coaching. We're still friends. We still talk all the time, every night, same as before."

Hayes still didn't say anything but now his silence took a disapproving slant.

"It's really fine," Zach continued. "I'm learning so much. And the team is winning."

Hayes sighed. "Zachy, you are so fucked."

"I am not," Zach argued, just because he hated how resigned Hayes sounded. Like he was hopeless, and he *wasn't*. He was an adult, making adult choices. He wasn't led around by his dick. Or his poor bruised heart.

"This is why I—" Hayes broke off, muttering a frustrated *fuck* under his breath. "This is why I cut it off with Morgan. I wasn't going to hang around for months or God forbid, for *years*, waiting for him to toss me a scrap."

"Yeah, you're totally doing so good with that, by the way," Zach retorted sarcastically.

"Fuck you," Hayes said, without heat.

"I'm not hanging around for a *scrap*. This is my *job*. I work for him." Technically he worked for Sidney and for the college, but he didn't need to go into the details of the chain of command for Hayes right now.

"I know, and I'm fucking proud of you for doing it," Hayes said. "But do you ever think that this is going to slowly kill you? Being that close but not close enough? You're never going to get over him without having some space."

Zach leaned back in his desk chair and squeezed his eyes shut, hating how his heart clenched at Hayes' soft question.

"Yeah," he finally admitted.

"But you're going to do it anyway."

"What else can I do, Monty?"

"Not let him that close?"

Zach debated asking that if Hayes had the opportunity to be this close to Morgan—but with nothing else—if he would take it. It would be a totally unfair question, because he knew how his best friend would answer.

He'd take all that intermingled joy and pain, no question.

"You know I'm not going to push him away," Zach said defensively.

"I know. Just think of how this ends," Hayes warned.

Zach knew exactly what he was thinking and not saying—*don't end up like me*—but even if he should be considering the possibility, he *couldn't*. Not now. "Me, becoming a great hockey coach."

Hayes sighed.

"Hey, I caught your game last night," Zach said, changing the subject.

"Oh yeah?" Hayes perked up.

"Man, that goal in the second? That was gorgeous fucking hockey," Zach said.

He'd had the TV on low as he'd talked to Gavin on the phone. He hadn't even realized Gavin was watching the same game he was, until they'd both made the same embarrassing screech as Hayes had woven his way between three opposing players, barely set up, and then hit the upper corner of the net like he was born to do it.

"Damn," Gavin had said. "That guy is good at hockey."

Zach had never been prouder.

"Thanks," Hayes said. "I think the team's gonna be good this year."

"Me too," Zach agreed.

They relaxed into a companionable silence.

"Got a long road trip coming up," Hayes observed.

"You'll be fine."

"Playing New York at the end," Hayes added. "God, I hate going there."

"No, you hate that even seeing his number in the rafters gives you a boner."

"You're the worst," Hayes said, his tone affectionate.

"Not true. Complete slander." Zach chuckled.

"Don't be a stranger again, okay? Don't make me call you when you fucking ghost me again." Hayes' soft amusement morphed into sternness.

"I won't," Zach promised.

"Good," Hayes said.

It had been four weeks since the conversation.

It was always The Conversation in Gavin's head.

Always the moment he sincerely, completely, utterly fucked everything up.

Not because he'd lied—the opposite in fact—but because of how Zach's hope had dissolved like sugar in water, drowning in the inevitability of disappointment.

He'd done that.

Gavin wasn't stupid; it was always going to really fucking suck to tell Zach the truth. That *yes*, he was attracted to him, but *no*, nothing was ever going to happen. But it felt worse because of what he'd done the night before.

What he kept fucking doing.

He told himself it was only because he'd closed the door firmly on anything happening, and this made indulging in every mental fantasy he had about Zach safe.

But it wasn't safe at all.

Didn't mean that Jon had stopped harassing him about it. Didn't mean he could stop doing it.

Didn't mean he'd stopped feeling way too fucking guilty about it.

"I'm going to have to talk to Mal, aren't I?" Zach asked from his seat on the couch. They'd just finished watching film of the last game. Analyzing the first line play in particular. How dynamite and dynamic Mal and Elliott were together.

Gavin leaned back in his desk chair, trying to pretend to himself that he wasn't counting down the minutes until he could leave this office and go home. Then get off. And talk to Zach. Or the other way around. He wasn't picky. He was going to be thinking about Zach no matter what.

"About the scouts?"

Zach nodded.

"Yeah, you probably should. They're really into Elliott. And well . . .the idea of keeping this going." Gavin gestured at the screen, where Elliott and Malcolm had thrown themselves into each other's arms. On the ice was the one place they really seemed to gel, though Zach kept insisting there was more going on these days.

Well, that had been the idea, anyway. There were other tutors that Gavin could have picked to help Elliott pass his class, but Mal had been the perfect, if potentially risky choice.

He still remembered when, after he'd broached the subject, Zach had told him his pet theory. They'd both been flushed, not because either of them were even remotely into the idea of their left and right wingers fucking, but because of the *fucking*.

Gavin tried very hard not to think about sex and Zach in the same thought, at least when he was right in front of him.

It was bad enough that it happened every night, when he was alone.

"It's hard to know whether I should push him to tell me what's going on." Zach sighed. "He should be talking to *someone*, though."

"Maybe he's talking to Elliott," Gavin offered optimistically.

Zach looked incredulous. "If what's happening is what I *think* is happening, talking is the last thing on their minds. You were twenty once."

God, he didn't even need to be twenty anymore to let even the idea of sex consume him. But the last thing he was going to do was confess that to Zach.

"Please, I really don't want to think about Mal and Elliott that way," Gavin said, scrubbing a hand over his face.

Zach grinned. "Whether you think about it or not, it's probably happening."

"God," Gavin groaned.

In some ways, Zach bringing it up and Gavin having to shut him gently down had been the best-case scenario, because he'd sworn to himself there would be no more mixed signals. No more almost-kisses. He'd toed the line, because anything else was unthinkable. He couldn't lead Zach on that way.

It was enough of a miracle that Zach hadn't gotten fucking pissed at him. Hadn't quit. Hadn't stopped being his friend.

They even still talked every night. Nothing had changed, except that he'd extinguished the hope in Zach's eyes.

Yeah, 'cause that didn't really fucking suck.

"I'll talk to him. Feel him out," Zach said. "After the game on Friday?"

"Maybe we should have Ramsey do it."

"He already pushed hard enough." Gavin heard the uncertainty in his voice. He'd told Ramsey not to get involved, and he hadn't *exactly* followed that directive, but Ramsey claimed he'd only given Elliott a much-needed nudge.

And they were still scoring goals. More than ever, in fact.

Gavin didn't need anyone to tell him, because he had plenty of emails from the Toronto scouts in his inbox.

Other scouts too. Sidney was practically foaming at the mouth, he was so goddamn excited.

Everyone was half in love with Elliott Jones, these days.

"Trust me, I've got this," Zach said, getting to his feet and on his way towards the doorway, he stopped next to Gavin's desk and put a friendly hand on his shoulder, squeezing reassuringly. Like touching was totally normal. Like it was No Big Deal.

Gavin had to give Zach full points for returning them to the status quo after The Conversation.

He wasn't sure he'd be able do it—or to do it so effortlessly—but Zach had managed it. Like maybe it hadn't mattered after all. But Gavin knew that was a friendly, easy lie to tell himself, because he'd seen the disappointment swamp Zach the second before he buried it.

"Thanks," Gavin said. "You'll let me know how it goes?"

Zach rolled his eyes, his smile affectionate. "Of course. When haven't I?" He gave Gavin one more shoulder pat, and then Gavin was watching his back as he walked out.

It was getting late, and he should head home, but he didn't want to let himself have what he craved *that* easily, so he made one more perusal of his inbox.

Slotted between an email from a Red Wings scout asking for a ticket to Friday's game and a forward from Sidney about this weekend's media schedule was an email from Jon.

He hadn't been *avoiding* Jon necessarily. He'd gone to his appointments. Dutifully answered in single words whether he was giving himself healthy physical release. *Yes.* Whether he thought about Zach when he did it. *Yes.*

Had even told Jon about The Conversation, even though it had been the last thing he wanted to admit to.

Had even accepted Jon's disapproving face, because he knew he deserved it.

But he also refused to discuss why he'd drawn the line he had, no matter how much Jon pushed him to talk about it.

Gavin opened the email, knowing he'd asked for every bit of the guilt trip that was probably awaiting him.

Let's have another call before the weekend, Jon had sent, **I want to really dig into this hangup you have about dating.**

Yeah that was not going to happen. Was *never* going to happen.

But he also didn't want to put Jon off. That would only make him more insistent in the end, and he wasn't going to ghost him the way he'd done in Michigan. That had been wrong, and *felt* wrong.

Gavin hit reply. **Why do I have to talk about it? You know why, and it's a valid reason. But we can schedule something Thursday.**

Jon's reply was nearly instantaneous. Before Gavin could even close his email.

Just because you believe it's valid doesn't mean it's actually valid. Thursday, 11:30 AM.

Gavin let out a heavy sigh and closed his laptop. Headed home, totally not already dreading what Jon was going to say to him on Thursday at 11:30 AM.

He had leftovers at home, which he pulled out of the fridge and stuck in the microwave.

After his chicken and rice was hot, he sat down on the couch and cleaned his plate because he knew he should.

Dealt with three more scout emails on his phone, as the Sharks-Kraken game played out on his TV. Celebrini and Smith were going to be something in three to five years. Just watching them like this, bringing young, hot blood to the sport, made Gavin glad that he was coaching again.

He was just debating whether he wanted to keep watching or turn it off after the last intermission when his phone rang.

Gavin didn't even need to check the screen to know who it was.

"Hey," he said.

He should get off the couch and go to the bedroom. He wouldn't want to do it after he was done talking to Zach, and he was trying not to be so fucking desperate to get off these days that he couldn't make it to the bed. But he didn't move.

"You have the game on?" Zach asked.

"They need better offensive pieces so they'll actually consistently play Celebrini and Smith together," Gavin said absently. "I get the idea of putting them on separate lines, spread the talent out a bit, but it's such a fucking waste of good chemistry."

Zach made an approving hum.

"Give them five years and the right pieces around them and they're the new Matthews-Marner," Gavin said.

And that got Zach's attention. "No way," he said. "Celebrini's not ever gonna be the natural goal scorer that Auston Matthews is."

"He's eighteen fucking years old," Gavin argued, enjoying riling Zach up more than he wanted to admit to. "Give him some time."

Zach harrumphed.

"You never think anyone is as good as Matthews. I think you're in love with him." As soon as the words were out of Gavin's mouth, knowing and teasing, he knew they were a mistake.

He's not in love with Auston Matthews; he's in love with you.

And Zach had never said that, of course, but it wasn't a stretch to imagine that Zach might believe that to be true.

Gavin wanted to apologize, but would that only make it worse? Probably.

"In love with his hockey maybe," Zach said hesitantly.

"Right. That's what I meant," Gavin said, even though that wasn't true at all.

On the TV screen, Smith sent a gorgeous no-look pass through traffic, and the puck hit Celebrini's tape like he'd been born and then *designed* to receive it, and a second later, the lamp lit.

"Okay, they're good together," Zach allowed. "Imagine how good together Mal and Ell are gonna be next year."

"I don't have to imagine it, I see it every day. The scouts in my inbox agree."

"More of them?"

"It's funny how Jones wasn't on anyone's radar when the season started."

"Because Nichols played him wrong last year."

"Or playing him with McCoy was the thing that unlocked his potential." Part of Gavin worried that was true, because if that was the case, then the opposite could be true, too. With all the interest in Elliott, the chances of him going to Toronto to play with Malcolm were slim.

Not for the first time, he thought of whether he was doing Elliott a disservice by not forcing him to play without Malcolm.

"I know what you're thinking over there." Zach's tone was soft but chiding. "There's enough time to figure that out. And do you really want to deal with the fallout of that decision?"

"No," Gavin said honestly.

Elliott was dramatic enough but when thwarted, Malcolm could be a total pain in the ass, too. And both of them together, riding his ass, if he separated them? Gavin wasn't inviting that kind of pain to his already complicated enough life.

"Good. Me either." Zach chuckled. "I have an early meeting tomorrow with my advisor at Koffee Klatch. You want me to bring you your regular?"

If Gavin was a better, stronger man, he'd say no. He'd say no to coffees, to shared breakfasts and lunches and dinners, especially to these phone calls. But he wasn't better *or* stronger.

"Yeah, that would be great. Thanks."

"Of course," Zach said.

Guilt pinged him. The same guilt that would evaporate in ten minutes, when he stripped off his clothes and let himself touch his half-hard cock, imagining the whole time it wasn't his fist wrapped around it.

"You know you really don't have to—"

"I *want* to," Zach insisted.

And that was the whole problem, wasn't it? He'd tried to make this easier, but he'd only made it harder. Because Zach didn't even act angry with him. Disappointed, sometimes. Once in awhile, he'd catch Zach looking at him, pensive and regretful, but he never seemed pissed.

It would be easier if he got mad.

"Alright, well don't let me stop you," Gavin teased, tongue feeling thick in his mouth. He pushed away the compulsion to ask what else Zach wanted.

Because nothing was going to send mixed signals like turning these perfectly innocent, if somewhat intimate, phone calls into phone sex.

Even if Gavin wanted it so badly his fingers shook with it.

"You couldn't, even if you tried," Zach said seriously.

Gavin *had* tried and look where that had gotten them. Back in the same space, Gavin's back to the wall, cornered in a hard place. No relief in sight.

Well, a *little* bit of relief.

The horn sounded on the game, and it ended.

"I've got an early morning like I said, so I should get some rest," Zach said reluctantly. He always sounded like the last thing he wanted to do was end the call, even though he was usually the one to instigate it.

"Yeah, you should. Me too," Gavin agreed.

A minute later the phone was on his bedside table charging, and he was stripping down in his bedroom, throwing his clothes in the hamper and the dry cleaning bin, letting himself *finally* fall to the bed.

Sometimes there were so many fantasies in Gavin's head that when he finally let himself have this, he couldn't pick just one.

But tonight, it was easy.

Zach had two to three inches on him, and at least twenty-five pounds of muscle.

It would be easy for him to crowd Gavin against the bed. Easy to push him down, *hold* him down. Wrap Gavin's wrists in his big, capable hands. He'd be gentle, but so firm. Not taking away Gavin's ability to decide, necessarily, but taking away all the noise in his head that claimed, over and over, that he *shouldn't*.

"So good for me," Zach would murmur as his head dipped low, a lock of his hair slipping down across his forehead.

Gavin's heart leapt and then raced away with the last of his self-control. He usually tried to wait a little longer, but he'd waited as long as he could tonight. His hand drifted down his torso, his skin already damp with anticipatory sweat. Between his thighs, his cock was so hard it was aching, and he wanted to touch himself more than he'd wanted anything in a very long time.

Anyone who claimed you hit a sexual lull at forty hadn't ever had Zach Wheeler around all the time, tormenting him with his sweet eyes and bright smile and wide shoulders and general *Zach-ness.*

But Zach wouldn't let him go the rest of the way, his fingers digging into his hip.

"Not yet," Zach murmured into his ear. His lips skated down the sensitive line of his neck, and it was so good, so fucking electric, Gavin actually groaned out loud.

He wasn't even feeling it, not for real, but that didn't matter.

This felt like the realest thing he'd felt in forever—at least since last night.

"Don't make me wait," Gavin pleaded.

The sweetness in his gaze dimmed, darkened. And that was so hot Gavin's hips nearly shot upwards. It was only the delusion that Zach was here, Zach was controlling every touch he got, that kept them flat against the bed.

"You gonna beg me?" Zach asked.

He didn't want to beg; but he wanted to beg so badly he was *dying* for it, at the exact same goddamn time.

"No," Gavin lied.

"I think you will," Zach said, cocky and smug and so fucking hot Gavin was dying with it.

Dying *for* it.

Gavin wet his lips.

Zach covered them, kissing him deep and slow, spinning it out until he didn't have a prayer of not sliding his fingers those last few inches or working his hips as he fucked up into his fist.

Zach lifted his mouth from Gavin's. "You wanna come?"

Gavin nodded, wordlessly, past speaking, because the white-hot clench in his stomach and the lump in his throat wouldn't let him.

"Then you'll have to beg me." Zach's lips teased the corner of his mouth again, little glancing touches, not giving him anything he wanted or needed, as the pleasure fizzed right up his spine.

"Please, *please*," Gavin finally groaned. "Let me."

Zach's smile was intimate, private, meant just for him. "Let go, G," he said gently, and that shouldn't have been as hot as it was, but he went supernova, shuddering as the orgasm crested over him.

Every single time he didn't think he could come any harder, but then he impossibly did.

With shaky hands, he wiped up his mess and then flopped back onto the bed.

Guilt was inevitable; it always filtered through the pleasurable endorphins no matter how good the orgasm was.

Maybe it would be different if it was *real*. If it was really Zach touching him, murmuring encouragement against Gavin's mouth, because he wouldn't be denying him and using him in the same breath. But it couldn't be real. He'd already decided that it couldn't. That it *wouldn't*.

But even the way it sort of felt like shit after didn't stop him from riding the high *during*, or from him chasing after it with every ounce of determination he had.

He should do better, *be* better, but he couldn't help himself.

And, it could always be worse. He could be leading Zach on by *actually* having Zach share his bed.

CHAPTER 11

December

"Finn's looking so solid," Zach said as he leaned against the boards. He'd put skates on today, so he was on the ice, as Gavin leaned over the edge, his chin nearly brushing against Zach's shoulder.

He shouldn't like it as much as he did, but that ship wasn't just sailed, it was out of the fucking harbor.

At the worst times he remembered all of Hayes' warnings. How if he didn't put some space between himself and Gavin, it would be impossible to move on.

And last month, when things had been fresh, he hadn't imagined that he'd ever want to. But as he dug in, getting ready for the long haul of having Gavin in a lot of ways but never as deeply or as completely as he craved him, he was beginning to wonder just how shitty this was going to be.

"Yeah," Gavin agreed. "God, on Saturday? He was on fire. I've never seen him play like that."

Zach nodded.

It was definitely shitty. And he was definitely still doing it.

"I wasn't sure about this thing with Braun. Thought it could get messy—"

"It could still get messy," Zach warned.

Morgan was a problem; he never stopped being a problem. Which Zach supposed couldn't be all that surprising, because he'd been a thorn in Hayes' side—in his *heart*—forever.

That was apparently just what he was. Persistent and annoying and always fucking digging himself in someplace he didn't belong.

"It could, but I don't think it will." Gavin sounded optimistic about this, which was cute but also naive, because everyone knew when Morgan found out that his greatest rival was coaching his son, he was going to lose his shit. It was only a matter of time and how long and how severe the shit-losing was going to be.

"You just like the results so much you're not worrying about the consequences," Zach said and felt rather than saw Gavin's smile against his shoulder.

"Yeah," Gavin admitted. "But that shutout! I was actually worried about the Phantoms' offense, but I shouldn't have been."

"Clearly," Zach said.

"We should run a shootout drill at the end of practice," Gavin said.

They still did them, because everyone needed them—not just Finn, but the offensive guys too—but they *had* been doing them less in deference to Finn's mental hangups.

But Zach agreed; that shutout was a natural extension of an undeniable growing confidence, and if that *was* Jacob Braun's doing, then he'd give the guy credit.

"Yeah," Zach said. "It's a good time for it."

"Agreed." Gavin rested his chin on Zach's shoulder for one last glorious minute and then he was rising, heading over towards center ice, where a knot of players had gathered, Ramsey starting to run them through a set of drills.

Ramsey was good. Always seemed to know what they needed to do before he and Gavin really considered it, and Zach hung back, observing as they worked on their power play. The first team was good—running like a machine these days, and it turned out, almost annoyingly, that booster at the bar had been right, because it was the best producing power play in the conference—but the second needed work.

Gavin beckoned him over as Ramsey gave the second power play team a gentle-ish ass reaming.

"I should move Mal to the second team," Gavin said.

He kept saying this stuff. Talking about how other teams, particularly NHL teams, were dividing up their good players. If Gavin brought up the Penguins' two-headed monster one more time, Zach was going to scream. Or pin him against the boards and kiss him so hard his mouth would be red and wet and bruised for a week.

"No, you shouldn't," Zach said.

"They need a better leader out there." Gavin sounded annoyed.

"Those guys are all just young." They were all freshman and sophomores, and he and Gavin had discussed, more than once, who was going to be the guy who stepped up and took a leadership role in that group. So far, it hadn't really been anyone.

"Hasn't stopped Jones," Gavin pointed out in a low voice.

And yes, Elliott was a sophomore, but he played like he was already in the pros. That was great, everyone was thrilled about it, but also, nobody had figured out yet how he'd made that jump. Zach knew Gavin was still worried it was because of Malcolm. And what would happen if Malcolm ever stopped being a factor.

"They'll get there," Zach said.

Gavin made a face as their third and fourth line centers totally missed each other on an easy pass and Ramsey's sharp reprimand cut across the ice.

"We need production from *everyone*, not just the first line," Gavin huffed.

"Maybe if Finn—"

"I'm not putting this whole team on his back," Gavin said.

"Fair," Zach agreed. Finn had enough pressures, without needing to be the savior all the time. Elliott and Mal—and to a lesser extent Ivan—didn't seem to mind that. But Finn did. Probably because Morgan Reynolds was a built-in pressure crank.

"Okay," Gavin said, when he'd finally seen enough, which was at least five minutes after *Zach* had seen enough.

"I'll go let Finn know we're going to do the drill," Zach said, and Gavin nodded.

Finn's helmet was pushed up and he was squirting water into his mouth from his water bottle.

"Hey," Zach said to Finn, "we're gonna run a shootout drill, for the end of practice."

Finn nodded. Zach swore he saw a shadow of *something* flicker across his face but before he could catalog and understand the emotion, it was gone.

Part of him wanted to go back to Gavin and tell him this was a bad idea, but if he did, then Finn would know why Zach had changed his mind, and that might push him even deeper into his own head.

No. They needed to do this. For the whole team, but for Finn, too.

Zach returned to the boards, leaning against them again, Gavin's elbow pressing against his arm. "Mal," he called out, when Finn was ready.

Mal was a deceptive shooter. He looked focused, but not particularly aggressive, until the last moment. It was a great strategy to lull goalies to sleep. Finn wasn't fooled by it, and he shouldn't have been. They'd been doing this since August. Finn should know everyone's tells by now.

Changing direction abruptly, Mal sped up, finding his zone.

"Come on, Mal," Elliott shouted from across the ice. "Stop fucking around!"

Gavin chuckled under his breath as Mal skated faster—nobody was unsure as to why—and then shot the puck, a dart right around Finn's knee pad.

Elliott yelled in excitement, and even Malcolm looked pretty pleased with himself.

The only one who didn't was Finn, who was frowning now.

Elliott went next, and used his speed the whole way, unlike Mal, and slipped a puck right between Finn's legs, quicker than he'd been anticipating, and now that was two.

"That's it," Zach called out, clapping his hands. If he didn't seem happy, then it would be worse. Finn would believe they all doubted him.

Gavin nudged him, and he didn't need to say why.

Zach glanced over at Finn, who was looking tense.

"You good?" he asked. Tried to make it a casual question. They *could* shut this down, no question, but Zach wasn't sure that would be a better option.

"Fine," Finn retorted.

"Alright," Zach said, nodding. He sent Ivan next, and then Ramsey. Finn got Ivan's shot, but not Ramsey's.

It was a great display by their offensive players, but Zach wasn't surprised that by the end of the drill, Finn looked like he was a mess, missing shots he'd normally have stopped, no question.

"Hey, Finn," Elliott called out, empathy written across his face as soon as the drill was over, but Finn wasn't having it, skating off the ice as fast as he could.

"Just let him go," Zach said, even though he knew he'd probably be the one following him. Trying to rebuild what they'd just broken.

"Shit," Gavin muttered under his breath.

"Should I—"

But before Zach could get the question out, Ramsey had joined them, and shook his head no.

"I've got this," Ramsey said.

"Andresen," Gavin warned.

But Ramsey just shook him off, like he usually did. "No, really. I've got this. I know what to say."

"Okay," Gavin said.

When Ramsey was gone, when they were the only two left at the rink, Gavin turned to Zach. "I fucked that up."

"If you fucked it up, so did I. I didn't know—I thought he was solid."

"He *was* solid," Gavin said, frustration leaking into his voice. "Morgan wasn't at the game on Saturday was he? Another sneak appearance?"

Zach shook his head. "Not that I was aware of. Besides, I saw him on ESPN when I got home after the game. He was on set. He wasn't here, in Portland."

"Well, maybe he opened his stupid fucking trap again," Gavin muttered.

"Or maybe he's already done the damage and now it's just a process to repair it," Zach said.

Gavin slid a look his way. "Yeah?"

"There's years of baggage here, G," Zach said. "You get that. It's not just a blink and you're better kind of thing."

Zach thought that nobody might understand it better than Gavin. Sure, instead of an overbearing parent or too much pressure it was grief and loss, but in the end the result was the same. He'd gone to Michigan to hide out, and he refused to even consider dating again.

And it had been *years*.

"I do get that," Gavin agreed. "Kinda wish I didn't."

Nobody probably wished that more than Gavin, but Zach figured he was probably a close second.

"Yeah," Zach agreed. They shared a look. The kind of look that he kept telling himself he needed to stop indulging in, but he couldn't quite make himself do it. Not when that look felt so good. Intimate and real and warm. Like Gavin's chest cracked open briefly and he let Zach see deep inside, to his heart.

It was impossible not to show Gavin his heart right back. Even if it would be better. Easier.

"Zach—" Gavin said in a low voice. Zach told himself it didn't sound seductive, and that Gavin wasn't looking at his mouth, but goddamn it, he was.

Gavin exhaled hard. Said, "Sometimes, I *do* wish things were different."

They'd been so good about this, for ages, for *weeks*, for more than a month now. A month and a half at least.

What he *wanted* was to lean in. To just *take* this time.

But he couldn't. He was frozen in place, by all of Gavin's stupid rules.

Zach steeled his brain. His heart. "Let's not do this again if you're not going to change your mind," he said with as much cold certainty as he could find.

Gavin straightened and looked away, and Zach said, before Gavin could apologize, "I'd better go make sure Finn's okay."

"Yeah. Yeah, you should," Gavin said.

And that was the end of it again.

If Zach had a stick in his hand to break, he'd have done it, right against the boards.

But he didn't, so he took one breath and then another, until his heartbeat was almost steady, and went to look for Finn.

"Team's looking great," Sidney said, setting his fork against his plate, "but I worry about that second team power play."

They'd exhausted polite small talk fairly quickly, and Sidney hadn't wasted any time bringing up the team.

Gavin barely tolerated these weekly lunches with Sidney. Zach had offered to come a bunch of times, but he never felt comfortable bringing him along, because this not only felt like Gavin's responsibility but Zach had so much on his plate already. He had classes and homework and also all the work he did with the team.

"Yeah, that's a concern," Gavin said as calmly as he could.

"Not that I imagine you aren't doing everything you can," Sidney said, patting him on the shoulder and sounding jovial and easy. "But what *is* the plan? Next year, you're losing a bunch of players. Who in this young group is gonna step up?"

Gavin's hand, resting on his lap, clenched into a fist until he forced it to relax, one fucking molecule at a time. He was probably frowning, but he wasn't sure it was avoidable.

Sidney was annoying; there was only so much he could do about it.

"That's a great question," Gavin said. "We're looking at this last stretch of regular season games closely."

He knew it was a political, noncommittal answer. A fucking *garbage* answer, but the truth was he didn't know.

Even if Brody played his senior year, like he'd committed to doing, before he went to med school, he was going to lose Ramsey. Mal and Ivan, for sure. There was almost no way whoever drafted Elliott would let him go back to college for another year. He was too good, too explosive.

They weren't even done with *this* year yet, and already people wanted answers to questions he'd barely started asking. And it wasn't just Sidney, though he was definitely the bluntest.

"I'm sure," Sidney said.

"Jones was barely on anyone's radar last year," Gavin reminded him, probably not as gently as he could have. He could hear the edge in his voice, and he already knew he'd be going to the gym after this to work out some of this frustration before practice. He told himself it was just this interminable lunch, but he knew that wasn't all of it. It was Zach, so close to touch, and yet untouchable.

"Because Nichols was playing him wrong."

"You've been talking to Zach, I see," Gavin joked awkwardly.

Sidney shot him a look. "There's a reason Nichols isn't in your chair right now."

Gavin decided this would be a terrible time to broach the idea he'd been toying with—moving Mal to the second power play team, even temporarily, hoping that his leadership and drive might give some of those guys a taste of where they needed to be. *What* they needed to be.

"Right," Gavin said. He finished up the last of his steak and hoped that now that their food was gone, he could make an excuse to get out of here sooner rather than later.

He'd known who was going to freak out about this idea—Elliott, first off, and Malcolm second off and probably the whole team for good measure—but he hadn't anticipated that Sidney would also lodge his own protest.

Fucking awesome.

"Any plans for the holidays?"

Gavin had been doing a shit job of pretending that Christmas wasn't coming up in a few days. It was always one of the hardest times of the year—it had been Noelle's favorite holiday—and when he'd been living at the cabin, it had been so easy to pretend it just wasn't happening.

It wasn't that easy now that he was back in the regular world, again.

"Uh, not really anything big," Gavin said. "What about you?"

It really said everything about how much he didn't want to talk about the second power play team—or next year's team—that he plowed ahead and willingly embraced Sidney's subject change.

"No family of your own to spend time with?"

"Uh, no," Gavin said. Maybe he *didn't* want to talk about this. "My parents are gone, and um, Noelle had a sister, but we're not close, at least not anymore."

Not since Noelle had died and he'd disappeared into the wilds of Michigan.

"I'm sure some of the team will be around," Sidney said placatingly, patting him on the arm again.

"I'm planning on catching up on work," Gavin said. "Prepping for the final push at the end of the season." He'd drown himself in game tape, instead of stupid action movies, like he'd always done at the cabin.

Maybe if he didn't leave his house, where it didn't feel like Christmas, it wouldn't *feel* like Christmas.

"Oh, but you need to take some time," Sidney said earnestly.

"I'm sure I will," Gavin said. He cleared his throat. "Well, I'd better be going. Thanks again for lunch."

"Of course," Sidney said, patting him on the back as they rose from the table. "Good luck this weekend."

"Thanks," Gavin said and escaped before Sidney could think of any more advice he wanted to impart.

His phone buzzed in his pocket on the way to the gym and when he pulled it out he wasn't surprised to see it was a text from Zach.

How was lunch?

Gavin wanted to pretend he didn't know why Zach had his schedule memorized as well as his own, but he knew.

Terrible. I'm going to the gym.

Zach sent him a thumbs-up and Gavin wasn't all that surprised when he was in the locker room changing into his workout clothes to see him walk in, too.

"That bad, huh?" Zach joked lightly as he sat down opposite him, his duffel dropping to the floor in front of him.

Gavin made a face. "It's not *bad*, he just doesn't quit pushing, even when we're winning. Even when we're leading the conference."

"Yeah?"

"Yeah, he's already asking questions about next year. And of course, he brought up the second power play team."

Zach grunted as he pulled his T-shirt over his head. Gavin wasn't looking. He *wasn't*.

He didn't need any more jerkoff material. His mind was already overflowing with it.

"They're gonna get better," Zach said and it was clear how much he was trying to be optimistic.

He glanced up and *God*, regretted that so much.

Zach was golden and muscled all over. His body was a work of art and Gavin wanted Zach to pin him to the nearest surface and gently demand Gavin worship him the way he deserved. Make him work for it.

Gavin cleared his throat. His mouth was so dry, the same kind of Sahara as his sex life.

"Yeah," Gavin agreed helplessly, though he didn't really feel the second team *would* get better, not unless he staged some kind of intervention.

"What else did you guys talk about?" Zach asked.

"Ugh, Christmas plans," Gavin said. "Which was somehow way better than discussing the power play."

Zach chuckled darkly. "I've noticed you haven't really talked about the break coming up."

"It's only a couple of days," Gavin said. He should ask Zach what he was doing. Not because he'd invite him to his own non-celebration if he was at a loose end. Zach had friends. A lot of friends, actually.

It shouldn't be going to Gavin's head or his heart or dick that Zach often picked *him* over all those friends, these days. He should gently push him away, but he was using up all his fucking self-control to not just cross the line and anything else was impossible.

"So you're going to work through it?" Zach asked.

Gavin leaned over to pull on his sneakers. "Yeah," he said. He didn't want to explain why and he hoped Zach might understand without him going into it.

Nodding, Zach turned, and Gavin got a brief glimpse of broad shoulders, muscles rippling.

Life was fucking unfair, that was the truth.

"You know I'm not going anywhere either," Zach said casually. But Gavin knew that it wasn't. He knew all of Zach's tones and all of his expressions by now, and he was *trying* too hard to act like it was no big deal.

"Not going home?"

"I've got a paper due, and then there's the team," Zach said.

Gavin wanted to tell him that the team would be fine. That he'd be working his way through everything they needed to do. He *should* tell him that. But he opened his mouth and something else came out. "You should come over," he said, failing just about as epically as Zach had at being casual, "watch some game tape with me. Eat pizza. Drink a few beers."

"That sounds great." Zach's bright smile, lighting up the whole fucking room—and Gavin's heart, too—told him it was a mistake.

But he didn't take it back. Because he didn't want to.

Gavin kept telling himself it was no big deal.

It was just a massive fucking holiday and he'd invited Zach over because he could deal with being alone for it—he'd managed alright the last few years, anyway—but Zach didn't deserve that.

He'd tidied up the living room. Ordered pizza, which he was keeping warm in the oven, and even added cheesy breadsticks, because he knew Zach loved them and it was Christmas.

There were four games cued up on his tablet, which he'd already hooked to his TV. His laptop was charged, ready to make notes or to look up various players or stats.

Gavin wiped his damp palms on his jeans and considered ducking into the bathroom again to check his hair, which was stupid.

This was not a date. It was a *work meeting*.

For a very stupid split second, he considered that he should've changed the venue from his living room to his office, because then he wouldn't be giving confusing signals.

But spending Christmas in his goddamn office was depressing, even for Gavin, and he wasn't going to subject Zach to that.

There was a knock at the front door.

Gavin wiped his palms again and walked over, opening it to Zach.

He was wearing a dark green Evergreens sweatshirt, the hood up against the drizzling rain, and the color brought out the green tint of his eyes.

He was so gorgeous even like this, pale and half-soaked from the rain, backpack slung over one shoulder and carrying a six pack of Gavin's favorite beer.

"Merry Christmas," Zach said as Gavin let him in.

"Oh yeah, Merry Christmas," Gavin said reflexively.

Zach shot him a look that was half sorrow and half under-standing, and Gavin wanted to fling himself on him, all over again.

"Brought you a present," Zach said, gesturing with the beer in his hand as he set his backpack down by the couch.

"Uh, thanks. You can put it in the fridge," Gavin said, trail-ing after him after Zach had slipped out of his shoes, moving through the house towards the kitchen.

Zach opened the fridge and froze. And yep, that was exactly what Gavin had been expecting when he saw what was sitting on the mostly empty shelf.

"I uh . . .might've got yours, too," Gavin said, shrugging and trying to act like them buying each other their favorite beer for Christmas wasn't weird. Or watching game tape for Christmas and eating pizza wasn't just as weird.

Zach glanced over at him, the look as intimate as if Zach had touched him. And *God*, Gavin wanted to be touched.

"Thanks," Zach said softly.

"We're . . .equally thoughtful," Gavin said stupidly. *Equally besotted*, his brain corrected.

"Yeah, we'll go with that." Zach grinned and slid a hand around his shoulders after he'd put Gavin's beer in the fridge next to his own. It was half a hug, or it would've been if he'd moved away, but he didn't, fingers curling into Gavin's sweat-shirt. He could feel the heat of Zach pressed against his whole side, even as the fridge's open door blasted him with cold.

"Maybe we should go . . .um watch the first game," Gavin said. He could hear the tremor in his voice—the desire to stay just like this. If he looked over, he wondered what he'd see in Zach's eyes.

Frustration, maybe, or affection? Or a mingled combination of both?

"Alright." Zach's voice was low, rough. He finally let go, and reached into the fridge, grabbing one of his beers. "You want one?"

Gavin should probably stay sober. Sober-ish, anyway. He remembered far too well what had happened this summer, when Zach had come to the cabin. He'd definitely gotten tipsy and that had definitely contributed to opening this whole can of worms.

But instead he nodded, and Zach grabbed him one too, opening both of them with the magnetic opener on the side of the fridge.

Their fingers brushed when Zach handed him the bottle and Gavin realized that he hadn't really stepped back, even when Zach had let go of him.

He took a step back now and didn't run to the safety of the living room, but he didn't look back either, to make sure Zach was following him.

But of course he was.

Gavin took his seat on the couch and set his beer on a coaster next to his laptop. Zach followed suit, and at least he kept to his side, pulling his laptop out of his backpack.

Gavin guessed that Zach was keeping his distance, making sure that their thighs didn't touch, even accidentally, but of course even when they weren't, it was all Gavin could think about.

He started the game, but he swore they were halfway through the first period before it even felt like he was watching the screen and not obsessing over the two inches between him and Zach.

"What do you think of that second center?" Zach asked, reaching over to pause the video.

God, the second center. Gavin tried to remember who that even was. If he'd even registered his presence on the ice.

"Um," Gavin said, hesitating, mind still racing.

Zach chuckled darkly. "You weren't even watching."

"I was too!" Gavin argued, even though he knew Zach was right. Maybe his eyes had been on the screen, but his brain had been somewhere else.

"Other team's skating circles around him. He's given away three pucks already." Zach looked over at him. "You gonna tell me what's on your mind?"

He really didn't want to admit the truth. Not when they were back on a couch and drinking beer, and so much of this reminded him of that night in Michigan.

"We should consider moving Mal down to the second line for this game," Gavin said, ignoring Zach's question. "Take advantage of this matchup. He'd demolish this kid."

Zach elbowed him. "I can't believe you're actually serious about that. If you split up the boyfriends, they'd sulk the whole game."

"They wouldn't. They're pros." Gavin hesitated. "Well, Mal is at least." Elliott would absolutely throw a hissy fit, which frankly made Gavin want to do it more.

"Just switch the first and second line—you probably don't need to do it for the whole game," Zach said.

"Yeah, probably not."

Zach flopped back against the couch and the motion made his leg brush up against Gavin's. Even through two pairs of jeans, Gavin felt it, and heat licked up his spine.

"You really gonna pretend you were actually watching?"

"Yes," Gavin said primly.

Zach laughed again. "Not gonna tell me what's on your mind?" He paused, his expression morphing into something a lot more serious. "Does it have anything to do with you pretending the holidays don't exist?"

Shit. Gavin almost wished it did. And he did miss Noelle, he'd never stop missing her, never stop that little flare of anger that rose in him whenever he thought about how her life had been snatched away from her way too early. But no, that wasn't why he was so distracted tonight and lying to Zach about it felt wrong on so many levels. He didn't think he could do it, even though he probably should. It would give Zach the wrong idea if he told him the truth, but he couldn't lie.

Not about this.

"No. No. I *don't* like to celebrate the holidays anymore. It's true that it's a habit now. But no, it's not why I'm distracted."

Gavin tried to ignore the hope flaring in Zach's eyes.

He'd sworn to himself when he'd had that horrible conversation that he'd only have to have it once. That he'd never give Zach any reason to think he might be changing his mind.

"You gonna tell me?"

If he said it out loud, then that would be breaking the promise he made to himself.

Gavin shook his head. "I . . .uh. . .it's nothing."

"Doesn't seem like nothing," Zach said, gaze skimming over Gavin, melting his insides.

But it had to be.

Clearing his throat, Gavin reached for the remote and re-started the video.

Unlike before, this time he paid scrupulous attention. Made notes.

After the first game, he grabbed them another pair of beers and the pizza.

Zach didn't ask again what he had on his mind, and Gavin told himself he was grateful for that, because he couldn't lie, and he couldn't tell the truth either.

They watched the second game, drank more beer, and made more notes.

At some point, Zach slung an arm across the back of the couch, and that should've made him tense, but it did the opposite. It was easier than it should be, to lean back, to imagine that if he moved even an inch to the left, Zach's fingertips might brush his shoulder. But right now, it was still fine. Right up against the line, maybe, but they weren't crossing it and that was all that mattered.

They started the third game, Zach murmuring as he got up to get them another pair of beers. When he came back, his arm went right back to where it had been.

Gavin settled even lower into the couch and told himself he was just imagining that he could feel the brush of Zach's fingers. He didn't keep them on his shoulder, just accidentally brushed them every once in awhile and that was fine too.

Accidents happened, right?

The room was warm, and then it felt like it got warmer, but Gavin didn't even mind. He even *liked* it. And if he liked it, why shouldn't he settle even farther into the cage of Zach's arm? So what if their shoulders were touching? They were only shoulders. Shoulders were perfectly innocent body parts, even when they were Zach's shoulders, which were big and broad and so fucking sexy.

Gavin finished his beer and couldn't figure out why he'd been so stressed about this. Zach was warm and hard and comfy, the cotton of his hoody scratchy-soft against his cheek, and it would be so easy to just drift off . . .

And he did.

Or he must have, because what could've been a second or an hour later, he was jerking awake, horrified to discover that he'd literally been sleeping pressed up against Zach's arm, a tiny patch of drool on his sweatshirt.

Zach was smiling down at him, affection and hope in his sleepy gaze. Looking like he wanted to wake up to Gavin like this for the rest of his life.

Fuck.

Gavin sprang backwards, blinking hard, trying to shake both the cobwebs and the thought—*I could do it, too, forever, just like this*—from his head.

"I . . .uh . . .I must've gotten tired," Gavin said uselessly, not able to meet Zach's eyes again.

When he'd woken up and done it, that had been bad enough.

"Yeah, me too," Zach said, voice rough but quiet. "I think we missed the last half of the game."

"I definitely got enough good notes from it." He hadn't gotten any notes on it all and would have to watch it again.

Alone. In his office. Without the unbearable temptation of Zach's hot body to fall asleep against.

"Right." He could tell Zach was smiling, even if he didn't see it.

"Well, uh, thanks for coming over?" Gavin heard how awkward he sounded.

Zach patted him on the arm. "It's alright, G. You've been working hard."

He had been. But there'd been no excuse for him throwing all his rules and the whole fucking line out like it didn't matter at all.

It mattered now, more than ever.

"Not that hard," Gavin protested.

"Yeah, sure," Zach teased. "I've *been* there. The final stretch of the season is tough, even for the coaches. You gotta take care of yourself."

Maybe you could take care of me, instead.

Gavin compressed his mouth together so he wouldn't ask. Because he was tempted, almost unbearably, to just throw caution to the wind and tell Zach he'd changed his mind.

But he hadn't.

And that was why he kept his mouth shut.

"Sure," Gavin said instead.

Zach put his laptop and notebook away in his backpack. Brushed off Gavin's suggestion that he call an Uber, protesting it was only a few blocks.

Said one last quiet *Merry Christmas*, pressing his fingertips to Gavin's shoulder, and then was gone, fading into the wet darkness.

Gavin watched his back as he disappeared into the night, and finally shut the door.

CHAPTER 12

ZACH WAS ALMOST DONE getting ready to head out for the boys' party on New Year's Eve—he and Gavin had agreed it was better to host something than to leave them to their own frat-party-fueled-desires, and so Gavin bought out the Star Signs arcade for their own party—when his phone rang.

He swore, grabbing at the phone in his pocket, nearly dropping it as he tried to finish fixing his hair.

"Happy New Year," Hayes drawled into his ear.

"It's only just after nine here," Zach said. He was running late. Gavin had already sent him two texts and Ramsey even more, wondering where he was.

"Yeah, well, welcome to the east coast," Hayes said.

Wherever his friend was, it was quiet.

"You do something fun tonight?" Zach asked, though he had a feeling if Hayes was calling him at 12:04 AM, he hadn't done *anything* fun.

"What do you think?" Hayes retorted.

Zach sighed, giving up on his hair and shoving a hat on. "I think you sound like you're in a hotel room."

"Bingo," Hayes said morosely. "I was at the party down-stairs. Couple guys with rooms next to each other. Had some drinks, played some video games. It was . . .well, you can tell how much I enjoyed it."

"Sounds like it wasn't the party, but *you*, dude."

Hayes made a dissatisfied noise.

"Let me give you Marcus' number," Zach said.

"You forget that he *also* doesn't live in my zip code," Hayes said.

"I'm sure he wouldn't be against a little career advancement, not if it meant he got a chance with Hayes Montgomery."

"Why would I want to drag someone else into this fucked up bullshit?" Hayes asked tiredly, and Zach was tempted to answer, but he had a feeling Hayes hadn't really wanted an answer.

He'd tried that before, and while the guy had been a douchebag, Zach wasn't entirely certain if his douchebaggery had been solely personality-based or because he'd gotten tired of Hayes being hung up on someone else.

Maybe Hayes had a point.

Zach grabbed his wallet and keys and let himself out of the apartment, jogging down the stairs. The arcade was only a few blocks away.

"Monty, I say this with love, but you gotta try to get over it," he said gently.

Hayes sighed.

"Someday," Hayes said, clearly making an effort to sound lighter. "You see your coach since Christmas and the epic cuddle session he didn't want to have?"

"It wasn't—" Zach broke off. "He just fell asleep on me. It wasn't anything." But it had re-lit the hope inside him, even as he'd tried to extinguish it.

Maybe Gavin didn't want to date again, but they were already practically dating, without all the physical benefits and Zach *really* wanted some physical benefits.

Even if that was just cuddling on the couch.

"Don't downplay it, Zachy," Hayes said sternly. "You're allowed to be excited that you're gonna get that happy ending."

"That's not a guarantee. He still freaked out."

"But it *happened*. And it's probably gonna keep happening. You seeing him tonight?"

"Yeah, we're hosting the guys at the arcade. Trying to keep them out of trouble," Zach said. It wasn't like Gavin was going to kiss him at midnight, but they'd be in the same room, and that was more than he'd even known to hope for, before.

"You didn't answer my question before. You seen him since Christmas?"

"Of course I have."

"Not for practice. Or in his office. I mean not for work."

Zach sighed. "No. But we still talk all the time. It's for work but it's . . .it's *more,* too."

Christmas and the last week—the clear affection in Gavin's eyes, the way he was touching him more casually now—was making Zach believe that something *might* be happening, no matter how much Gavin denied it.

"Lean into it," Hayes told him.

"But—" He didn't want to push Gavin too hard. Make a move Gavin didn't want him to make.

"You want him or not?" Hayes interrupted.

Zach couldn't help his exasperated groan as he turned the corner, nearly to the arcade. "You know I do."

"Then don't let him deny you," Hayes said.

This was the first time Hayes had ever suggested he push Gavin. Every other time, he'd warned Zach to be patient. To let Gavin set the pace.

"Why are you saying this now?"

"Because I'm thirty fucking years old and I'm in love with someone who doesn't love me back, who other than the shit he's required to say on ESPN, hasn't even said my name in years. It's so shitty, and I don't want this for you, too."

Zach squeezed his eyes shut, stopping in front of the door to the arcade. "Hayes."

"Don't," Hayes said sharply. "Don't fucking feel sorry for me, okay?"

Zach almost said that maybe Hayes was wrong; maybe Morgan did love him but even if he did, that wasn't any better. Maybe it was even worse. Because Hayes was still alone.

"Okay," Zach said softly.

"If I had to relive things, I'd . . .I think I'd do them differently," Hayes said. "That's why I'm telling you to do this. You don't want to end up like me, alone on New Year's Eve and wondering what the fuck happened to your life. What it might be like if you'd made different choices, taken a risk that you didn't think would pay off, but *might've*."

"You could always reach out. He's retired now," Zach suggested.

Hayes' laugh was sharp. Hard. "And look desperate and pathetic? Like I can't take a hint? Fuck no."

"But you want *me* to—"

"I want you to make a move, because you both want each other and it's fucking stupid to just *not*," Hayes said.

"Alright, I'll . . .I'd consider trying again, maybe a little more directly this time," Zach said, heart beating a little faster at the thought of it.

"Good," Hayes said. "Now go do it. *Make it happen*, Zachy."

The front door to the arcade opened, and Ramsey stuck his head out, making a face. "There you are," he said. "Where've you been?"

"I gotta go," Zach told Hayes.

Hayes hummed and then added, right before Zach hung up. "Remember, you promised."

Like he was going to forget that, anytime soon.

"Sorry," Zach said to Ramsey as he followed him into the arcade, skirting past the sign that said it was rented out for a private party. "I was talking to a friend."

"Montgomery, yeah?" Ramsey asked.

It was a miracle anyone ever kept anything from this guy.

Of course, it wasn't exactly a state secret that he and Hayes were friends.

"Yeah," Zach said, nodding.

"You're not dating him—" Ramsey shook his head, before he could even finish his sentence. "Of course you're not dating him."

"Why the *of course*?" Zach asked, even though he probably shouldn't. He wasn't sure he wanted to know what Ramsey had observed about him and Gavin that he deliberately wasn't mentioning.

Ramsey shot him a look. "Because you're fucking obsessed with our coach, dude."

Right. *Right.* God, was it so obvious *everyone* knew?

"I mean . . ." Zach trailed off.

"Are you kidding me? You're not in denial about this," Ramsey said. "You two are like horny sharks circling each other."

Zach's jaw dropped. "We are not." Even though he could see exactly why Ramsey might call them that.

"Two alpha dogs, who love working together, who can barely stop looking at each other? Oh yeah, you're both sharks and you're fucking hungry." Ramsey nudged him with his shoulder. "Please tell me there's some blood in the water, soon. 'Cause the sexual tension is *thick*, man."

"That's . . .that's Elliott and Mal," Zach argued, even though it was a fucking weak argument. Yeah, Elliott and Mal had their share of sexual tension, but after they'd gotten together it had calmed considerably.

They only looked like they wanted to eat each other alive maybe thirty-five percent of the time now.

Ramsey cocked his head. "Not the same."

"Sure," Zach said as Ramsey led him to the bar. He ordered a beer and tilted his head towards Ramsey, who nodded back. Zach added a second one to his tab.

Ramsey leaned against the bar after the bartender slid two bottles across the wood.

"Ell knew he wanted Mal, though he certainly didn't *want* to, because Ell's got an ego. On the other hand, Mal was in major denial mode." Ramsey tapped his fingers against the bar, off-rhythm with the music playing. "You and Coach are different."

"We shouldn't be talking about this," Zach said sternly. *Especially not here.*

"Oh, I know. He's my coach, etcetera etcetera." Ramsey absently waved a hand, like this wasn't a big deal. Like he was used to getting chastised for saying more than he should. And *well*, he probably was.

Zach rolled his eyes. "Yeah, we're both your coaches, asshole."

"Hey, if you need a push in the right direction, I'm still gonna do it." Ramsey paused. "*Do* you need a push in the right direction?"

"Isn't that something you're supposed to be telling me?" Zach muttered.

Ramsey grinned. "Okay, let me rephrase. This is me pushing you in the right direction."

"A common theme tonight," Zach said morosely.

"Well, I'm glad I'm not the only one," Ramsey said. He nudged Zach. "He's over by the pinball machines, probably trying to stay between Elliott and Mal so they don't run off and fuck in the bathroom."

Zach sighed. "Remember when McCoy was the responsible one who never took a step out of line?"

"I do. And it was a damn shame," Ramsey said.

Zach wanted to argue with him, but he could see Ramsey's point, too. That Malcolm had been penned in by his own expectations, by his own rules, and maybe he was a little wilder now, but he was also freer. *Happier.*

"Yeah."

Ramsey shot him a knowing look. "What are you waiting for, dude? Go distract him from his task. Everyone'll be happier. You. Coach. Definitely Elliott and Malcolm."

If he wandered in that direction—and that was a big *if*, still—would Ramsey take that as silent approval of everything he'd said? Of course, Zach had always intended to find Gavin, at one point or another tonight. They always circled each other, and he knew New Years Eve wouldn't be any different.

Like two horny sharks, Ramsey's voice supplied in Zach's own head.

It wasn't like Hayes had been particularly subtle, but Ramsey had been even *less* subtle. Which tracked, really.

"I guess I should go say hi to everyone," Zach said and Ramsey shot him an incredulous look like they both didn't know exactly who he'd be looking for.

He found Gavin exactly where Ramsey had said he would be, leaning against a wall by the bank of pinball machines. Elliott was racking up major points on a Star Wars themed one, Mal practically pressed up against his back as Ell's fingers flicked over the controls, nearly too quick to make out.

Jacob Braun was standing next to Gavin, and Zach wasn't particularly surprised to see him there. He'd heard around the grapevine—though Finn hadn't come to them and told either of them specifically—that they weren't just coaching now, but dating. Zach might've been more concerned, but it was so obvious how much the new relationship suited Finn. His smiles came quicker, bloomed easy as breathing across his face, and his play had never been more confident, like he was finally figuring out how to exist in his own skin.

If Jacob had anything to do with that, then Zach wholeheartedly approved.

"Hey," Zach said, approaching them.

"Hey," Gavin said, and Jacob nodded.

"Good to see you, man," Zach directed at Jacob.

"You too." Jacob gave him a friendly pat on the shoulder.

"Where's Finn?"

"Dominating Ivan and a bunch of the rookies at foosball," Jacob said, sounding proud as hell.

"We were reminiscing," Gavin said.

"I didn't realize you two knew each other before," Zach said, glancing between Gavin and Jacob.

"I coached him once. The Four Nations tournament."

It took Zach a moment, and then he realized what tournament Gavin was referring to. *That* tournament. The one where Morgan and Hayes had played together, Hayes scoring the winning goal in the championship game. The one that had sent his best friend tumbling down a black hole of misery that he had yet to drag himself out from.

"Didn't realize you and Reynolds ever played on the same team," Zach joked.

"Honestly, we avoided each other," Jacob admitted. "Which was better for everyone."

Gavin chuckled under his breath, like he agreed.

Zach tipped the rest of his beer down his throat, uncomfortably aware that he was the only one who knew what had *really* been going on at that tournament.

"Hey, another round?" Jacob said, gesturing with his bottle.

"Sure," Zach said, and Gavin shrugged his agreement.

He was gone in a minute, leaving him and Gavin alone. Of course, Elliott and Malcolm were only a dozen feet away, at the pinball machines, but they were so wrapped up in their own world it was like nobody else existed.

Zach slipped closer to Gavin, nudging his shoulder against Gavin's. "How're you doing?" he asked in a low voice. Not that anyone was paying attention to them.

A bomb could've gone off right now and Elliott and Mal probably wouldn't have noticed. Elliott was gazing up at Mal, and he was looking down, like Elliott was the best thing in the entire world.

Zach wanted to say he didn't know what that felt like, but goddamn it, he did.

"Oh, fine," Gavin said. His eyes cut to where Elliott and Mal were laughing together. "Just keeping an eye on those two."

"Amazing at the beginning of the season that they didn't like each other."

Gavin made a scoffing noise. "I wouldn't believe it if I hadn't had to witness it. You're later than I expected you to be."

"Hayes called," Zach said. "It's after midnight where he's at. Boston? Toronto? I can't remember."

"I don't really miss those days," Gavin said. "A different hotel room every other day."

"Me either," Zach agreed.

After Christmas, they'd gone back to their regular routine like nothing had happened. They'd talked last night and the night before and the night before that. Every night since it had happened.

But Hayes was right that this was different. The first time they were together in the same room, and it wasn't *technically* for work-related reasons.

Gavin looked hesitant, too, kind of like Zach felt. Like he was trying to figure out if they should talk about it. Or if they should pretend that Gavin waking up in his arms wasn't a thing they both wanted.

"I . . ." Gavin swore under his breath. "I don't love the holidays."

"Really?" Zach teased with faux earnestness. "I had no idea."

Gavin shot him a glare, and the heat of it crawled under Zach's collar and slid down his spine.

"I know you can see it, but I want to tell you that this year was . . .better. Better than I expected."

Zach had been trying to play it cool, still half-afraid he was going to scare Gavin off from this new closeness, but there was no way he was hiding the thrill that sent through him. Or his smile.

"Yeah? I'm glad. Really glad." Zach dipped his head down, making his voice low and intimate. Gavin flushed.

And oh yeah, it was on, baby. Hayes was right. Gavin wanted this, and he just needed Zach to push them over the finish line.

How perfect would it be if they finally got together on New Years Eve? A new start and a new beginning, all for them.

"You ever play these?" Gavin asked, gesturing towards the bank of pinball machines.

"Yeah," Zach said. "I'm okay."

Gavin held out his hand and Zach wasn't sure what he was doing until he was taking Zach's wrist with a light touch and tipping a few quarters into his hand. "Give it a go," he said.

Zach half-expected Gavin to stay over where he was at, but to his surprise, he followed Zach as he picked a machine at random. He didn't drape himself over Zach like Malcolm did to Elliott, but he was close enough Zach could feel the heat of his body.

He dropped the quarter and dragged his mind back to the machine in front of him.

For a few minutes, Zach focused on the game, figuring out the good spots to hit, the idiosyncrasies of the paddles. By the time he was on ball three, Gavin leaned in and said, "Better at this than you said."

Zach glanced over. Felt his fingers tremble on the controls at the look in Gavin's eyes. Heat, singeing him. Pupils dilated. Hands shoved into his pockets like he might reach for Zach if he thought he was allowed to.

Swallowing hard, Zach nodded. "It's been awhile."

"Doesn't seem like it."

"Just . . .uh . . .riding a bike," Zach said.

"Right." There was a glimmer of mischief in Gavin's expression, like he was thinking of something else.

And okay, it had been awhile for Zach, not just playing pinball but flirting with intent and wanting badly to take it farther. Ever since the summer, when he'd gone to Michigan, he hadn't even been vaguely interested in anyone else or even hooking up. But it had been *years* for Gavin. And he hadn't ever done anything with a guy before.

Zach would be the first.

It made his breath short and his skin hot.

He missed the ball completely, pulling the paddle a whole half-second too late.

Shrugging, he turned to Gavin. "You wanna go?"

"I've never done this before," Gavin said.

But with Hayes' words echoing in his head—*lean into it, and make it happen*—Zach put his hands on Gavin's waist, gently pulling him over, where he'd been standing a second ago.

Gavin tensed, but then he relaxed.

"Have a little fun," Zach suggested slyly.

"If you insist." Gavin shot him a smile, a little shaky around the edges. But determined, too.

Like maybe he was scared, too, but the fear mattered less because he wanted this as much as Zach did.

"I do," Zach said. He inserted a quarter into the machine.

Gavin *wasn't* as good at it as Zach was, but it was fun to watch his brow furrow in concentration and to witness as his reflexes came to life, again.

Between balls two and three, Gavin turned to Zach, astonishment creasing his expression. "This is a little like hockey."

"A little?" Zach raised an eyebrow.

"Okay, a lot like hockey. It's a wonder Mal's not better at it."

"He's still learning to let go and play with instinct instead of focusing on the skill he knows," Zach said. "But he's gonna get there."

"Imagine how many points he's gonna put up when he does that."

"Nobody's gonna be able to stop him out there," Zach agreed.

They played half a dozen more games, exchanging machines, laughing together.

It was only then that Jacob arrived back, a sheepish expression on his face. "Shit, sorry," he said. He was flushed and Zach wondered what he'd been up to—and if Finn had been involved. "I got distracted by the foosball tournament."

But he handed out new beers and hung out for a minute or two before Finn arrived, too.

Jacob didn't hesitate to wrap an arm around Finn's waist and drag him close. "You two enjoying the pinball?"

"It's fun," Gavin said. He scratched at the label with his thumb nail. "More like hockey than I expected."

"If you think that, you should come join us at the foosball table. Brody's there. And his boyfriend. Don't let anyone tell you that football players are better than hockey players," Finn said. The tops of his cheeks were pink, and he looked happy.

Like he'd just won and also like he'd gotten to claim whatever he wanted as a prize.

"Sure, we can do that," Gavin said, and Zach tried not to be disappointed that they were joining the rest of the team.

He'd get Gavin alone, again. They both wanted it, and Zach just had to figure out a way to make it happen.

They spent the next hour making the rounds of the arcade, joining in Finn's foosball tournament, then watching as Elliott and Ramsey took each other on at DDR, Ell wiggling his hips suggestively at Malcolm after, who looked equal parts embarrassed and thrilled.

Before Zach could really realize how close it was, Ivan announced that it was only five minutes to midnight.

Zach wasn't stupid enough to think he was going to get a kiss, but he'd at least expected to be in the same room as the clock ticked down.

"He went to the bathroom," Ramsey said under his breath, like he'd totally figured out why Zach was looking around.

"That—I wasn't," Zach tried to protest, but Ramsey just rolled his eyes.

"Maybe if you go grab him now, you can delay him until twelve," Ramsey said.

Zach knew he should think this through.

But how many times had Zach waited for Gavin to be ready? To be willing to follow through? He was done hesitating right on the threshold and never getting to cross it.

He took off for the bathroom, which was in a little hallway tucked in the back, near the pinball machines.

It was quiet, nobody over here, the whole team gathered around the bar, waiting for the final countdown to start.

As Zach turned down the hallway, he looked at his watch. Two minutes to twelve. All he had to do was waste one hundred and twenty seconds. Easy.

But then the bathroom door opened and Gavin's eyes widened as he took Zach's appearance in. Like the last thing he'd expected was to see him right now.

"Oh, hey," Gavin said awkwardly.

It was really a very tiny hallway. Barely enough room for two people. Zach stopped right in the middle and didn't budge, even as Gavin sidled up to him, like he expected him to move out of the way.

Like Zach had come to piss, and not to find Gavin.

"Hey," Zach said. "I was looking for you."

"Right, it's . . .uh . . .almost midnight, isn't it?"

Zach didn't want to look down at his watch, but he thought they'd probably wasted at least forty-five seconds.

"Yeah, I think so."

Gavin took a step closer, and Zach still didn't move.

"Are you—" Gavin broke off, taking a deep breath. His head tilted back and he looked right at Zach.

"Yeah," Zach said.

The noises from the team were filtering through the hallway, getting louder by the second. A countdown, Zach realized, his brain finally picking out the numbers from the raucous cheers.

He and Gavin stared at each other. Gavin had to know what he wanted, what *he* wanted, but he didn't move. Zach decided that was permission enough.

And then, *finally*, a final noisy yell.

"Uh, Happy New Year?" Gavin said nervously, licking his lips.

Zach broke first. He stepped closer, his hands rising to cup Gavin's cheeks. Felt the scrape of his late night scruff along his jaw and tilted his mouth against his own.

Zach was kissing him.

Gavin had known it was coming. He'd known the moment he'd opened the bathroom door and Zach had been standing here in the hallway.

It wasn't hard to figure out what he wanted.

But what do you want?

That wasn't so much the question as *what am I allowed to want?*

It was only then, staring at Zach, who had him practically held hostage, not moving, just looking, just *waiting*, that Gavin acknowledged to himself that he'd come to the bathroom for exactly this reason.

He hadn't wanted to watch the clock tick over to midnight and stand next to Zach and just keep fucking pretending that he didn't want to kiss him.

He wanted to kiss him.

So Gavin kissed Zach back.

Zach's kiss had been soft, almost hesitant. Like he was asking a question he hoped he knew the answer to.

Gavin tilted his head and kissed him back, deeper.

He didn't know if the kiss was so different because it was a man, or because it was Zach, but it lit Gavin up from the inside out, electricity humming through every bit of him—to his fingertips and then all the way back to his toes.

Zach gasped into his mouth, and then there was his tongue, sliding against Gavin's own, as his hands cupped his cheeks and held him there, just for him to kiss.

It shouldn't have been so good, but it was actually fucking incredible.

Zach pulled back, and Gavin nearly reeled him right back in. He wanted to keep kissing, keep *feeling*, and not worry about thinking anytime soon.

But Zach took another step back, lips red and wet, and Gavin's brain kept short-circuiting.

But one thought stood out from the jumbled, heated mess: he'd been five seconds from grabbing Zach's arm and dragging him back. Not just into Gavin's arms, but to the bathroom with its single room and the lock on the door.

With nearly the whole team just outside.

Zach didn't say anything, and Gavin didn't know *what* to say.

He couldn't pull out the *that was a huge fucking mistake* card, not when he wanted so badly for it to be the opposite.

But desire didn't equal reality.

He'd promised himself, a hundred times, a *thousand* times, that he wouldn't do this. Always before, he'd managed to pull back at the last moment, but he hadn't this time. He wasn't stupid; he'd known exactly why Zach cornered him in the hallway. Zach had given him plenty of outs. Plenty of chances to leave. To laugh it off. But he hadn't.

Instead, Gavin had been an exposed nerve of pure fucking *need*, and he'd just given in to the onslaught, when he should've been remembering all the very good reasons he had to keep his distance.

"Oh, there you two are." A voice echoed through the hallway. Gavin was afraid to look and see if it was Ramsey, because God knew, he could probably figure out immediately what they were doing.

But it wasn't Ramsey. It was Brody, who flicked a glance between them, a crease between his brows, like he thought he might know what he was witnessing but some part of it didn't quite compute.

Thank God for small favors.

"Yes," Gavin said, clearing his throat. "We're right here."

"Right here," Zach said, voice rough.

"You missed the ball drop but it's okay. There's still some champagne left."

"Right, okay." Gavin nodded. "Lead the way."

He could feel Zach following him, could feel Zach's eyes on him, burning right into his skin, as they rejoined the rest of the team.

Forty minutes later, the party was breaking up, and Gavin could *still* feel Zach's eyes on him. Even though he'd been talking to Finn and Jacob, and Zach had been on the other side of the group, chatting easily with Mal and Elliott and Ivan, Brody and Dean chiming in every few minutes, he just *knew* Zach was watching him, carefully.

Watching and waiting for an opportunity to come over and say casually, "Oh, we're going the same way? I'll walk with you."

Then somehow, they'd end up in Gavin's house, and they'd kiss again, and probably more, and it would be simultaneously glorious and the worst thing Gavin had ever done.

He had to tell him something—but maybe that could wait. Maybe he could put it off, for a few days. At least until his lips didn't taste like Zach's every time he licked them.

At least until the memory wasn't burning a hole in his brain.

But of course, that wasn't how it worked out.

Ending up standing outside the arcade with Zach as Finn and Jacob said their goodbyes and melted into the night was probably karma intervening and paying him back for touching Zach in the first place.

The sidewalks around them were empty, with absolutely nothing to distract from the fact that it was just the two of them.

"So, uh, well," Zach said, giving him a bashful glance from under long lashes. Like he hadn't been the guy pushing right into Gavin's space and kissing him first less than an hour ago.

Gavin steeled himself. There was a part of him that knew he could just talk around it. Say he was tired, they had an early morning, etcetera, and then put this horrible conversation off for another day or two.

But another day or two wasn't going to change anything, and maybe it was better to just plunge right into the fire.

"Zach, we need to talk." His tone wasn't gentle just for Zach; he was trying to take it easy on himself, too.

Zach's face, eager and boyish, fell so fast. Gavin ignored the spreading pain soaring through him in a dizzying wave.

"Are you really going to do this again?"

"I shouldn't have done that. I shouldn't have—" He couldn't say *I shouldn't have let you do that,* because Gavin had been a full and enthusiastic participant. He'd known exactly what Zach was going to do, and he'd let him do it anyway. "It's my fault. I keep letting this happen and I shouldn't. I'm sorry."

There was a flash of the same agony that Gavin felt across Zach's face, then it was wiped clean. He shoved his hands into his pockets and shot Gavin a stony glare.

"You really are, I guess."

Gavin didn't know what to say. How to even explain. He couldn't even fucking explain it to *himself.*

He just knew whenever he thought of keeping this going—of seeing it to its natural conclusion—hugging Zach and kissing him and *dating* him, he felt so sick to his stomach with guilt and horror he knew he couldn't. How could he ever face himself in the mirror knowing that he'd just moved on, easy as that?

"Zach—"

"No, don't. Don't." Zach glared at him again, hotter this time. Angrier. "You want this, you want *me*, I know you do."

It was impossible to deny it. "I do," Gavin said, "but—"

Zach's gaze was burning, *boring*, into him. "There doesn't have to be a *but*! It just is. We weren't expecting it but it happened, and it . . ." Zach looked away then, like he couldn't bear it.

Gavin couldn't bear it either, but he *had* to, because he'd created this whole fucking mess. No matter how shitty this felt, he had to just stand here and *feel* it.

"I want to say I shouldn't have taken this job, because I was afraid of this, but we've been good together," Gavin said.

Zach threw his hands up. "We could be good together, *period*. If you would fucking let us."

"I'm too old for you. Too old and too . . .fucked up," Gavin said quietly.

"If any of that was actually true, then this wouldn't already be working," Zach argued. He still looked pissed but he took a step closer and then another. Gavin wanted to run away, but he deserved this. So he stayed put. "You say we can't date, that you *won't* date, but we're already dating."

Gavin wanted to argue. But his mouth was so dry. Zach was so close. "No. *No*."

"The only thing we're not doing is kissing and—" Zach broke off with a muttered *fuck*. "We're just not touching each other like that, but we both want to. We're doing everything else. We spend like fifteen fucking hours together and then *after,* we talk to each other every night. Like we can't get enough."

"That's . . . that's . . . that's *work.*" But Zach wasn't wrong.

And Zach knew it too, because he wore an unimpressed expression that told Gavin he knew just how much of a liar he'd turned into. It was work, yes, but it had evolved into something else, too. Friendship, affection, companionship, attraction. Even lust.

"It's not wrong to want more," Zach said, and suddenly he was gentle, soft, again, palm pressed against Gavin's cheek and God, he wanted to lean into that touch more than he'd ever wanted anything, ever.

But that wasn't true, was it?

Because the thing he'd wanted, the *one fucking thing* he'd needed and never gotten was for Noelle to come back.

Guilt surged, and Gavin shook Zach's hand off. "No," he said roughly, turning away so Zach couldn't see the glitter of moisture in his eyes.

He never should've permitted things to get this far, but now that they had, he could at least take responsibility and finally, put his foot down.

"Are you serious—you *are,* you're fucking serious," Zach said incredulously.

He didn't reach for him again.

"I told you." Gavin hated how raw he sounded, like his throat had been scraped with glass.

Zach stared at him for one beat and then another. "Yeah, you did." And then he turned and walked away.

CHAPTER 13

It was not the dawn of the new year that Zach had wanted.

He didn't sleep. Stayed up, sitting in the same spot on the couch he'd collapsed onto the moment he'd walked into his apartment after the worst night of his life.

The best, and then the worst.

But even if it wasn't what he'd anticipated, what he'd desperately craved, it could still be a new start.

A fresh beginning.

When his alarm blared at eight-thirty, Zach lifted himself off the couch, feeling every one of his twenty-seven years, and hobbled into the bathroom.

He took a long hot shower. Pretended that a few tears didn't fall, mixing with the water as it swirled down the drain.

When he got out, he didn't think he could talk about it, still, because even the thought of discussing it made his throat close over with despair and sadness and panic, but he did find his phone and type out a text.

Tried it your way, he sent to Hayes, **and I don't want to talk about it, but it's over.**

It's over, Zach thought. *It's really over.*

He'd never entirely understood why Hayes had cut Morgan off hard and fast. Why he'd refused to accept even the scraps of time they could've stolen together, because Zach had always assumed that having something of someone you loved was better than having nothing.

But no, Zach got it now. Something was *worse* than nothing.

The scraps only made him ache for more, to have *everything*, and he couldn't keep going with that bottomless pit of desire opening up inside him all the time. Even if it took the rest of his life to fill it, he had to start now, one shovelful at a fucking time.

There were six weeks left of the regular season and then play-offs, if they made it that far. It was unfair to the team to bail on them now, but the idea of spending the next two months with Gavin like nothing was wrong, like nothing had changed between them, made him physically sick.

Zach had put his teams first his whole life, right up until he'd walked away from the NHL, and that had felt so much like the right decision, at the time and every single day after, he'd sworn to himself he wouldn't ever go there again.

He wouldn't carve himself out and leave nothing behind just to satisfy some impossible need that other people had for him.

It was shitty, but he was going to have to walk away.

The email to Sidney was shockingly easy. A handful of polite garbage sentences and there was his resignation, staring back at him from the screen. He could cc Gavin, but then Gavin might take it as a passive aggressive threat to change his mind or Zach was gone.

But Zach loved Gavin and he didn't want someone who had no love left to give.

In another year he'd be done with his Master's, and then he could leave this town behind. Really start fresh.

Hayes texted back. **What happened? Are you really not going to tell me?** Then a second text, coming in nearly on the heels of the first. **Are you okay?**

Zach flopped back on the couch. This adulting shit was the worst. He wanted to crawl in bed with a bottle of vodka and never leave.

I kissed him. He kissed back, then said no. I'm quitting.

It was the most clinical straightforward analysis of the situation Zach could provide. And somehow it sucked even more than any dramatics he could've texted Hayes. Seeing it all there, in black and white, cut him like a knife.

For a long second, he stared at Hayes' second question, not sure how to answer. Of course he wasn't fucking okay. Hayes should know better than to even ask.

Finally, he typed out, a letter at a time, slow and deliberate, giving himself a chance to change his mind, but it only felt more right the longer he looked at it: **No, but I will be.**

He watched as Hayes' typing bubbles appeared and then disappeared half a dozen times.

Yeah, you will be, he finally said.

Of course, that might just be Zach's own stupid optimism reflected back at him, because it wasn't like Hayes had ever really gotten there. But he still might, and if anyone deserved it, it was him.

But it wasn't just him. They *both* deserved it.

Zach reminded himself of that one more time and sent the email.

He went to the student gym instead of the staff one, enjoying the feeling of anonymity, of just being another student here, regretting the decisions he'd made the night before. Sweated out all his sadness, and it sort of worked.

Showered, and then hit the library.

He'd turned do not disturb on his phone, and didn't bother looking at either his inbox or his texts. Though he couldn't imagine anyone sending him anything he might want to hear. Even if Gavin changed his mind, even if Gavin begged him to come back, Zach knew this was what he needed to do.

Hayes had told him once that he didn't have to put up with any of Gavin's baggage—that it wasn't *his* baggage—and even though part of Zach still wanted to help him carry it, he wasn't going to sacrifice his own peace of mind to do it.

Gavin was never going to accept wanting him. He'd never be easy if they got together, and Zach decided he deserved *better*.

It felt like the righteous decision, the *best* decision, all the way up until he was done at the library and he headed back to his empty apartment.

He usually filled up the long silences at night with music or a game playing on TV—or his favorite way, which was Gavin's voice, hushed and intimate as they talked on the phone.

There'd be none of that.

None of that ever again.

The thought struck him and Zach felt unmoored, destroyed. He staggered over to the couch and cried for the second time.

It wasn't the most terrible day of Gavin's life, but it felt like it crept into the top five, maybe even cracked the top three, which was a fact Gavin was studiously ignoring.

He only got through it because he knew he deserved it and because he'd learned, the hard way, that tomorrow had to be better.

Sometimes it wasn't a whole lot better, but even marginally better would be an improvement he'd accept.

It wasn't better.

It was worse.

His phone rang way too fucking early, just past seven, blaring on his nightstand, waking him out of a listless, restless sleep that he'd only found after he'd blearily seen the clock hit three AM.

Gavin scrambled for it, thinking, for a single heart-stopping moment, that it was Zach.

He didn't know what Zach would be telling him, but he only knew he wanted to hear his voice.

It was not Zach.

It was Sidney, and he was blustering, clearly upset and ranting so fast Gavin could barely follow what he was saying.

"What's going on? Slow down," Gavin finally barked.

"Did he not tell you?" Sidney demanded.

"Did who not tell me what?" Gavin asked flatly.

"*Zach Wheeler. Your* assistant coach. Sending me his resignation! He can't quit now. You're leading the conference and he's a big part of that. You told me he runs the power play. Who's going to fix the second team power play now?"

Gavin nearly dropped the phone. He couldn't believe he'd never imagined that this could happen. Maybe he and Zach wouldn't work out personally but *surely* he wouldn't quit this job. This job he loved that he was so fucking good at. It had been killing him enough that he'd let Zach down romantically, emotionally. But now Sidney was telling him that he wasn't going to get Zach in *any* way. He was removing himself from Gavin's life, completely, and there was suddenly no question.

Solidly top three worst days ever.

That was the only excuse for what Gavin said next. Or at least that was what he told himself.

"Fuck the second team power play," Gavin snapped.

Sidney made a noise like a dying whale.

He realized he shouldn't have said it, and he *especially* shouldn't have said it to his boss, but he'd been reeling, barely holding it together, and then Zach had just hit him with the knockout punch.

"I mean," Gavin said, grappling for some kind of dignity, "*I* can fix it."

"Fix the power play or fix your assistant coach quitting?" Sidney asked in a steely voice.

"I . . .uh . . ."

"There's only one right answer here, and it's not the fucking power play, though that's not me saying it's *not* a problem," Sidney said.

Gavin could tell Sidney that there was no salvaging this situation but he couldn't tell him why. The thought was incomprehensible.

"If he's quitting," Gavin said, "I can't imagine I could change his mind."

"No?" Sidney challenged. "I find that very hard to believe. I saw you two less than a week ago, and you were fine. The team's playing great. *Fix this*, Blackburn."

Gavin winced. "I'm not sure there's anything I can say—"

There was one thing he could *do*, but he couldn't imagine that, either. Or, he could imagine it far too well, and that was the whole fucking problem.

"I don't care. Fix it," Sidney barked again.

"Maybe *you* should—"

Sidney cut Gavin off. "When I hired him, I didn't want to let him go off to the god forsaken place you'd buried yourself in. I told him he was crazy, that you'd never want to coach again. That everyone knew that. But he never, ever let it go. He begged and pleaded and threatened and coerced. He never gave up on you, not once."

Gavin shut his eyes, guilt swamping his already painfully guilty conscience. He didn't want to hear this, but there was no way to stop Sidney.

"I can't believe you'd give up on him *this* easily, without even trying to get him back. Without even trying to fix whatever it is you two broke."

It's me, he wanted to tell Sidney, *I'm the broken thing, and I can't be fixed.*

"I'm really not sure there's anything I can say," Gavin said diplomatically.

"Find something then," Sidney said. "What even happened?"

"It's . . ." Gavin licked his lips. Still tasting Zach there, even though it was heaven and hell. "It's complicated."

"Then uncomplicate it!"

Gavin laughed humorlessly. "I wish it was that easy."

"He never gave up on you. Even when I was insisting to him that he should." Gavin could hear the reprimand in Sidney's words. "You're going to give up on him *that* easily?"

Gavin was lost for a moment. He didn't want to give up on Zach, of course. Not now. Not *ever*. Every part of him was dying to walk—no, *run*—over to Zach's place and beg him to reconsider. That he was sorry. That Zach was right, about everything.

But he *wasn't*, and that was the only persuasive argument that Gavin thought he might even be tempted to listen to.

It was a problem.

"I . . .no. No. Of course not. I'll . . .I'll see what I can do." It would basically kill him but he could go over there and ask Zach to reconsider. Repeat his commitment to keep things professional—this time he *would* stick to it. There'd be no more late night phone calls, no more early morning breakfasts, no more surreptitious glances at Zach's gorgeous body in the gym. No more fantasies while he touched himself.

"Good," Sidney said. "See that you do."

He hung up, leaving Gavin to contemplate all the things that had to come to an end. And even then, even if he promised none of that would ever happen again, Gavin didn't think Zach would reconsider.

But Sidney was right. Zach had come to Michigan this summer even though everyone doubted him—even though *he* even doubted—but he'd done it because he'd felt compelled to try to convince Gavin to change his mind.

He owed Zach for that, because maybe he was wrong about Gavin being ready to date him or Gavin being worthy of him—or that they were already dating—he'd been right about hockey.

Gavin hadn't been done with hockey, after all.

But if he was right about hockey, could he have been right about him, too?

It wasn't the first time the thought had occurred to him, but it was the first time Gavin didn't dismiss it immediately out of hand as wishful thinking.

He was hurting so much, maybe that was why he didn't?

But he'd promised Sidney—and promised Zach too, in more than just words—that he'd try. If he didn't at least attempt to figure out if Zach was right about *everything*, then he wasn't holding true to that. And no matter what else he believed, he knew Noelle would be disappointed if he didn't keep his word.

It was easy and also terrifying to email Jon and ask for an emergency session.

Because, what if Zach was right?

He was almost hoping Jon wouldn't email him back right away—he didn't, actually. But ten minutes after he'd sent his SOS email, his phone rang.

"Everything okay?" Jon asked as soon as Gavin picked up.

Gavin made a face, which he could do because they weren't on the video chat. "No," he said.

"You want to tell me what happened?"

Gavin hesitated, and that was all the opportunity Jon needed to pounce. "You should get on a video session first."

"So you can hold my lack of poker face against me?" Gavin asked petulantly.

"You caught me."

Gavin tried not to sulk as he dragged out his laptop. A minute later they were set up on a call, Jon leaning back in his desk chair, concern creasing his face.

"Okay, now, tell me what happened," he said.

There was no way around it. Only *through* it. Gavin told himself to stick to the most straightforward recitation of events, nothing dramatic. Nothing about how good the kiss had been. How terrible the aftermath had felt. How he'd wanted to reach through the phone and strangle Sidney with one of his dumb ties this morning.

"Last night, we were at a team party, for New Years, and Zach kissed me and I kissed him back. I told him after it was a mistake and we couldn't do this." Gavin took a deep breath. "And now he's resigning."

Jon's eyebrows inched upward. "You turned him down *after* you kissed him?"

Why was Gavin not surprised Jon was stuck on that part?

"Of course," Gavin said impatiently. "You *know* I can't date. I told him that too. Before."

"I do remember that." Jon's voice was still very even. Super calm.

Gavin didn't feel calm. He was freaking out, suddenly not sure his skin could contain everything he was feeling. Zach was *quitting*.

On the team. On *him*.

"I know I've probably given him a few mixed messages," Gavin allowed. More than a few. Even though he'd tried so fucking hard to keep his attraction under wraps.

"Possibly," Jon said.

"I just . . ." Gavin floundered, *knew* he was floundering, but he didn't know how to stop. "I should try to stop him, and I don't know how. What could I possibly say to make him stay?" He didn't say it but he was thinking it. *How can I ask him to stay when I don't deserve it?*

"Well, I imagine there's one thing," Jon said dryly.

"Not that. Obviously."

Jon sighed. "Listen, the only thing that's obvious is that he likes you, romantically, and you like him, romantically. Why shouldn't you explore that? I'd assume he's not asking for a lifelong commitment."

"I don't know what he wants."

"Because you've never let it get far enough to actually discuss it," Jon said bluntly. Gavin was reminded of why he kind of hated him sometimes.

So he changed the subject.

"Sidney was telling me how hard he fought for me, to even get the opportunity to come out to speak to me, even though Sidney didn't think I'd take the job." Gavin took a deep breath. "Even though he didn't think I'd agree, he still made the effort. I . . . I don't want to pay him back by doing nothing to stop this. He was right about the job. About me taking it."

"And now you wonder if he's right about the dating, too," Jon said shrewdly, going there, even though Gavin hadn't.

"Well . . . yes." It wasn't easy to admit he might've been wrong. "What if he is?"

Then Gavin was going to launch himself into the fucking sun.

No, really, he was going to melt right through this floor.

It would be humiliating and terrifying and exhilarating and Gavin wasn't even sure what he'd do about it.

"Then . . .I don't know. I really fucked this up," Gavin said, scrubbing a hand across his face. "How do I know that, though, without trying it?"

"Dating?"

"Yes, ugh," Gavin retorted. "Zach said we were *already* dating, but surely I would know if we were?"

"I don't know, would you?"

Gavin made a face, before he remembered that Jon could see.

"Answer the question," Jon added firmly. "You can't keep pretending that you're clueless. Or that you don't know why even the thought of dating makes you want to quit therapy or fuck up this new life you're building."

"I don't know why—"

"Bullshit," Jon said frankly.

Gavin took a deep breath. Tried to calm his racing heart. He didn't want to say it out loud. He didn't even want to *think* it.

"It's . . .it's wrong to move on. It means I didn't, that all that grief was for . . ." He swallowed hard, past the lump in his throat. "It means that all that grief was for *nothing*."

Jon's expression softened. "Gavin, it doesn't."

"It does, it *does*," he choked out. "She'd be so angry."

"She wouldn't. I wasn't ever lucky enough to meet your wife, but from the way you've talked about her, she seemed like a generous, kind person who loved you a lot and I think . . ." Jon paused, stared at him even though Gavin could barely meet his eyes on the screen. "I think she'd be really happy that you're happy, again."

Gavin couldn't speak. Reminded in force, in so many ways, of every way Noelle *had* been generous and kind. Funny, too. Never taking herself too seriously. Always poking gentle fun at him. Making him laugh. Getting him out of his own head.

Kind of like Zach did.

Gavin bowed his head and tried to swallow his tears down.

"I don't know if I *can* be," he choked out.

"That's not true," Jon said, "because I can tell you, from where I'm sitting, in the two and a half years since we started talking, I've never seen you this happy."

"That's . . ." Gavin gulped air. Wiped his eyes. "That's awful. But great."

"Guilt is a very common feeling in these situations," Jon soothed. "But you don't *need* to feel it, Gavin. You mourned deeply and completely. None of your grief was a waste. But I told you when you took this job, you were going to come back to life again. Feeling attraction and dating? That's normal. That's part of it."

"Then why does it feel so *awful*," Gavin whined.

"Does it really, though?" Jon questioned. "Or do you *want* it to feel awful so you don't feel guiltier?"

Gavin hated it, but Jon had a point. When he was with Zach—when Zach was smiling at him, and they were talking and sharing a table at the diner or at the sub shop or even Gavin's couch—it was *amazing*.

Everything that Gavin wanted.

Except . . . he could admit that wasn't entirely true. He wanted more, too. Why else could he not stop thinking about Zach every time he touched himself?

The more he thought, the more Gavin realized how much time they'd been spending together. The more he'd looked forward to it. Zach's face in the morning, at the gym, his voice echoing in his ears at night.

How much he'd wanted every moment of it, and *more*.

"I think . . ." Gavin scrubbed a hand across his face. "I think you might be right. I think . . . *God*, I think Zach might be right."

"Possibly," Jon said, but he was smiling now.

"I really, really fucked this up, didn't I?"

"Positively, I don't think it'll be that hard to win Zach's forgiveness," Jon soothed.

"You think?" Gavin had thought it was impossible to do what Sidney had asked and convince Zach to change his mind—and maybe he still couldn't. Maybe he'd made Zach so angry, pushed him away so hard that he wouldn't be willing to rescind his resignation. But he could at least apologize. Tell Zach he wanted him. Tell him he wanted to kiss him again, and *more*.

Jon rolled his eyes. "He's clearly crazy about you, Gavin. He didn't quit in a fit of pique because you turned him down. He quit because he can't be around you and *not* date you."

"How do you know that?"

Jon shot him a knowing look. "It's not that hard to figure out. He didn't quit before, when you told him point-blank you weren't going to date him. He only quit now because he'd tired of watching you pretend that you're just coworkers. Just friends."

They weren't just friends. Gavin could acknowledge that to himself, now.

They *were* friends, yes, but almost from the beginning, when he'd arrived back in Portland, he'd felt more.

Wanted *more*.

"I think you just need to lay out your feelings, your concerns, and your mental state. See if he's still willing," Jon said. "*And* additionally, we're going back to two appointments a week."

"What?"

Jon made an impatient noise. "You're not suddenly fine because you've figured out that you want this, Gavin."

"I've done years of therapy, I do get that," Gavin said dryly.

"And if you want this to work with Zach, I recommend you keep doing it," Jon said. "That means *actually* talking about the shit you don't want to talk about. Like your guilt. And why you didn't want to date again in the first place. That shit doesn't just go away."

"Right. Yeah." Gavin sighed. "So you think I should just . . .apologize? Say I've changed my mind? Grovel?"

"Maybe a combination of all those? Have some honest and open communication," Jon said, smiling knowingly.

"You would say that," Gavin said, rolling his eyes. "Such a fucking therapist."

Jon barked out a laugh. "You're not wrong. I'll send some times and dates, to set up the appointments, alright? And keep me posted."

"I will." Gavin took an unsteady breath. "If I need an emergency session again . . .I don't want to fuck this up even worse with him . . ."

"I've got you," Jon said warmly. "And you've got this. Your heart's in the right place, Gavin."

"I hope so." *God, I hope so.*

After getting off the call, Gavin took a quick shower, threw some clothes on, and set off. First he checked the library, weaving his way through the stacks and tables, checking each study room to make sure he hadn't missed Zach. But he wasn't there. Next he swung by Sammy's, and then Jimmy's, but their regular tables were empty.

He had to give himself a pep talk after dropping by the gym. Still nothing. Classes weren't starting up for another week, so he couldn't be there.

Gavin supposed Zach could be at his apartment, but it felt like he was *never* there during the day, unless he couldn't help it. He always complained it was too quiet. Too lonely. Gavin had never hesitated to give him his company in the evenings, when he couldn't avoid going back there, during their nightly phone calls.

Unless you made him so fucking miserable he doesn't want to leave.

Taking a deep breath, Gavin switched directions and headed towards the small complex Zach lived in.

His heart was racing, barely contained in his chest, when he knocked on Zach's door.

Thirty seconds passed. He pounded on it again. And again. No answer.

He was going to go out of his goddamn mind if he couldn't find Zach—couldn't see him and talk to him and make this right again.

Just when he'd about given up and pulled his phone out of his pocket to call Zach and ask where he was, the door opened.

Zach's hair was messed up, practically sticking up, and he squinted against the light pouring into his apartment.

"G?" he asked, his expression blossoming into hope before it shut down completely, leaving Gavin more worried and nervous than he'd been even a minute earlier.

"We need to talk," Gavin said. "Can I come in?"

Zach hesitated.

"Please," Gavin said. He wasn't above begging. In fact, he wasn't above it at all.

He *wanted* to beg. He wanted to show Zach that he was willing and ready to do whatever it took. Whatever Zach needed to believe that Gavin was serious, that Gavin cared about him, that Gavin wanted to make this right.

"I don't know," Zach said heavily. He looked like he wanted to shut the door in Gavin's face. Like he was five seconds away from actually doing it. "Are you just here to get me to change my mind?"

At one point, if he hadn't gotten his shit together, Gavin might've been. He might've come here just because he'd promised Sidney—given his word. Felt guilty because Zach had given so much and Gavin should at least meet him halfway.

But no, that wasn't why he was really here. Not anymore.

His eyes had been opened and Gavin couldn't deny it any longer.

Maybe this would mean Zach would take his resignation back. Maybe it wouldn't. But that felt secondary to everything else.

"No," Gavin said, "I'm here because *I* changed *my* mind."

Zach's lips parted, like he was shocked, and that hurt, but it was an easy hurt to push away. He was going to make this right. Felt the certain weight of it.

"Alright, I guess you can," Zach said and opened the door wider.

Gavin walked two steps in, heard the door close behind him, and he knew he was going to do it only a second before he did.

He fell to his knees, right in front of Zach, like his strings had just been cut.

"I'm here for you," Gavin said, gazing up at him. Zach was beautiful, even like this, and so much everything that Gavin wanted and had been purposefully denying himself.

He wasn't going to do it a second longer.

CHAPTER 14

Zach blinked, then blinked again.

He knew what he was seeing, but he couldn't quite believe it.

Had he hallucinated or was Gavin here and was he *kneeling* at Zach's feet, like he was pleading for Zach's forgiveness?

"What—what are you doing?" He could barely get the question out.

"Begging you to forgive me. To reconsider. To . . ." Gavin gazed up at him. "I'm trying to tell you I fucked it up. I want to say I changed my mind, but it's not even that. I didn't change my mind . . .I *saw* it clearly, for the first time."

Gavin pleading on his knees wasn't something Zach had even thought to want, but now that it was happening, he couldn't deny the heat pouring through him, the nearly savage satisfaction at having Gavin like this.

"You want me?"

Gavin choked out a laugh. "You make it sound so simple."

Zach gazed down at him. He looked so fucking good like this. He'd look even better in Zach's bed. "It *is* that simple."

His head bowed then, his dark hair curling against the pale nape of his neck. If Zach had seen him like this back in Michigan, that skin would have been tanned from the sun, but after five months in Portland, with its overcast skies and drizzling weather, it was bleached white.

Zach realized he wanted to see Gavin's skin in all its shades. Wanted to trace the subtle curve of his neck with his thumb so he reached down and did.

The skin there, on Gavin's nape, was velvet soft. Gavin let out a hiccupping breath. "I fucked it all up," he murmured, not looking up and not dislodging Zach's fingers as they stroked him.

"Yeah, kind of, but I get it. I forgive you," Zach said. There was no universe he could imagine where he wouldn't. His other hand moved to Gavin's shoulder and squeezed it. "You don't need to do this, like uh . . .this."

The problem was Zach didn't even know what *this* was. Was this something Gavin was into? Was it something *Zach* was into? Before this, he'd have said no, absolutely not, but now he wasn't entirely so sure.

Gavin didn't move. The air between them grew thick, heavy.

"What if I like it?" Gavin asked, so quiet Zach could barely hear him.

There was no way if Gavin looked now that he'd miss that Zach's cock was getting hard in his sweatpants. He was eye level with it, which honestly, it was a fucking miracle Zach hadn't gotten hard *before* now.

But it was one thing for Gavin to say he wanted him, that he'd changed his mind, and another entirely for Zach to shove his dick into Gavin's face.

"Then *I* like it," Zach said and used the hand curled around Gavin's shoulder to lift him up. "I like *this* too," he added in a soft voice, leaning in. He slid his hands down his arms and tangled their fingers together.

It was almost terrifying, no matter what Gavin had just said, to lean in and kiss him again.

What if he changes his mind again? What if he pushes me away after it's over?

Zach wanted to believe that Gavin wouldn't. That part of what him pounding on the door and then going to his knees meant was that he *wouldn't*, not ever again.

That he'd made up his mind and he was sticking to it.

Gavin swayed towards him, his gray eyes intent on Zach's face. "You still want this?" he asked quietly.

Zach knew what he was asking. *Do you still want me?*

Part of him wanted to say, *I've wanted you since I was eighteen and stupid,* but that would probably freak Gavin out and they'd just got done *un*-freaking him out.

So instead of answering, Zach leaned in the rest of the way and kissed him.

Gavin's mouth was hot and lush against his, Gavin groaning into the kiss as Zach pulled him in close, hands tightening around his waist.

As Gavin's tongue slipped into his mouth, tangling with Zach's, he wondered, dimly, if he should try to slow them down. Focus on some nice polite making out. Not shove his hard cock against Gavin's hip, reminding him that he was a guy, and *if* they had sex, it wouldn't be like any sex Gavin had had before.

But then Gavin pulled back, mouth red and wet and pupils swallowing his eyes, and he said breathlessly, "I've thought so much about this."

Jesus fucking Christ. Was Zach supposed to control himself when Gavin was basically serving himself up on a silver platter?

"Yeah?" Zach heard the rough, desperate edge in his voice as he asked the question. "You wanna tell me about it?"

Gavin flushed bright red. "Uh . . ."

Zach lifted a hand, stroking that soft skin at the nape of his neck again. Toying with the ends of the hair that curled over it. "Come on," he cajoled.

"Kissing, yeah," Gavin said with a soft exhale of resignation. "And uh . . .more. Definitely more."

Zach's eyebrow rose. "More?"

Gavin licked his lips. "Do I have to ask for it?"

"I don't know, you were pretty eager to beg a few minutes ago," Zach teased gently. And yeah, maybe this was out of his sphere of experience, but he kind of loved it.

"Is that what you want me to do?" Gavin didn't look like he'd call him a sick fuck for it, or slap him or leave if he asked for it. Even if Zach demanded it.

"It sounds like a great start."

Gavin nodded, like he was telling himself it was okay now, to do it. Because Zach had said it was okay. And suddenly Zach was lightheaded, arousal surging through him, making him harder than he could remember being in ages.

He'd always known Gavin could demolish him, but he'd never imagined Gavin would do it this easily, or with soft pleas falling from his lips.

"Zach, please take me to bed. I want it so bad. I wanted it before I even knew what it was, before I could even know how good it could feel."

"Yeah?" Zach's fingers found bare skin underneath Gavin's T-shirt, stroking lightly at his sides. He was soft and firm and Zach wanted to touch him all over.

Actually, he wanted Gavin to ask him to touch him all over. Beg him, even.

"I want it," Gavin said, flushing again. He could barely meet Zach's eyes but he had a feeling it wasn't a lack of desire but a surplus of it.

"What do you want me to do?"

Gavin made a face. "Do I have to say it?"

"Oh yeah, you sure do," Zach said, smiling, because he couldn't *not* anymore. This was hot as hell, no question about it, but it was wonderful too, filling him with a buoyant happiness until he felt like a balloon, about to float away into the clouds.

Gavin leaned in, kissed him again. God, his mouth was incredible. Soft and wet and perfect, his tongue slipping into his mouth like there was where it belonged. Zach couldn't get enough of kissing him, so he dragged the kiss out, one melting into the next.

He only pulled back when he felt Gavin begin to pant unsteadily, and then his hips flexed against Zach's once and then twice.

Yeah, Gavin was definitely as into this as Zach was.

"I want you to touch me," Gavin murmured. "I want you to give me an orgasm I'm going to think about every single night you're not next to me."

Zach's brain shut down.

"Cute you think you're going to have any nights alone after this," he said roughly. Probably it was too much to assume they were spending every night together, but Zach had wanted this too long and he felt insane with just how *much* he needed.

He pushed Gavin towards the bedroom and thanked God his apartment was small and the bedroom wasn't that far away.

He could push Gavin right down onto the couch and blow his mind, but the bed would be better. More room, more options. Because he had a lot of things he wanted to do. A lot of ways he wanted Gavin to feel.

"Guess you like that," Gavin observed, his hand sliding down Zach's back and cupping his ass. Squeezing it. "God," he exhaled sharply, suddenly, like the touch affected him as much—or more—than it had affected Zach.

And that was saying something.

"I fucking love it," Zach said and pushed Gavin right up against the edge of the bed. "I fucking—" He almost said it and only saved himself in the last moment by mashing their mouths together again. Zach had told himself if he ever got a chance to do this, he'd have some finesse, but the urge to take and take and *take* was shredding his self-control.

Or maybe that was the way Gavin had fallen to his knees right in his fucking doorway.

Either way, Zach was basically losing the fight to get his hands on Gavin *right now*.

He broke the kiss for just long enough to pull Gavin's shirt off, hands trailing down his curved collarbones to his pecs, lips finding the sharp perfect angle of his neck.

Gavin moaned, lighting up all of Zach's nerves, as his fingertips found his nipples and circled. He'd done enough fantasizing of his own, and even in those daydreams, Gavin had never felt this good. Been this responsive, like warm putty in Zach's hands.

"More, more," Gavin groaned.

Zach could do that.

He pushed Gavin up onto the bed, made quick work of his shoes and socks, and then slid his palms up his calves, his thighs. Gavin's hips twitched when he stopped just short of where he clearly wanted them—if the long hard length of his cock, so obvious in his jeans, was any indication.

"Oh, not yet," Zach said, not sure if he was tormenting Gavin or himself. Or if it was a wicked combination of both.

Gavin whined, high and insistent in the back of his throat. "I can . . .I'll beg again," he promised.

And God, that did sound good, but maybe next time. Zach already knew what he wanted *this* time.

He resumed his upward movement, sliding up along Gavin's gorgeous body, until his hands found his wrists. Grasped them firmly and then kept going, until they were stretched out together, their intertwined hands above Gavin's head.

Gavin's breath was coming in shallow, desperate pants now, so Zach had to assume this was doing it for him too.

But he wasn't ever going to just *assume*. Not with G.

"You like this?" he asked, dropping a kiss against his mouth, then sliding his lips across his scruff to his neck. Nibbling there. He wanted to leave a mark, so everyone knew he'd been here, like planting a goddamn flag on an unexplored island, but he held back. For now.

"Yeah." Gavin sounded even more wrecked than Zach imagined.

"Think you could keep your hands up there like that?"

Gavin let out a shuddering breath. "Um, yeah. Yes."

"You *want* to keep your hands up there like that?"

Gavin arched up into him again. "God, yes."

"Okay, then. Be good for me."

Gavin swore but Zach couldn't even pay attention because his own brain was short-circuiting, his cock twitching in his sweatpants, because they both knew Gavin was going to do whatever Zach said.

That he was going to be *good*.

Zach released Gavin's wrists but true to his word, they didn't move an inch. He took his sweet time making his way back down to the waistband of Gavin's jeans.

If Gavin thought he was going to go quicker now because of how fast he tugged down the rest of his clothes, he was going to have to think again.

Especially once Zach got his first glimpse of Gavin's cock. Hard and pink, leaking against his stomach. It had a nice thickness to it, and Zach's mouth went dry, imagining all the things he wanted to do with it.

"God, please, *please*." Gavin's voice was thready, whining.

Zach tore his gaze away from his cock and met Gavin's wild eyes. "I thought you were going to be good," he said casually.

Watched as Gavin's cock twitched.

Settled his hands on Gavin's thighs and squeezed. Loving the strength of them, the corded muscle, the faint scratch of the dark hair against his palms.

"I can be, I *will* be," he swore.

"Alright. See that you are," Zach said. He hadn't realized how much this was turning him on, but he was aching in his sweats, sweating through his T-shirt. He stripped it off and Gavin groaned again.

"So gorgeous," Gavin panted.

"Yeah, I know you think so. Caught you watching me in the gym." Zach shot him a cocky grin. "Bet you wanted me to do this to you every time you looked when you shouldn't have been."

He leaned in and swiped his tongue across the head of Gavin's cock, just tasting his precome. Gavin made a noise like he'd just been shot.

And *that* was hot, too.

"Remember, you're being good and not moving," Zach said, leaning against and toying with the head with his tongue. Just teasing, a little, enjoying the tiny aborted twitches of Gavin's hips as he desperately tried not to chase the pleasure.

"I am, I *am,*" Gavin gasped out.

Zach gave him one last look before sliding him into his mouth. He was so hot and perfect, filling his mouth and making Zach realize just how long it had been since he'd done this.

Nothing else would've compared though. He'd wanted Gavin's taste in his mouth, the weight of him on his tongue.

Gavin was shaking all over and Zach knew it wasn't going to take very long for him to lose it, so he sucked hard and took him as deep as he dared, feeling his throat close around him.

"Fuck," Gavin shouted and trembled, a second later shooting down Zach's throat.

Zach worked him through it, mind full of hot static, finally letting his softening dick slip from between his lips.

Panting a little, he finally rose up and pulled his sweats down. At the first touch of his hand against his sensitized cock, he hissed.

"Wait—" Gavin said, finally trying to rise.

"No, just like this," Zach said, climbing onto his hips, straddling him, and with his other hand, found Gavin's lips, until he was sliding two fingers into his hot mouth.

Gavin groaned and sucked around his fingers as Zach stripped his cock.

He was so close, and then Gavin bit down, just on his fingertips, and his orgasm hit him like a thunderclap, making everything go white and dark as he shot off, all over Gavin's chest.

"Fuck," Zach said, trying not to collapse with all his weight onto Gavin's body. He was a few inches taller and probably forty pounds heavier and he didn't want to crush him.

"Oh my God," Gavin exhaled in a shaky voice as Zach barely managed to fall to the side, landing on the bed with a soft thud.

So much for finesse. Zach wanted to feel bad. He knew he should probably apologize for how rough he'd been. But that had been the hottest sex of his whole life, and when he looked over at Gavin, almost afraid of what he might see on his face, he looked equally as floored.

Okay. At least he hadn't scared him away.

"I . . .uh . . ." Zach tried to make his brain come back online. "Just give me a minute and I'll clean us up."

"No rush," Gavin said, like he was perfectly okay to lie there with jizz all over his chest.

Then he slid a fingertip down through it, swiping through the trails, and made Zach's brain permanently shut down when he slid it into his mouth, humming with satisfaction the whole time.

"You can't . . .*I* can't," Zach said, shaking all over. "You're killing me."

Gavin's expression was guileless, and so fucking innocent. "Me?"

Zach couldn't ask him if he'd been this down and dirty with his wife. She was definitely not a subject he was going to bring up in this bed, considering that she was the reason G had barely made it here at all.

"You know what you're doing," Zach said, tracing the bulge of Gavin's bicep with his fingertip.

"Guess I do," Gavin said. He huffed out a slightly embarrassed breath. "Not with anything else, though."

"No?"

Gavin flushed again. "I . . .I didn't mean to do it that way. I just . . .I'd been thinking about it. Thought it might be easier if I wasn't in my head."

"Was it?" Zach wasn't offended. He could only imagine how tough it might have been for Gavin to even consider sleeping with someone else. Even if he wanted to, and clearly he'd wanted to.

"Yeah, it was. But it was . . ." Gavin was bright red now. "Better than I expected."

Zach nudged him, grinning. "Don't tell me you thought I'd be shit in bed," he teased. Gavin had said that he hadn't wanted to be in his head, and maybe that was something Zach could do for him—not let him fall too deeply into the circle of his own thoughts.

"The opposite, actually." Gavin's confession was hushed, reverent. "You're good at everything, and I knew you'd be good at this. And you were. . .it was fucking incredible."

Zach's fingers tightened around his arm, squeezing gently. "For me too, G." He leaned over and pressed a kiss to his lips, brief but intense.

"I meant it, you know," Gavin said earnestly. "I fucked it up before. When we kissed . . .I should have handled that differently."

"Differently how?" Zach knew he should get up and clean them up, but he didn't think he could move until he heard Gavin's answer. Maybe he shouldn't be testing Gavin, but there was a part of him that *needed* to, because he couldn't go back again, not after what they'd just done.

Gavin knew exactly what Zach was asking. *Are you going to do this tonight and in the morning tell me you regret it? That it's not happening, all over again?*

He picked his words carefully. "I should never have kissed you and then claimed after that nothing had changed. Honestly, I shouldn't have told you nothing had changed after the night we *almost* kissed. I freaked out, and that wasn't fair to you."

"Was it fair to you?" Zach wanted to know.

Gavin should've known that Zach would be like this, because he'd always asked the tough questions. Didn't let things slide. Went after what he wanted with a single-minded focus Gavin had always admired.

"No, it wasn't. But that wouldn't be the first time," Gavin said wryly. "At least according to my therapist."

"Well, stop that," Zach joked, nudging him with his shoulder.

"I'm . . .I'm trying," Gavin promised.

Zach pulled himself up, but Gavin reached out before he could think it through, held onto his arm. He didn't want Zach to go, even to the bathroom, until he was sure Zach understood what he was trying to say.

Until Zach *believed* it.

"Hey," Gavin continued in a low voice, "I *do* want to do this again. I want to do this lots of times. And all the other stuff too. The breakfasts and the lunches and the late night tape watching. Falling asleep on you, on my couch. Phone calls every night."

Zach smiled, eyes crinkling at the corners. "Yeah? Good. Cause I want to, too. But I don't think we're going to need the late night phone calls, anymore, G."

He got up and went to the bathroom.

Zach had said something along those lines before they'd had sex. *Cute you think you're going to have any nights alone after this.* Gavin's heart had hiccupped when he'd heard that.

He knew Zach meant it. Zach meant it all, it was obvious from the way he gazed down at Gavin, like he was something precious and special that was worth waiting for.

And he wanted Zach to know the reverse was true, too.

He wasn't letting Zach go. Not this time.

A minute later, Zach returned with a damp washcloth, but he didn't hand it over. Instead he leaned over Gavin's body, cleaning his chest and his stomach himself, gently wiping away all the evidence they'd finally done this.

Gavin was almost sad until he realized that maybe that had been the first time, but they had an infinite number after this.

Maybe that was too serious of a thought, but he didn't know how Zach could think this was casual for him.

After tossing the washcloth in a hamper by the door, Zach resettled in bed, tugging Gavin over until his face was resting against Zach's bicep.

Gavin curled his fingers into the golden trail of hair leading down to Zach's soft cock. Saw it twitch a little and felt an echo of heat pulse through him.

But before they went at it again, he still felt like he had things to say. An understanding they needed to come to.

"I'm in this," Gavin said quietly, "but I can't say I'm always going to be perfect at it."

Zach chuckled. "Don't need you to be perfect. Just need you to be *you*. That's all I ever wanted."

"Since Michigan?"

Zach tensed a little, and then he turned, looking Gavin square in the eye. "If we're being honest, no."

"Since I came back to Portland?"

Zach sighed. "Don't freak out. But I had like an enormous fucking crush on you before, when I was in college. I wouldn't have done a thing about it. Was more embarrassed about it than anything else, if I was being honest, but I don't want to pretend. Not anymore."

Gavin deliberately didn't spend a lot of time thinking about the past, for obvious reasons. But he still cast his mind back now, remembering how Zach had been during the two years he'd coached him in college. Zach, an eager and sweet eighteen-year-old puppy of a guy, who worked hard, who never told Gavin that he couldn't do something.

Who'd always gazed at Gavin like he was someone worth following.

"I can see that, actually," he said, chuckling under his breath.

"Noelle . . ." Zach hesitated, like he suddenly wasn't sure he if should say her name or not, "she knew. She told me I was cute. Ruffled my hair about it more than once."

Gavin froze. She'd never mentioned it to him, and even though she hadn't, he knew her silence hadn't been the disapproving sort. No, she'd probably been hoping not to embarrass Zach even more than he already was.

Still, something unwound inside Gavin. More of his guilt losing its tenacious grip on his heart. "Yeah, sounds like something she'd do."

Zach's whole face relaxed. "You're not upset?"

"No. Never. It's . . ." Gavin tried to pinpoint exactly how he felt about Zach's youthful crush. "It's sweet."

"I thought it had faded, honestly, then I went to Michigan, and it was like we were meeting for the first time, even though we weren't. Like our relationship was fundamentally different."

"You'd grown up," Gavin said, thinking but not saying how *well* Zach had grown up, and how he'd noticed from the first moment he'd spotted him. The attraction that had blossomed so naturally.

"And you'd changed. I didn't realize it at first, or I dismissed it 'cause I thought you wouldn't take the job, but then you did, and it was obvious how good this could be, between us."

It was hard to admit, even though it shouldn't have been. "I saw it too, immediately. I almost didn't take the job, because I thought I couldn't keep my hands off you."

Zach's squawk of outrage was adorable. "Are you freaking kidding me?"

Gavin laughed. "No."

"Oh my God, and here I was freaking out when you showed up because you kept talking about how you'd been my coach." Zach groaned under his breath. "Hayes was right, you kept trying to put me back into that box."

"And it never worked," Gavin added. "No matter what I tried."

Zach made a satisfied noise as he tugged Gavin closer. Gavin was leaning half on Zach's chest now, and it made perfect sense to rise up and kiss him again.

It only took a minute or two of making out for Gavin to end up in Zach's lap, naked skin pressed to naked skin, grinding their increasingly interested cocks together.

"Fuck, you're so hot like this," Zach groaned, his mouth gliding down Gavin's neck.

Personally, Gavin thought that was *Zach*, with his messed-up hair, half sticking straight up, and the beard burn on his neck and his red swollen lips.

If he'd known it could be like this, could feel this fucking good to touch and be touched again, he wasn't sure he ever could have resisted it.

"Though maybe nothing will ever be as hot as you walking into my apartment and going straight to your knees," Zach mumbled against Gavin's neck.

"Yeah, you liked that?"

Gavin was out of practice with sex in general and inexperienced with men, specifically, but even he'd noticed that Zach had *definitely* liked it.

It had been sort of tough to miss, considering what had been right at his eye level.

Zach pulled back and shot him a knowing look. "I keep telling myself the innocent look isn't doing it for me, but it totally is."

"Noted," Gavin said, laughing. He leaned in and kissed Zach firmly, then realized what he wanted. What he should have asked for, before. "Would you . . .uh . . .be interested in doing that again?"

Zach's eyes widened. "Yeah?"

"I want that." Gavin decided that if they were doing this, if they were going there, he was going to need to use his words. "I want to get on my knees for you and suck your cock."

Not just because the words were important and necessary, but because of how they worked Zach up so easy.

Zach's jaw dropped. And a second later, he was hustling them both off the bed, his cock fully hard now, Gavin getting a front seat view of it as Zach gently pushed him down to his knees at the side of the bed.

"Goddamn it," Zach hissed as Gavin inched closer, sticking his tongue out. "This is way too hot."

"Do you want to stop?" Gavin asked quietly. *He* didn't want to stop. It was amazing how much this was doing it for him, too. His whole body felt lit up, with just the weight of Zach's hands on his shoulders as Zach leaned forward, briefly touching his dick to Gavin's outstretched tongue.

"Hell no," Zach said, exhaling hard as he finished closing the distance between them. "But if you want to stop, all you have to do is say the word."

Gavin nodded, brain fizzing as Zach slid his cock an inch at a time into his mouth.

He'd thought about this occasionally, back when he'd been married. He'd always liked something in his mouth. Noelle had teased him about his oral fixation, and how much she'd enjoyed that. But it felt so different. Then after Michigan, he'd thought about this more than he should've. Fantasized about it, even, as he touched himself at night.

How it would feel for Gavin. If he'd enjoy having a cock in his mouth. If he could do a good enough job for Zach to enjoy it.

Zach looked like he was enjoying it now, face creased with pleasure, bottom lip bitten between his white teeth, aborted groans barely making it out of his mouth as Gavin sucked him deeper.

There was a weight and a purpose to this that he discovered very quickly that he loved. A power, too. He'd heard people talk, of course, of the power you could find on your knees, but he'd never imagined he'd experience it.

Or that it would feel so fucking amazing.

He wasn't doing anything particularly special. Just suction and relishing the weight of Zach's cock in his mouth, trying to take him in deeper. He had a gag reflex so he imagined he couldn't go much farther, but Zach was shuddering above him, hands a solid weight on his shoulders, grounding and reassuring him.

Then one of Zach's hands slipped up and cradled his head, and that blew the top of his skull right off.

Gavin pulled off for a second, groaning. "That, *that*, please," he begged.

Zach blinked slowly, like this whole thing had pulled him right under, until he was drowning with it.

"This?" he asked, tangling his fingers more insistently into Gavin's hair.

Gavin nodded, leaning forward, tongue out, and letting Zach's hand on his head guide him right back where he was meant to be.

He thought Zach mumbled something about going to hell, but how could this be hell, when it felt so goddamn good?

When Gavin felt like he was going to come just from Zach's cock in his mouth and the pleasurable bite of pain on his scalp from Zach holding his hair just a little too tight?

But Zach was into it, just as into it as Gavin was, if the way his cock was twitching and blurting precome was any indication. It probably wasn't the world's best blowjob, but he was trying, and that clearly meant something to Zach, who kept pushing him harder and faster.

Then he accidentally went a bit too deep, and Gavin choked.

He expected panic, but all he felt was satisfaction, and even as Zach backed himself out, murmuring sweet apologies, he wanted Zach to do it again. And again. Until Zach came down his throat.

It was unclear if Zach would allow him to touch himself, to give his cock a taste of the pleasure he was giving to Zach. He didn't doubt Zach would rock his world after, but his cock was aching so badly, his whole body burning and shaking with how aroused he was, and so he took a chance and took a palm and just pressed down. Anything to relieve the nearly unbearable pressure.

Zach swore and said, "God, yes, touch yourself. Make yourself come as you're sucking me."

It was total fucking end game after that. Gavin sucked harder, pawing at himself, already feeling his orgasm sizzling in his balls, and a second later, Zach was pulling back, even as Gavin tried to keep him close.

But Zach batted him away, but it was a near enough thing that a stripe of come landed on his tongue, then the rest hit his face, hot and insistent.

"Oh God," Zach groaned, and that was all it took for Gavin's orgasm to hit him hard and strong, leaving him trembling and gasping as he shot into his fist.

He slumped down on the ground and tried to catch his breath.

Zach leaned in and used a finger to swipe through the stripes of come on Gavin's face, half-cleaning him up and half-rubbing it in.

"So good like this," Zach murmured. "So gorgeous. So perfect."

"Thought you didn't care if I was perfect," Gavin gasped.

"Turns out you are, anyway." Zach's touch was reverent. A second later, Gavin was sort of, mostly clean, and Zach tugged him back onto the bed.

They didn't move for a long time after that, and that was perfect, too.

CHAPTER 15

"I keep worrying that this is a bad idea," Gavin said under his breath, leaning in as Morgan Reynolds, finished reading the lineup card, was making his rounds through the locker room, acting like he practically owned it.

Zach wasn't unhappy about it; Gavin could complain about Morgan all he wanted, if he was going to do it this close to Zach.

They'd been trying to keep some distance between them at the rink, and around the guys, but ever since a few nights ago, Zach had felt like he was five seconds away from pinning Gavin to the nearest flat surface and ravaging him.

Because he could now. It was not only allowed, it was *encouraged*.

"We both talked to Finn about it. He's solid, he and Morgan are doing so much better. Besides," Zach added, "he's still Morgan Reynolds. Maybe he can inspire the guys."

"I think they know Finn a little too well to let Reynolds go to their heads," Gavin said. He was probably not wrong.

Zach shrugged. Morgan was finishing up, nudging Elliott, the pair of them laughing together. Malcolm was next to Elliott in his stall, looking like he wanted to forcibly remove Morgan's hand from Elliott's arm.

"Score one for me," Morgan said laughing, and Elliott just cackled. Malcolm relaxed a fraction.

"You got it, boss," Elliott said.

Morgan made his way over then. "Team's looking good," he said to Gavin.

"Thanks," Gavin said dryly.

"Wheeler," Morgan said, inclining his head in Zach's direction, expression more guarded.

He had to know Zach was Hayes' best friend; it was not exactly a secret they'd played together for the Mavs and that they'd been close.

"Hey," Zach said, shoving his hands into his pockets so he wouldn't be tempted to punch Morgan in the face.

"I was surprised to see you retired so young," Morgan said, because of course he fucking did.

Zach shrugged. "It was time. Got other things to do."

"Or you worried you wouldn't be able to produce without Monty," Morgan said, his smile suddenly lethal.

Gavin reached out and grasped Zach's arm. Like he too was suddenly afraid that Zach might do something he wouldn't regret at all.

Honestly Zach didn't know what pissed him off more—that he'd implied Zach's success had only been because of Hayes or that he'd called him *Monty*, like he deserved to have any bit of Hayes in his mouth at all, nevermind a nickname that only his friends called him.

Morgan had never been Hayes' friend.

"Come on," Gavin hissed under his breath. "Don't be an ass, Reynolds."

Morgan shrugged. "*I* never thought it, I was just wondering if *Zach* thought it."

"Zach doesn't," Zach said flatly.

"Well, there you go." Morgan grinned like it was one great big joke.

"God, I hate that guy," Zach said as soon as he was gone.

Gavin looked over at him, surprised. "Really?"

Okay, maybe he'd sounded a little vehement for what had only been a pretty mild chirp. He'd heard hundreds of things way worse when he'd played.

"He's just an asshole," Zach muttered.

"It's weird he brought up Hayes," Gavin said thoughtfully.

Gavin would think it was weird. Zach didn't think it was weird at all, and he definitely wasn't going to tell Hayes, because if he did, Hayes would probably correctly assume Morgan hadn't been able to keep his name out of his mouth.

Which begged the question—if he was that desperate, why had Morgan not gone to Tampa and done his own share of begging for forgiveness?

"Not really," Zach said flatly.

Gavin looked over at him. "No, *no*," he said, comprehension dawning on his face.

"You said it, not me." Zach pushed off from the wall. "Come on, it's nearly warmups."

It was easy-ish to let the flow of warmups and then the game empty his brain of anything that wasn't hockey.

The first period started slow, both teams feeling each other out, until Elliott grabbed the puck and flew across the ice. It felt like the whole arena held its collective breath. Elliott held it a breath longer than he normally did, maneuvering around to the goalie's right side and then shot. He pulled it a little too much, and it bounced right off the post. Ell made a face, and then the lines were switching again.

"Find some urgency," Gavin told the guys the intermission after the first period ended. He sounded calm, like he wasn't really worried, and Zach wasn't either.

This was a beatable team, and the Evergreens had overcome slow starts before.

But a slow second period was a different story. Mal took a great shot, and by some fucking miracle, the goalie managed to deflect it, a miracle of a save that would probably end up on his end of season highlight reel.

But it piled up. Shot after shot, some of them even high quality, none of them going in. Zach could tell Elliott was getting frustrated, because he barked at Mal the next time they were on the bench, Ivan leaning over and putting a reassuring hand on his arm.

Finn was playing great, too, beautiful in the crease and not looking perturbed at all when they headed out for the third period. But it didn't matter how good of a shutout he was putting together. They couldn't win the game if they couldn't score goals.

It was only late in the third, when Brody stole the puck and sent it Ramsey's way. That was the beginning of a lot of their best setups. With his chess-master's brain and the way he saw the ice, he always knew the best place to send it after that.

But this time he didn't pass it. He took the shot himself, finding the perfect angle through all the traffic between him and the goal.

The goalie hadn't expected Ramsey to take it and wasn't ready, the puck hitting the back of the net.

The arena erupted, Ramsey flinging his arms in the air, Brody crashing into him.

Zach let out the breath he hadn't been aware he'd been holding, and next to him, he felt Gavin fractionally relax.

Now they just needed to hold the lead for the next few minutes.

The Sabretooths pulled their goalie in the last minute, but it didn't matter, because the Evergreens' crushing defense, led by Ramsey and Brody, stifled them before they could get anything going, even a man up.

Elliott looked unusually subdued in the locker room after the win, quiet as he pulled his equipment off.

Gavin didn't have to send him over—or even give him a glance. Zach saw and he was already planning on taking care of it.

"Hey," Zach said, heading over and knocking a fist against Elliott's. "Great game."

Elliott didn't look convinced. "We were fucking ineffectual out there."

Next to him, Malcolm grunted his agreement.

"You weren't bad. Sometimes no matter how many shots you take, they just don't go in," Zach said. "You had some good setups, especially on the power play—"

"Yeah, exactly," Elliott retorted.

Zach wasn't going to bring up the second power play team; he wasn't *that* stupid.

Elliott would just demand for the hundredth time they double shift him.

"We're the top line on the team," Mal said in a low, frustrated voice.

"The top line in the *conference*," Elliott reminded him.

Zach sighed. "And sometimes that means jack shit."

"We're gonna get it together," Mal promised Zach. "More drills. More practice."

This was not what he'd come over here for. "It's fine," Zach said, but he had a feeling nothing he said was going to stick. Maybe if they went and fucked out their frustration after this, they'd see what had happened more clearly.

Zach could only hope.

"I'm gonna practice that shot a million goddamn times," Elliott said under his breath.

"And you'd make it ninety-nine percent of the time," Zach said.

But Elliott was already turning away.

When Zach finished making his rounds—high-fiving Ramsey and Brody, thanking them for the goal and the extraordinary defensive effort, and congratulating Finn on another killer shutout—he headed to Gavin's office.

Sure enough, there he was, slumped on the couch, in the dark.

Not a great sign.

"Finished with the media?" he asked.

Gavin shrugged.

Zach perched his ass on the side of the couch. Nudged his hand right up next to Gavin's thigh, as close as he dared, when they were here, at the rink. "Don't tell me I'm gonna have to give *you* a pep talk, too," he teased.

Gavin rolled his eyes, but then he asked, "What kind of pep talk?"

"The one where I tell you that we take the win. That Ivan's line will sort itself out. That Finn was so fucking solid out there."

"Yeah," Gavin agreed, but the confidence that was always in his voice was not quite there.

"We'll have to keep them from over-practicing this week," Zach said. "Ell in particular."

"He should've made that shot," Gavin said. Zach smacked him on the thigh.

"Not you too."

Gavin shot him a helpless look. "He wants to make it, he needs that shot."

"He *has* it," Zach reminded him.

But Gavin didn't say anything.

"Hey, let's go grab a late dinner," Zach said.

Gavin's forehead creased. "You want to go have dinner?"

"I don't want to go over the tape. Not tonight. Dinner," Zach said and shot Gavin the most predatory smile he could muster, "and then dessert after. No thinking about hockey."

"Like a . . .like a date?" Gavin looked uncertain.

Zach's heartbeat didn't flutter with concern. It definitely did not. They hadn't used the d word. They'd used the *other* d word frequently enough in the last few days, but *dating* was not *dick*.

He remembered, a little too well, how adamantly Gavin had been against dating. He didn't seem adamantly against dick, enthusiastic in a way that had practically short-circuited Zach's brain.

"Yeah," Zach said hesitantly.

But Gavin's face melted into a smile. "That sounds . . .actually, that sounds really nice."

"Yeah? We'll head over to Sullivan's, then," Zach said. "I'm sure they've got a quiet corner for the Evergreens' famous hockey coach."

Gavin flushed, and Zach loved it, tapping him on the leg. "Come on, let's go."

⤜≫≫⑃ ⑄≪≪⑊

Gavin didn't like trading on his name, but when it came to Zach, he'd do worse, with zero compunction.

It turned out that Sullivan's was only too happy to find them a quiet, dark corner for their late dinner.

Zach ordered them a bottle of wine, claiming that even someone without a decent palate would enjoy it. Gavin made a face but found himself lighter than he'd been even an hour ago, sitting on his couch and wondering if this was when the other shoe finally dropped.

Zach was right, it had just been an off game, and they'd *still* won.

He could relax. That was not only allowed; it was *encouraged* on dates.

"Hey, thanks for suggesting this," he said as Zach examined the menu, even though they both knew what he was going to get. A steak, practically still mooing. Baked potato. Sour cream, but no butter. Roasted Brussels sprouts. And if they had something decadent and chocolate on the dessert menu, he wouldn't even try to resist.

They'd shared so many dinners, nearly just like this one, not just since Zach had come back to Portland U, but even when he'd been his player, it was kind of amazing that Zach hadn't smacked him upside of the head and told him that they were already dating before this.

"You're welcome," Zach said. Under the table, his foot nudged Gavin's. "You deserve to be wined and dined before you get dicked down."

Gavin flushed. They hadn't done anything like that yet—unless they counted Zach pressing on his taint when he'd blown him last night. He had a feeling Zach wouldn't count that.

It was hard to be disappointed, because even the handjobs and blowjobs they'd shared were so damn good. Hot and overwhelming and intense every time, like the moment they got their hands on each other, it was too hard to not get carried away.

Zach gave him a steady, incendiary look. "Or maybe before you dick *me* down."

Gavin shifted uncomfortably, all too aware of how hard he was in his slacks. All because Zach had said *dick* twice and then looked at him like that.

"That . . ." Gavin's voice was rough, and he cleared his throat. Tried to clear his mind. He'd worried he wouldn't be able to clear it after the game, but it turned out that hadn't been very hard for him—or for Zach. "Uh, yeah. That um . . .both ways."

Zach chuckled. "Good. Me too. Now what are you getting?"

His doctor had whined about his cholesterol last time he'd had a physical, so he decided on the sea bass.

After they ordered, Gavin searched for something they could discuss that wasn't hockey or how badly he wanted Zach's foot to travel all the way up his leg, to where his cock was still pulsing against his zipper.

His brain grabbed the first topic it could find. "That was weird, tonight, when Morgan came by the locker room," he said.

Zach shot him a semi-agonized look. "Do we have to talk about him on our date?"

"You really don't like him." Gavin was still surprised by this. Not that he'd really believed Zach *liked* Morgan, but that his dislike was so pronounced, yes.

"Is it about . . ." Gavin dropped his voice. "Hayes?"

"I'm not supposed to talk about it," Zach said. But he sounded like he wanted to.

"Honestly, I didn't even know they knew each other that well," Gavin said.

Zach shot him a look. "Are you kidding me? You were there, front and center for it."

It took a moment, but Gavin realized what he was talking about. "Are you talking about the Four Nations tournament? That was *five years* ago."

"Oh, I know," Zach said, rolling his eyes.

"Did they—" Gavin stopped suddenly. The memories were five years old, but he could remember some things—and one thing in particular.

One early morning, when he'd come out of his room to go for a run, and Morgan had been there, in the hallway, even though Gavin knew his room was two floors up. Morgan had brushed it off, claiming that he'd had to check in with a teammate about their upcoming game that afternoon, but Gavin realized that Morgan had never said *which* teammate it had been.

"Yeah," Zach said. "And Hayes would hate that I'm telling you this, but we're . . . well, we're . . ." He pursed his lips and blew out a short breath. "We're together now. So you should know. Or know it all. It fucked Hayes up. It's currently fucking Hayes up."

"After five years?"

Zach sighed. "Is there a statute of limitations for loving someone who doesn't love you back?"

"No wonder you looked like you wanted to kill him," Gavin said. "Well, we knew Morgan was an ass."

"Yep, we sure did, and Hayes knows it too," Zach muttered, picking up his wineglass and taking a long drink.

"Probably better than anyone else," Gavin guessed, and Zach nodded.

Their salads arrived then, and they were quiet for a long minute, eating.

"I thought I might end up like him," Zach said out of nowhere, while they were waiting for their main dishes.

"Like Hayes?"

Zach nodded. "In love and no chance of it ever being returned." He flushed then, like he'd just realized what he'd said. "Shit, I didn't mean—"

But it wasn't surprising. Gavin knew what it was like when you were with someone when love and desire were intertwined, and nothing about this thing with Zach felt casual. He didn't think he ever could have *done* casual. Could he say it back yet? Gavin didn't know, but he could at least reassure Zach.

"It's okay." Gavin reached across the table and took Zach's hand, squeezing it. "I care about you, too. A whole lot. I'd never have done this otherwise."

Zach's embarrassment finally seemed to fade. "Yeah?"

"This isn't just some flash in the pan thing for me. I've only ever wanted to be with two people, and you're one of them, Zach," Gavin said quietly.

In fact, the last thing Zach looked now was embarrassed. His flush seemed to be more of the "incredibly turned on" variety. Gavin was a fan.

"I feel like I've wanted you most of my life," Zach agreed, squeezing his hand back. "This is like a dream come true."

And it wasn't a lie, not even stretching the truth for Gavin to say back, "For me, too."

They did manage to finish dinner—only because Gavin teased Zach about needing to eat his protein so he'd have enough energy for later—and Zach even bypassed the dark chocolate mousse on the menu, giving Gavin a long speculative look as he told the waiter they had dessert waiting for them at home.

"So you've got something decadent and delicious back at your apartment for me to eat for dessert, huh?" Gavin asked as they walked out into the night air. It was cold for January, and their shoulders brushed together as they turned down the sidewalk towards Zach's place.

"I think I can come up with something," Zach said, the look he shot Gavin both earnest and scorching.

Gavin's mouth went dry.

When he'd ever let himself consider what dating Zach would be like, he'd never imagined it would be like this. Easy and fun and intense and so hot it was a miracle Gavin's brain didn't just melt.

But it also wasn't much different than what they'd been doing before. Sure, the flirting was new—or not *new*, but neither of them were shying away when it got to be too much—and the sex was *definitely* new, but other than that, the dinner tonight could have been like a dozen others they'd shared in the last few months.

He told you, you just didn't want to listen.

"Hey," Gavin said, hesitantly. Zach liked it when he used his words. *He* liked it when he used his words. "I think . . .I think you might've been right."

Zach smirked. "You don't want to save that for later? Sounds like pretty hot pillow talk."

Gavin had no doubt that at some point in the evening, Zach would have him babbling out much dirtier things. And not only would Gavin not feel a hint of shame, they'd both probably enjoy it a little too much.

"No," Gavin said, "this isn't about sex." He flushed. Ironically he could dish it out in the bedroom, once they were both naked, but right now? Walking down a street where anyone could see them and hear them? Just the word made him hot under the collar. "It's about . . .well, the dating thing. I'm glad you told me the truth. I think it probably sucked to do it, but you were right. We were already dating. I just didn't know it yet. Or I didn't want to acknowledge it."

"Yeah it did suck," Zach agreed, his gaze warm on Gavin's face. "But it's okay, because you listened. Eventually."

"Eventually," Gavin muttered.

"Hey, before you say anything about yourself that you're gonna have to take back—don't," Zach said, nudging him with his shoulder.

Gavin kind of wished he could reach down and squeeze Zach's hand. But the publicness of the situation made it impossible, at least right now. At some point, they'd tell Sidney and, to a lesser extent, inform the team, and maybe he'd never be *out* out, but he wouldn't worry about holding Zach's hand.

"I just wanted to say . . .I'm glad we did this all those times before. All the breakfasts and lunches and dinners and film sessions. And glad we did it tonight, too."

"Felt different and also the same, yeah?"

Gavin nodded.

They reached Zach's apartment building and Zach motioned to the stairs, a knowing glint in his eyes as Gavin walked up them, Zach close behind.

"You're totally staring at my ass right now," Gavin said, cheeks flaming, wondering exactly what Zach was thinking. What he was *planning*.

"It's an ass worth staring at," Zach said frankly, no shame whatsoever.

Gavin liked him that way. It was why he trusted him to always get Gavin out of *his* head. To stop worrying and agonizing and just *enjoy*.

"Yours is pretty good too," Gavin murmured.

"Glad you like it." Zach sounded downright smug now. "Wanna see it a lot more?"

"*Yes*," Gavin said, and that was all he got out before Zach was unlocking the door and pushing them both inside, pressing Gavin up against it.

He didn't kiss him, which was disappointing. What wasn't disappointing was the way his thigh pushed hard between Gavin's, the full weight of him pinning him to the door. His stare, intent and incendiary, added even more weight.

"Just deciding what I want," Zach said absently, reaching up and popping one of the buttons on Gavin's shirt and then another, spreading it open and then stroking his collarbone once it was exposed.

"Me, I hope." Gavin's voice came out strangled, desperate.

Zach just chuckled. Way too composed for Gavin's liking. "That goes without saying."

"Good." Gavin swallowed hard.

He leaned in farther, but still didn't kiss him. Gavin knew he was thinking about it from the way his eyes kept flicking to his lips, and Gavin tilted his head up, asking without asking for it. But instead, Zach went for more buttons, flicking each one open slowly until his shirt was open to the waist. Zach spread it open and then tugged it out from his pants.

Gavin twitched as he continued to undress him with a casual deliberateness that was making his cock leak.

Zach didn't say it, but his dark eyes, not missing a thing, were easy to read. Gavin was going to get whatever Zach *chose* to give him, and he was going to like it.

Gavin wanted to tell him that he *did*, that he *would*. That he could be patient and good.

But then Zach dropped to his knees. At first Gavin was sure he was taking care of the rest of his pants and then his shoes and socks, and he *did*, but then he still didn't move as he just rocked back on his heels and stared at Gavin's naked body.

It shouldn't have been a turn-on for Zach to be fully clothed and for him to be the exact opposite. It should have made him feel vulnerable and weird, the awkwardness crawling over his bare skin, but he felt anything but. Gavin felt good. *Powerful*.

Then Zach leaned in, swaying so close to where Gavin's cock was hard. "Don't come," was all he said.

That was all the warning he got before Zach's mouth closed over him, hot and wet and perfect.

A groan rippled out of him, but Zach's firm grip on his thigh reminded him of what he'd demanded. The order that Gavin would do his best to follow.

It wasn't *easy*, because Zach was damn good at this, sucking him down like he was born to do it, cheeks hollowing out. It might've been a fraction less amazing if Gavin had been able to tear his eyes away from the vision of Zach doing this, but he couldn't. He looked too goddamn good, the visuals multiplying the pleasure cresting inside of him.

Zach's hand squeezed down tight, fingertips digging into his thigh muscle, and maybe the bite of pain was supposed to be a reminder, but it only cranked Gavin up more.

"Good?" Zach questioned, after he pulled off, tongue flicking out to lick the head of Gavin's cock.

"Fucking amazing," Gavin said, trying not to shudder at how easy it was to just *let go*.

"Wanna come?"

"Yes." That was a no-brainer.

"Are you gonna?" Zach challenged.

That was even simpler. "No."

"Good."

Then after one last leisurely suck, Zach rose and, framing Gavin's cheeks with his palms, kissed him hard and deep.

They kissed for long enough that Gavin almost forgot he was on a hair trigger, so close to coming he could nearly taste it.

It was effortless to just slide into the give and take of Zach's mouth against his. When they kissed like this, it felt different, like Zach didn't mind if Gavin was aggressive too, sliding his tongue against Zach's.

"God," Zach groaned out, leaning back a fraction, licking his lips and making Gavin want to chase him. He ground against

Gavin's bare thigh, his black pants slick against his skin, his cock a hard insistent weight. "Want you."

Gavin kissed him again, but before they could devolve into another makeout against the door, Zach was pulling him away, hand wrapped insistently around Gavin's wrist.

He tugged them into the bedroom, gently pushing Gavin down onto the bed. "Stay here," he said and took his sweet time stripping down.

Gavin barely remembered to blink, his arousal spiking again as he watched Zach get naked just as slowly as he'd done to Gavin.

Finally, they were equally naked. Gavin hoped Zach would come back. Kiss him some more. He'd told him not to come, but Gavin needed something, the desire an insistent hum under his skin.

But instead of crawling onto the bed, Zach detoured to the nightstand by the bed, Gavin watching as he pulled out lube and condoms. He swallowed hard.

"I want to ride you, watch as you just take it," Zach said. The look on his face was full of heat, but also tenderness. "Is that something you want?"

"Yes." Gavin's throat felt like a desert it was so dry, but there was no question in his mind. He *wanted* that.

"You're still not going to come," Zach said, "not until I say."

Gavin nodded.

Nonchalantly, like Gavin's blood pressure wasn't spiking at the whole concept, Zach dribbled lube on his fingers and after climbing onto the bed and making a spot for himself between Gavin's thighs, slipped his fingers behind him.

Gavin swore loudly. "That's so . . .that's so . . . God, you're so
. . ."

Zach grinned. "Yeah?"

"You're killing me here."

"But you love it," Zach said smugly, and yeah, Gavin was.
There was no denying it.

"Yeah," Gavin agreed in a rough voice.

"I don't know if we need the condoms, but it might be easier,
this first time," Zach said, his voice hitching as he continued to
do whatever he was to his ass.

Gavin wished he could see, but even more than that, Gavin
wished he could be the one doing it, even though he probably
wouldn't be very good at it.

"Okay." Gavin took a deep breath, then another. Trying to
calm down. If he said the things he was thinking out loud, he
was going to fucking lose it. But he wasn't going to stay silent,
either. "I want to see. I want to *do*."

Zach froze. "Yeah?" And suddenly he didn't sound quite so
calm and collected either.

"Come here," Gavin said. His voice barely even sounded like
his own.

Zach didn't argue. Just straddled Gavin, and Gavin wasted
no time slipping his fingers back to where Zach's were. Wet and
God, moving inside of him.

He was plenty wet, wet enough for Gavin to carefully slide
one along Zach's two.

"Fuck," Zach cried out. "God, yes, please."

It wasn't quite as good as seeing it—they would get to that,
Gavin would make sure of it—but this was unbearably hot

too. Feeling the soft heat of Zach, and his own fingers against Gavin's. Feeling as he opened up. It was almost *more* intense because he couldn't see it. Could only experience the visceral sensation of it.

"You're just so incredible like this," Gavin ground out. His cock twitched against his stomach, maybe as hard as he'd ever been when he was eighteen, and all because Zach—big, brawny Zach, with those wide shoulders and kind eyes—was falling apart in his lap.

"Feels so good," Zach panted. "But it could feel better. Put the condom on."

Gavin's fingers were trembling as he ripped the packet open. It had been forever since he'd worn one but muscle memory was a thing, and he got it on, gasping a little as he touched himself just to roll it down his length.

Zach repositioned himself, stroking Gavin's cock with his lube-wet fingers, which was a whole other brain-melting exercise in hotness. "Remember," he said, "don't come. Not yet."

Gavin promised himself that he wouldn't, but then Zach began to drop down, his heat scorching and undeniable as he slowly swallowed Gavin up.

"Oh my God," Gavin said, his eyes nearly rolling back in his head.

"Yeah, it's so good." Zach's voice was breathy and desperate, and it worked Gavin up even more.

"Can I . . ." Gavin gasped as Zach's gorgeous ass hit his thighs. "Can I touch you?"

Zach leaned in and caught Gavin's bottom lip, nibbled there. "You'd better," he murmured.

As Zach slowly began to move, Gavin wasted no time reaching behind, cupping Zach's ass in his hands, loving the play and flex of the muscles as he sped up. Then he reached in, feeling where Gavin was splitting Zach open, and if he'd thought he was enjoying this before, that sent it straight into another stratosphere of *holy shit, this is incredible.*

"You feel so good," Zach gasped out. "God, I'm going to come. It's too good. You're too—"

"Yes," Gavin demanded.

Who was in charge right now? He didn't know, but maybe it didn't matter. Unable to stay still one second longer, he thrust his hips up, and Zach groaned again.

"Yes, more," he begged.

They found a rhythm and then Gavin reached out, fingers brushing Zach's cock as they fucked.

"Shit, shit," Zach said. "Touch me please. I'm gonna—"

Gavin made what he hoped was an encouraging noise, and then the top of his head nearly exploded right off when Zach tightened around him, shooting between their chests.

Nearly, because he was barely hanging onto his self-control.

Gavin didn't think he'd ever needed to come so badly in his whole goddamn life.

Zach slumped onto his chest, smearing the mess between them, but Gavin didn't care. He was stretched thin, vibrating with need.

"Come on, baby," Zach murmured then, "take what you need. Come for me."

It only took two unsteady thrusts of his hips and he was exploding, everything going black and bright brilliant white around the edges.

He felt Zach get up, his cock sliding out of him, and a few moments later, he was back, grinning irrepressibly and wiping them both down with a wet washcloth.

"Good?" Zach asked, even though he had to know he'd just short-circuited Gavin's whole self. He tossed the cloth into the laundry basket and resettled back on the bed.

Gavin let out an unsteady breath. "Incredible," he said.

Zach beamed even brighter. "We're good together," he said, his voice low, intimate.

It was impossible to disagree with that statement when it was so profoundly accurate.

"You wanna hear you were right again?"

Zach chuckled. "I wouldn't be against it."

"You were right," Gavin said drowsily. "And you were right about us not talking—or even thinking—about hockey, tonight."

Zach's arm tightened around him, nudging him even closer. As good as the sex was, this was almost better. "There's always tomorrow for hockey," he said.

CHAPTER 16

Zach barely registered his phone going off, he was concentrating so hard on the video clip on his laptop from the team's last game—specifically the Evergreens' first power play unit. He didn't glance over until the second text came through, his phone beeping insistently.

The first was from Gavin. **Picking up a sub at Sammy's. You want your usual?**

Zach sent a thumbs-up.

The second was from Hayes. The Sentinels were on a long road trip west, playing the Kings, the Sharks and the Mavs—the team that he and Hayes had been on together.

Got a free minute finally, want to chat?

They hadn't been able to do much more than exchange texts since he and Gavin had gotten together over a week ago. This always happened deep in the season, when hockey took over Hayes' life—and now Zach's life.

Yeah. In my office. Call my laptop? Zach texted back.

A minute later, his laptop dinged, and then there was Hayes, looking exhausted with dark circles under his eyes and a droop to his mouth. But he smiled when he saw Zach.

"Zachy, good to see you, man."

"Ditto," Zach said, leaning back in his chair. "How's the road trip?"

"Hell," Hayes said, but he was still smiling. "You know how it is."

Zach nodded. He knew. It was one of the reasons he'd learned that the NHL was not for him. He'd found zero joy in the endless fucking grind.

"We're playing the Mavs tomorrow, and that's fun and also . . ." Hayes winced. "It kinda sucks."

Hayes had told him once, just once, that he'd imagined playing for them his whole career. Being drafted a Mav and then retiring a Mav.

It hadn't happened, and even if Hayes was happy as a Sentinel now, even as the Sentinels' captain, Zach had to imagine the trade still stung, somewhere deep.

"But enough about me," Hayes said. "How are your boys doing? I caught a game the other day."

"Yeah?"

"It was some absolutely shitty stream, but yeah. They look good. Solid defense."

Zach heard what Hayes wasn't saying. They'd scored two goals in three games, starting with the first after the holiday break. Even though they'd gotten three points—one win, one loss, and an OT loss—everyone on the team was tiptoeing super carefully around words like "problem" and "slump" and "losing streak."

"Finn looks great," Hayes continued. "I hate to say it—"

"No, you don't," Zach argued. Hayes would never lay the faults of the father on the son. It was why he'd never worried about the strong possibility that Hayes would end up as Finn's captain. He'd take care of Finn, even if Finn's dad had broken his heart.

Hayes sighed. "No, you're right. I don't hate to say it. It's great. He's great. Coming along really fucking well."

"He is," Zach agreed. "Now if Ell and Mal can get their shit together."

"They're taking good shots," Hayes said, "they're just not going in. It happens sometimes. Don't let them overthink it."

"Gavin wants to shuffle the lines," Zach said under his breath. If Gavin was walking over to Sammy's and grabbing them lunch, he'd be at least another twenty minutes before he showed up at Zach's office door, but he wasn't going to be stupid about this.

"Really?" Hayes looked surprised. "Didn't you tell me that those two are basically inseparable these days?"

Zach nodded. "And they're *always* better together than they are apart."

"He needs to just let them ride it out," Hayes said.

It was what Zach kept saying, but he had a feeling Gavin didn't want to wait and see. Wanted to *do* something. Sometimes the toughest part of coaching was just doing nothing.

"I know," Zach said.

"It's not creating a problem between you, is it?" Hayes wondered.

Not yet it wasn't. They talked about it, round and round, Gavin hardly sounding convinced either way, and then Zach would kiss him, and they'd melt into each other all over again.

"No," Zach said.

"But you're worried," Hayes said astutely.

"We're in a weird spot. I'm his assistant coach. I'm here to support him. Support his decisions."

"Even when they're stupid ass decisions?" Hayes chuckled darkly. "And no, you're not just there for that, Zachy. You're there to be a sounding board, to pull his head out of his ass when he shoves it in too deep. Not just to automatically agree with every choice he makes."

And Zach did know that, but he'd also never imagined that he and Gavin would ever seriously disagree about how to handle something.

Not that they had. *Yet.*

"It wouldn't be such a problem if the second power play team or some of the other lines could create some decent offense," Zach grumbled.

"They'll get there. They're young," Hayes said optimistically. "Remember what we were like when we were that age."

"Stupid," Zach said, and Hayes laughed.

"Not sure we ever grew out of that," Hayes said. But he sounded lighter and Zach *felt* lighter.

"Fair," Zach agreed, chuckling now too.

"But it's going good, you and your coach?" Hayes said. "I can see you're in your office so I won't make you give me a play by play."

"Oh, just 'cause I'm in my office, huh?" His door *was* closed, but he wasn't going to tell Hayes he wouldn't have done it regardless. Hayes already knew it. Sharing details of meaningless hookups was one thing, but it was another to tell each other when it mattered. Zach had never gotten more than a few tight-lipped sentences out of Hayes about Morgan Reynolds and he was *fine* with that.

Hayes flushed. "Hey if one of us is having sex, I feel like it's a responsibility to share. Some of us are going through the dry spell of a century."

Zach shot his best friend a look. "You know that's *your* choice, Monty. You're hot. You're rich and famous. You're single. You could walk into any bar in the LA area and get as much dick as you wanted."

"Thanks," Hayes said dryly. "I'm going to say that the next time a reporter asks me what specifically I'm doing to win games. *Being hot. Being rich and famous. Getting as much dick as I want.*"

Zach laughed. "You might've five years ago."

Five years ago, they really had been young and stupid, practically rookies, barely over twenty-one, buzzing at just the thought they were playing in the NHL.

But the trade had settled Hayes' outrageous streak, and then the A and then the C the Sentinels had bestowed on him had seemingly eradicated it completely.

"Five years ago," Hayes said, rolling his eyes. "That feels like a fucking lifetime ago."

"I'm serious though," Zach said, "you have to get back out there."

Hayes looked suddenly suspicious. "Is this your second attempt at an intervention?"

"No, it's my attempt at giving a shit about you," Zach said firmly.

"I don't think you have much room to talk. You got the guy after what, only six months of pining?" Hayes waved a hand. "That's fucking nothing."

He didn't sound angry or bitter or even jealous.

"Monty," Zach said quietly.

"I'm just going to be single forever," Hayes said. Which was stupid because Zach was right—he was a *catch* and wasting his whole life pining away after Morgan fucking Reynolds was practically criminal.

"Don't do that to either of us."

"The least you can do is tell me if it was worth the wait," Hayes said, ignoring Zach's reproving comment.

"I already told you that." Via text, several times.

Hayes huffed in frustration. "Seriously that's all I'm getting?"

"It's . . . it's not what I expected, in a good way. In a *great* way." Zach wasn't going to go into any more detail than that. But it was safe to say that the power dynamic between them cranked him up more than he'd ever dreamed it would.

"No more widower freakouts?" Hayes asked it lightly but it was impossible to miss the worry in his gaze.

"He seems to be . . . all-in, I guess? We've even been on a few dates. He keeps saying he's going to tell our boss. With things being the way they are with the team, we haven't discussed telling them yet, but I think that's only a matter of time."

"Good, I hoped he'd treat you right 'cause I really didn't want to come all the way there just to kick his ass," Hayes said.

Zach rolled his eyes. "Like you could."

"Hey, I've been in like . . .what . . .three fights?"

"Yes, three fights in seven-plus years in the NHL. You're practically a goon, Monty."

"I think one of those was actually an accident." Hayes grinned goofily then, suddenly looking years younger. Zach wanted to reach through the screen and hug him.

Convince him, any way he could, that his life hadn't ended. That he wasn't just playing hockey games and marking time.

But what else could he say that he hadn't said already? Hayes had to decide for himself that he was done waiting.

"Well, you can come here, and 'accidentally' stumble across G if he ever fucks up," Zach said.

"Good, I'm gonna." Hayes hummed in approval.

For a second, they were both quiet. Sometimes when they'd played together, when the noise of the NHL got too intense, they'd hide together in dark arena corners, in their hotel room, and just sit in silence. Soaking up the comfort of each other's presence.

They were a long way from being those rookies, but Zach discovered it worked the same way.

But before the quiet could drag on too long, there was a soft knock on his door.

"Oh, I think Gavin's here with lunch," Zach said, suddenly feeling awkward. Should he keep Hayes on the line? Should he say he had to go?

"Oh, good, I can give him the shovel talk now, then," Hayes joked.

Zach flushed. "Monty," he warned.

"I'll be nice."

"Accidentally or on purpose?"

Hayes laughed out loud as Zach called out, "Come in."

Gavin stuck his head in. "Hey," he said, "I thought I heard you talking to someone."

"Come 'ere," Zach said, waving him in. "I'm just talking to Hayes."

"Oh, I don't want to—"

Zach grinned and gestured at him again. "Come over. Say hi."

Hayes looked very smug on the screen, arms folded across his chest. "Hey, Coach," he said as Gavin rounded the desk, coming into view.

"Good to see you," Gavin said, depositing the bag of sandwiches on the desk next to Zach's laptop. "You two catching up?"

"Yeah, Monty's on a shitty road trip," Zach said.

"Like an eight fucking day road trip," Hayes complained.

"Sucks," Gavin said.

"Yeah, I'm pretty worn out but . . ." Hayes' lips curled into a grin. "Not too worn out to make a detour up to Portland if I need to."

"Ugh, Monty," Zach groaned.

But Gavin just smiled. "I get it. If I was on the other side, I'd absolutely come kick my ass if I screwed up again."

Hayes nodded firmly. "Glad you understand the score, Coach."

"I'm not going to screw up again, though," Gavin said earnestly. "Not if I can help it."

"Hmmm." Hayes didn't sound won over yet, though. "Guess that means if you 'accidentally' screw up then I can 'accidentally' kick your ass?"

Gavin laughed, for real then. "Sure. Why not."

"Monty thinks he's a real goon, now. With his whole three NHL fights," Zach joked.

"And how many did *you* have?" Gavin asked, looking delighted. Zach was probably gazing at him like he was wildly, crazily in love.

Which he was. No question.

"More than three," Zach said wryly. He'd gotten into more than his share. Usually because some opposing player was shitty to Hayes and he wasn't going to stand back and let any of that crap go.

"But you're built for that, baby," Gavin teased, patting his bicep.

Zach flushed.

Hayes made an obnoxious cooing noise in the back of his throat. "You two are adorable. I'm happy for you, really. Now go have your lunch date, I've got lunch too. Not a date, so I'll try not to cry into my turkey club."

After Hayes had hung up, and Zach was opening the Sammy's bag, spreading out the paper-wrapped sandwiches on the desk, Gavin asked, "He didn't really mean that, did he?"

"About crying into his turkey club?" Zach asked, reaching into the mini fridge behind his desk and grabbing a can of Diet

Coke for Gavin—that he'd started stocking just for him—and a bottle of water for himself.

"Yeah," Gavin said. "Is he okay? He looked exhausted."

"Dregs of the season. You know how it is." But Zach couldn't say he wasn't worried. That he wasn't *always* worried, in some way, about Hayes.

"Yeah, still. He's . . .it's not going to make him feel worse, to hear about us together?" Gavin asked, as he picked up half of his ham and cheddar sandwich.

"He's happy for us," Zach said. He wondered if that ecstatic thrill that they were an *us* would ever stop cascading through him.

Gavin cracked his Diet Coke open. "I didn't think he wasn't."

"I just wish he'd decide it's time to move on," Zach confessed. "Morgan isn't going to miraculously become not an asshole."

"I don't know, he's trying pretty hard with Finn these days to keep that shit at least under wraps," Gavin pointed out. "I wouldn't have believed it, but I've *seen* it. Even watched him getting along with Braun, like they might actually be friends. I'm just saying crazier things have happened."

"Don't tell Hayes that," Zach said morosely.

"I wouldn't," Gavin said, expression earnest. "I can't say he and I get along all that great, but maybe I should—"

"Oh my God, G, *no*," Zach said and suddenly he was laughing. Not because it would be funny, but because of how catastrophic the dumpster fire would be. "*Nobody* knows. Just them and us. Can you imagine how much he'd freak out if you knew he'd fucked Hayes Montgomery five years ago."

"Might get him out of his head, to scare him like that," Gavin muttered.

Zach grinned. "You're so evil. I love it."

"Yeah?"

"God, I love *you*," Zach said, and he realized what he'd said only after Gavin's eyes went wide. And surely it couldn't have been that much of a surprise? He'd said it before, during their dinner date. He hadn't intended to say it again, but it had just popped out of Zach's mouth because it was such a part of him now, had been practically since the day he'd shown up here in Portland, that it almost didn't even make sense to *not* say it, though he had been trying to keep those three words under wraps not to freak Gavin out.

"Oh, um, yes," Gavin said awkwardly.

Here was the thing: it was almost impossible to be mad that Gavin didn't say it back right now, because of Gavin's history, and how long and hard he'd resisted dating again.

He wouldn't love again easily. But he *would*. Zach believed that with every fiber of his being.

After all, G had said it best himself; he'd dated two people ever. His wife, and Zach.

"Sorry if you . . .uh . . .didn't want to hear that again," Zach said, trying for chill and ending up somewhere else.

Gavin cleared his throat and set his sandwich down. "Not at all, Zach. I just . . ."

"I get it," Zach said, putting a hand on Gavin's arm and squeezing. "I really get it."

Gavin didn't say anything.

"I can be patient. I just wasn't before, because you clearly wanted this as much as I did, and you kept pretending you didn't. That was frustrating, and I couldn't do it forever. But waiting for you to get comfortable, while I *have* you? In my bed and next to me while we eat lunch and across from me at the dinner table? That's a no-brainer. I'm there and I'm *happy* to be, as long as you need me."

Gavin swallowed hard. "You mean that."

"I said it, before. I can say it again. That's why I don't mind being patient. Waiting until you're ready."

"I . . ." Gavin winced. "Is it selfish to ask you to do that?"

"Is it selfish to expect you need more than ten days of time after we get together to love me?" Zach laughed and shook his head.

Gavin cracked a smile then, too, and something deep that had tensed inside Zach relaxed again.

"Maybe not to *actually* feel it," Gavin said softly. "Maybe to accept it. To say it."

They hadn't done this at the rink, but Zach couldn't help it. He leaned in and kissed Gavin briefly, tasting the honey mustard from his sandwich.

"Well . . .uh," Gavin said eloquently when he pulled back. "Should we talk about the power play?"

Zach laughed. "Do you really want to?"

Gavin made a face. "I really don't *want* to, but I think we've got to."

"You know how I feel about it," Zach said. He hadn't made a secret of his opinion, and maybe Monty was right, it wasn't his responsibility to merely parrot back Gavin's opinions, but to challenge them.

Gavin had never struck him as someone who wanted a yes-man around him.

"I want to move Mal to the second unit," Gavin said.

"Don't do it," Zach said. "Putting a good winger on that unit isn't going to make any fucking difference, and it's going to piss them all off."

Gavin looked like he wanted to argue. He just picked at his sandwich, instead. "We need to do something. I knew it was a problem when the first line was scoring, but now that they're not, it's blatant there's a gap in our game."

"It's just a slump," Zach said. He'd been avoiding saying that word, but it was impossible not to call a spade a spade right now. Not when G was right, and it was staring them in the face. Continuing to deny it only made it harder to deal with.

"I know, but how do we *fix* it?" Gavin asked in a frustrated voice as he ran a hand through his hair.

"I don't think you can, G," Zach said gently. "They gotta sort themselves out. They're taking the shots. They've got good puck movement, good angles. At some point one's just gonna go in."

"Hopefully more than one," Gavin grumbled.

"Okay, more than one," Zach promised.

"You really don't think I should move Mal to the second power play?"

"If you want Elliott to freak out, sure," Zach said. "And then Elliott's not focused on scoring, he's focused on how Malcolm's not on the ice with him."

Gavin's lips pursed. "He's very possibly going to have to get used to that, anyway."

"He knows it, or at least he acknowledges it in the back of his mind. Does he think about it? I doubt it, and you know what? He shouldn't be thinking about it. He should be focused on *this year*."

"I'm just saying," Gavin said. "He can't always be good only when Malcolm's playing on his line."

"That's a conversation for whoever drafts him," Zach said bluntly. He wasn't trying to be cold about it, but that was the truth. And if things shook out the way they were looking, it was very possible Elliott would end up back with Mal, and other than yearly trade rumors, they'd never have to worry about it.

Gavin sighed. "I still think we should try it. At least for the power play in the next game."

"If you're gonna do it, you've got to do it now, so we can spend the next few days working on the new configuration during practice," Zach warned.

"Not a few days so Elliott can get his drama queen act out of the way?" The corner of Gavin's mouth quirked up. "I suppose you think I should be the one to tell Mal."

Zach nearly said, *it's your team and your idea, so yeah, I'm gonna let you take this one.*

But the more he thought about it, the more he knew it should be him.

"Actually no. I'll do it."

Gavin looked shocked. "Really?"

"I'm in charge of special teams," Zach said.

"But it's—"

"Yeah, it *is* your idea, and I fully expect you to concede it was a bad idea when it doesn't help," Zach said.

"You're angry with me," Gavin said, a crease forming between his dark brows.

"No. No. Not like . . ." Zach huffed. "Not like you think. Do I think you're wrong? Yeah. But I want you to know I'd be saying this regardless of what's going on between us. It's not . . . it's not personal. I'm not angry with *you*, G. Obviously I'm frustrated too, with our lack of scoring depth. I want to fix it, too."

"Okay." Gavin nudged him with his foot. "As long as you're not gonna punish me." He flushed bright red then, and oh yeah, he could be into that.

Zach might be into that.

"I mean, not like *that*," Zach teased. He heard how low and rough his voice sounded. "Definitely not the 'banishing you from my bed' kind of punishment, anyway."

Gavin went even redder, all the way to his collar. If Zach pushed it aside, he thought that flush might go all the way down.

"As long as it's not a doghouse kind of thing," Gavin said.

"Would that change your mind?" Zach wondered.

Gavin chuckled. "No? Probably not?"

"You don't sound too sure about that." Zach shouldn't be delighted about this—they were supposed to be professionals, supposed to be keeping their personal relationship away from the rink—but it was hard not to be. Not when he was so wildly in love it was difficult for him to keep his feelings partitioned away from the work they did here.

"Let's not test it," Gavin said, ducking his head, but not enough for Zach to miss his fond smile.

"Sure thing, boss," Zach joked, enjoying the way the color on Gavin's cheeks deepened again.

Zach texted Mal to meet him at Koffee Klatch before practice and to bring Elliott.

Funny, Mal texted back, **I don't think I could've kept him away.**

And that was true. In the last few months, Mal and Elliott had become like a matched set, rarely seen without each other.

Zach pushed down a spike of guilt that he should've done more to convince Gavin this wasn't a good idea.

Maybe it *was* a good idea. Maybe shaking up things would help break everyone out of this weird scoring malaise they'd been in since the beginning of the year.

He was at the coffee shop five minutes early, but Mal was already sitting there, Elliott at the counter, chatting with someone by the espresso machine.

"Hey," Mal said, as Zach slid into a chair opposite him. "What's up?"

He looked a little apprehensive, but then this was Malcolm, and *a little apprehensive* was pretty par for the course for him.

"I just wanted to give you a heads-up about something Coach is changing," Zach said gently.

Mal sighed heavily. "We're *trying*, I swear to God, and if you'd let us, we'd be at the rink—"

"No," Zach interrupted him. "I get that you're trying, and Coach gets that you are. But sometimes things need to be shook up."

"Shook up how?"

Zach looked up and Elliott was standing there, a frown on his face and an enormous iced coffee in his hand.

"You're not drinking that," Mal said bluntly to Elliott. "You're gonna be hyper for fucking forever if you do."

"I need a pick-me-up before practice," Elliott said blithely, sitting down, kitty corner to Mal and tucking his legs under Mal's chair.

Zach didn't look but he was pretty sure Elliott had hooked his ankle around Mal's.

"Uh, well, shook up like . . ." Zach hesitated again.

"You're moving me back down to the second line." Elliott said it bluntly, flatly.

"Actually, no," Zach said.

"I told you." Mal elbowed Elliott gently. "You're too good. Coach B would never do that to you."

"We *are* moving Mal to the second power play team," Zach said, finally getting it out.

Elliott digested this information, not looking particularly put out, but not pleased either. "Permanently or temporarily?"

"Temporarily, of course," Zach said hurriedly. "And I want to make it clear, of course I support this decision, because Coach B is my coach too, but I don't necessarily think it's the right call. You two play the best hockey when you're together."

"We know," Elliott said smugly.

"Yeah, if you know, how come we're not then?" Malcolm complained, shooting Elliott a look that Zach couldn't quite interpret. There was affection, sure, and the kind of bone-deep certainty you felt when you knew you loved and were loved in return, but it was also tinged with frustration and something else.

Resignation?

"It's just for the power play, Mal," Elliott said, reassuring him.

Mal made a face.

Zach wasn't sure he'd expected this.

"We moved you specifically, Mal, because we think the second power play team needs some additional leadership."

"Yeah, 'cause Ethan can't lead his way out of a paper bag," Elliott groused.

Zach wanted to disagree with that assessment, but if it wasn't true, they wouldn't be moving Mal.

"It's 'cause I'm playing like shit, right?" Mal said heavily.

"Actually you're not at all. We're just . . ." Zach cleared his throat. "Trying to spread some of the wealth around. Hope it sparks some goals for everyone."

"Right," Mal said morosely.

"You're not moving him off my line, are you?" Elliott demanded.

"No, no, of course not." Zach would absolutely go to bat for that, if Gavin ever seriously suggested it.

"You'd better not," Elliott said.

That was more in line with what Zach had expected from this conversation—Elliott alternately sulking and making demands.

Not Mal looking like someone had just kicked his puppy.

He'd actually expected Malcolm to understand.

"It's not meant to be a punishment," Zach said as gently as he thought Mal could stomach, laying a hand on his arm.

"Right," Mal said. "Hey—I gotta—I gotta go."

He was up in a flash, and out the door before Zach could even hope to stop him.

Elliott's stare grew heavier.

"You're not going after him?" Zach asked.

"I know where he's going, and I'll catch up with him," Elliott said. "You really aren't punishing him?"

Zach choke-laughed. "No. *No.* God, we're just trying to bring some steady leadership to the second team."

"Move me instead," Elliott demanded then, and there it was, the demand that Zach had expected. Though not *what* he'd expected. He'd fully anticipated that Elliott would throw a fit and demand they not do it at all. Not that they move him instead of Malcolm.

"But—" Zach wasn't sure how to say, with any kind of tact, that Elliott was definitely not the steadying force that Mal was, but he never even got a chance because Elliott interrupted him first.

"I can be that same presence that you want Mal to be," Elliott insisted stubbornly.

Zach probably looked faintly dubious at this assertion before he blanked his reaction, because Elliott's jaw jutted out even farther.

"I *can*," he said. "Maybe I'm not scoring, but I *will*. I know I will, I just need . . ."

"Yeah, you will," Zach reassured. "Of course you will."

"Just move me, okay? Not him."

"You'd be okay moving to the second power play team?" To some extent, every guy on the team had some kind of ego; Elliott's was healthier than most, and almost entirely deserved. He couldn't imagine a situation where Elliott would *choose* to move.

"Yeah," Elliott said, without hesitation. "If it was me or him, yeah."

Zach sighed. "Ell, it's got to be Malcolm."

"Seriously?" Elliott made a face, and Zach nodded.

"It's just, he takes these things so personally. He wouldn't want anyone to know, but you're Zachy, so maybe it's okay. But he's sensitive, you know? He wants so badly to be good, to live up to his expectations. Not even everyone else's, but his own."

Zach understood, maybe better than Elliott imagined he did.

"I get it, I felt that way too, once," Zach murmured.

But that didn't stop Elliott. "Even if you didn't mean it that way, to make it a punishment or make him feel lesser, he's gonna, and I just . . ." Elliott's lips clamped together. "I would take that for him, if I could."

Zach understood that, too. He'd never minded carrying some of Gavin's burdens, had even invited it more than once. Tried to deal with crap and keep it off Gavin's plate, so he wouldn't be bothered.

"I really do get it," Zach said. "But this is the way it's gonna have to go."

Elliott shrugged. "I had to try."

He'd known, of course, that Elliott and Mal had some serious feelings for each other—it was difficult to miss these days, honestly—but he'd not expected to come face to face with the pure selflessness of their love today.

"You love him," Zach said.

Elliott gave a single nod. "Yeah, I do."

"Then help me remind him that he's a great fucking hockey player, okay?"

"How are you gonna do that?" Elliott wanted to know.

"By giving him a task to accomplish."

Elliott groaned. "You're gonna challenge him to get the second power play in line."

"Yep."

"You're gonna create a monster. Even *more* of a monster," Elliott warned him.

"Yeah. Well, you're gonna have your hands full, too. Conrad is moving to your team."

"Fuck. Well, it could've been worse," Elliott said with resignation.

CHAPTER 17

It was their second practice after Gavin had decided to shake things up, and he wished he could tell himself it was working.

Be patient.

He knew chemistry took time to build, but so far, Malcolm was just bullying his players into submission, until they were afraid to even shoot the fucking puck. As for the first team, Elliott had turned into a mini Malcolm, riding Conrad until he just reflexively sent the puck in Elliott's direction, even if he wasn't particularly open.

"You just missed Ivan, who was *right there*," Zach barked out across the ice. Not sounding particularly patient.

Maybe it had been unfair of Gavin to give him this burden, when he hadn't even wanted to do this in the first place.

Part of him wanted to head over to where Zach was standing, just inside the blue line, as he tried to reason with the five players on the ice, and tell him to forget this whole fucking thing.

There had to be easier ways to get out of this slump.

But you did this, you have to see it through.

Ramsey skated his direction, as Zach argued with Elliott and Conrad.

"What do you think, Coach?" he asked, picking up his water bottle.

Gavin rolled his eyes. "You can see it as well as I can. It's a clusterfuck."

Ramsey just shrugged though, like he *hadn't* noticed it. That was ridiculous because Ramsey noticed everything.

"Giving Mal a job to do with them was a good idea. But the problem is that none of those kids have Ell's backbone, so instead of rising to the occasion, they're just folding."

Gavin pursed his lips.

"And," Ramsey continued, "Elliott's not a bad leader, but it doesn't come naturally to him. Not yet, anyway. So instead of figuring out how to make Conrad listen to him, he's pushing him too hard."

"I saw," Gavin admitted.

"Not too late to fix this," Ramsey said casually.

"We've spent two days trying this out," Gavin said. "It's worth running for one game. Maybe it'll go better than we think."

Ramsey raised an eyebrow and shot him a dubious look before skating over to rejoin the group.

They ran the play again, and this time it did go better, Elliott skating circles around one of their younger, more inexperienced defenseman, threading the puck between skates, and once he was deep in the zone, passing it to Ivan, who passed it reflexively right back to Elliott and he shot it, top shelf, just clearing the other goalie, Nick's, glove.

Elliott cheered and even went out of his way to celebrate with Conrad but Gavin wasn't stupid. Conrad had been there, by the net, as a precautionary measure in case they needed the rebound, but he hadn't really been involved in the play. That had been all Elliott, because he was so goddamn good.

"Well, that was better," Zach said, skating back over to where Gavin was leaning against the wall.

"You don't need to placate me," Gavin ground out.

"I'm not," Zach insisted. "It *was* better."

"Only because that was classic Elliott-Ivan," Gavin grumbled.

"Hey, Conrad did what he was supposed to do, and that's all that matters. He could've gotten in the lane, drifted right where Ell was gonna shoot it, and then what would we have done?"

Gavin shrugged, because there was no good answer to that. And also because Conrad *had* ended up in Elliott's shooting lane at least twice—and that was just during today's practice.

"You're grumpy," Zach pointed out, sounded half-amused and half-concerned.

"I'm just worried," Gavin said. "You're right—this might not fix anything."

"And maybe it's just the shakeup they all needed to re-focus and figure out how to bring their A game," Zach said.

"You don't really believe that," Gavin retorted.

"Actually . . .I'm not sure anymore. They're all working harder. Maybe you were right, they got a little complacent because everything was going so well and we were so good."

"We *are* so good," Gavin reminded Zach—and himself.

But as practice drew to a close, Gavin was still thinking about it. How good this team was, and how it had the potential to be extraordinary.

How he never wanted to be the reason that they never reached their real potential.

After Zach came off the ice, he nudged him and said, "I'm gonna go to the gym. See you later?"

Zach nodded. "I've got a study session but I'll head over after?"

"Sure."

Gavin wasn't sure they'd spent a night apart since getting together almost two weeks ago, and he wasn't sure he wanted to start now. Especially not when he was already so uneasy about all the crap surrounding his team.

Some moments, some *days*, Zach felt like the only steadiness Gavin possessed.

You know other things, too. Lots of other things.

He reminded himself of that, over and over, in the gym. Lifting until his arms burned and running hard on the treadmill until sweat stung his eyes.

After showering, he headed home, heating up leftovers and eating them on the couch as the Sentinels and Mavs played.

Hayes was already two goals in, skating like a man possessed against his former team, but Gavin was only half-heartedly watching as he sorted through his email and tried to pretend like he wasn't already eager and waiting for Zach to show up. To kiss him. To put his arms around him. To reassure him. And then to do more . . .

It wasn't that late, but with arousal already beginning to simmer in his veins, Gavin took himself to bed—not to *do* anything; he couldn't actually imagine not waiting for Zach, now that he was allowed to touch him and be touched in return—but because he thought maybe if he did, the waiting wouldn't feel so interminable.

He'd read the same page of his book, some bullshit crap about leadership that Sidney had recommended, when Gavin finally heard the front door open and close.

He'd texted Zach his front door code a few days ago, but this was the first time he'd actually used it, and his heart began to race as he heard the noises of Zach closing the door, shucking his shoes, dropping his bag down on the couch, and then heading in towards the bedroom.

When Zach finally appeared in the doorway, his face was half-shadowed, the only light coming from the lamp next to the bed.

"Hey," Zach said, grinning. "Hoped I'd find you here."

"You happy to be right?"

"Yeah." Zach's gaze dipped from Gavin's face down his bare chest to where the blankets were barely rucked up around his hips, exposing a strip of his boxer briefs. "I used to imagine you lying here like this when we talked on the phone."

Gavin swallowed hard. Remembering all the times he'd done exactly that—and even more, the moment he'd hung up, touching himself, and wishing there'd been some way, *any way*, it could be Zach's hands instead of his own.

"It happened pretty often," Gavin admitted, and Zach groaned in the back of his throat, soft and earnest.

"You're killing me, here," he said. But he sounded like he'd willingly go to the grave.

"Then I guess I shouldn't tell you what else I used to do," Gavin teased.

Zach froze in the middle of taking off his sweatshirt.

"Are you fucking kidding me?" Zach demanded, after he regained movement again, his T-shirt following the sweatshirt. Gavin almost joked that *yeah*, his clothes did absolutely belong on Gavin's floor, but heat blasted through him at the thought, because they sure fucking did.

Zach's breath was coming out in shallow pants, his chest rising and falling.

"I'm not kidding," Gavin said. He swallowed hard, meeting Zach's intense gaze.

After shucking his jeans, Gavin fully expected Zach to crawl up on the bed, to blanket his very willing body with his own. But even though Zach put a knee on the bed, absently cupping where he was clearly hard in his briefs, he didn't move up farther.

Instead, Zach waved at him, casually, like his eyes weren't blown dark and hungry like he could eat Gavin alive. "Well, then," he said, "what are you waiting for?"

"What am I—" Gavin broke off. "You don't want me to—"

"Oh, I do," Zach said smugly.

"I'm not touching myself in front of you," Gavin hissed, suddenly flushed with embarrassment *and* unexpected arousal.

"You're not, huh?" Zach grinned. "I bet I could convince you to do it."

"No way," Gavin scoffed. He wasn't going to take that bet. Maybe he was soft for Zach—eager, really—hungry, like he'd been starving for years and years. Zach had to know that, but he wouldn't use it against him.

Would he?

The look on Zach's face said he absolutely would, without a single qualm.

Especially when he palmed his cock, with more purpose this time.

Like all it was going to take for Gavin to break was Zach touching himself.

It was crazy hot, lighting Gavin up inside, but he had self-control and *dignity*.

Sort of, anyway.

Part of what he liked about sex with Zach was that dignity usually ended up being the last thing on his mind. There was too much Zach in it, a litany of pleasing him and Zach pleasing him back, there was just no room for it.

Zach reached up with his other hand, tucking his fingers into his mouth and licking them. Making a showy mess of it, honestly, and Gavin could feel his heartbeat in his fucking ears.

"You still good?" Zach asked innocently, then practically deep-throated three of his fingers. Thrusting them once, then twice, until they were soaking wet. Then he shoved his briefs down without a single hesitation, groaning as he fisted his cock.

"No," Gavin squeaked out. His cock was aching and hard, twitching against the cotton of his underwear. He'd never wanted to touch himself so badly in his whole life.

"No?"

"I want you to . . ." Gavin trailed off.

"Use your words," Zach said bluntly when he couldn't finish the sentence.

"I want you to touch me."

"And *I* want you to show me what you looked like. I know what I imagined, but I want to see the reality." Zach's expression softened. "You don't have to be embarrassed."

"It's embarrassing, though," Gavin said.

"Is it though?"

Gavin groaned again. Trying not to watch as Zach's hand circled around the base of his cock and squeezed.

"Just let me suck your cock," Gavin said. Like demanding Zach's cock in his mouth was somehow less embarrassing than just putting a hand on himself.

Zach didn't have to even point it out. He just raised an eyebrow, like he knew it and wasn't even going to bother saying it.

"Fine, *fine*," Gavin said, horribly flustered. "I'll . . ." He shoved his boxer briefs down his thighs before he could chicken out.

"Go on," Zach encouraged, smiling now, like he'd really gotten everything he wanted.

Gavin made a face as he gave his cock a tentative stroke. It was dry and hardly flashy but it lit him up with pleasure. Just because Zach was watching, his gaze practically a caress.

"Feel good?" Zach asked softly.

"Yeah, but could . . .uh . . .feel better," Gavin said.

"What did you think about, when you did this before?"

Gavin flushed again. "You, obviously."

"What about me?" Zach asked with a smug grin.

"Uh." He was already doing this, surely it couldn't get any more awkward, even if he told Zach the truth. "You're leaning over me. Kissing me. Touching me. Not letting me do anything but *take it*."

Zach hummed under his breath, and suddenly there he was, *finally* climbing over Gavin, lips meeting Gavin's and kissing him thoroughly.

The kiss spun out into long wet presses of their mouths until Gavin thought he might actually be losing his mind, and maybe he should've kept touching himself, because maybe he would've already come.

"Like you like this," Zach murmured against his lips. "Pliant. Horny. All mine."

Gavin had a vague idea that should embarrass him too, but he was too far gone to find that particular emotion anymore. Fuck dignity, anyway.

"I like it too," Gavin confessed, the words dredged up from deep inside him.

"Maybe you'll like this even more."

That was all the warning Gavin got before Zach was sliding down his body, mouth closing around his straining cock, all perfect wet heat.

Getting exactly what he'd wanted—what he'd dreamed about, lying here alone so many times—was overwhelming, in the best possible way.

Zach sucked him hard and deep, and Gavin choked, already right up to the edge, trying to hang on to prolong the pleasure.

"Don't come," Zach said, letting Gavin's cock slip out of his mouth. "Okay?"

"Okay." Gavin heard the strain in his voice.

That was not going to be easy but if Zach was asking him, it was for a good reason. He'd gone along with all of Zach's ideas so far, and Gavin didn't want to stop now.

"Get me the lube in the drawer," Zach said, and that was something that lived next to Gavin's bed now—lube and condoms. He'd flushed when a few nights ago Zach had deposited them matter-of-factly there.

They hadn't used them yet, and as Gavin scrabbled to open the drawer with uncooperative fingers, he wondered if that was about to change. He should be nervous, but there was no room for nerves, not when Zach was teasing the head of his cock with his tongue.

But Zach just took the lube and ignored Gavin handing him the condom.

"Don't need that," he said, and Gavin let it fall to the comforter, groaning as Zach took him deep again.

Squeezing his eyes shut, he tried to focus on the pleasure and yet not let it overtake him until he was back at that knife's edge of orgasm again.

Just feeling made it a little easier, because watching Zach *always* unwound him. He was so *Zach*. Hot and focused and intense. Like he was getting every single thing he'd ever wanted handed to him.

He was so busy *not* watching Zach he nearly jumped out of his skin when he felt the first touch against his hole.

"Fuck, are you—" Gavin bit off when he just swirled it around, not even pushing it in yet.

"Relax," Zach said.

"Are you gonna fuck me?" Gavin asked again. He was totally relaxed.

Zach chuckled, the noise vibrating around his cock. "I told you *relax*. I'm not going to do anything you don't want me to do."

This was Zach so it was entirely possible by the time he let Gavin come, he was going to be begging him to fuck Gavin. That every bit of nerves and anxiety would be gone, washed away in a flood of desperation and desire.

But he didn't. Only toyed, which was the best word Gavin could come up with, with his brain full of hot static. Zach's finger dipped in, but only the tip, a handful of times, as he continued to suck Gavin's cock.

Gavin realized he was babbling words, *pleading* for it, honestly, when Zach chuckled and said, "Want it now, huh?"

"*Yes,*" Gavin said with a sharp exhale.

Zach didn't respond with words, only slid his finger in, with slow intent, and Gavin let out a moan.

He'd wondered if he *would* want this. But it turned out it was the hottest thing in the universe, and he was being burned up from the inside out.

"Wanna," Gavin cried out as Zach finally slipped a second finger in alongside the first, hitting a spot inside him that made him see fucking stars.

"Not yet," Zach coaxed.

Gavin ground his teeth together and tried to hold on. It felt so fucking good. Zach had nearly given up actually giving him any suction on his cock, was just teasing up and down its length with his tongue as he finger-fucked him so expertly Gavin wanted to cry with how good it was.

"Please, please," he begged.

"Tell me one thing," Zach said, and he was breathing heavy too. Maybe making Gavin lose it was making *him* lose it, and somehow that wrenched everything inside him tighter and hotter.

"What?" Gavin gasped.

"Was this what you imagined when you lay here alone, getting yourself off?"

Was it?. He couldn't even *think* right now. "I…uh…I don't know."

"G," Zach reprimanded, twisting his fingers in more insistently, making Gavin groan.

"I couldn't have, because I didn't even know, I couldn't have even fucking *imagined*," Gavin said in a rush. "I didn't even know to want this."

"But I gave it to you," Zach said smugly.

Gavin could only nod helplessly.

Zach fit another finger inside him, Gavin biting his lip hard as he felt the stretch. He was so close to coming he didn't know how he hadn't yet.

"You close?" Zach murmured.

Gavin tried not to laugh. If he did, he probably *would* come. "*Yes*," Gavin said.

Zach's tongue did something absolutely devilish, and then he said, in a rush, "Then come."

Gavin only had a moment to register it before he was letting go, pulse after pulse shooting down Zach's throat.

It was the hardest orgasm he'd ever had—and that was before Zach twisted his fingers again and the pleasure kicked up again.

Gavin knew he should do something, *help* Zach get off, but he was a limp rag lying on the bed, as Zach crawled up again.

"Good?" Zach asked, and that smirk on his face was absolutely one-hundred-percent deserved.

"Yes," Gavin panted. "I should—"

"Open wide," Zach said and crawled up farther, legs bracketing Gavin's shoulders. A moment later, he was opening his mouth and Zach was gently pushing his hard cock against Gavin's outstretched tongue.

He'd just come his brains out, but something about this made another flash of heat pulse inside him.

"That's it, I'm so fucking close already. It's 'cause you're so hot. So perfect. So mine," Zach murmured.

He thrust once and then twice, Gavin trying his best to suck him, and then a second later, he was tensing and coming in Gavin's mouth.

He swallowed, and a moment later, Zach collapsed next to him.

Zach's finger tapped Gavin on the shoulder. "You good?" he asked breathlessly.

"Uh, *yeah*," Gavin said, still feeling a little out of it. "That was . . .wow."

"It was pretty good, wasn't it?" Zach still sounded smug, and Gavin still couldn't blame him.

"Insanely good." Gavin sighed happily as Zach curled into his arm. Zach might be bigger than him—taller and broader—but it didn't matter like this. He just wanted to touch him.

Zach didn't say anything for a long time, and Gavin listened as their exhales evened out and synced up, like they were one person, breathing for two bodies.

Gavin glanced over, then, and found Zach watching him. His expression happy and content, mirroring that same feeling blooming warm and undeniable inside Gavin's chest.

He'd thought when he reached this point that he would be afraid. Terrified, maybe, of feeling this way again and losing it. But all he felt was lucky. He'd felt this way once before, and now he'd gotten somehow blessed enough to feel it a second time. Gavin wasn't sure he was special enough for that, but maybe it wasn't about deserving it. Maybe it was more about *accepting* it.

Making sure that every day going forward, he never took it for granted.

Gavin wanted to believe that he'd never taken his wife for granted, but he knew he'd done it more than once. Gotten busy, gotten preoccupied with his job, with hockey, because he'd known she would be there whenever he managed to get free of the ice clogging his brain.

Their marriage hadn't been perfect, but it had been happy.

And now, he was happy again.

"You make me really happy," Gavin told Zach. "Happier than I ever thought I'd be again."

It was worth pushing that last little bit of guilt away to see Zach's face light up at his words. "Yeah? You make me really happy too."

"I was thinking . . .I want this to be serious."

Like it was mirroring his words, Zach's expression didn't dim exactly, but it took on a more thoughtful flavor. "I kinda already thought it was."

"It is. I just . . .I don't want to hide it. Hide you."

Zach barely blinked. "We just started dating."

"I said it before; you were right. We *didn't* just start dating. We just started taking advantage of all the benefits of dating," Gavin said. "And if you meant what you said about um . . .your feelings . . ."

"I did, obviously," Zach said. He pressed a kiss to Gavin's shoulder. "I love you."

"Then I want to tell Sidney about us. And maybe the team, too, if he's good with it."

"And if he's not?" Zach raised an eyebrow.

"He's going to be," Gavin said confidently. "And if he doesn't want us to tell the team, well fuck him."

Zach laughed. "Alright. Fuck him, then."

Gavin wondered if he should tell him the rest—that he was pretty sure he loved him, too, because that was the kind of emotion that made you *want* to take these big wild swings—but he wanted to give it a bit more time. He was sure, but he also wanted to do this right.

Besides, Zach had said he wasn't going anywhere, and Gavin believed him, as much as he'd believed anything, ever.

Zach couldn't say this game was going *badly,* but he also couldn't say it was going particularly well either.

Ivan had opened the scoring by hitting a sweet rebound shot around the net only a few minutes into the first period, and it had been impossible, even from the bench, not to feel the sheer relief radiating off Elliott and Malcolm that the line had scored.

They'd both gotten an assist on the goal, and the crowd had cheered extra loud as the announcer's voice had boomed across the ice, listing off their names.

"Let's go, baby," Elliott crowed as they settled back on the bench, smacking his gloved hand against Mal's knee.

Mal rolled his eyes but he looked a fraction more relaxed.

The real test came near the end of the first period, when the Evergreens went on the power play for the first time.

Mal nearly got up and then sat back down, the motion clearly automatic as Elliott and Ivan rose to join Brody and Ramsey on the ice.

Zach reached over, settling a hand on Mal's shoulder, squeezing him through his pads.

Mal didn't say anything but he didn't shake him off either.

It wasn't the worst power play Zach had ever witnessed, but it did lack the finesse that the first group usually relied on. Still, it would be hard for them to be *bad* out there, with a man advantage and the amount of talent the Evergreens were putting on the ice.

Gavin had told him before the game he was going to play it by feel, if he'd let the first team take the whole two minute shift.

They had about four good pushes towards the net. The last attempt was by far the best. Ivan set up the great way he always did, calm and steady, Brody and Ramsey on the back end of the zone, and Elliott grabbed the puck after a sweet little back pass and charged in.

In front of him, Zach felt Mal tense, and yell, "Shoot it, Ell," and then he did, sliding around to the far side of the goalie and flicking the puck right in.

Mal leapt to his feet with the rest of the guys on the bench, celebrating, and if Zach hadn't watched hundreds of hours of tape and practices and games, he might not have noticed that Mal wasn't quite as happy as he might've been.

Even when they'd been sniping at each other, fighting constantly before they'd gotten together, Zach had never seen Mal be less than thrilled whenever Elliott found the net.

Gavin pulled him aside as they walked to the locker room in the first intermission. "What did you think?" he asked.

Zach didn't roll his eyes. But he wanted to. "That doesn't mean anything," he said. "That was all Ell, and we all know it."

Gavin didn't say anything, just made a humming noise, shoving his hands into his pockets.

"Elliott might have done it even better if Mal was out there," Zach said.

"Sure," Gavin scoffed. "Better than that beauty of a goal."

"Don't tell him that, his ego's already inflated enough." Zach hesitated. "And don't say it in front of Malcolm either."

Gavin looked up at him, surprised. "Why not?"

"I told you, he feels that the root of this decision is you telling him he's not good enough."

"That's crazy," Gavin said. "He got moved to the second group so he could make them *better*. I told him that. Multiple times."

Zach nodded. He knew. He'd said it too.

But then he remembered the tenseness in Mal's shoulders. The way Elliott occasionally made offhand comments in the locker room about Mal's dad. He never said straight out that he was an unsupportive shithead, and clearly he wasn't as bad as Morgan Reynolds either, but there was a pain point there. Some old wound that had never really closed, and then he and Gavin had gone and started pressing on it.

"What do you want me to do?" Gavin said with a resigned sigh. "I'm not gonna switch things around in the middle of a game."

"Send them out first next power play."

Gavin looked at Zach like he was crazy.

"We're up two to zero, and we've got a really solid defense. It won't kill you to give Mal that."

"I don't want to take our foot off the gas," Gavin said under his breath.

"Then don't. Send them out there with the motivation to put the pedal to the metal. Mal's got plenty of fire. He feels like he's got something to prove, now."

Gavin looked like he was considering it. "I'll think about it," he said.

Zach nodded, knowing he couldn't push any harder. It was his responsibility to put the special teams together and plan their execution but Gavin's job to deploy them. He'd made his feelings clear enough and part of why he'd known Gavin would be perfect to coach this team was that he was willing to be unconventional at points.

They *were* up to two to zero, so Gavin only made a handful of comments in the locker room after they walked in. Zach went over and checked in with Finn, who seemed solid and totally locked-in.

Ramsey flagged him down. "How do you think it's going?" he asked, under his breath.

"Seems like we got some juice tonight," Zach said.

Ramsey nodded. "You gotta know—anyone could've been out there on that power play. That was all Elliott."

Oh, Zach knew it. Him knowing it wasn't the problem.

"I'm working on it," Zach said.

"Are you though?"

Zach shot him a look.

"Just saying. Mal's tense."

"I noticed." Zach wasn't blind.

"You think Coach's noticed?"

"I made sure of it."

"What about *your* tenseness?" Ramsey teased. "You two still circling each other?"

Zach supposed he shouldn't be surprised or disappointed that Ramsey had decided between the first and second period was a great time to bring up Zach's sex life.

"Are you serious?" Zach retorted.

But Ramsey just shrugged innocently, like his question was no big deal.

"Knowing you, I'd imagine you knew what happened before we even did," Zach muttered.

"Oh, I assumed," Ramsey said with wide eyes. "But thanks for confirming."

"You're a fucking menace," Zach said without heat.

Ramsey grinned then, like nothing made him happier than hearing that. "Yeah, probably."

"When are you gonna chess-master yourself?"

"Never, man, *never*," Ramsey said.

And as Zach walked away, he was pretty sure Ramsey meant that—believed it completely, in fact—but that was the funny thing about life, and even more about love.

It liked to throw curveballs.

Gavin didn't say anything about the power play until they were nearly through the second. The third line had actually managed to miraculously shoot something into the net, and they were now up three goals.

But then one of their players high-sticked Ivan, and with the first line already out there, maybe halfway through their shift, it was the perfect opportunity to put a set of guys who had mostly fresh legs.

Malcolm obviously wouldn't be, but Zach had seen him work a four or five minute shift before. He could handle it.

Gavin looked over at Zach. Then at the guys who were milling around the bench, waiting to hear what he wanted.

"McCoy, get your guys out there," Gavin barked.

Elliott was still Elliott, so Zach half-expected him to make some kind of token protest but instead of arguing, he only lifted himself back over the wall and shot his boyfriend a bright, proud smile, tapping him on the helmet. "Go get 'em, baby," he said. "Score one for me, huh?"

Mal blushed. "Yeah, yeah," he said, but he looked pleased. Glowing with it, in fact.

"Damn it," Gavin said less than ten seconds later, when Ethan won the faceoff, slid the puck to Mal, and he just shot it right in with a flick of the wrist, before the goalie could even dream about blocking it.

Elliott was yelling—something about what he was going to do to Mal later, and Ivan elbowed him, hard. "Shut up," Ivan said, but Zach didn't have to see his face to know he was smiling too. "Nobody wants to know what you two get up to."

"Yeah, no shit," Brody said.

"Like you're so innocent," Ivan grumbled. "I saw you and Dean at Gamma Sigma the other night, practically humping against the side of the house."

Brody blushed. "That was . . .we thought we were being subtle."

Ivan rolled his eyes. "You two have never, ever, in your entire fucking lives, been subtle."

Zach laughed.

"Hey, we're not Elliott and Mal, at least," Brody protested.

"Yeah," Elliott crowed, "you're not fucking us!"

In the last minute of the game, the opposing team pulled their goalie, even though they were down four goals, and that was the only way they managed to slip one right by Finn.

Still, it was a great game and a great score, and there was plenty worth celebrating about.

Gavin leaned in and said to Zach as they were watching the guys shed their equipment, "Okay. Maybe you were right. Maybe we just had to wait out the slump. Maybe I fucked this up when I tried to switch it up."

"Yeah, huh, maybe you did," Zach said, trying not to grin too broadly.

"Ugh, don't be smug about it," Gavin muttered.

"But you *like* it when I'm smug," Zach argued, unable to hold back his smile any longer.

"Yeah, yeah. You wanna help me tell Mal?"

"Sure," Zach said. He stopped by Mal's stall, let him know he and Coach wanted to see him. Mal just nodded his dark head.

Nobody was surprised that when he showed up at Gavin's office thirty minutes later, Elliott was also with him.

"Maybe better that you're both here," Gavin said. "I told you both this was an experiment we were going to try."

"Shitty experiment," Elliott mumbled under his breath and Malcolm elbowed him in the side.

"I said it was something we were gonna try," Gavin started again, "but I'm thinking that maybe it might be better to go back to our regular power play units."

"Good," Elliott said, tilting his chin up.

"No," Malcolm said bluntly.

Gavin's eyebrows crept up. "No?"

"With all due respect, sir," Mal said, proving again just how completely opposite of Elliott he was, "I don't think it's a good idea to switch back."

"Mal!" Elliott exclaimed sharply, shooting him a glare. "What are you saying? Of course you need to come back to our power play unit."

"No," Mal repeated firmly. "Those guys have to get better, and nobody's gonna do it if I don't."

"It's not *your* job," Elliott argued.

Zach opened his mouth to say something, but Gavin nudged him hard.

"I'm a leader on this team, and an A, so yeah, it sure is my job. And I get it now, Coach." Mal slid a look over towards Gavin. "I didn't at first, but you didn't move me because I let you down."

"No," Gavin agreed.

"You moved me because those guys need someone to force them to get their shit together."

Gavin nodded.

Mal turned back to Elliott. They were a very touchy-feely couple, despite the many lectures they'd been given about PDA, but Zach realized it was more often Elliott touching Mal than Mal touching Elliott. But Malcolm touched Elliott now, on the shoulder, sliding his hand across to his neck and squeezing. "But Ell, you gotta know. We might not always play together, all the time."

Elliott sulked. "I know."

"We gotta get used to it in case—"

"Don't say it," Elliott warned.

Mal's lips quirked up. "Okay, I won't. But honestly I love watching you play. You're such a star, babe. When I'm on the bench I've got the best seat in the house."

Elliott smiled at him, soft and easy, full of love. "Flatterer."

"Just telling the truth," Mal said, shrugging, but he looked pleased.

"So you want to stay on the second power play, then?" Gavin asked.

Mal nodded.

"Alright then," Gavin said. He looked over at Zach. "Make sure they get plenty of practice this week. They're still shaky out there."

"But getting better," Zach said, maybe more optimistically than he felt. But if Malcolm could commit to this, so could Zach.

After Elliott and Mal were gone, Gavin turned to Zach and put an arm around his waist, tugging him in.

It wasn't the first PDA they'd ever indulged in at the rink, but it was the most obvious. "Am I supposed to tell you that *you* were right, now?" Zach asked in a low, teasing voice.

"Nope," Gavin said. "You were still right, though I maintain I had the right idea."

"You were trying to go old-school when I only ever wanted you to break all the conventions," Zach pointed out.

"A little, yeah," Gavin agreed. "But it's alright. We're good."

Zach pressed his mouth against Gavin's temple. It was just a graze, barely even a kiss, but it lit him up with happiness and joy.

"Better than good, I'd say," Gavin said.

CHAPTER 18

"Honestly," Sidney said, poking a fork into his salad, "we couldn't be happier with how this has turned out."

Gavin told himself not to roll his eyes. This was his *boss*, and even though he was a bit of a patronizing dick, he was going to need all the goodwill he could get in a minute.

"Me too," Gavin said.

"You seem to have fixed things with Zach," Sidney said. "And the second power play. I never would've imagined moving Mc-Coy to the second team would change things."

Gavin nearly said that he'd been just about ready to move everyone back to their original positions, but Malcolm had argued against it. But if Sidney thought he'd waved his magic wand and fixed everything, he wasn't going to pretend otherwise. Not right now. Not when Sidney had given him the best way to broach the subject he needed to discuss.

"Yeah, everything's good with me and Zach," Gavin agreed. Hesitated, took a deep breath. He hadn't told Zach he loved him yet, but wasn't this him doing it just without using the specific words? "Better than ever, actually. That was what I wanted to talk to you about."

"You and Zach? I figured you didn't want to meet up for lunch just to hear me blather on about how good the hockey team is," Sidney said, his gaze knowing.

And *ugh*, it was worse, knowing that Sidney was aware of just how much Gavin disliked their lunch meetings, but Gavin pushed that embarrassment aside and went on.

"Yes, me and Zach. It's actually, it's really . . .uh . . .me *and* Zach, now," Gavin said. Prayed that he wouldn't have to go into anatomical detail in front of his boss just how much it was him *and* Zach, now.

Surely Sidney would appreciate him being circumspect, if a little vague, about the specifics.

"Wait," Sidney said. "Are you saying what I think you're saying? You and Zach are *together*?"

There was nothing else Gavin could do but nod.

"Well, that certainly adds clarity to why I got that crazy resignation from him a few weeks back." Sidney shot him a jovial look. "You two get into a fight?"

"Uh, something like that," Gavin said. *God, please don't ask. Please, please don't ask.*

"You're sure it's not going to interfere with your work again?" Sidney questioned.

Gavin internally groaned. "Really, no. Everything's fine now. We worked it out, and I can promise you, there won't be any more of that."

"Good." Sidney nodded sharply. "You two are too valuable to this organization to possibly lose one of you."

"You won't. Not over this. I can guarantee that."

"So you're asking for . . ." Sidney trailed off, eyeing him steadily.

"Not permission, necessarily, since it's already happening," Gavin admitted. "And I suppose, not your blessing either, but I wanted to make you aware. And I *did* want to ask your opinion on us telling the team."

Sidney set his fork down. "You're very serious about this," he said.

"Yes," Gavin admitted. "Our guys have been very honest about their own lives, and I don't want to hide in return."

"As long as you're sure the dramatics are over, I don't see an issue," Sidney said thoughtfully. "You're leading by example, and I've always been a fan of that."

"Very over," Gavin reassured.

"Alright," Sidney said, not looking particularly convinced by it, but then he'd been the one to receive Zach's resignation and his phone call the next day, apologizing and saying he'd made a mistake.

Gavin thought that particular phrasing had been pretty damn generous of Zach, because it hadn't been *his* mistake, but entirely Gavin's.

When Gavin had pointed this out, Zach had only laughed and hugged him, saying he was so happy he'd have been okay claiming responsibility for just about anything.

Gavin had laughed, too. Happy, too, and relieved and so many other emotions filtering through him.

He should say something else to Sidney, now, so Sidney wouldn't continue believing that Zach had nearly quit the team in a fit of breakup pique.

"To be clear, just so you're aware, I . . .it was all my fault," Gavin said.

Sidney raised an eyebrow.

"And it wasn't a breakup," Gavin continued, internally wincing at how he'd suddenly transformed into a gossiping teenager. "We weren't together before, and now we are."

Sidney chuckled under his breath. "You don't owe me the details, Gavin."

"I know. I was just . . ." He swallowed hard. "I was married a long time, and I didn't think I'd be with anyone else. That I'd even want to be with someone else. This thing with Zach took me by surprise, and I didn't handle it well, at first."

"But you've got a handle on it now?" Sidney asked.

"Yes," Gavin said confidently. He didn't add, *I wouldn't be telling you otherwise,* but he thought it sort of went without saying.

If I'd fucked this up, Zach wouldn't be here anymore, and I'd be alone and miserable and we'd probably be losing, and I'd be sitting here in front of you for an entirely different reason.

"Good," Sidney said, nodding. "That's all that matters."

"We appreciate the understanding and the grace to . . .live how we want to," Gavin said. Because Sidney didn't have to be this accepting. Gavin wasn't stupid enough to believe it came from anything other than a desire to keep both of them happy, employed, and winning.

Sidney smirked. "I'd be stupid to piss you off when you're about to take us to the Frozen Four."

"That's not a guarantee—"

"Come now, Blackburn. You know what the team's chances are. How they're playing. Even the second power play team is better."

"It is," Gavin agreed.

"I'm just saying, winning covers a multitude of . . .I'll say *sins* but I certainly don't consider what you're doing anything of the kind. We accept everyone here, at Portland U."

Gavin nearly rolled his eyes and asked if they printed that on a T-shirt, but he'd gotten what he'd wanted, and it was better not to create additional waves.

"That's great," Gavin said instead and returned to his salad.

"I was thinking, there's this other podcast we could get you on—"

He didn't even think. He just lifted his eyes up, spearing Sidney with a look. "Don't push your luck."

For a second, Gavin worried that he *should* have kept making nice, but Sidney just laughed, slapping his arm and making some kind of foolish noise about how Gavin should never change.

Well, Gavin didn't intend to.

Except for one important detail: now that the impossible had happened, and he'd fallen in love for a second time in his life, he was never letting Zach go.

It took Gavin ten minutes to figure out exactly why Jon was being so fucking cagey.

At first, he'd been sure it was *him*, because they were discussing his sex life, and Gavin hated that every single time it came up, in every single iteration.

Now that he was actually sharing it with Zach and it was so good, *unexpectedly* good, discussing it was actually worse.

He could barely tell his therapist with a straight face that he'd jerked off.

Nevermind explaining to him that apparently it made his dick as hard as it had ever been when Zach pinned him to the bed and didn't let him come, no matter how much he begged for it.

"Have you discussed how far you two want to take things?" Jon asked.

He'd been weird, off almost, since the moment Gavin got on the call, like he kept expecting him to explode with some emotional drama that Jon would have to deal with. But there was nothing.

Unless you counted Gavin being required to discuss his sex life.

"Some, yeah. But I think we're both pretty happy with how things are right now. Like . . .uh . . .I don't want to be tied up, and I don't want to tie *him* up. It's just good sometimes, when he tells me not to move, and I can . . ." Gavin internally squirmed. "I can let him take all of it from me."

"Take what exactly?"

Gavin exhaled and scrubbed a hand across his face. "I want to say my consent but that's not true either, because he knows I'm consenting."

"Did you have that conversation about safe words?"

"Yeah, and I get why it might be something that could be needed, but for us—if I say stop, Zach knows I mean stop."

"Does he?"

"Ugh, I hate it when you do that," Gavin grumbled.

"Ask about your sex life? Force you to talk about it?"

"Answer a question you already know the answer to."

"I think the most important thing is that *you* know the answer," Jon said.

"Well, obviously I do," Gavin retorted and then realized a second later, why Jon had even asked. He laughed, feeling that buoyant happiness seep through him again. "You wanted to know if I did."

Jon nodded. "Was there anything else you wanted to talk about?"

Gavin shook his head. "Honestly, I'm . . .I can't even believe I'm saying this sometimes, but I'm so happy. I didn't think this was in the cards for me, again."

"I'm glad it was," Jon said, but he was hesitating again. Gavin could see it on his face. Maybe Jon was the therapist and Gavin was just the client, but for as long as Jon had been looking at him, Gavin had been looking back. And there was no question in Gavin's mind that something was up.

"Are you concerned about what Zach and I are doing in bed?" Gavin asked it bluntly, because maybe he was. Normally he'd never expect Jon to hold back an opinion, but it was also such a weirdly awkward topic.

"No, no, though I don't think it would be a bad thing, if you're both into it, to try having some vanilla sex every once in awhile."

Gavin had considered that. He wanted Zach to fuck him, next time they were in bed together, and he had a feeling he wasn't going to want it to be anything else other than what it was. Him and Zach, together, giving and taking.

"Alright," Gavin said. Then *he* paused. "Are you really not gonna tell me what's bothering you? Is everything okay?"

Jon chuckled awkwardly and rubbed a hand across his jaw. "I kept expecting to have to ask *you* that, Gavin,"

"What, why?"

Jon winced. "Gavin, it's February 1."

It was.

Gavin had thought about it when he'd fallen asleep last night, listening to Zach's soft snores next to him, feeling the warm press of his body against Gavin's. And he'd thought about it this morning, when he'd first woken up, ten minutes before the alarm.

He'd had that ten minutes to mull over the fact that it was his anniversary, his fifth without Noelle, and for the first time, he'd been sad, but he'd also been . . .accepting. There was a bittersweet flavor to his thoughts, no question, but he hadn't felt once like crawling back under the covers and disappearing from the world. And if he *had*, he knew he'd have wanted Zach to be right there with him.

"Yeah, it is," Gavin said.

There was no hiding it; Jon's jaw dropped. "You remembered?"

Gavin shot him an incredulous look. "You thought I forgot?"

"Well, *no*, not necessarily but I wondered. It's a day you've historically struggled with. I thought it was why you'd made the appointment today."

Gavin realized, suddenly, why Zach had been quiet today. Why he'd told him he'd be in the library all afternoon and evening. Why he'd kissed Gavin goodbye this morning and then essentially disappeared.

Yes, he had homework and his classes, but it was the first time he'd been so silent.

God, this was why Gavin loved him so much. He was giving Gavin the space to grieve, even if Gavin didn't need it anymore.

He'd had his ten minutes, and that had been enough for today.

"Shit, I think Zach was thinking the same," Gavin said, groaning. "He's been quiet all day. Especially after I mentioned I had therapy."

"You really don't want to talk about it," Jon stated rather than asked.

"I . . .it's not that I don't miss her. Or I didn't love her. I did and I do, every day. But . . .you know how you sometimes tell me about the fullness of grief? I let it invade my whole life and run it, no questions, no checks and balances, for years. I couldn't do it anymore. Not only that . . .I didn't *want* to do that anymore."

Jon smiled.

"And I think," Gavin added, before Jon could say *I told you so*, "that this whole time, every time we talked, for years, this was what this was leading to. Me not wanting grief to run my whole life anymore. For me to accept it and give it a corner in my mind and in my heart and to say, leave the rest of me alone."

"Yes," Jon said. He was smiling bigger now, maybe bigger and brighter than Gavin had ever seen him smile before.

"Well. Damn." Gavin felt it too but then he wasn't blind enough to believe that he hadn't been here, even without realizing it, for some time.

"Proud of you, Gavin," Jon said.

Gavin took a deep breath and said, "Proud of me, too."

"That guy of yours is good for you. And you're good for him, too. You did a lot of the hard work, the toughest work, before you met him again, but because you did, you were ready for it."

"I . . ." Gavin trailed off. If he was going to say he was in love with Zach, he was going to do it to Zach first, not his therapist. He was too emotionally healthy to fuck this up, now. "You know how I feel about him but I haven't told him yet so I think I'd better wait."

"Good call. And, Gavin?"

"Yeah?"

"Don't doubt it, okay? Because I've seen it in your face, every time you talk about Zach, for months now. He's special, and even more than that, he's special to *you*."

"Don't have to tell *me* that," Gavin said.

He barely was hung up with Jon before he had his phone out, sending Zach a handful of texts.

Where are you?

You're not avoiding me because it's February 1, are you?

If you are, we need to talk. I'm home. Will be home the rest of the day. Come find me.

Zach's phone buzzed on the desk next to his laptop. He was trying to get ahead on his reading—taking notes, outlining possible essay topics, anything to avoid thinking of what *Gavin* was going to be thinking about today.

He glanced down at his phone, surprised the texts were from Gavin.

It wasn't that he hadn't realized February 1 was approaching. He had. But they'd also been so busy with the team and the power play changes and then there had been their relationship—which was incredible and so much hotter in the bedroom than Zach had ever anticipated.

It had been so easy to lose himself to it, to pretend that everything was going to be okay—that it *was* okay—then all of a sudden, the next day was February 1, and Gavin was casually mentioning having a therapy call in the afternoon and everything inside Zach had frozen.

He'd *seemed* fine, kissing Zach goodnight with the same sweet enthusiasm that he always did.

Zach had spent a mostly sleepless night trying to figure out what the fuck he should do, and the only answer he'd come up with was maybe it was for the best if he gave Gavin the space he needed.

He'd told Zach that he wasn't going to be perfect at this. Zach had understood that to mean he was still going to grieve for his wife, and that was more than okay, it was totally expected.

He never once felt like Gavin wasn't really happy with him, now, and that was all that mattered, really.

But still, he'd spent the whole day with a knot in his stomach. Not worried, exactly, that Gavin would live through this anniversary and decide, at the end of it, that he didn't want to be with Zach after all. But that he'd be sad. That he'd remember how it felt to be so miserable.

If Gavin's mind was that changeable, he never would have told Sidney about them. They wouldn't be planning the best way to tell the team.

No—Gavin was in this.

And if his texts were any indication . . . *come find me*, Gavin had said.

That was the easiest thing in the whole damn world.

Zach shoved his laptop into his backpack and took off like a shot.

He half-jogged, half-speed walked to Gavin's house, and once he got there, hesitated on the porch. He had the door code now and let himself in all the time, but this was *February 1.*

But then, what had Gavin said? Zach fumbled for his phone. **You're not avoiding me because its February 1, are you?** was written there, right in black and white. Like Gavin was *surprised* that Zach would give him space. Like he was goddamn surprised that Zach might think he *needed* space.

Zach opened the door.

Gavin was on the couch, the Knights-Oilers game on the TV, playing at a low volume. He glanced up as Zach toed off his sneakers and set down his backpack.

"Hey," he said.

"Hey," Zach replied, shoving his hands into the pockets of his jeans. He didn't move to take the seat next to Gavin, even though he knew he should.

Zach didn't know why he was suddenly so nervous. He'd been *trying* to do the right thing in a prickly situation.

He could never be Gavin's wife. He didn't think Gavin even wanted him to be Noelle, but if he could only be Zach, what did that *mean*? Before today, he'd thought he'd known, but the deeper they got into this, the harder the question was to dismiss. The more impossible it was to answer.

Gavin raised an eyebrow. "So this *was* about you avoiding me today, then?"

Of course Gavin would cut right through the awkwardness with blunt honesty.

"Um, yeah, well, sort of," Zach said, grimacing at his own indecision. He took a deep breath. If Gavin could tell the truth, he could, too. "Yeah. It was."

Gavin patted the couch next to him. "Come. Sit down. Let's talk about this."

What else could Zach do but what Gavin asked? He didn't even *want* to fight it. He understood, maybe a little better now, when they were in bed, pressed together skin to skin, kissing like it was going out of style, why Gavin let him take control.

"First off," Gavin said and leaned in, brushing a tender kiss across Zach's mouth. "Hi, again."

He pulled back, but Zach chased him, kissing him more firmly, now that he knew it was okay. Gavin made a soft, rumbling noise of satisfaction in the back of his throat as they kissed, Zach's tongue in his mouth, Gavin's fingertips digging into his shoulders.

But just when Zach began the internal debate of whether they should take this to the bedroom or just fuck on the couch, Gavin pulled back.

"I said we should talk," Gavin said, looking amused and also aroused. He licked his lips, and Zach almost leaned in again.

But he was trying to be an adult about this, not just a horny teenager who'd finally figured out that his crush was mutual.

"We can talk," Zach said.

Gavin took a deep breath, settling back on the couch, too far away from Zach already. "I know what you were trying to do, and I appreciate the gesture. I can't say this day *wasn't* hard for me, every other year."

Zach didn't say anything, because what was there to say? Gavin was always going to grieve his wife, and part of Zach didn't even want it to be different because that loyalty, that depth of feeling, was part of what made Gavin *Gavin*. Part of what made him the man that Zach was so gone for.

"But," Gavin continued, "I didn't need you to give me space. It wasn't . . .it's gotten easier to compartmentalize the grief. To feel it and then put it away, where it belongs, in a box on the shelf. I'm probably never going to *not* feel it, but it doesn't need to run my life, anymore."

"That sounds . . .really healthy," Zach said slowly.

"My therapist told me I put the work in, and he's right. I did. That was a lot of it. But you also reminded me that I wasn't dead yet, either. As a friend and as more." Gavin exhaled, his gaze so soft. "So much more. You have to know . . .maybe I brought myself back, most of the way, but that last ten percent? I did it, because you were so freaking irresistible."

Zach grinned. "Yeah?"

"Yeah." Gavin rolled his eyes, but he was so fond. "I told myself I didn't want to feel this way ever again, but it happened anyway. I couldn't even stop it, and the truth is, I didn't want to. It feels so good. *You* make me so happy."

"You make me happy too." It felt like the right thing to do, to lean in, and kiss Gavin again. Just so Zach didn't confess his love again. He'd done it a handful of times, but he was trying not to push Gavin. It *sounded* like he loved him, but things were so good, Zach couldn't say he missed actually hearing the words.

Their lips brushed together, firm and sweet, but then Gavin pulled back again, one of his hands reaching up to cup Zach's cheek. "What I'm trying to say is I love *you*."

Zach had just told himself he was fine not hearing the words, but the moment Gavin said it, he realized that was total bullshit. He *had* needed them.

It was why he'd felt so uncertain today; not entirely sure where he'd stood.

But Gavin had just made it as plain as he could.

He was with Zach now; he *loved* Zach now.

"God, I love you too," Zach said roughly and pulled Gavin in, mouth moving against his own, until he was nearly squirming into Zach's lap.

"Come on." Zach slid his hand down Gavin's back, resting against the tantalizing curve of Gavin's ass. "Let's go to bed."

"Before we do . . . I . . ." Gavin took a deep breath, suddenly looking awkward again.

"What is it?" Zach pressed their foreheads together. "You can tell me anything. Whatever you want, I'm going to do my best to give it to you."

"First off, I *do* want you to fuck me," Gavin said.

Zach chuckled, heat winding its way through him, making his dick even harder. "That's not going to be a problem."

"And . . .I really enjoy what we do most of the time, but I want this to be different. Just me and you."

Gavin didn't need to say the words, or ask for it, but Zach understood what he wasn't saying: *I want you to make love to me.*

And Zach had meant what he'd said earlier, that he'd give Gavin anything he wanted, but this was the easiest request he could've ever made.

"Yes," Zach said softly, and leaning in, kissed him again. It was sweet and tender and hot, too. He didn't think they could be anything else together.

Gavin slid off his lap and, reaching for Zach's arm, tugged him up. "Come on," he murmured into Zach's mouth, his body pressed against Zach's, until he could feel every aroused inch of him. "Let's go to bed."

Zach didn't need to be asked twice.

He let Gavin pull him into the bedroom, and felt his heart beat faster as Gavin pulled his polo shirt off, then slid his pants down, toeing his socks off.

Zach could see the outline of his hard dick in his dark blue boxer briefs, and Gavin hissed out an unsteady breath as Zach reached out, palming it.

"Your turn." Gavin smirked, the corner of his mouth quirking up.

Zach hadn't been able to predict just how much he'd like taking control in the bedroom with Gavin, but he discovered this was just as good, too. Their movements soft and deliberate, their edge dulled by the sweetness blooming between them.

He pulled his sweatshirt off and slid his sweatpants down. The moment they hit the floor, Gavin was on him, straddling his thighs, pushing him back onto the bed, mouth on his.

They kissed for a long time, Gavin's hips making little circular grinds against his own but other than that, he seemed content enough to kiss until Zach's lips felt swollen and he might just drown in a sea of desire, the air between them warm and thick, like syrup.

His fingers slid under the waistband of Gavin's briefs, feeling the muscles of his ass clench and then relax.

"Come on," Gavin mumbled into his mouth. "I want it. Want *you*."

But Zach had been hanging back, trying to let Gavin set the pace, because that was what he'd thought he'd been asking for earlier.

"I don't wanna—"

Gavin pressed a kiss to his mouth, and Zach groaned a little as he swiveled his hips even more insistently, feeling his cock brush against Gavin's. "It's a give and take, baby."

Zach didn't waste time, then. He knew what he wanted. What Gavin wanted, too. Tensing his muscles, he flipped them and eased down Gavin's body, taking his briefs with him as he went.

Gavin's cock twitched against his stomach as Zach wrapped a hand around his thigh and pressed it open. "This what you want?" he asked.

Shooting Zach a hot, affectionate, nearly exasperated look, Gavin nodded. "But *faster*," he added.

Zach chuckled. "Impatient, much?"

"I've been *wanting* you," Gavin protested.

"Well, get the lube, then," Zach said. "Can't fuck you without it."

Gavin grumbled again, but he leaned over, stretching his lean, muscled body to get to the drawer, and Zach could only sit there, between his legs and think, *God, that's all mine.*

"No condom," Gavin said resolutely, handing the bottle to Zach.

"You sure?"

Gavin's voice dipped low. "I want to feel you. All of you."

Zach swallowed hard, arousal surging through him, his cock aching. "Fuck, that's hot," he admitted.

The pupils in Gavin's eyes dilated even further and yeah, he thought so too.

Zach knew Gavin had enjoyed his fingers the one time he'd used them before, but he still took his time. Warmed up the lube on the pads of his fingers and gently worked up to even sliding a single one in.

By the time he finally did, Gavin groaned and Zach realized he'd made a similar noise at the white-hot clenching heat around it as he gently thrust in.

"Another," Gavin begged. "Come on. I'm not delicate."

"But precious," Zach argued. "Important. *Gorgeous*, like this."

Gavin's head flopped back onto the bed. "You're gonna kill me."

"And you're gonna enjoy every second of it," Zach promised.

But he did give Gavin another finger, relishing the way his body tightened and then loosened around him. Then twitching as Zach curled them, and hit that spot that made Gavin cry out.

"Oh yeah, baby, let me hear you." Zach could hear the guttural roughness in his own voice. How close he was to just thrusting into that soft, sweet heat. Making Gavin cry with how good it was.

Gavin made a choked noise. Like he was embarrassed. That wasn't going to fly, at all.

"I wanna hear it," Zach said. "Tell me just how bad you want my cock." He slid a third finger in and stroked the edges of Gavin's hole with his thumb. Making him groan.

"I want it," Gavin begged.

"Better." This was turning Zach on so much it was becoming a hardship to not just thrust mindlessly into the mattress, desperately craving that friction against his hard cock.

"Please," Gavin demanded. "I'm ready. So ready. I love you."

And like hell Zach wasn't going to give it to him after he said *that*.

"Come on, turn over for me, baby," Zach said, and Gavin shook his head in protest.

"I want to see you."

"Trust me, it'll be easier this way," Zach said. "I'll make it . . ." *I'll make it special.* But the words felt trapped in his throat. *I love you, too. So fucking much.*

"I do trust you," Gavin said, so softly, the truth of what he was saying so undeniable Zach couldn't miss it.

He turned over, rising to his knees, tensing and then relaxing as Zach's hands caught his hips, rearranging him exactly where he wanted him.

Zach finally got rid of his underwear, slicking up his dick with only a few quick movements, because if he touched himself any more than he did, he was going to lose it. And he wanted to be so good for Gavin. The *best*.

"You ready?" Zach murmured, leaning over and draping himself across Gavin's warm back. He ran a soothing hand up and down his flank before he returned it to his hip.

"Yeah." Gavin sounded anticipatory. Breathless. A little nervous.

Zach took it easy, carefully fitting himself to Gavin and then sliding in achingly slow. Absorbing every gasp and groan Gavin made, every keen of disbelief at how good it was.

And it was really fucking good. Gavin was hot and tight around him, under him, the two of them plastered together with barely any room for Zach to even breathe as he finally slid the last inch in.

Zach patted Gavin's hip reassuringly, trying to get himself back under control. He'd never felt so close to the edge, but he'd promised and Gavin *trusted* him.

"I'm good. It's so good." Gavin's voice was high and breathy and incredulous. "God, *please*."

It only took a few slow, measured thrusts for Gavin to start working his own hips, moving with Zach, and then suddenly, it wasn't slow or controlled at all, but frantic, both of them chasing their pleasure.

Sweat slid down Zach's spine, down his abs, dripping onto Gavin's skin and he didn't care. He only wanted to be closer, deeper. He reached around, groaning under his breath as he found Gavin's cock hard and dripping precome, making the slide easy as he began to stroke him.

Gavin tensed and then let out a shout, clenching around Zach, his orgasm overtaking him.

It only took a few more strokes for Zach to follow right behind him, both of them collapsing onto the bed together.

"One second," Zach said, sounding like he'd just run sprints, breath gusting in and out of his chest. "I know I'm heavy."

"I like it." Gavin's reply was muffled by the comforter but clear enough.

"I *love* you," Zach mumbled back.

Gavin laughed, breathlessly. "Ditto. Wow."

Zach finally found the energy to pull out and collapsed next to Gavin. Sliding an arm around Gavin's back, tugging him closer. Gavin's face was relaxed, and so happy. "Good?"

"I think that's an understatement."

Satisfaction curled through Zach. He'd done that. He'd made Gavin sound that way, happy and peaceful and totally fucked out.

"I should get up and clean us up. We're probably uh . . .going to have to change the sheets."

"In a minute," Gavin said, tilting his face closer to Zach's. "First, I wanna do this." He leaned in and kissed him, soft and earnest. And Zach wasn't ever going to argue about that.

CHAPTER 19

"You feeling good about this?" Gavin asked Zach as they walked into the rink.

Zach glanced over at him. "Yeah. Actually. Yeah. I thought I'd be . . .nervous, I guess? But I'm not. They're all gonna be supportive. How could they not be? You were supportive of them, G."

"That's not why I was supportive," Gavin grumbled. He wasn't expecting to be paid back in loyalty, just because he'd been a decent person who believed people shouldn't be defined by who they loved.

"I know that, and they know it, too," Zach reassured him, nudging him with his shoulder. "I'm just saying, they're probably going to be more excited than anything."

Gavin groaned in the back of his throat. He didn't think Zach was wrong, which was why they were doing this now, after clinching their conference title, assuring their spot in the Frozen Four. They had two regular season games left, but he and Zach had agreed that if they were going to tell the team, this was the time to do it.

"We're just going to do it and then move right along," Gavin reminded him. He didn't think the team would be so disrespectful as to ask for details, but it wasn't like *they* ever shied away from sharing plenty of their own.

"Right," Zach said, shooting him a grin. "Sure that's gonna happen."

They'd called the meeting before the last practice before their final back-to-back games. They didn't need to win these, but Gavin wanted to win them anyway, because if they did, they'd set a Portland University record for the number of wins in a single season, and that meant that even if their Frozen Four dreams didn't come true, they'd still be in the history books, memorializing this incredible season.

"It's happening," Gavin retorted.

"You're still good with this, right?" Zach asked.

Not for the first time.

"I'm just saying," Zach added, "I'm not coming out of the closet. Just telling everyone I coach how I just punched up, big-time."

Gavin rolled his eyes, charmed despite the fact that he *should* know better. "Oh, yeah? Somehow I don't think that's how they're gonna take it."

"That's how they should take it," Zach joked, nudging him again. His smile was wide and bright, zero hesitation.

"Honestly telling Sidney was more nerve-wracking than this," Gavin admitted. "And that went fine enough."

"Everyone's just happy that you're happy, including me," Zach said. He hesitated, glancing around, and once he was convinced there was nobody in this corridor, he leaned and pressed a quick kiss against Gavin's cheek. "*Mostly* me, to be perfectly honest."

Gavin flushed. "Don't start anything you can't finish."

"Oh, I'm gonna finish it, baby," Zach teased.

It wasn't easy to drag his mind back out of the gutter, but Gavin managed it, but it took the rest of their walk to the locker room.

Zach pushed the door open, and Gavin was pleased to see that pretty much the whole team was already there, getting changed for practice.

"Hey, guys," Gavin said, and they all looked up, nodding their greetings. "Just wanted to get together real quick before these last two games and check in."

"We're ready, Coach," Ramsey said. He looked properly respectful, but Zach had already told him that Ramsey had guessed what was going on between them. Had even encouraged Zach to go for it on New Years Eve. He probably knew exactly what this meeting was about.

Gavin wasn't surprised; he'd known what he was getting when he'd asked Ramsey to be the captain of this team.

"Last two regular season games. Chance to set the Portland U record, and put our stamp in the record books before we head to Wisconsin for the championship." Gavin glanced over at Zach. He seemed relaxed, totally at ease, hands shoved in the pockets of his sweatpants, a smile on his face. "We don't *need* these games, but I want them. For me, for sure, and for Zach too, but also for us, as a team. This is a special team, and I don't want anyone to forget us."

"They wouldn't," Brody said, speaking up. He wasn't the most vocal in the room, but always the most quietly supportive.

"And they won't," Ramsey agreed, sharing a glance with his best friend. "We're gonna make fucking sure of that."

"Good," Gavin said, nodding. "But here's the thing—this team hasn't just been special because of how we've won on the ice. We've won off it too. Forging a new era in Evergreens athletics, not just saying we're supportive and that everyone can play, but leading by example. Ramsey is the first captain of the Evergreens who's openly queer. Zach the first assistant coach, and . . ." Gavin took a deep breath. He'd just told Zach that telling Sidney the truth had been tougher than this, but now that the moment was here, all those expectant faces looking at him, he realized it wasn't *easy* to do this, either.

"What Coach B is saying is that you should pat yourselves on the back for practicing what we've been preaching. You were examples in the way you always played hard, and in the way you lived your lives," Zach said, coming up to stand next to Gavin. He looked over at Gavin, giving him a little nod of support.

It was now or never.

"In that vein," Gavin said, "Zach and I wanted to tell you something, even though it's a little unconventional. Despite that, we hope this won't really be a big thing—" Zach laughed out loud next to him, and yeah, maybe that was wishful thinking. "We wanted you to know that we're . . .uh . . .together now." Gavin reached out and took Zach's hand, squeezing it, hoping that would be the visual cue they all needed to understand exactly what he was saying.

Gavin watched as jaws around the room dropped and a shocked silence descended.

"We're very happy, thanks," Zach joked.

"Well, shit, you weren't *already* together?" Ivan asked.

Gavin froze.

"Told you," Ramsey retorted, shooting Ivan a triumphant look.

"Fuck—does that mean you won the pot?" Brody questioned Ramsey.

"I told you we should have gone later," Elliott said, leaning over to nudge Mal. "I told you they didn't have their shit together, yet."

Mal just shrugged.

"Actually," Finn said, speaking up, "I think *I* won the pot."

"What?" Elliott exclaimed. "When did you say?"

"Technically, Ramsey said the new year. *I* said the end of the season."

"Wait a second," Gavin said, not sure he was following. Hoping that he wasn't, actually. "Did you *bet* on us getting together?"

"Yeah, Coach, neither of you were very subtle." Finn shrugged.

"No way, not even remotely," Elliott agreed.

"That's fucking rich, coming from you. One half of the least subtle couple in history," Ivan complained.

"Hey," Elliott protested. "Mal and I figured our shit out on our own!"

"Yeah, Jones, but not before we had to witness your months-long mating dance," Brody retorted.

"This is slander," Elliott grumbled. "Total fucking slander. Tell them, Mal."

Mal just shrugged. "They're kinda not wrong, babe?"

"Ugh," Elliott grumbled.

"I think the real question is, who won the pot?" Ramsey said, his voice cutting through Elliott and Brody's argument.

Gavin looked over at Zach, who just shrugged.

"The only way we're gonna be able to decide is if we know *when*," Finn said.

"Oh God," Zach said. "That's none of your business."

"It sure is," Ramsey argued. "We need to know who won the pot!"

"It's not a small amount of money," Ivan said, nodding.

"No shit," Finn said.

"Dude, shut up, your dad is a multi-millionaire and you're dating *another* multi-millionaire," Elliott said.

"And most of the room gets some kind of NIL money," Ramsey inserted. "Nobody's hurting."

"Uh, we're not comfortable discussing the details," Gavin said, hoping that maybe he could head this off at the pass. "Maybe we could donate the pot to charity? Maybe Jacob's charity?"

Ramsey looked unimpressed by this plan. "It's not about the money. It's about bragging rights."

God. Their relationship details were now part of the *bragging rights* of the team. If he'd thought answering Jon's questions about their sex life was uncomfortable, this was worse.

"Yeah, that's right," Brody said, and Finn chimed in his agreement.

"Shut up," Ivan told Finn. "You're only saying that because you think you won."

"He *did* win. He's fucking Jacob Braun," Elliott said.

"Hey," Mal said. "And *you're* fucking me."

Elliott shot him a look filled with love and affection, batting his eyelashes. "And oh, baby, I love it. Every single moment of it."

Gavin scrubbed a hand across his face. "What would settle this?"

Next to him, Zach was chuckling under his breath. At Gavin? At Gavin's clearly delusional idea that he'd be able to tell the team the basic fact that they were together now and they'd leave it alone? *Probably.*

God, Gavin loved him anyway. Even the annoying bits. *Especially* the annoying bits.

"Obviously we need to know when you really got together," Ramsey said.

"Not the nitty-gritty," Ivan said hurriedly. "Just the timeline."

"I don't know, I could stand to hear a few details," Elliott muttered.

"Shut up, you horny monster," Brody retorted. "It's amazing Mal manages to satisfy you."

"Not so much of a surprise," Elliott announced.

Ivan groaned. "Don't fucking get him started, okay? Because he *will* tell you exactly how Mal does, in explicit detail."

"A timeline. Okay." Gavin looked over at Zach, who was still grinning. "You okay with that?"

"Hey, it's your show, G," Zach said, raising his hands like he wasn't half of this.

Gavin sighed.

"That's what we need, Coach," Finn said. "What date was it?"

"January 2," Gavin finally admitted.

The room burst into noise again, Ramsey trying to argue that January 2 was basically the same as January 1, which was the New Year and Finn making the point that the fact it was *after* January 1, plus that Gavin and Zach were telling them two games before the end of the regular season meant he should win.

"I guess believing this would be no big deal was wishful thinking," Gavin said under his breath.

"Yeah, a little." Zach slung an arm across his shoulders. And *God*, he could do that now, in full view of the team. Of course, it seemed like he probably could've done that before, too, since they'd all assumed it was already happening without being told.

Gavin was actually *not* going to think about that, because if he did, and really considered how obvious they must've been, he'd die of embarrassment.

"Coach," Ivan said intently, "you gotta give us more than that."

"More than that?" Gavin's eyebrows raised.

"Like, was there *something, anything,* before that?" Ramsey questioned. The knowing gleam in his blue eyes made it clear he believed there had been.

"Uh," Gavin hesitated.

"Ivy," Brody hissed, elbowing him in the side. "You're being an ass."

"We need to know who wins!"

"You're not even in the running," Brody argued.

"I have a side bet going," Ivan admitted.

"Oh my God," Brody said, burying his face in his hands. "You guys are *all* assholes."

"No arguments from me," Zach said mildly. "And you're not getting any more details."

"You're really telling me that *nothing* happened on New Years Eve, when you *both* disappeared for the countdown?" Ramsey asked archly.

Gavin exchanged a glance with Zach. Was Zach also remembering how they'd been discovered in that hallway at the arcade? It hadn't been Ramsey who found them, but Brody. Ramsey's best friend.

Brody, who might've mentioned it to Ramsey. Who probably *had* mentioned it to Ramsey.

"Wait a second," Brody said, realization dawning across his face, and shit, there it was. "You two were—I *saw* you."

"What?" Ramsey exclaimed. "You saw them and you didn't say anything? Not to *me*?"

"Well, I didn't *realize*—it was New Year's, dude—"

Ramsey rolled his eyes. "And Dean was there."

"Of course Dean was there!"

Gavin inwardly groaned. "Last detail," he said in a loud enough voice it cut through the bullshit—Ramsey giving Brody shit about his boyfriend and Brody dishing it right back, pointing out that Ramsey had been the one to set them up—"But uh, yes, something happened that night."

"But you didn't get together then. The bet wasn't if they fucked in the bathroom, it was when they got *together*," Finn said, leaning forward, teeth gleaming as he grinned at Ramsey.

"Fuck you, I won," Ramsey argued.

"We didn't—not in the bathroom . . ." Gavin argued, hating himself and hating that he hadn't managed to shut this conversation down yet.

"Don't worry, Coach," Elliott said reassuringly, "you wouldn't be the only one."

Zach was just straight up cackling now.

"Thanks for being helpful," Gavin murmured to him. "What do we do?"

Zach glanced over at Gavin and finally stopped laughing, clearing his throat.

"Okay, we're going to give Ramsey twenty-five percent of the pot, for the New Year's guess. Finn gets the rest," he said, finality ringing in his voice.

Ramsey started to argue—but Zach shot him a look. "We can either accept my decision," he said, "or I can go into additional detail about collusion."

"Collusion?" Finn asked, mid-high five with Ivan. "What about collusion?"

"Nothing about collusion," Ramsey muttered.

"That's better," Zach said, nodding. He looked over at Gavin. "You good?"

Gavin tried to paste on an expression that wasn't flustered. He wasn't sure he managed it. "Yeah, yeah. Great. Let's uh . . .let's talk about the game tomorrow."

"Game tomorrow," Zach repeated, raising his voice again.

"Yeah guys," Ramsey added, his voice rising to meet Zach's, "game tomorrow. Let's get focused."

If Gavin had ever needed to know if Ramsey was the right choice to wear the C, the way the whole locker room went right back to getting ready for practice, suddenly locked and dialed in, that was the evidence he would've needed.

But he hadn't ever needed it.

Ramsey had been the obvious choice from the moment he'd shown up, and he'd only ever proven that gut instinct right, over and over again.

He finished getting ready first, and as he passed by Gavin on the way to the ice, Gavin reached out and grabbed his arm. "Hey," he said in a low voice, "thanks for the support."

Ramsey shrugged. "It's not a big deal."

It *was*, actually, but Gavin was okay pretending if that was what Ramsey wanted.

"We could play it easy the next two games—"

"No," Ramsey said, shaking his head abruptly. "No. We're not taking our foot off the gas."

"Good. *Good.*" Gavin hadn't realized how much he didn't want to until Ramsey agreed.

"We got this, Coach," Ramsey said, patting him on the arm. Then he shot him a knowing look. "More than twenty-five damn percent, that's for fucking sure."

When Zach wandered back after talking to Finn, Gavin was still chuckling.

"What's up?" he asked.

"Oh, just . . .Ramsey being Ramsey," Gavin said.

"He ended up being pretty perfect for this team, didn't he?"

"I couldn't come up with any way he could be any better," Gavin said, and meant every word.

The second to the last game had *just* ended—literally Gavin and Zach were still in the tunnel, following the players as they headed towards the locker room, when a figure peeled itself off the wall.

"Gavin," the figure called out, and Zach looked over, pausing in his tracks as the guy joined them.

Of course it was Morgan Reynolds.

"Morgan," Gavin said steadily, "what can I do for you?"

"Jacob mentioned Finn getting tomorrow off to rest for the playoff run, but that's a mistake. You want him to be in the net tomorrow."

"I do, huh?" Gavin asked, and Zach couldn't tell if he was trying not to smile or trying not to throttle Finn's dad.

"You want to set the record. You've just tied it. But if you don't win tomorrow, you're not the sole leader in the record books. You'd be just meeting history, not setting it."

Gavin shoved his hands in his pockets, eyed Morgan up and down. "I'm so glad you're here to tell me how to run my team," he said bluntly.

Morgan's face flushed dark red. "I'm—I'm right here. You know I'm right."

They'd been up five to one at the end of the second period, and he and Gavin had already started to discuss that if the lead held, how they'd approach the next game.

Gavin had already told Zach that he was going to put Finn in. Of course, they hadn't had time to tell Finn that, yet.

"Are you right?" Gavin said casually.

Morgan squirmed, and that was impressive because he was famous for never flinching under pressure. But Gavin was making him squirm now, and it was impossible for Zach to ignore just how insanely fucking hot that was.

Even hotter was the fact when they finally got home tonight, if Zach told Gavin to get on his knees, he'd do it, gladly and gratefully, lust in his eyes and love in his touch.

"You know I am," Morgan muttered. "You want to win tomorrow's game."

"We could win with Nick in the net," Zach pointed out.

Morgan rolled his eyes. "Nothing against Nick, he's a fine goalie, but he's not Finn, and you guys both know it."

"He's solid, for sure," Gavin said.

"He's going to ask you himself. I know he will. He wants to play." Morgan didn't need to say it for both of them to know it.

Finn hadn't been particularly into the idea of resting for the playoffs when Zach had broached the subject. He wanted every start, every minute of experience, and Zach couldn't blame him, because he was growing leaps and bounds every time he was in the net, his crisis of confidence solidly in the rearview mirror.

"I'm sure he will," Gavin said. "And how's he gonna feel when he finds out that you showed up here before we can even *think* about tomorrow's game, demanding that we put him in?"

The red faded from Morgan's face suddenly, bleaching it white. "Shit. I shouldn't have said anything. God, no, don't tell him. He'd be so pissed at me."

Gavin patted Morgan on the arm. "Your heart's in the right place, but you're kind of an asshole."

Morgan sighed, clearly resigned. "I'm trying not to be." He glanced over at Zach and for the first time, really met his eyes. Zach had always wondered if Morgan knew that *he* knew, but now he was sure. It was all there, regret hard-coded in his gaze. He didn't know how to not be a dick. Not to his son. And not to Hayes.

"Well, do some more work on that," Gavin said, patting him again.

"Thanks," Morgan said, rolling his eyes.

When they headed into the locker room, without Morgan following them, Gavin turned to Zach. "You wanna go talk to him?"

"Finn?"

"Yeah. When the time seems right."

"You could've told Morgan you'd already decided to put him in," Zach pointed out.

Gavin just grinned. "And miss the opportunity to put that guy in his place? Hell no."

They were still feeling out the limits of their relationship, in various locales, but this was the locker room—still a semi-sacred space where everyone who needed to know already knew they were together—and it felt very natural to lean in and press his lips against Gavin's. "You're hot when you're cutthroat," he murmured against Gavin's mouth.

"Yeah?" Gavin didn't sound like he hated that at all.

"Oh yeah," Zach said. "Gonna show you how much, later."

"I'm holding you to that."

Historically, Gavin had always felt like teams were *his*. Technically he supposed the players were their own, and he could also possibly make the argument that the teams he'd coached also belonged to the leadership—guys who wore the C and the As.

But he'd never looked out across the ice, watching his players as they warmed up, and felt the weight of expectations and ownership settling over not *just* him, but someone else too.

Zach stood next to him, not only bearing half that weight but also half the joy. Taking and giving and sharing until he didn't know where he ended and Zach began.

"No matter what happens tonight or in Minnesota, it's been a hell of a season," Zach said quietly. Like he was feeling the nostalgia of watching their final warmup on home ice the same way Gavin was.

"Couldn't have done it without you," Gavin said, glancing over and meeting his eyes. Some days he could only see the twenty-seven-year-old Zach, the man who'd arrived at his cabin this summer in the broadness of his chest and shoulders, the occasional shadows in his blue eyes. But other days, he could see a whole progression of Zachs, overlaid on top of each other. The grownup Zach, and the eighteen-year-old he'd coached for the first time, the nineteen-year-old he'd sent off to the NHL. The twenty-three-year-old who'd clawed his way up in the Mavs organization, making himself more valuable after each minute of ice time he earned with his blood, sweat, and tears.

In different ways, he'd loved all those Zachs.

But he couldn't deny he loved this Zach, *his* Zach, most of all.

He was so goddamn lucky, to find this kind of life-altering, life-defining love, twice, and to get to share his favorite thing in the world with him, too. Maybe a less selfish man would let this record go. Decide that having it all was truly an embarrassment of riches. But Gavin wanted it all, still.

Wanted to carve their names, *this team*, so deeply in the record books nobody could ever think of forgetting them.

"Literally you couldn't have done it without me," Zach teased lightly, nudging him with his shoulder. "If I hadn't gone and begged you to take the job, everything would be different. You wouldn't be here at all."

"Different and so much worse," Gavin said. "Come on, let's go win this, okay?"

Zach grinned. "We got you, Coach."

Gavin knew it wasn't only that—he had them, too—but always before, he'd have made a point of it, that he was the coach and the leader. That it was only *his* team.

But it wasn't anymore, and he knew it.

So he only smiled back.

Elliott and Mal were on fire from the moment Ivan took the first faceoff.

It wasn't the last time they'd ever play together. There was Minnesota and the Frozen Four coming up, and there'd be other games. But none like this.

They felt it, pushing deep into the opposing teams' offensive zone as easy as breathing, Elliott literally skating circles around one of the defensemen, flicking the puck around his skates, passing it to Mal, then receiving it back, tape to tape like they were sharing the same brain, the same physical body.

He made an aborted move like he was going to shoot it, let the goalie sink into his block, before sending the puck Mal's direction and he sank it in the opposite side of the net.

The way it started was the way the game kept going.

The Evergreens were up 1-0, then 2-0, then the second power play team scored, Ethan, the youngest rookie at seventeen and the one center on the team Gavin thought might have the most upside, grabbing the rebound from one of Mal's deflected shots.

It was a great game. Easy and *fun*, Finn looking almost bored at the nearly abandoned end of the ice.

Between the second and third period, Elliott danced around the locker room, Mal smiling at him, looking lighter than Gavin could remember him *ever* looking.

"Those two," Ramsey said to Gavin as he walked up next to him, shaking his head. "They're absolutely going to do something against the rules after this game."

Gavin shot him a look full of disbelief. "What do *they* think is against the rules?"

"Not what *we* think is against the rules, or God forbid what *Elliott* thinks is against the rules, but what does *Malcolm* think is against the rules?"

"I'm not sure I want to know," Gavin said, scrubbing a hand across his face. "Maybe don't tell me anything more."

"Just a hunch, Coach. Might want to clear out of the locker room early and leave it that way," Ramsey said, laughing.

"God."

"Don't think he's gonna be around much, either," Ramsey cackled.

The third period started, and the Evergreens kicked it off with a power play. Their opponents came out of the intermission apparently deciding that if they couldn't beat them with their sticks and the puck, they could do with their fists.

"Sloppy and shitty," Zach hissed under his breath, as one of the team's biggest defenders went right after Brody, slamming him up against the boards.

Brody shook it off, but a look crossed Ramsey's face that promised retribution.

Gavin just hoped it was the scoring kind of retribution.

"Ivan," Gavin said, giving the first line center a nod. "Get your guys out there."

"We got this, Coach," Ivan promised, exchanging a knowing look with Ramsey.

"Don't lose your temper," Zach reminded them. "You've got them exactly where you want them."

Ramsey grinned evilly and smacked Brody's back. "Believe me, I know it."

Gavin couldn't ever doubt Ramsey's defensive bonafides. He was a smooth, effortless skater, quick and lethal out there, but when he decided he wanted to go on an offensive push, he was almost as effective. And he wanted it today, Ivan passing him the puck like they'd already agreed on this.

"Did you draw this one up?" Gavin asked Zach, who just shrugged.

"Well, I'd say by this point they know what they're doing," Gavin murmured. Also they were up 3-0, and they were clearly having fun, so there wasn't much harm if they wanted to work out something new.

Maybe some coaches were into that micromanagement shit, but not Gavin. He'd never been big into it, but this year had taught him to mellow in even more new and unique ways. It was why Zach had known he was perfect for this team—and they were perfect for him, too.

Zach grinned as Ramsey wove his way through defenders like they didn't even exist, breaking ankles like he had been holding back before now. He passed the puck to Elliott, who shot it right back. "I'd say."

Ramsey found an opening a second later, and the goal horn blared, making it 4-0.

The players surrounded him, pushing him into the boards as he laughed and pointed right at the bench at where Brody was grinning right back.

"Well, that went well," Zach said, and that was the fucking understatement of the century.

Gavin couldn't say he held his breath for the next ten minutes, because while they weren't in the habit of blowing a big lead, weirder things happened.

Finn did give up a goal nearly at the end of the game, but it was a fluke, him shrugging a little helplessly as he pushed his helmet up after.

Mal shot another beauty in, right after that, going on a breakaway, keeping their four-goal buffer.

"That was damn impressive," Zach said to him, leaning over him when he settled back down on the bench.

"No shit," Elliott retorted fondly, his gloved hand patting Mal on the upper thigh and just resting there after he was done.

Normally Gavin might clear his throat, force Elliott to actually *not* be groping his teammate during a game, but there was only a minute left, and maybe it made him a pushover, but he was too happy to say a word.

Besides, wasn't his shoulder pressing right up against Zach's in a way he'd normally never allow?

Gavin decided there wasn't anything wrong with making a few exceptions.

Especially tonight.

And when the final buzzer sounded, he turned to Zach and the smile on his face lit up a space inside Gavin that he wasn't sure anything had ever touched.

Pure joy cascaded through him, and he didn't lean in to kiss Zach, but it was a near thing. Cupping his face and staring in his eyes, trying to tell him everything he felt, everything new and strange and perfect blooming inside him, while the bench dissolved into chaos and celebration, was enough.

"Love you," Zach said roughly, leaning into his hand.

But it wasn't just enough, it was *everything*.

EPILOGUE

THEY HANDED GAVIN THE trophy first.

He knew there was a protocol to these things—he'd literally sat through the meeting where they'd described to him and the opposing coach how the end of the final championship game would work, so everyone would know what to do, win or lose. But Gavin didn't give a shit about protocols. He wanted to share this win with his team. With *Zach*.

Not in five minutes. Not when it was deigned "permissible" to pass the trophy around. *Now*, damn it.

He waited ten seconds, which he personally felt was about nine seconds too long, so the press corps could get their photos, and then he turned to Zach, their hands brushing.

There was a press release sitting in the Evergreens' head of PR's outbox, ready to hit send whenever Gavin decided he was ready.

Staring at Zach's perfect, private smile today, as the anarchy of winning surrounded them, Gavin realized that he'd *been* ready, and there was no reason to wait anymore.

"We're the champs, baby!" Elliott screamed to his left, Mal laughing so hard he almost drowned him out.

But Gavin couldn't hear anything, couldn't see anything else but Zach. He leaned in and kissed him.

Zach's mouth was warm and tasted like the Gatorade he'd been rolling around in his hands during the last intermission as he'd sketched out the power play design that had won them the game, Ivan from the faceoff to Ramsey to Elliott, hanging around on the other side of the net, so quick that the goalie hadn't had a moment to even get in position.

That had been four minutes left in the game, and because of Elliott's goal, there'd been no overtime, because they'd held the lead, Ramsey and Brody skating the last shift with as much purpose as they'd skated the first, protecting Finn and their net like it wasn't just the game on the line, but their lives.

Zach's mouth moved against his, with intent, and the rest of the noise around them faded away.

Gavin was pretty sure someone yelled, "Get it, Coach!"

It might've been Ramsey. Honestly, it was probably Ramsey.

Gavin smiled against Zach's mouth and then pulled back, their hands against each other on the trophy.

He didn't even have to ask Zach, it just felt natural to turn to that voice and pass it onto him, sweat and what Gavin thought might be tears, dripping down Ramsey's face as he hoisted the trophy up, skating out onto the middle of the ice, the rest of the team streaming behind him, all fist pumps and supportive screams.

"We did it," Zach said, and Gavin nodded, because he'd never heard anything more right in his whole life. Not, *I* did it, or *you* did it, but *we* did it, *together.*

"It's gonna be like this forever," Gavin told him. "Us."

"Even when someone tries to hire me away?" Zach teased.

"Someone tries to hire you away, they're getting a package deal," Gavin said. Maybe it was crazy. But he never wanted to do this alone again, not without Zach.

Zach didn't argue, he just glowed, affection and fondness pouring out from his expression. "Us, together," he said, and Gavin had never heard anything better in his whole goddamn life.

Even the final buzzer today, giving them the championship win.

June

The air was slow and muggy, Zach moving through it like his limbs were coated in honey.

He and Gavin had been up at the cabin for over a week now but he couldn't say that he was even remotely used to the intense humidity yet. Maybe he wouldn't ever get used to it.

Zach tugged out the shirt that he'd tucked into the waistband of his shorts and used it to wipe his face then his sweaty chest. He'd just been on a long run, thinking that with the sun falling lower in the sky, the heat would be less of a problem.

That had been wishful thinking and he was imagining a long, cold shower and an even colder beer, in that order.

When he turned the corner and the cabin came into view, he saw Gavin on the porch, bare legs stretched out in front of him, and clearly he'd had the same idea because there was a fresh beer, condensation sliding down the bottle, on the small table next to him.

His head was tipped back, eyes closed, but the moment Zach opened the squeaky screen door, his gaze met Zach's.

"Hey," Gavin said. "Have a good run?"

"Ugh, no. It's hot as fuck out," Zach complained, leaning against one of the columns of the porch, debating if Gavin would argue if he just stole his beer for himself instead of going all the way in the house to grab one.

"Hey, your choice to go now instead of going this morning," Gavin pointed out. He lifted the beer and took a long drink, his throat working as he swallowed. His skin had already begun to darken, though he wasn't quite as tan as he'd been last June when Zach had shown up at the cabin uninvited.

"Yeah, can't imagine what I was doing this morning instead of dragging my ass outside for a run," Zach shot back, grinning.

This morning they'd been tucked up in Gavin's double bed together, legs tangled together, enjoying the silence and each other. The long, slow kisses they'd exchanged had felt sweet and soft, too precious to break up to get out of bed except for anything but the most pressing reason—and going for a run definitely hadn't been on the list.

"It was good," Gavin agreed, smiling. He handed the bottle to Zach, who took it and finished it off. "I was thinking about starting dinner. Throwing some chicken and veggies on the grill."

"Sounds good," Zach said. He needed to take a shower, still, but he didn't move yet. It felt too good, too right, to be standing here on the porch, nearly a year to the day since he'd done it the first time.

Back then, he'd been a mess, worried and anxious and more than a little terrified his old crush was making a valiant comeback, but now all he felt was a bone-deep satisfaction. Happy in a way he'd never imagined being and now couldn't imagine being without.

"Your phone buzzed a bunch of times," Gavin mentioned. "I glanced at the screen. It was Pat."

Pat was still Zach's agent and never knew when to just leave a good thing alone. Zach groaned.

"He still fielding offers?" Gavin wondered, his voice carefully neutral.

Zach knew what Gavin had said a few months back, when they'd won the championship, but he'd wondered at the time if Gavin really meant it.

"Yeah," Zach said.

Their relationship was still pretty new, and Zach was honestly still satisfied enough being Gavin's assistant that he felt no reason to even bother entertaining any of the offers Pat was getting. But that wouldn't always be the case. Someday he might want to try being a head coach on his own, and when that happened, what was Gavin going to do? Just follow him, like a puppy dog? Become *his* assistant?

Zach didn't know, and maybe that was okay.

They didn't need to have all the answers, especially to questions he wasn't sure he was ready to ask yet.

"You know you can talk to him about them, right?" Gavin asked hesitantly. Too hesitantly. Like he thought Zach was already ready to move on. And *yes* since he'd retired from the NHL, it felt like every single year had seen him moving on, moving *up*. But he wasn't ready to keep doing that now. Where he was at felt right, so right, and not just because of Gavin.

He had more to learn, and he didn't feel even remotely ready to shoulder a whole team, even if it was college or juniors, and the best place to learn was at Gavin's elbow.

"Of course I know. I just . . . there's no reason to do it yet. I'm not ready. You know I'm not ready."

Gavin scrunched up his face. "I don't know if I'd say you're *not* ready, because you're already a great coach, but yeah, I can't say I'm eager for you to move on."

He shouldn't ask. Hadn't he *just* thought that they didn't need all the answers right now? But he asked the question anyway. "What would you do if I did?"

Gavin lifted himself out of the chair and wrapped a hand around Zach's waist, tipping his face up. "I meant it," he said softly. "I love you. Where you go, I'm going. But that's not why I said it."

"I'm . . ." Zach felt a little breathless, the happiness punching him right in the solar plexus. "I'm good where we're at. Really good."

Gavin nodded his agreement. "I don't want to leave either. We're doing good work in Portland. Can do some more, next year and the year after. But I don't want to hold you back, either."

"You'd never," Zach said.

Gavin smiled then, slow and knowing. "It's probably gonna have to be me kicking you out of the nest, if we're being honest."

"Probably." Zach chuckled. Gavin probably *would* think he was ready before Zach himself thought he was. "And then what are you gonna do? Become *my* assistant?"

"Yeah. Sounds good, doesn't it?" Gavin's expression was totally serious.

It did. But Zach hadn't thought he was necessarily in earnest but it appeared he was.

"Listen," Gavin added, "I don't care what I do. I don't have an ego that way. I don't give a shit who they say is in charge, officially. I could care less if some media asshole theorizes that I'm regressing or taking a position that isn't as important, or whatever. I want to be with you and I want hockey. That's it. I've learned what's important and yeah, don't get me wrong, the accolades are nice. I like winning. But I love you more."

Zach pressed his mouth against Gavin's. It was easy and hot and sweet. "Love you more, too," he agreed, pulling back a fraction. "Might be fun, too, to boss you around."

Gavin grinned, his smile suddenly turning filthy. He kissed Zach again, nibbling with his teeth on his bottom lip, making Zach groan. "Don't need a new job title to do *that*."

-

I loved writing this universe and hockey so much I couldn't stop here – don't miss Hayes and Morgan's standalone book, *Breakaway Goals*, coming late summer 2025.

-

If you'd like to read about Zach and Gavin finally getting that phone sex they've both been thinking about, click here to download the bonus scene.

INTERESTED IN READING MORE OF
BETH'S BOOKS?

CHECK OUT A FULL LIST OF TILES
BY SCANNING THE QR CODE
OR VISITING HER WEBSITE

WWW.BETHBOLDEN.COM/BOOKLIST

WANT TO FOLLOW BETH?

MAKE SURE YOU NEVER
MISS A RELEASE?

SCAN THE QR CODE BELOW
OR VISIT HER WEBSITE
FOR A SOCIAL MEDIA LIST,
NEWSLETTER SIGNUP,
AND SO MUCH MORE!

WWW.BETHBOLDEN.COM/ABOUT